Xin Publishing

Exile

Clive K. Semmens

Xin Publishing

Published by Xin Publishing
an imprint of Xin He Ltd.
83 Ducie Street
Manchester M1 2JQ
United Kingdom

http://www.xin-publishing.uk/

Story © Clive K. Semmens 2017
Cover artwork © Anjula J. Schaub
                    & Clive K. Semmens 2017

All rights reserved. No part of this publication
may be reproduced, stored in a retrieval system,
or transmitted in any form or by any means,
electronic, mechanical, photocopying, recording
or otherwise, without the prior permission of the
publishers and/or authors.

ISBN: 978-3-942357-29-6

Chapter 1

I was so exhausted by the time I landed that as soon as I'd tied everything down I just fell asleep in my harness.

Even in thick clothes, sleeping half hanging in a harness, propped up awkwardly against a rock on a cold hillside, is not ideal. I have no idea how long I slept like that. I woke from terrible nightmares.

My left arm was numb and completely unresponsive, and it took me some minutes massaging it with my right hand to get the circulation going. The cold, stale blood invading my innards made me feel very ill, and my head pounded.

With my left arm still feeling rather wooden it was difficult to get out of my harness, but eventually I succeeded. I drank some water, stuffed some clothes into my rucksack, and headed down the hill.

I met an old chap in the village. He seemed friendly, but we didn't have any language in common. As far as I could make out he was telling me in mime that if I took a right turn further down the road, I'd get to a railway.

At the end of the village there was a muddy track to the right. I thought, *that can't be it*, and walked on. After what seemed a long way I reached a crossroads, and took the road to the right.

I rounded the shoulder of a small hill, and found I was entering a narrow valley. Further down I could see houses with rough dry-stone walls and flagstone roofs, their backs built into the valley sides, and their fronts straight onto the road. As I approached, ragamuffin children ran into the road in front of me, stared at me for a moment, then dashed back into the houses before I reached them. I saw no sign of any adults, but suspected they were watching me from the dark openings of their glassless windows, or out of their open doors. It was cold, but I couldn't smell any smoke. I didn't think anyone had lit their fire for the evening yet.

It didn't seem a very welcoming place. *With luck there might be a railway in a mile or two.* I pressed on.

It was a long mile or two. *It'll get dark before long, and I'll have to find somewhere to stay.* I was just considering going back to that last village, when I saw a flickering light high on the hillside, and a rough track leading towards it. In the gloom, I could make out trees around the light – the first trees I'd seen since I landed.

I headed up the track, hoping the people would be hospitable.

The woods were thick on each side of the track, and almost closed overhead, forming a dark tunnel; but the track was better here, and I could see the firelight ahead.

The house was much grander than those in either of the villages I'd seen. The walls were dressed stone, straight and tall, and the entrance was a double door of finely carved wood, glazed in the upper half with small panes of clear glass. I could see through them into a grand hallway, lit by a fire in a huge fireplace.

I knocked at the door – it had a heavy iron ring for a knocker. The sound echoed, but there was no response. I pushed the door gently, and it opened quite easily. I went in, and called softly, "Is there anyone at home?"

There was still no response, but I could hear a murmuring, as of many people chattering at some distance. I stood in front of the fire for a while, wondering what to do next, and hoping someone would come and find me.

The floor was featureless – a dull, dark red, very smooth and almost waxy looking, but not at all slippery. I'd no idea what it was made of. I was pretty sure there was nothing like it back in England.

A wide passageway led from the hall, dimly lit by oil lanterns with glass chimneys that disappeared through the ceiling. I decided to investigate. After ten metres or so there was a half-glazed door on the right, similar to the entrance door, followed by a series of windows in a similar style. Through the windows I could see people sitting at candlelit tables, chattering and laughing. Opposite the windows the passageway opened out into another hall, similar to the first, but larger. I stood for a moment in the hall, wondering whether to approach the people in the adjacent room, or wait for them to approach me.

Then there were people issuing from another passageway.

A tall, middle-aged lady came over to me. Her clothes were like nothing I'd ever seen before, patterned in seemingly random blotches of strong, dark colours. Her skirt hung like a curtain, with deep folds, and brushed the floor. Her blouse puffed out around her body and upper arms. She seemed to be about to speak, then stopped, as if not knowing what to say. She made a gesture that I took as an invitation to speak.

"I was hoping that you'd allow me to lie by your fire for the night."

She stared at me, then turned to a lady beside her and spoke in a language I didn't recognize, much less understand.

Suddenly I was surrounded. They didn't look unfriendly, just perplexed. They all stared at me, then turned to each other and began talking earnestly. Finally a tall, elderly man pushed through the throng, and said, in English, "I am Haarig. You speaking English?"

I almost collapsed with relief; but he scarcely understood a word I said, and wasn't able to say much in English. I thought he confirmed the existence of the railway, but I wasn't sure. But I didn't sleep by the fire. They fed me well, and gave me a comfortable bed.

Striding down the track in the morning, my mood was much lighter. I'd slept better than I had in a long time. Above all, however little they and I had understood each other, I felt cared for. It was even colder than it had been the previous evening, but the sky was blue, and I'd had a nourishing, warm breakfast. My rucksack felt lighter on my back, despite having a generous packed lunch in it.

Back on the road, I tried to make good time. I wondered what the train service would be like when I finally reached the railway – and how much further it really was. And how I was going to pay for my ride. If there was really a railway at all.

I came out onto a high, steep escarpment, overlooking a vast plain. The road descended in a series of hairpin bends.

At the foot of the slope was the railway, a single narrow-gauge track. I could see where the road crossed it at an unmarked, ungated crossing. There was no sign of a station as far as I could see in either direction.

It took me about half an hour to get down to the railway. I was relieved to see that the track was well used: the running surfaces were bright and shiny, completely rust free. There was a footpath alongside. But which way was the station?

I was about to choose a direction at random when I heard what I thought was a distant train. I looked both ways, but couldn't yet see anything. I climbed onto a rock close by the line to see further, and saw the train coming from the east. On an impulse, I decided to wave as it approached – and was astonished when the driver waved back, and brought the train to a squealing halt.

It wasn't a passenger train. The wagons were windowless vans. The driver beckoned to me, and gave me a hand up onto the footplate. Without a word, he turned to his engine, pulled a huge lever, and with a hiss of steam we were off again. He reached over the railing behind the cab, picked up a couple of lumps of wood, and shoved them into the firebox. Finally, he turned to me and spoke.

Again, we had no common language. But he was smiling, and seemed quite happy to take me wherever he was going. I hoped we were going in the direction of some city, rather than further out into the wilds, but I'd no means of knowing.

We travelled a while in silence. Well, not silence – the engine was very noisy – but not trying to communicate. We weren't going very fast, maybe twenty-five miles an hour. Every now and then the driver shoved a couple more lumps of wood on the fire, but most of the time he was just leaning out of the side of the engine, first on one side, then on the other, mostly looking ahead, but occasionally glancing behind. I spent most of my time watching the countryside.

The driver pulled a metal ring above the firebox. There was a long, piercing whistle – and suddenly we were in a tunnel. The sound of the engine, echoing from the tunnel walls, was deafening. The smoke made me cough a little.

After what seemed a very long time we emerged into the sunlight. The driver touched my arm, and pointed ahead. There was another train, waiting for us in a passing loop. The driver pointed at the other train, covered his eyes briefly with his hands, and then pointed at me. Then he looked over the side of the train, pointed at me again, and made a walking movement with his fingers towards the side of the train. I realized that he didn't want the driver of the other train to see me, and was indicating where I should hide. There was a narrow walkway above the engine's wheels, and a handrail above it. I was to crouch beside the boiler, on the side away from the other train.

We slowed as we came into the passing loop, and stopped. I could hear the drivers laughing – and then my driver was beckoning me back into the cab.

Introductions were a lot of gesturing, smiling, and uncomprehended speech. His friend seemed to have brought food for my driver as well as himself, and I was cordially invited to share their meal – so I produced my packed lunch and offered to add it to the feast. Each took a morsel, but they made me keep most of it for later, making it clear that they thought they'd got plenty for the three of us without. Although I was careful not to eat more than an equal portion, I was certainly well fed by the end of the meal. I hoped they were too – they indicated so, anyway, with a pat of their stomachs and a motion of their hands around imaginary big bellies.

It was at least half an hour after we arrived before we parted with a hug – how different from England! – and were off.

The line continued more or less level for a couple of miles, then we began climbing. With a whistle we went into another tunnel, still climbing. It wasn't a long tunnel, but when we came out we were on a rocky plateau. In the cab it was warm, but it looked cold outside despite the sunshine.

We were going faster than we had been, running level, sometimes in a cutting through rock, sometimes on an embankment, often close to ground level. For a while a crow flew alongside us, keeping exactly level with the cab. The driver pointed to it, and hugged the air as though hugging his friend again, saying, I presumed, that the crow was being friendly. I nodded. *But maybe really it's riding our bow wave, the wind blowing around the train. It's still flapping its wings, but maybe it's getting a boost from us.* I couldn't think how to express that thought in mime, and kept it to myself.

In the distance, I could see a line of hills. We were heading for a gap in them, but even the gap seemed to be quite a bit higher than the plateau we were crossing. Several of the highest peaks were capped in snow, brilliant white in the sunshine.

As we approached the gap in the line of hills, we began to climb again, first on an embankment, then on a high viaduct. The viaduct began on a long, gentle curve, and I could see that it was a series of huge stone arches, a really beautiful piece of architecture. As we climbed, the ground dropped away beneath us as well – there was a wide valley between the plateau and what I could now see were substantial mountains.

Long before we'd finished crossing the valley, the viaduct straightened up and I couldn't see it any longer, so that we seemed to be flying. We were still climbing hard, and we'd reached a dizzying height before the ground began to rise to meet us. Ahead I could see the mouth of a tunnel.

I saw the line of another railway climbing up the wall of the valley, then disappearing into its own tunnel. The driver saw where I was looking, pointed to the other track, and described in hand movements how it passed beneath our line, then doubled back, climbing all the way, and joined with our line some distance further on.

Just before the end of the viaduct, I looked down and could see that the other line had two parallel tracks, narrow gauge like ours.

We were in the tunnel for some time. We emerged into a different world – a gorge on a grand scale. On both sides, almost vertical rock walls rose a hundred metres or more. Our viaduct took us around a curve to join the rocks ahead, where it clung to the cliffside on a series of stone arches, like half a viaduct built into the rock. Far below us, a huge river ran amongst jumbled boulders.

There were now two tracks, and I guessed that the other line had joined ours somewhere in the tunnel.

We were heading downstream. At first I thought that this river
must feed into the broad valley we had crossed earlier, and that
we'd soon leave the river again, perhaps through another tunnel;
but no, we continued following the river, descending gently at
first, and then quite steeply. The river descended below us in a
series of rapids and waterfalls. Our line curved back and forth,
sometimes following the wall of the canyon, occasionally
tunnelling through a spur or bridging a side valley, or crossing
from one side of the canyon to the other on what must have been
fantastic bridges or viaducts, but most of which I was unable to
see from the train.

We were descending steeply, but the river below us was
descending much more steeply still, and we were getting higher
and higher above it. For a while we clung to the left side of the
gorge, then we were out of the gorge and I began to get distant
views again. We'd passed right through the mountains. Far
ahead, I could see the towers and spires of a city, and beyond it
the sea, shimmering in the evening sunshine.

I looked at the driver, and tried to ask in mime if that was
where we were going. He looked puzzled for a moment, then
slapped his forehead.

He patted his breast pocket, pulled a piece of paper from it,
then pointed to where my pocket would have been if I'd had
one; but of course I didn't have any papers. He showed me his
paper. There was a lot of incomprehensible writing on it, and a
thumbprint in one corner. He pointed to the thumbprint, then to
his dirty thumb, and laughed. It was evidently some document
he needed to pass some checkpoint, and I needed one too; but he
spread his hands as though to say not to worry, and turned back
to his engine.

The line steepened yet more, onto a long incline diagonally
across the face of another huge escarpment. We were running
faster than we had all day, but we'd not used any fuel since we
came out of the last tunnel. The fire was burning very gently. We
flashed through cuttings lined with cut stone, and over
embankments and viaducts.

We thundered across a bridge over a ravine, and the slope
began to level out. Then we were flying along between fields of

maize, wheat, and other crops that I didn't recognize. The driver began to make up his fire.

The sun was almost down to the horizon, and I realized that we'd not reach the city until after dark. I wondered what would happen when it was discovered that I didn't have any documents, and where I'd spend the night. But the driver seemed to understand the situation, and didn't seem to be worried.

Our pace slowed as we lost the momentum we'd gained in the descent, and the mountains shrank behind us. Gradually the light faded. Here and there I could see firelight in the distance.

We stopped in a village. The driver jumped down from the engine, indicating I should stay where I was. He returned a while later with food, and we ate together as the train gathered speed again. I again offered my packed lunch, and again he took just a morsel, and made me keep the remainder.

Long after dark, we passed through several larger villages quite close together, and then began to cross a long, clattering metal bridge.

The driver lifted up a panel in the floor of the cab. Underneath, I could see rough wooden boards spanning the chassis. I had to hide there! It was a very cramped little space, made all the more cramped by the presence of several sacking parcels bound with coarse string.

Shortly after the end of the bridge – I heard the changed sound – we began to slow, and finally came to a halt. Someone climbed into the cab. There was a short conversation, and then the sound of someone climbing down again.

We proceeded at what I guessed was about walking pace for some time, then the panel above me opened again, and there was the driver grinning down at me, his grubby face illuminated by the light of the fire. He helped me out of the hole. I ached all over.

He began to pull the parcels out of the hole. Dimly, I could see a woman walking alongside the engine. The driver passed the parcels to her without a word. She disappeared into the night, then a moment later reappeared and climbed into the cab. She and the driver talked quietly for a while, she looking me up and down every now and then, and he smiling and patting her hand. Then she climbed down again, and beckoned me to follow.

Climbing off a moving train, even one moving very slowly, wasn't something I was used to. In the dark, I missed my footing on the rough ballast, and fell awkwardly towards the train. I fended myself off, and fell the other way. There was a yelp, and somebody leapt to my aid, catching me before I hit the ground. I could barely see him, but it seemed to be a young man or a large boy.

The woman said something to me; judging by her tone of voice she was asking if I was okay. She and the boy helped me to my feet. I'd twisted my ankle and bruised my hand, but I wasn't badly hurt, and said so, but I was sure they didn't understand a word. The boy put my arm around his shoulder and half lifted me.

We set off along the track, then in almost complete darkness turned into a narrow, muddy alleyway between high walls. The last few wagons of the train rumbled past behind us. The sound of the train slowly faded, and I gradually became aware of the sounds of the city.

The alleyway turned a right angle, and then another. There was a little more light here. We emerged onto a narrow, dimly-lit cobbled street between high, scruffy buildings. Most of these seemed to be shops of some kind, with open fronts and oil lamps hanging inside. Above the shops were several storeys of windows, many dark but a few illuminated from within. The street was full of people.

We crossed the street diagonally, and went into a dark passageway between two shops. Almost immediately we began to climb a staircase, too narrow for the boy to support me. He went ahead, and the woman followed me. It wasn't easy climbing steep, slightly irregular stairs, in almost complete darkness, with a twisted ankle, but the handrails on both sides helped a lot.

We reached a landing after about fifteen steps, but the staircase doubled back towards the street. A little light came in from the street through a window at the top of the second flight, and I could see doors on each side of the next landing. We continued up another six short flights, and reached the top of the stairs. I could see lamplight under a door to our right, but the boy opened a door on our left and we went through. He turned up the wick of an oil lamp that was hanging above him, and I could see a large, dim, cluttered room. We were just under the roof. Four huge, roughly hewn beams spanned the room above head height, and the ceiling sloped right up to a high ridge above them. On each side, between the middle two beams, there were large dormer windows.

Opposite the door was a rough brick wall with a fireplace in the middle, and a fire burning very low. A tiny old woman was sitting by the fireplace, picking at the knots on the parcels I'd been smuggled with. She'd evidently been doing this by the light of the fire until the boy turned up the lamp, which I realized she probably wasn't tall enough to reach.

One of the parcels was already open. It was full of cloth like that of the clothes the woman had been wearing at the house where I'd spent the previous night. It seemed so long ago.

The younger woman stirred up the fire, added some wood to it, and got a good blaze going. Then she planted me firmly in a comfortable chair by the fire. She lit another oil lamp and put it on a table in the corner, then she and the boy sat on benches each side of the table and started to prepare some vegetables.

The old lady looked at me. Then very tentatively she began speaking, saying a few words, then looking at me apparently for signs of comprehension, then trying a few different words. I guessed she was trying different languages. After a while she gave up.

I tried all my languages. We didn't have a single language in common, despite seemingly having half a dozen each. She laughed, and spread her hands in a gesture that said, "Oh, well."

The younger woman said something to her, and the old lady got up and came over to me. She seemed very sprightly for her age. She sat on the floor by my feet, and made me pick up my injured foot. She removed my boot carefully, and peeled off my sock. My ankle was quite swollen and discoloured. She examined it and clucked disapprovingly. She said something to the younger woman, who got up and came over to the fire.

There was what I could only call a cauldron beside the fire. The younger woman picked up a large bowl and a jug, half filled the bowl from the cauldron, and put it on the floor in front of me. The old lady gently put my foot in the water, which was very pleasantly warm.

The younger woman brought a little bottle from a shelf in the corner, and poured a small amount of bright red oil into the old lady's hand. The old lady lifted my foot out of the bowl, and began to rub the oil around the swelling. A feeling of heat spread through my foot. It felt wonderful, and I smiled. The old lady smiled back.

The boy brought a pot full of vegetables and hung it on a hook over the fire. The younger woman worked the fire back up into a good blaze again.

As she was doing this, I heard the creak of the door behind me, and turned – and there was the engine driver, with another man.

The two men went to the corner where the table was, picked up one of the benches, brought it over to the fire, and sat down. I realized I was in the engine driver's chair, and started to get up, but he waved me back down. The two of them stretched their hands out to the fire. How much that was for physical warmth, and how much psychological, I wasn't sure: it was very noticeable how much warmer it was than it had been the previous night. Whether this was a change in the weather, or because we were in a city, hundreds of metres lower down and a couple of hundred miles or more further south, I didn't know.

I guessed the other man was also an engine driver. Both of them were pretty filthy, and similarly dressed.

The engine driver said something to the boy, who went back to the corner. He took down a huge jug and several mugs from the shelves, and poured out a dark brown liquid into the mugs. He brought three large mugs. He handed one to me first, then one to the other man, and finally one to the engine driver. I held my mug, wanting to see whether others would engage in some ceremony before drinking. The boy went back to the table, and brought another three, somewhat smaller mugs. He gave one to the old lady, then one to the younger woman, and finally sat on the end of the bench next to the engine driver with his own.

The engine driver raised his mug and made a short speech. Then everyone lifted their mugs, so I did likewise. Everyone laughed, and indicated that I shouldn't have raised mine. Then they lowered their mugs, and the other man immediately raised his, and made another short speech. This time nobody else raised their mugs – but the younger woman indicated to me that I should, so I did; then she made a gesture as though speaking, and pointed to me. It was evidently my turn to make a speech, so I said "Thank you. I wish I could speak your language!"

The other man muttered, "English!", and smiled at me. I lowered my mug, and the younger woman indicated that I should drink first, so I did, just a sip at first.

The drink was quite a surprise. It didn't seem to be very alcoholic, if at all. It was a kind of fruit drink, but it was very spicy and sweet, which made the fruit or fruits hard to identify.

Then everyone lifted their mugs with an exclamation, and drank, but it was clear that they intended to make their drinks last. They just took sips at intervals, so I did the same.

Conversation resumed, but everyone was looking at me much of the time. Finally the other man turned to me, and said, "You English talk." I replied that I did, and he said, "Very sorry, English I not much, I try."

The people at the house where I'd stayed the previous night were friendly in a remote kind of way; these people were much more interested in what I was doing there. They all kept trying to talk to the man who knew a little English, getting him to say things to me or ask me questions. It was obviously quite hard work for him – and it was quite hard for me, too. Often he didn't understand what I was saying, so I had to rephrase things; and he was often lost for words, too. We resorted to mime quite a lot.

Before he started to work on the railways he'd been a sailor, and that was where he'd learnt a little of many languages. Initially, he assumed that I wanted to try to get back home, which really was not what I wanted to do at all.

What I wanted to do was find somewhere where I could do something useful, earn my keep, and settle down. Getting this idea across wasn't easy, and a meal of spicy vegetable stew and hunks of bread was ready before we'd reached that level of understanding.

I had learnt who everybody was. The engine driver was Peyr, his friend was Judd, Peyr's mother was Yaana, his wife was Yaani, and their son was Grim.

They had a daughter, Aila, older than Grim, too; but she was working somewhere out of the city.

By this time it was well into the middle of the night, but no-one seemed to be thinking of sleep at all, apart from Yaana, who was fast asleep, and had to be woken up for the meal.

When we'd finished the stew and bread, Judd said that Peyr wanted me to get out my packed lunch, and share it round. It was evidently luxurious fare. Everything was exotic to me, so I couldn't tell what was ordinary and what was special. Everyone seemed very pleased with it, which pleased me of course.

Conversation continued over the meal, and well into the night thereafter.

At first I was a bit reticent about telling them my story, but they made me feel very much at ease. Gradually they came to understand my situation better.

Through the big dormer windows, I could already see the light beginning to appear in the sky when Judd said Peyr thought we ought all to get some sleep. Beds were simply piles of cloth on the floor, and there was no sort of privacy at all.

Chapter 2

It was broad daylight when I woke. Peyr was still asleep, but everyone else was sitting at the table, eating and drinking and talking softly together. When they saw that I was awake, they showed me where to get washed, and invited me to a breakfast of bread, fruit and water.

They'd obviously been awake for a while, and had been discussing my situation. Judd told me that everyone was saying there'd be no problem me staying with them a while, but that even if I learnt the language it would be very hard for me to earn a living in the city. Without identity papers I wouldn't be able to get a decent job. Some people had false papers, but they didn't know how to go about getting them, and it was certainly very risky.

Some people managed to work without papers. Yaana had none, and worked at home, making clothes. Peyr smuggled the cloth in, then smuggled the finished clothes out again.

Judd suggested that I should stay long enough to learn enough of the language to get by, and then either try to get work on the ships that plied in and out of the city, or travel with Peyr to Briggi, the smaller town at the other end of the line, where people didn't have identity papers and things were much more relaxed.

I wondered whether any of the ships travelled as far as England, or anywhere else where I might be in danger of being recaptured by the English authorities. Judd said that in all his days sailing, although he'd met quite a few English-speaking sailors and even been in ports where everyone spoke English, he'd never heard of a place called England.

I'd worked on small boats, but never on a ship. I really rather wanted to settle down anyway, so I said I thought I'd try the town at the other end of the line.

Although I was very grateful for the invitation to stay long enough to learn the language a little, I felt it would be too much of an imposition on them all. But Judd assured me that they were all very understanding of my plight, that they understood very well about authoritarian regimes and the consequences for those who rebelled against them, and that it would be much easier to find a niche in the other town if I already knew at least the basics of the language.

With Judd as interpreter, Yaana said I could help her. Even if I couldn't sew well, I could cut cloth to a pattern. If it enabled her to make more clothes, Peyr could smuggle more cloth easily enough. She laughed, and said I could earn my own keep for a few weeks or months, but wouldn't be able to raise a family like that!

I'd never thought about raising a family, but I'd have been pleased to earn my keep.

I wondered where the other railway, the double-track one, went. Judd said it went to a bigger city, Meyroha, and that I didn't want to go there: the authorities there were much more efficient than they were here. A small town had to be best for me. Cities, at best, were like this one, Laanoha – with an oppressive regime, but chaotic enough for non-citizens to disappear down the cracks – and at worst might be as bad as going back to England.

In the countryside, there'd be no problem with the authorities, who didn't really attempt to keep control there. However, the poor lived a very hard and insecure life, and while the rich might be hospitable enough as long as I was a novelty, I wouldn't be able to find a niche with them. There wasn't really anything between poor and rich in the countryside.

Of course our conversations weren't really as fluent as I perhaps make them seem. But we got the meanings across somehow.

At first, I stayed the whole time in their room. Judd came round and helped to teach me the local language, Laana, as much as he could, but he worked long hours in the railway workshops. Most of the time there was just Yaana and me at home. All the others went out to work. Judd was very helpful, but I learnt more from Yaana, not just Laana but the local customs as well.

Judd said that once I'd got the basics of Laana there'd be no problem me going out in the city with any of them – there were plenty of strangers around who didn't know Laana very well, but someone who didn't know it at all would attract a lot of attention. Judd lent me some of his own clothes. "Yours do look very strange. You'll be less noticeable in mine."

I couldn't go out on my own. Whoever was with me had to keep a weather eye out for officials who might want to see my papers. For one thing, I might not spot them in time, and for another, I wouldn't know my way around well enough to get away from them – certainly not without attracting attention. It sounded a bit scary, but I was used to some uncertainty about the future, and none of my new friends seemed unduly worried about it.

Yaana had lived in the city for fifty years without papers. "But she knew Laana quite well when she first arrived, and by the time she'd reached an age where a sweet smile wouldn't get her out of trouble, she was a well-known figure around the place," said Judd. "That's true," she said, "except that I reckon I can still smile sweetly." And she could.

I wondered how her children had managed to get papers when their mother hadn't. "There's only Peyr," she said. "His dad took him to the office to get his papers when he was ten. His dad had papers." I could see what they meant about disappearing down the cracks!

I rather missed Peyr when he went away only a couple of days after I arrived. By the time he got back several days later, I'd learnt to cut cloth to a pattern. I'd tried my hand at sewing, too, and managed to do a reasonable job, but I was very slow. Yaana laughed at me. "You'd learn if you had to, but it'd take quite a while to get up speed. It's not worth it."

On his third trip after I arrived, Peyr took me along. "It'll be good for you to get out of the city for a while – and come and see Briggi. Get some idea of the place before deciding whether you really want to settle there. It'll be good for me to have some company, too."

Before dawn, Yaani and Grim took me down to the side of the track. I managed to clamber aboard the moving engine without twisting my ankle again! Then I was secreted away under the footplate along with several parcels of clothes.

Formalities leaving the city were evidently less stringent than on entry. We didn't even stop, we just slowed to a crawl while Peyr had a shouted conversation with a couple of officials.

Once we were clear of the city, Peyr let me out of my hiding place. The sun hadn't risen yet, but it was just beginning to get light. We were crossing a wide, lazy river with numerous sand bars, some of them with lines of bushes growing on them.

Leaning out over the side of the engine, I could see the bridge below us. It was a metal lattice supported at intervals on stone piers. I wondered how deep beneath the sandy bottom of the river they'd had to dig to get a good enough foundation for the stonework. Peyr didn't know. The bridge had been built before he was born.

At least, I think that's what he said. My grasp of Laana was still rather limited – I'd only been learning for just over three weeks. Total immersion, every waking moment, is a pretty good way to learn, but three weeks isn't long.

I looked back at Laanoha. The spires and towers that looked so impressive from afar still looked pretty impressive from this distance, but along the bank of the river I could now see the more ordinary buildings. They were a motley collection of different designs, mostly rather dilapidated and seeming to lean on each other for support. Most of them were four or five storeys high. Alleyways just wide enough for a cart pierced the line at intervals, each leading to the end of a long jetty.

At the other side of the river the flood plain far below us was in intensive use, with what looked to be vegetable patches. Beyond that were badlands of ravines and rough scrubland and then a large village before we entered the rich farmland of the plains.

Whistle, village – whistle, level crossing – rattle, rattle, rattle, another bridge over a river, not as big as the first one, but still pretty big. It also was flowing east, so it wasn't the same river.

Then we were slowing down for a village where Peyr said we were going to stop.

A young woman ran alongside for a little way, and then clambered up into the cab. Peyr said something to her that I didn't understand – apart from my name. Then he turned to me, and said more slowly and clearly, "This is our daughter, Aila."

We stopped in the middle of the village. Some men started to load a stack of wooden boxes into two of our wagons.

The three of us walked down a road away from the railway line, Peyr and Aila talking all the while. I couldn't follow the conversation, but found I was picking up the odd word here and there. Aila glanced at me every now and then. I kept looking sidelong at her – she was a very pretty young lady. I'm sure my embarrassment showed in my face when our eyes met, but she just smiled a smile that was oddly like her grandmother's.

I didn't only look at Aila; I did take in some of the features of the village, too. Every now and then Peyr broke off from his talk with Aila to point out something or other to me. On each side of the road there were small, single storey houses – mostly built of wood, but a few brick ones – each with a vegetable garden around it. The road finished at a pair of imposing wrought iron gates in a high brick wall. Aila went to the gate as though to open it, then seemed to change her mind, and set off up a path along the foot of the wall. Peyr and I followed her.

The path led away from the houses. Soon we were between the brick wall on our left, and a field of maize on our right, both too tall to see over. The path continued like this for a couple of hundred metres, and then we emerged onto an area of rough ground, dropping away into a deep ravine. Several goats were grazing on the far side of the ravine. I guessed the boy standing near them was keeping an eye on them, but he seemed to be more interested in playing with a couple of sticks.

Aila led the way along the edge of the ravine, which gradually widened and deepened. After a short way it angled left, and led down to fields at a lower level, by the side of a wide, slow river. To the right I could see a long bridge that I assumed was the railway.

We reached a point where we either had to scramble down a steep slope to those lower fields, or turn back. The view across the river and its flood plains was fabulous. Aila made a sweeping gesture to show that this was what she'd brought me to see. I said it was beautiful – well I thought that was what I said, but she smiled a shy smile and ran over to me, reached up and kissed me on the cheek, then ran back down the path we'd come along.

Peyr laughed, and said that we'd better get back to his train. He led the way along a different path, that took us directly back to where the men were just finishing loading the boxes.

We climbed back into the cab, Peyr built up the fire again, and we set off.

"Aila works in the big house there."

"Ah – the one with the big iron gates?"

"That's right. They're quite decent people, as rich folks go. Well, Gamaara is, and Tiiram is okay as long as you're on the right side of him."

I thought to myself that the rich people I'd stayed with the first night seemed to be decent people, too – but of course I didn't know how they treated people who worked for them, or their tenants, if they had any.

"You made me laugh when you said Aila was beautiful!"

"Ah. Is that what I said? I meant to say the view was beautiful."

Peyr looked puzzled for a moment, and then laughed again.

"That's the wrong word. You can't say that about a view. That's for people."

Language is funny, but I knew enough of a few languages to understand what I'd done.

"A lucky accident. Aila is beautiful. You have a beautiful daughter."

"Only a foreigner would say that in front of a girl so soon after a first meeting!"

"That's okay. I am a foreigner."

Laughter.

"What does she do at the big house?"

"She looks after the children mostly, but she does some cooking and cleaning too."

As we neared the mountains, we slowed down and stopped behind another engine. Peyr jumped down and went and coupled the two engines together.

Even with two engines and a half-empty train, going up the incline was slow.

It felt very different going back up into the mountains. I almost felt I knew where I was going, but the mountains looked different somehow, looking forward as I approached them, rather than looking back at them as I was leaving. Laanoha, too, appearing behind us again as we climbed, looked different from a distance now I'd seen it up close – even just the fact that I knew its name seemed to make it look different. *Or maybe it's just the different light, the different time of day.*

At the top of the escarpment, where the gradient diminished somewhat, we began to pick up a little speed. We might have got up to eight or ten miles an hour. In the gorge, the labouring of the two engines made a thunderous noise, somehow bigger and more impressive coming from something that seemed so small and insignificant in that vast space between those towering rock walls.

As the line levelled out at the summit, we slowed down and stopped. There was a strange feeling of silence. Only gradually did I become aware of the sound of the river below us, actually making quite a lot of noise, but of a very different character, really quite soothing.

Peyr uncoupled the engines. The other driver moved his engine forward a short way, then set off backwards, crossing over onto the other track and back down the way we'd come.

The tunnel didn't seem as long as it had coming up the gradient, and it seemed like no time before we were on the long, high viaduct, then speeding across the plateau beyond it.

There was a train waiting in the first passing loop already. I hid down the side of the engine until Peyr was sure Laar, the driver of the other train, didn't have any awkward passenger with him. He didn't, so I joined in the job of loading wood onto Laar's engine.

Peyr had brought food for Laar as well, and we all sat on the wood stack to eat. The weather wasn't warm, but it was sunny and the breeze was light, and we had a very pleasant half hour sitting there chatting. Then we all took turns at the pump, filling Laar's engine's water tank.

I was still thinking about Aila, and how she'd kissed my cheek and then run away; but I was too shy to want to talk about her with Peyr. Peyr had no such inhibitions, but he was sensitive to my shyness.

"It's Aila who gives me dinner in the evening in the other direction. But I have to go and get it, because she doesn't know when I'm coming. In this direction, we're still not too far from Laanoha, so she knows pretty much what time I'm going to arrive."

"Does she cook it in the big house? Don't they mind? Do they know?"

Peyr laughed. "Yes, they know, and they don't mind at all. I think it might have been their idea, in fact. They're some of Yaana's best customers, too. Good arrangements all round!"

We arrived at the next loop about half an hour before the other train. "If I'd known it would be so long, I could have taken you to see the waterfall. But if Rodd had come and found my train and me not here, he'd have wondered what had happened to me. The down train nearly always arrives here at least half an hour before the up, but you can't rely on it."

I was a bit puzzled for a moment why Peyr couldn't have left a note for Rodd, and then realized that I'd never seen any of them reading or writing; and that Peyr's identity papers carried a thumbprint, not a signature. I was glad I'd not said anything.

I knew that some people in Laanoha could read and write. There were written signs outside some of the shops, and street names and numbers on buildings, and while Peyr's papers carried a thumbprint, there was also a lot of writing on them. But I wondered how many people were literate, and how many weren't. Back in England, illiteracy was quite unusual – certainly you couldn't get a job like Peyr's without at least basic reading and writing.

I suspected that Judd might be literate. He'd not introduced me to written Laana, but perhaps he just thought that an unnecessary complication, or that maybe I wasn't literate in English. I'd have liked to learn to read street names and shop signs at least, but I'd not thought to ask. At least I could read numbers – they were roughly the same as in England.

Was Aila literate? Suddenly it seemed to matter to me. But I couldn't ask Peyr, for two reasons: I didn't want to insult him, and I didn't want to embarrass myself.

Rodd didn't even stop. He didn't slow down at all. Peyr got us going again.

It seemed to be no time before we were at the point where Peyr had first stopped to pick me up. Peyr waved to a lady sitting in a gig waiting at the crossing. She waved back. "One of Yaana's customers!" said Peyr, "She wants me to stop on the way back to pick up an order."

"She doesn't live in a big house in woods at the top of the escarpment, does she?" I wasn't sure whether she might have been one of the people in the house where I'd stayed. She wasn't one of the people who'd taken a particular interest in me, but she did look familiar.

"I don't know where she lives."

"How do Yaana's customers know to come to you?"

"Oh, that's the grapevine. It's very efficient!"

I didn't feel able to ask about how the grapevine could be so good at putting customers in touch with Peyr without also risking the authorities in Laanoha discovering the smuggling.

We were now heading into country I'd never been in before. A few miles after the crossing, we pulled into another passing loop. We had to wait again for the train coming the other way.

This passing loop was different from the other two, in that there were a few buildings close by. A young man in rough clothes came out of one of them, carrying a dish. Peyr called out to him, and he went back into the building, reappeared with two dishes, and brought them over to us. Peyr paid him, and he left us to eat our meal, returning a short while later with drinks. He waited while we drained our mugs, then took the dishes and mugs away.

We could hear the other train approaching by this time, and Peyr built up the fire again. "I don't know why Shiim is so late. He's got a good engine, and it's usually the up train that has to wait for the down here anyway."

But it wasn't Shiim, and it was a different kind of engine from all the others I'd seen.

"That explains why it's late," said Peyr. "That's a train off the Sirimi branch, a load of stone. Shiim won't be happy."

I hid down the side of the engine as usual, but only for a moment. Peyr didn't know the driver of the other train, but their talk was friendly. The other driver declined the meal he was offered. "I need to get out of the way," he said. "The regular train's following me up."

We had to wait in the passing loop for Shiim as well. I thought that seemed pretty irregular, but Peyr said, "No, it's the way we always cope with the extra trains off the Sirimi branch. There aren't too many of them."

Shiim's train was appearing in the distance as the Sirimi train left. He steamed straight through without stopping. He waved and blew a double blast on the whistle. "Like I said, he's not happy, but it's one of those things. If the Sirimi branch ever gets busy, they'll have to double the track from here to the junction. The Briggi traffic nowadays is really as much as the line can take. Shiim's missed his dinner anyway, he'd normally get it here."

"What time will Shiim get to Laanoha? It's later than when you picked me up there."

"There's only two more stages today. He'll stop at Veglid – that's where we load fuel and water for the pass, just before the long viaduct. He'll get to Laanoha about midday tomorrow. The Sirimi train will have to go right through though. There's nowhere to stop on the main line."

"Where will he sleep at Veglid? There's nothing there at all!"

"Oh, there is. There's a whole village – Veglid. It's about half a mile from the loop, that's all. It's an old coaching station, but its main trade now is handling firewood for the trains. And overnighting one or two engine drivers every night, of course."

"You said, 'an old coaching station'. Aren't there any coaches any more? Are there passenger trains? I've not seen any."

"You're about to. There's one every other day."

"So where do the passengers sleep? The passing place this side of Veglid is surely in the middle of nowhere, isn't it?"

"Yes, it is. That's why it's the passenger trains that stop there. They sleep in the train, and there's a kitchen on the train, too. They could stop at Raamba of course, like we do, but they're safer at Elbrouha. With a kitchen on the train, they don't need a café."

I thought that maybe I'd learn the names of all the stops in the end, if I came this way often enough. I wondered whether I would. But Peyr had raised another question in my mind.

"Safer at – what was its name? What's the danger at the other place?"

"At Raamba? Bandits. The goods train is pretty safe. The wagons are very tough, and what is there to steal on the engine? If they knew where to look there's Yaana's cloth or clothes, but a couple of parcels of clothes isn't much of a prize for a bandit."

"Are bandits a big problem here?"

"No, but they would be if people didn't know what to do about them. They used to be."

"So why's the other place safer?"

"Elbrouha? It's almost completely inaccessible except by train. It's real break-a-leg country for miles around, vertical cliffs up or down each side of the line for more than two miles in the Veglid direction, and a tunnel the other way."

We had to wait in the next passing loop for the passenger train. It only had four short coaches, and a smaller engine than ours. It didn't stop, but whistled.

The junction for the Sirimi branch was just at the beginning of the loop.

"Sirimi is little more than a village, but it's an old place, and has some pretty nice solid houses compared with most places in the hills. Big quarry – that's why it's got a railway."

A big quarry? Old stone houses? That sounded like the village where I first landed. Pretty much in the right place, too. If it was, then that muddy track at the end of the village, where I thought, "that can't be it," probably did lead to the railway, in only a short distance. How my perception of the world had changed in just three weeks!

I'd walked a lot further than I needed to – except that I might have waited a week for a train in Sirimi, by the sound of it. It would have been a quarry train, and the driver wouldn't have been Peyr, and who knows whether he'd have given me a ride, or been willing or able to smuggle me into Laanoha? How very lucky I'd been.

"I think I've been there. That's where I first landed, I reckon."

"That's something that's been puzzling me. How on Earth did you get here in the first place? How can a foreigner arrive anywhere but a port? Or somewhere on the coast at any rate. Sirimi is bang in the middle of nowhere, not even up at the ice, although how anyone would come all the way over the ice anyway I don't know."

Well, I knew I was going to have to explain myself a bit more some time. Evidently now was the time, and at least Peyr was a sympathetic audience, with a fairly good understanding of engineering. I hoped I wasn't going to make him think I was a magician, or telling tall stories, but I was going to have to tell him the truth.

"I flew. It was the only way I could get out of England, but I'd no idea where I was going to end up. It was very risky, I could have ended up landing high up on the ice, or falling into the sea, or just falling from a great height. But it was my only chance."

Peyr looked very puzzled. Then the light dawned.

Just as there are unrelated words for beauty – one for a beautiful person, another for a beautiful thing or view – so there's only one word for flying, and that's for birds.

Apart from the fact that I'd used a word that didn't go with humans, there was another problem with what I'd said. Birds – the Laana word covers bats and flying insects as well – don't talk, so they don't say "I flew", and there's no word "I flew." I'd made it up the way some other "I did so-and-so" kind of words seemed to be made up, but it didn't exist until I made it up.

If that sounds as though Laana is a linguistic straightjacket on thought, there's some truth in that. But English is also a straightjacket on thought in its own ways. Every language is.

Peyr was illiterate, but highly intelligent. It didn't take him long to work out what I meant. He also believed me, which was a relief. He could see that it was the only way I could possibly have arrived where I had, and was desperate to know how I'd done it. He knew it wasn't magic, and he wanted to understand the technology.

Explaining *how* I'd flown was a problem of a different order. Peyr had never heard of electricity, and he'd never seen plastic film. I'd filled big plastic bags with hydrogen that I'd made by electrolysis. Peyr didn't even know about gases – but he did know about steam, and he knew about hot air. He'd played with little hot air balloons: paper lanterns, lit by a candle, that floated into the sky.

Floated! That was the word I wanted. I hadn't flown, I'd floated on air. Hanging from balloons – not hot air balloons, but something a bit like them. We were getting somewhere.

I'd floated like a lantern, with no control over where I went. I hadn't flown like a bird, who can go wherever it likes.

"So you were very lucky not to land in the sea, on the ice, or high up in the mountains!"

"Quite lucky, but it wasn't as bad as it sounds. If I didn't like where I was coming down, I could go up again. I started out with nearly half a ton of water, and dribbled a bit out of the tank if I wanted to go up. If I was getting too high, I detached one of my smaller balloons. My biggest worry was if I ended up in high mountains or over the ice. I'd got a lot of warm clothes, but it gets very cold when you get really high. Even if you're warm enough, it doesn't feel good being too high, you feel funny inside, you don't seem to be able to breathe, and you can get an awful headache. I don't know why. Maybe it's because it's so scary just thinking about falling so far, but it seems to be more than that."

The next passing place was right in the middle of a village – Belgaam, Peyr told me. There was a train going the other way already in the loop, but that was where both trains would stay for the night. Gomaal, the other driver, had already gone to the inn. We found him there, sitting by a roaring fire and eating his evening meal.

The atmosphere in the inn was very congenial. Half the village must have been there, all drinking skiir, and many of them eating a meal. There was a terrific hubbub of conversation, and a great deal of laughter. Everyone wanted to know who I was, but Peyr realized I didn't want to talk much. "He's a friend of mine, a foreigner. He doesn't speak much Laana."

Our meal arrived. It was a meat and vegetable stew – mutton I think. It was the first meat I'd had in weeks. There was plenty of fish in Laanoha, but very little meat, and we couldn't afford it. "I sometimes smuggle a bit of salt meat in for a special occasion," Peyr had said, "but fresh meat is impossible for anyone but the rich in Laanoha. Even salt meat is very expensive – there's a big import duty on it."

Gomaal finished his meal. He curled up in a pile of old cloth in a corner, and was soon snoring, despite all the noise. Peyr and I soon followed suit. It had been a long day.

I woke once in the middle of the night.

I'd been dreaming. I didn't recall a lot of my dream. It was very confused, but I know it featured Aila, and my room back in England, and sailing, and flying, and riding an engine. Especially Aila, she kept turning up again and again. I remember that much very clearly.

Apart from the quiet breathing of several sleepers, the room was silent. The fire was a barely visible red glow, but otherwise everything was pitch black. All the candles of the previous evening had been extinguished.

Chapter 3

It was still night when Peyr woke me, gently shaking my shoulder. There were a few candles lit, the fire was roaring again, and there was a delicious smell of breakfast frying. The same two girls who'd served the meals the previous evening were cooking over the fire.

There were just the first hints of light in the sky as Peyr and I went outside and disappeared into the darkness in the corner of a field with little pots of water to clean our backsides. So different from arrangements in Laanoha, or the posh house where I'd stayed the first night, or most of my experience in England! But just like I remembered at my Granny's farm on the banks of the Thames near Frenchport when I was a child.

We washed at a pump in the yard behind the inn, and went back into the inn for our breakfast. Gomaal was a few minutes ahead of us.

Potato fritters, made with quite a lot of egg. And a hot drink! The first hot drink I'd had here; a bit like the dandelion tea that's so popular in England nowadays, but less bitter. I wondered what leaf it was made from. Peyr told me the name in Laana, but I couldn't recognize it from the description. Maybe it was something that doesn't grow in England.

The girls gave us a hot fruit stew and a piece of cheese to finish. I'd seen goats by Aila's village, and there had been cheese in my packed lunch from the posh house, but there was no milk or cheese in Laanoha. Nor eggs. Not for the likes of Peyr and his family, anyway.

The inn was on contract to the railway and Peyr didn't have to pay. Yaana had given me some coins, and I asked whether I should pay for my stay. Peyr said no, so far as anyone knew I was the railway's responsibility. It didn't make any difference to the railway, they paid a set amount anyway. It would just make it more complicated if I tried to pay.

I thanked the two girls as best I could. They just smiled broadly and said they looked forward to seeing me on my way

back. I left with a warm feeling about Belgaam. I'd been made
to feel very much at home.

After Belgaam, the valley got steadily narrower, and we
began to climb again. The fields were smaller, with hedges
between them, and each one a little above the last, but the land
still had crops rather than livestock.

We and another train arrived almost simultaneously at a
passing loop. Both trains slowed almost to a halt, but neither of
us stopped completely, the timing was so good.

"Preysh likes to judge passings as nicely as possible. Just
here, on a clear day like today, we can see each other from a
long way off; and since it's our first passing of the day, we've
got a fair chance of timing it to get here at the same time. You
have to slow right down, though – you need to be able to stop if
you have to, you can't take a chance of clipping the last wagon!"

Peyr and Preysh blew a few short blasts on the whistles in
greeting as we passed, or so I assumed; but Peyr told me it was
drivers' slang congratulating each other on a perfect passing.

Preysh had spent the night at the next passing place, another
one in a village, Kaahes. Men from the village helped us load
firewood and fill our water tank. We were fully loaded and ready
to go before the next train in the other direction appeared in the
distance.

"It's the other Laar. He's got the last of the old, slow engines.
It was supposed to be retired last year, but one of the new ones
has been taken for main line duties. They've added an extra train
on the Meyroha run. They've got three passenger trains a day on
that route now."

"Doesn't it slow the whole branch line down, having one
slow train?"

"He's only slow on a couple of stretches. He pulls a short
train, so he can climb just as well as anyone else. But he doesn't
have the top speed the rest of us have. Most places that doesn't
make any difference, because downhill stretches are uphill in the
other direction so they have to be short anyway. But this next
stretch is nearly level, so it's long, because most of the trains can
go quite fast in either direction."

"They're building another engine, then?"

"Yes, they are. But they might have to build two before we can retire Laar's engine, because they're talking about adding one more train every other day, so that half the passenger trains can get all the way through to Laanoha with just one overnight. If they started them early enough in Briggi they could do that anyway. But it's funny, you can finish a passenger train as late as you like, but you can't start it early in the morning."

I laughed. "People are just the same in England."

"I can understand it on the main line, where there are several passenger trains a day. Given a choice, most people wouldn't catch the early train. But when there's only one passenger train a day, they don't have a choice. I don't know why the railway thinks it has to start them late. But who am I to fathom the minds of the committee?"

"Maybe it's the committee who don't like to get up in the morning?"

"They don't use the passenger train anyway. They've got their own coach, and attach themselves to a goods train whenever they feel like it. They're a damned nuisance. You have to do a shuffle in the passing places because you're too long. Either that or take a couple of wagons off the train for the whole run, both ways, and they wouldn't like that."

As Peyr had said, this stretch was long and level, and we got up a good speed. The river was meandering about lazily in a wide, flat valley, but this wasn't rich cropland like the plains lower down. There were a few sheep and even fewer goats grazing on rough pasture.

Peyr seemed thoughtful, so I didn't trouble him with questions. I spent most of the time gazing out at the landscape, trying to spot any signs of human life other than the railway. Well, the sheep and goats were presumably a sign of human life, but that was about all. They were looking after themselves, but I suspected that they couldn't do that for the whole year. If it was as chilly as this in autumn, what was it like in winter? Buried in snow was my guess.

Peyr extracted Yaana's bundles of clothes from their hiding place, and put them on the wood pile. "Our best customer's at the next stop."

There was a train waiting in the next passing loop when we arrived.

Beside the line there was a single large building, built of huge, rough blocks of grey limestone, and with a roof of large gritstone slabs. It looked almost as though it had grown out of the ground. The sides of the valley had been littered with similar rock for miles.

"Faahiha will be in the inn. She'll have been here nearly an hour by now."

"She? A lady engine driver?" It didn't seem to fit with the local culture.

"Yes. Why not? We've got three lady drivers on this line. But you're right, it's an unusual job for ladies. There aren't any lady drivers on the main line. There's a bit of history about it. I'll tell you later, but we'd better not be talking about it just now!"

We went into the inn. There were half a dozen people sitting on benches each side of a rough wooden table, sipping skiir, chattering and laughing.

"So! You've arrived at last!" *She must be the lady driver*, I thought.

"Are you in a hurry, or do you want to eat here? I've got a packed meal ready if you'd rather get on." *He must be the landlord.*

"We'll eat here. We're holding no-one up now. We're in no hurry to get to Briggi. There's some parcels for you from Yaana on the back of the engine. Your lad can go and unload them."

"I'll stay and chat for a while too. Jinni will get her dinner at Kaahes without me if she's there before me, but she'll probably be late as well anyway. Who's your quiet friend?"

"This is Owen. Owen, this is Faahiha."

Peyr also introduced me to the family who ran the inn. I remember Tambuk's name, because that's also the name of the inn, and of the village half a mile away, but his wife's name and those of their three grown-up children escaped me. Tambuk and his wife busied themselves preparing food, and their son and two daughters went off somewhere.

"Have we driven them away?"

Faahiha laughed. "No, they're going to round up the goats."

"I saw a lot of sheep and a few goats on the way, but they didn't look as though they were going to get rounded up."

"No, most of them won't be. But Tambuk has some milking goats here. Tambuk's famous for cheese. Just you wait and see!"

We'd just got our food when there was an earthquake. It wasn't a very bad one – I'd been in much worse, and so apparently had everyone else – but it was enough to make me jump up and start to run outside.

Peyr laughed. "Sit down, Owen. We're not in Laanoha here. This place won't tumble down round your ears from a little tremble like that. Tambuk's been here a thousand years and it's not fallen down yet."

"I don't think it's as old as that, really, Peyr. Graamon says there weren't any earthquakes in the old days, before the ice. That's less than a thousand years ago. And Tambuk was built with the likelihood of earthquakes in mind."

I felt a bit stupid. Faahiha was right: I could see that Tambuk was built to withstand a pretty vigorous shaking. And whoever this Graamon was, he knew what he was talking about: back in England, that's exactly what they used to say about the earthquakes. Well, what some of them used to say, anyway – the ones I reckoned knew what they were talking about.

"Who's Graamon?"

"Graamon's a friend of ours in Briggi. He's someone you ought to meet – he'd love to hear about your ballooning. He's someone who'd probably understand how you did it, or at least have a better chance than I have! But I'll tell you more about him on the way. We'd better get moving. That wasn't much of a quake, but any quake can bring rubbish down onto the line. I don't want to have to crawl along in the dark for hours, and neither does Faahiha."

"I'd rather stay the night here, to be honest, Peyr. Nobody will blame us if everything's late tomorrow, they'll have felt the quake. Even in daylight you can't go fast safely after a quake, not until the line's been checked, so it'll be dark before we get anywhere anyway."

"Okay. I don't need much convincing about that. Owen and I can stay here too. Briggi will still be there in the morning. And our meal's nearly ready."

"And I'll get to hear Owen's story!"

I got to hear Faahiha's story, too, and how the Briggi line came to have three lady drivers.

Faahiha's family lived in Briggi. Her mother died when Faahiha was still quite small, and her father, who was an engine driver, took to taking Faahiha with him nearly every trip, only leaving her with her elderly grandparents occasionally. She became a favourite with all the drivers. An observant little girl, she soon knew all about the railway and the engine.

When she was older, she had to spend more time looking after her grandmother, but still felt very attached to the railway. She became involved with a young engine driver, Berraam, and after her grandmother died, she started accompanying him to Laanoha and back.

There was an earthquake just after they'd left Tambuk at the end of one trip. Faahiha was six months pregnant and it was snowing. The earthquake was a bad one, and they were in a rock cutting when it struck. A rock fell on the engine, crushing part of the cab, and killing Berraam outright.   Faahiha could see immediately that he was beyond help.

Naturally she was distraught, but she knew she had to save herself. It was very lucky for her that she knew the engine and the railway well. She brought the train to a halt as quickly as she safely could.

She either had to walk back along the line to Tambuk, or somehow drive the train to Briggi. Walking four or five miles back to Tambuk in what looked likely soon to be a major snowstorm didn't appeal, but she couldn't be sure the line to Briggi would be passable.

It had been quite a powerful quake. Would any of the bridges and viaducts have been damaged? Might there have been landslides onto the track? Either way was a bit of a gamble, but driving the train seemed the better option. She told herself that the line was built to withstand quakes, and that the falling rock was a very unhappy bit of bad luck. She walked back up the line to inspect the train.

Her fears were well founded. Halfway along the train, several wagons had derailed. She tried to uncouple the rear of the train, but couldn't shift the coupling. She returned to the engine and inched it forward a little, hoping to take the pressure off the couplings so she could undo one of them. She walked back along the track to the first derailed wagon. She still couldn't shift the coupling, which she quickly realized was jammed by the misalignment. The next one forward was free enough to undo.

She'd never actually driven the engine before, but she'd watched Berraam and her father doing it often enough. She was very nervous about the condition of the line, so she drove very slowly. She'd almost reached Briggi when she found the line flooded.

She knew that the flood wasn't very deep, because she knew the line was almost level at that point, and began to climb again at the other side of the river as it went into the town. But she couldn't see whether the line was intact under the water, and anyway she couldn't be certain the flood was shallow enough for the engine to ford safely.

She wondered why the river had flooded, and whether it was getting deeper or draining away. She didn't want to wait for it to drain away, even if that was going to happen.

If it hadn't been snowing, she'd have been able to see Briggi – and people in Briggi would have been able to see the train. She wondered if they'd heard it.

There was a road bridge about a mile upstream, that would be above the level of the flood. On the other side of the river, the road would take her into Briggi, but what was the country between where she was and the road like? In the snow...

Then she realized that they'd hear the engine's whistle in Briggi, no problem.

They did. There was an answering whistle from the other side. Faahiha knew they would think it was Berraam driving the train, but she thought they must realize he wouldn't attempt to take the engine blindly through the flood. She was right.

She waited. She knew they'd come across to her before long somehow, and she was right about that, too. It was an hour before a four-handled trolley appeared out of the blizzard, the water halfway up its wheels, four men – two of them engine drivers Faahiha knew – pumping the handles, and two sitting on the front of the trolley, feeling for the rails under the water with poles to make sure the line was sound.

Knowing that the line was sound, and knowing that the water wasn't too deep, the two experienced drivers drove the train slowly into Briggi, pushing the trolley.

There was one other fatality amongst the railwaymen in the big quake. Faahiha's father's engine derailed at speed near Embrouha, and fell forty metres into the gorge. Faahiha had lost everybody, but not her spirit. She was tough.

There was a lot of damage to the line. It was three weeks before it was reopened, and there were speed restrictions on several sections for a good deal longer than that.

Just two months later, Faahiha gave birth to twin daughters – Berraami and Jinni. The Briggi line drivers decided that they'd club together to support Faahiha and her twins, but Faahiha wouldn't have it. "I've proved I can drive an engine," she said, "I'll earn my living."

The railway company didn't want to employ her, but they made the mistake of trying to make the excuse that the other drivers wouldn't like it. They were utterly wrong about that.

Berraami and Jinni grew up on the footplate, even more than Faahiha had. It seemed inevitable that they too would be engine drivers, and they were.

I told Faahiha and Peyr all about my escape from England. She agreed with Peyr that he must introduce me to Graamon in Briggi, and that he would want to know all the technical details of how to make balloons capable of lifting a man.

I rather suspected that the technology to do it was beyond anything available here, but I didn't want to sound too certain about that – I wasn't completely certain myself. But I'd seen no sign of anything electrical, and suspected that even if there was electrical apparatus hidden away in workshops anywhere it wouldn't be able to produce the currents needed to generate large volumes of hydrogen. I didn't know any other method. Add to that, I didn't think there was any plastic sheeting here. I couldn't imagine what else you could make the balloons out of, unless you could make a single really huge one out of the heavier materials that were available – and then how would you control ascents and descents?

Faahiha and Peyr were much more interested to hear about the trip itself.

I'd floated up from the garden at home on a dark, foggy evening, deliberately choosing a time when no-one would be able to see me. Happily it seemed that no-one had taken any notice of the forest of balloons I'd collected, tethered to a couple of big trees in the garden. I was under house arrest, but what I was up to no-one seemed to care. With guards all around the area, it was obvious that I couldn't escape. I'm pretty sure no-one witnessed my departure.

What they must have thought when they found I'd disappeared, I don't know. I very much doubt anyone worked out how I'd escaped, or where I'd got to. I'd wanted to get far, far away, where no-one would know who I was, and I'd certainly succeeded in that.

I'd never been off the ground before, and nor had anyone I knew. As far as I knew, no-one had since ancient times, when according to legend, some sort of controlled flight had been commonplace. How much truth there was in the legends, I wasn't sure – but I suspected there was more truth in them than most people believed.

I had no idea what I was letting myself in for as I floated up into the fog. Would my methods of going up and down work as planned? Would the wind take me too fast? Where would I drift? How long could I keep aloft, if I didn't like the look of any of the places I passed? How high would I go, and would it be very cold, as it was in high mountains, or even colder if I had to go right over the top of the mountains? How high could I go? Might I end up forced to land high in the mountains, in the sea, or on the ice?

How big was the risk of my balloons catching fire? I'd made sure there was a good vertical separation between them, but if one low down caught fire, would the wire to the upper ones survive? Or would the rising fire ignite the upper balloons anyway? From the lowest balloon upwards, I'd used wire rather than rope to minimize the risk of it burning through, but would that make me vulnerable to lightning? I didn't know.

There were so many unknowns. I consider myself very lucky that none of the dreadful things I'd imagined came to pass – they so easily could have done. But it was the only way I could think of to escape, and I couldn't bear the thought of spending the rest of my life under house arrest. They were supplying food and water and fuel, and no doubt they would have supplied clothes when my wardrobe began to get ragged, but they read all my letters, and my friends and colleagues couldn't visit me without a guard present. I was suffocating.

Fortunately I'd had the foresight to stock up with materials at home, suspecting that I might be placed under house arrest. It was fortunate too that they didn't cut my electricity supply, and didn't seem to think about how much electricity I was using. I used a lot making all my hydrogen. Godfrey reckoned that the ancients had had much more powerful electricity supplies than modern England, to judge by some of the archaeological finds he'd examined. How they'd produced so much electricity he'd not been able to fathom.

Faahiha and Peyr were fascinated to hear how I'd floated right up through the fog and out into the clear sky above it, seeing the fog from above like a blanket of clouds *below* me, and the stars in a clear sky above me even though it was a night of thick fog in the town below. It was eerily quiet, and the top of the fog was only dimly illuminated by the starlight.

It was very cold. I was glad I'd anticipated that, and brought plenty of warm clothes.

There wasn't much wind, and I drifted very slowly southwards – not realizing I was moving at all until I floated over the edge of the fog, and the ground beneath came into view. Really it was the disappearance of the white fog I could see. The ground was utterly black.

I was very high by then, but I didn't know how high until first light, well before dawn. I'd seen a few lights on the ground, but just points of light, nothing recognizable. I could see light in the sky before I could see anything on the ground, but it wasn't long before I could make out fields and houses. The houses were barely more than specks.

I considered letting one balloon go, to float a little lower, but decided just to float on. I wasn't too high – it was cold, but not unbearable. I liked that I probably wasn't very noticeable from the ground, and the fewer balloons I released, the further I'd be able to go.

I didn't know how far I'd come, but I was sure I wanted to go a great deal further before I could be confident of being beyond the reach of the English authorities, or their spies and friends in neighbouring countries. I guessed I was doing fifteen or twenty miles an hour, judging by how fast the scenery was passing below me. Despite my speed, I felt very still.

By the light in the sky I knew I was heading south, and before long I knew exactly where I was. The view from the sky was surprisingly easy to relate to the maps I'd seen of southern England and northern France. I was crossing the river Thames, just upstream of where the chain ferry runs between Frenchport in England, and Louvigny in France on the south bank.

I told Faahiha and Peyr how the French have a different name for the Thames, and how there's a joke argument about which is correct; that there are a lot of serious arguments between the English and the French, but that the language difference isn't really one of them. The difference between English and French is much less than between either of them and Laana!

The wind changed during the morning. It had been from the north, but was now from the west. I sometimes floated over towns and villages, but mostly it was farmland. Late in the day I began to see snowcapped mountains far to the south, and knew they were the Alps.

For a long time, far below me there was a big river, nothing like as big as the Thames, but a good size nonetheless. I saw several large boats on it, some apparently trading up and down it, others seemingly ferries plying across it. Then the line of my drift and the line of the river diverged, and it disappeared off to the south.

Gradually the proportion of woodland to fields increased, and towns and villages got smaller and more widely separated, until eventually I was floating over apparently uninhabited forest, broken only by a few rivers and bare-topped hills.

As the sun got lower in the west, I began to descend. This didn't look like a good place to land, almost uninhabited, and anyway I wanted to get much further, well away from England. I opened the tap at the bottom of my tank of water for a few moments, and was relieved to find myself rising again without having to lose too much of my water.

I hadn't slept the previous night, and although I wasn't doing much but watch the scenery, I was exhausted. I dozed on and off, but was afraid of losing too much height and crashing, or getting too high and maybe freezing to death in my sleep.

At one point I woke to find myself skimming the treetops – I think it might have been my feet brushing the top of a tree that woke me. In a panic, I released too much water before I'd really woken properly, and then I rose quite fast and got very high. It was really cold, I began to feel light-headed and nauseous, and I had a pain in my ears. I wasn't sure whether that was caused by fear or the cold or both, or something else entirely; certainly breathing felt hard.

I released a small balloon from the very top group, and down I went again. I had to release more water to avoid crash landing, but I was careful this time not to release too much.

Over the next few days I learnt to control my height quite well. I don't know how many days I was in the air though; I was so tired I completely lost track of time.

I found that I almost never needed to release a balloon, but needed to get rid of a little water quite often, especially at night. It seemed that my balloons were leaking steadily.

Another time I had to release a balloon, I'd climbed to a great height to avoid a thunderstorm. Lightning was one of my greatest fears. A couple of hundred metres above the ground, I was being drawn towards the storm, but as I climbed it drew me less, and before I reached the top of the thunderhead, I was being blown away from it. I knew Godfrey would be very interested in such information, but I was sure I was never going to see him again.

"Graamon would be interested to know that, too."

But escaping the thunderstorm I'd climbed too high again, and had to descend after only a little while because it made me feel so unwell.

Most often I seemed to be drifting eastward, but sometimes I'd drift in other directions for a while. Of course I don't know which way I went when it was dark, or when I was dozing, and I wasn't always thinking about which way I was going anyway. Often I could see ice in the north, but I was relieved to find that I never approached the ice closely, nor did I approach very high mountains, although I saw them in all directions at one time or another.

I did cross a huge area of bare rock and sand for a while, and hoped against hope that I wouldn't have to land in it – but I wasn't much happier at the idea of landing in the vast empty grasslands I crossed, either, or the apparently uninhabited forest.

Finally and most worryingly, as the light revealed the scene below me one morning, I found myself over the sea, with no land and not even a ship in sight. I was out of sight of land for at least several hours, but it could have been much longer, I'd lost track of time so badly by then. When land did finally appear, I was so disoriented and confused that I didn't know which direction I was approaching it from. I hoped it would be inhabited.

The coast was rocky and bare; inland was unbroken forest. Then there was a line of rocky hills, and at the foot of the hills a broad band of what looked like fields, and unmistakably, a village, with a large quarry beyond it.

I released a balloon, and another when it seemed I might end up high on the rocky hills beyond the village. Then I seemed to be descending too fast, so I released a little water, but I didn't dare release too much for fear of starting to rise again. I had quite a rough landing on a rocky slope a mile or so from the village, but luckily I wasn't seriously hurt.

I tied my remaining balloons to a large rock in case I decided I needed to move on again – I'd still got some water in my tank, so I knew I could still go at least a little way, but I hoped I wouldn't have to, because I'd completely run out of food.

"So your balloons are still tied to a rock near Sirimi? I wonder if anyone's found them. I wonder what they'll make of them if they do?"

"There's a very odd water tank, too – it's made of plastic, a material I don't think you have here. And a lot of warm clothes. The hydrogen's most likely all leaked out of the balloons by now, so they'll just be plastic bags tied to bits of wire. Odd enough anyway."

"You left some clothes there?"

"Yes. I didn't want to carry them all. There are a lot more than I needed once I'd landed, even allowing for being out in the cold at night."

"We should go up to Sirimi sometime and see if they're still there. I'd like to see your plastic stuff, and it'd be a shame to lose your clothes."

"I don't know if I'll be able to find them. I was pretty confused when I left them."

"And yet you walked half way to the Sirimi Road crossing before you got to sleep?"

"No, I slept right there, still in my harness, tied to the rock along with the balloons. I don't know how long I was there, my guess is about twenty-four hours, because it was early afternoon again by the time I unharnessed myself and walked into the village."

This conversation took much longer than you might think if you forget that I was still at an early stage of learning Laana. The candles were nearly burnt out before we blew them out and rolled ourselves up in the piles of cloth in the corner of the inn. Tambuk and his family had been asleep in another corner for hours. How much they'd heard of my story I didn't know, and it didn't seem to matter; but I think they'd probably given up listening when Faahiha and Peyr were telling me Faahiha's story, which they knew already.

Chapter 4

It was still dark when we woke to the smell of frying meat. Tambuk and his wife were preparing breakfast. It was goat, and it was delicious. There were fried potato slices, too.

"All being well, in a couple of hours you'll be in Briggi, and Faahiha will be at Kaahes. But I'm making you packed lunches in case there's problems on the line."

"Thanks, Tambuk. It'll be a good four hours anyway, even if the line's clear, because we'll take it really slow. We can't afford to risk hitting a rock that's big enough to derail us, but too small to see until it's too late."

We set off as soon as it was light enough to see the line clearly. Before long we were in a rocky cutting, and Peyr told me it was where Berraam was killed. The line was clear for us.

Closer to Briggi, there was a cutting through softer ground where there were a couple of minor landslips, but they didn't quite reach the line. Peyr couldn't be sure of that from a distance, so we had to approach them very slowly, but they were no trouble to us.

"I'll report them, and they'll send a team out to clear them. The cutting's wide and shallow to keep landslips like that off the line, they always happen even in minor quakes."

"I wonder what the line south was like for Faahiha?"

"I expect it'll have been okay. Quakes usually get stronger the further north you go. They'll have felt last night's even right down in Laanoha, but it'll scarcely have made the roof tiles rattle there. It's usually noticeably less even in Kaahes than in Briggi."

"Aha. I wondered when you said about Laanoha being less quake-proof than Tambuk."

"A big quake in Briggi usually gives Laanoha a bit of a rattle, and there's often more damage in Laanoha than there is in Briggi. But that's only because there's a lot more of Laanoha, and Briggi's built to live through them, just like Tambuk. A proper Briggi quake would flatten half the buildings in Laanoha. There'd be thousands killed."

We emerged from the cutting onto a curve on an embankment, and then onto a low viaduct over a broad meadow with a river meandering across it. "Faahiha's flood was here."

At the other end of the viaduct the line disappeared between buildings. I guessed – correctly – that this was Briggi. We'd arrived at last – about eighteen hours late.

There was a train ready to leave. The driver had started to raise steam as soon as they heard Peyr's whistle approaching the town, but he wanted to hear from Peyr about the condition of the line first. "Clear as far as Tambuk, anyway. I don't know beyond that, we were already at Tambuk when the quake struck."

I realized that he'd meet someone at Tambuk who knew what the next stretch was like – or if he didn't, he wouldn't be able to go on at all anyway. The drivers obviously knew that without a moment's thought.

We met up with a couple of other drivers for lunch at an inn right by the railway yard. They wanted to know who I was, but Peyr didn't tell them very much beyond the fact that I was foreign, and I didn't say much. They wanted to know if the line had been damaged by the quake at all, and of course Peyr only knew about the first stretch. One of them was due to take a train out as soon as Jinni arrived, but we'd no idea when that would be. It was going to be a couple of days before everything was back on schedule, even if the line was undamaged everywhere.

On this shift, Peyr should have had two nights in Briggi before returning, but we'd had one unscheduled night at Tambuk, so we only had an afternoon and an evening to take a look at the place. The contrast with Laanoha was striking, but I got a good feeling about Briggi.

I also got a good feeling about the people. People in Laanoha were friendly enough in private, but out on the street most people seemed very wary. It wasn't like that in Briggi at all. There was a universal openness and friendliness, even on the street.

Peyr delivered the last bundle of the clothes Yaana had made to a house in a back street, then we went on to Graamon's lodgings. He wasn't at home. His landlady said he'd gone to Meyroha, and she wasn't sure when he would be back. "He often goes to Meyroha nowadays, I'm not sure why. He's usually back in less than two weeks, though, so he's not staying there long. Maybe he's got a girl there!"

Peyr laughed. "That wouldn't surprise me a bit. It's time he had. He'll make a good father if he ever gets round to it. Oh, and tell him I've got a foreign friend he ought to meet – Owen here. He knows my schedule, or can find it out easily enough. If he gets a chance, he'll make the effort to catch me, and then we can arrange something."

"I don't know why, I thought Graamon was about your age, Peyr."

"He's not all that much younger than me. Maybe ten years at most. I'm not sure how old he is. He had a girlfriend for years, long ago, but she was sickly and wouldn't marry him. She said she couldn't raise a family, she wouldn't live long enough for them to grow up. She was right, she died in her late twenties. Graamon took a long time getting over it. I'm not sure he ever really has. But he's got the sharpest mind of anyone I know. He's the brains behind the new engine design, amongst other things."

"But he lives here in Briggi? I thought they were building them in Laanoha."

"They are. Doesn't stop him doing the designs here, although he does have to visit the workshops from time to time. But he likes it better here, and the bosses don't dare to tell him where to live, he's too valuable. They can't afford to upset him."

We walked all the way along a street of shops, and took a look in several of them. Peyr bought a couple of silky scarves. "Yaani and my mother'll like these. The winds are beginning to get chilly again, even down in Laanoha, and last year's scarves are looking about ready for the bedding pile."

"Won't you get one for Aila?"

Peyr laughed. "I thought you could get her one. She'd like that." So, shyly, I did. I got the nicest one I could afford, and the shopkeeper said, "It's a present for your young lady? Would you like me to wrap it nicely for you? No extra charge."

I was about to say, "No, thanks," but Peyr was quicker. "Yes please. She's not exactly his young lady, though. Well, I'm sure he'd rather you didn't put it like that, anyway."

Peyr was right, I would rather she didn't put it like that. I'd met Aila once, for about three quarters of an hour. In the presence of her father, and with a significant language barrier. But I'd definitely felt something, and Peyr had obviously seen that and thought Aila felt it too. Or was it just Peyr's sense of humour? Or some cultural thing I'd not picked up on?

For our evening meal we went to an inn down by the river. Before we went in, Peyr took me to look at the boats. They were very different from the boats on the Aaha at Laanoha. There, the boats were beamy, with tall masts – there was plenty of room in the river, plenty of height under the bridge, and the bigger boats were designed to sail up and down the coast, as well as up and down the river. Here, the boats were more like English barges – narrow to fit in locks, with a hinged mast to go under low bridges, but seemingly with a deep draught.

There was a short spur of the railway right down to the dockside. A group of men were loading logs from a barge onto some railway wagons.

Peyr seemed to know people wherever he went. I tried my best to follow the conversation over the meal, and I could understand a lot of what Peyr said, but the clientele in this inn seemed to have a very different dialect. I'd had little difficulty understanding people elsewhere in Briggi, but here they might have been talking a different language. If so, Peyr understood it – but was replying in plain Laana, without apparently causing any reaction.

After the meal, we went back to the inn by the railway yard for the night. We drank skiir with other railway workers and the innkeeper and his family, laughing and joking well into the night. "We're due out of here at one tomorrow afternoon, but everything's still running hours late. Goraal hasn't arrived yet, and he was due at four this afternoon. I doubt he'll come tonight now, but I expect everyone will make an extra early start tomorrow, so we'll have to be ready to go on time. It could be another day or two before things are back on schedule though."

Faahiha's daughter Jinni had apparently arrived a few hours after us okay, but we'd not met her. Being a Briggi resident, she'd gone home.

The pile of old clothes in the corner, that was the typical bedding arrangement in this country, here smelt rather of wood smoke. "They've not had enough dry weather recently to dry them out of doors, and you can't leave them unwashed forever," Peyr explained. "Especially in an inn. Most inns have a drying room upstairs around the chimney, but here they use the engine shed. Briggi's not an easy place to have upstairses."

"What do they do at the waterside inn?"

"I don't think you'd want to sleep there unless you were pretty desperate!"

I thought he was saying the bedding pile might not have been very wholesome, but there might have been more to it than that. Reading between the lines of the conversation earlier in the evening, I guessed that Peyr had taken me down to the waterside inn deliberately to introduce me to a community it was best to be on good terms with.

I dreamt about Aila again that night. At one point it was dark, and snowing, and I was trying to rescue her from a flood. At another she was running away from me as if to make me chase her, but she kept disappearing into the driving snow and I was afraid of losing her.

Then somehow we were in a maze of old alleyways between wooden buildings in Laanoha. There was an earthquake, and the buildings were shaking and seemed about to collapse around us; and always Aila was running away from me, looking back at me, smiling that shy smile and laughing.

Chapter 5

Goraal had arrived at Tambuk pretty late and stayed the night, but he'd left there very early and the train that should have gone the afternoon before was ready to go as soon as he arrived. "With luck the whole line's back on schedule now. At least we know it's all clear, there's just some very minor landslips to clear up, nothing that affects normal working."

A goatshed roof had collapsed at Belgaam, killing a couple of goats, and a landslide into the river at Embrouha had caused a wave that swamped a couple of small boats, but as far as Goraal had heard, nobody had been hurt anywhere. It had been a fairly minor quake – it was rather unlucky that even a goatshed had suffered.

Peyr explained how it had been a landslide into the river, combined with a damaged dam further upstream, that had caused the flood at Briggi after the quake when Berraam was killed. It had been very lucky that Briggi wasn't flooded. It was only saved by the fact that the dam hadn't been very full. Half the men of Briggi had worked like madmen for a couple of weeks to clear the blockage in the river before the thaw, which they knew would have flooded Briggi badly.

Our first wagon was taken over by the workmen going out to the landslips. Every train for several days was going to have one wagon reserved for the workmen. We had to stop several times to drop a few men off at each place where there was work to do, and were a bit late at Tambuk; but Diraan was late too. He'd been dropping workmen off here and there on the run from Kaahes as well; but beyond Kaahes the line was apparently unaffected.

"We'll probably be back on schedule before we get home," Peyr said.

Before we left Tambuk, Tambuk's son brought several big parcels of cloth, and Peyr hid them away under the cab floor. "Is there still room for you in there, Owen? Or should I get Tamun to take one of the parcels back until my next trip?"

"Oh, I'll squeeze in somehow. I know the routine now, and it's not for long."

After Tambuk, we had to stop several times to pick up workmen going home to Kaahes after their shifts.

We stopped for lunch in Kaahes. Peyr warned me, "Watch out for those two girls at Belgaam. We'll be staying there again tonight. I saw how they were eyeing you up. They're both on the lookout for a nice young man. There's no-one the right age for them in Belgaam who's not already spoken for, apart from a couple of lads who are a bit dim, to put it mildly. And they'll guess this may be the last chance they'll have to get at you for ages."

I wondered what exactly Peyr thought they might do. Try to get into bed with me and then insist that I had to marry them? Perhaps with the threat of violence from their family? I didn't feel able to ask. I was getting into aspects of culture where I needed to know the rules but was unable to find out.

Or did he have his eye on me for his own daughter, and didn't want competition? He didn't have to worry on that score. Those two girls seemed nice enough, but they'd not had the same effect on me that Aila had had, not in the slightest. Whether I really wanted to get involved with Aila or not I really didn't know, but I knew that I didn't want to get involved with anyone else just at the moment.

I wondered how on Earth I could find out the things I needed to know without asking directly, without letting Peyr know what I was fishing for. Things had seemed so simple, by comparison, in Laanoha – but probably only because I'd been shut up in their room most of the time, or out on the street where everyone was a bit wary of strangers.

I needn't have worried. Peyr realized I'd gone a bit thoughtful, and guessed why. Back in the cab, he broached the subject again. "You don't know the rules of the game here at all, do you? Don't worry too much. They won't try to blackmail you or anything like that. They'll try to find out as much as they can about you, and advertise themselves to you as subtly as they can, but that's all. They'll just try to make sure you want to be in Belgaam as often as you can, nothing more than that for the moment. They'll know they're winning if you land there for the night with one of the other drivers, when I'm on one of the other shifts! For the time being, they'll be allies, but if once they think they've hooked you, they'll each be trying to catch you for themselves."

It seemed to be more a bit of a laugh to Peyr than anything else, but I suspected there was a serious undercurrent in relation to his own daughter. But that question could wait for the moment.

Forewarned is forearmed. Whether I'd even have noticed the girls' behaviour if Peyr hadn't said anything I don't know. He was right that they'd be subtle, but he was also right that they'd be trying to impress me, and trying to find out as much about me as they could. I spoke less than I could have, hiding behind my limited knowledge of Laana. Peyr played along with them, seeing that I was taking heed of his warning, and not wanting to sour the atmosphere.

After an excellent dinner, we all chatted late into the night, but they learnt little about me beyond what they knew already: that I was a foreigner. Everything was very friendly though, we slept well, they made us an excellent breakfast, and we parted with a friendly, "See you soon!" with no actual mention of when or even whether I'd be travelling that way again.

Then we were gaining speed again, leaving Belgaam behind. "You actually understood quite a lot of the chatter, didn't you? I think even the locals could tell that. They'll think you're the strong silent type rather than really not understanding. Those girls have probably got even more interested now!"

"Maybe. Things don't always work out the way one intends. But as long as I don't get flirty with them, everything should be all right, shouldn't it?"

"Hmm. I don't know. For a while, certainly, but it could get awkward if you spend the night here often. A pity, this shift gives more time in Briggi than the other shifts – two nights and a whole day rather than just one night and two bits. I think you liked Briggi, didn't you? Even though we didn't get as long there as we should have done. It'd be good to get to know it better, and better to meet Graamon on his own territory in Briggi than in Laanoha."

"I rather wished I'd met Graamon on this trip – but maybe it'll be better if my Laana improves a bit before I meet him really anyway."

"That's good thinking. I have a feeling that Graamon may be the man to find work for you, with your technical knowledge, and the better your Laana is when you first meet him the better, for that. Maybe it's a pity we asked his landlady to put him in touch with us!"

"Maybe, but what's done is done, and it seemed the right thing to do at the time. I don't suppose it matters a lot anyway. You could waste an entire lifetime waiting for the right time to do something. I'll do my best to improve as fast as I can, anyway."

I rather wondered whether at this stage my knowledge would improve faster, and be more impressive to Graamon – I was already thinking in those terms! Oh well – if I learnt to read and write Laana as well. But how could I broach the subject without insulting someone? I'd seen no evidence of any of my friends reading or writing. I had a suspicion that Judd might be able to. But only a suspicion, no actual evidence.

And what about Aila? I was sure that Graamon must be literate.

"How often would 'too often' be? Do you think it'd be okay to overnight at Belgaam maybe twice more? Once next trip, to get a better look at Briggi, then miss one trip, then one more to try actually to find somewhere to stay? That's if Graamon hasn't sought us out by then, of course."

"Oh, I'm pretty sure he'll either visit us or get a message to me to send you to him before that. You might manage that first trip in three weeks' time, but I'd be very surprised if he leaves it nine weeks."

We must have met someone at Sirimi junction, but I really can't remember who, whether we had to wait for them or vice-versa. It was all getting to be such a familiar routine – and it's got so much more familiar since, of course.

We must have had lunch at Raamba, too, or picked up a packed lunch to eat in the cab, I really don't remember which.

I do remember stopping at the Sirimi Road crossing, though. The lady who'd waved from her gig was there. Peyr was already slowing down before the crossing came into sight, because he was expecting her. Her horse was waiting patiently with the gig, by the big rock I'd stood on three weeks and two days earlier, and she was standing on the road, right by the railway. Peyr's control of his train was perfect: he rolled to a halt with the cab right beside her, with only the tiniest touch of the brakes at the last moment – not like the time he'd stopped for me, when he wasn't expecting anyone, and he'd stopped with a great squealing of brakes.

She held out a paper note, and Peyr reached down to take it, but as she reached up to give it to him, she spotted me in the cab. She looked surprised, and said to Peyr, "A moment – don't set off straight away. I know your friend!"

So she was from the big house!

Peyr climbed down from the cab, and beckoned to me to climb down too. The lady startled me greatly by giving me a big hug, and then held me at arm's length by the shoulders, and said, "I'd ask you how you were, if I thought you'd understand!"

Peyr laughed, "You'd be surprised how much he does understand, lady, with him only having been learning Laana for three weeks."

I was abashed, and stammered, "I'm very well, thank you. Peyr and his family have been looking after me very well."

The lady looked me up and down, and said, "Your pronunciation is very good! Someone has been teaching you well, not just looking after you. But you must be a good student, too. Maybe we should have tried to keep you at Siroha. But what's done is done, it seemed right to let you go when you seemed to want to go. But you must visit us some time! Everyone will want to hear your story now you can talk, and there are always interesting people here for you to listen to as well. When will you be able to come?"

I didn't know what to say. I quite liked the idea of visiting the big house and its people again, but I wasn't sure what Peyr would think, and didn't want to upset him. However interested I was in the big house and its people, I valued Peyr's friendship far more.

Peyr saw my confusion. "I'm sure Owen would love to visit you some time, lady. Just now he has commitments in Laanoha, but I'll be here again on my next trip and we'll work out when would be convenient for him and for you."

"Very good. I'll be here. We have some of his things up at the house, too. Owen, did you say his name is? Owen's things. One of the shepherds found them up on the hill. I could bring them down on the big cart if you like, but I don't know how you'd carry them on the train, unless you can open one of the wagons."

The shepherd must have been totally mystified by my things, but it must have been immediately obvious to the people in the big house that they belonged to me, once they'd seen them. No wonder they wanted to hear my story! They'd probably been very puzzled by the sudden arrival of a foreigner so far from the coast or the border anyway.

"I'd be very grateful if you brought me some of my clothes. We could carry them on the train easily enough. But if you don't mind keeping the other things for the moment that would be kind – I'll have to work out what to do with them."

I was thinking that Graamon would want to see them, and would know how to move them; but I didn't want to say anything about Graamon, at least not without talking to Peyr first.

"That's fine. There's plenty of storage space at Giroha, it's no trouble at all. I'll bring your clothes down here and meet you on your next trip."

"It might be just me, Owen might not be with me for a few weeks. But I can take them anyway, that's not a problem."

I don't know whether the lady noticed the meaningful glance Peyr shot at me, but she didn't react at all even if she did. I kept quiet.

"We'd better be getting along, anyway," Peyr said, "Don't want to keep Berraami waiting at Elbrouha. See you in four days' time then."

"Okay. I'll have Owen's clothes for you. Bye."

"It's good they've found my things. It'll be nice to have some more of my own clothes – and there's more warm clothes than I'll ever need, if any of the rest of you would like some of them. And I expect Graamon will be interested to see some of my ballooning equipment."

"I'm sure he will. I'd quite like to take a look at it myself, but he'll understand what you did much better, I'm sure."

"Some of the stuff is too big to carry on the engine, and I presume we can't put anything in a wagon. Do you think Graamon will have some method of moving it? Or maybe he'll be quite happy to look at it where it is – I don't really want it all for anything other than showing to him. Or to anyone else who might find it interesting, of course."

"Oh, lots of people will find it interesting – but it'll only be idle curiosity in most cases. Graamon may be only person to really make use of what he learns from you. And he'll find a way to move it if he decides he wants to – he could commandeer a wagon on a train any time he wants, they wouldn't dare to refuse him. Oh, another thing is that if Graamon wants you to work for him, he'll tell the railway to get papers for you. That would be really good – they'd be pretty good papers, and you could come and go whenever and wherever you like, all open and above board. I think there's a pretty good chance of that."

I wondered how, or whether, to raise the question of visiting Siroha, and decided not to say anything for the moment. Peyr definitely hadn't seemed keen on the idea of me going there, and I didn't want to seem keen if he wasn't. He might or might not say anything sooner or later. I thought it might be best if we'd discussed it before he met the lady again in four days' time – I didn't think I'd be there then.

At Elbrouha there was no friendly, "All clear. Berraami's on her own." from Peyr. I had to stay hidden down the side of the engine. I heard Peyr talking with two other men, but there was no trace of a woman's voice. I waited. I knew there must have been a stranger on the other train, someone who couldn't be allowed to know about my presence in Peyr's train. I would have to wait quietly where I was until we set off, before I'd be able to go back to the cab.

It seemed an eternity. I was sure we'd not stopped long at Elbrouha before, but the waiting just went on and on.

It turned out that Berraami and Laar had been asked to swap shifts because a special passenger had asked to travel on that train, and the company didn't want even to raise the question of whether he minded sharing the cab with a woman for two days. Then the special passenger had insisted on having a packed lunch at Elbrouha instead of getting a cooked meal at Raamba, "We arrive at Raamba too late for lunch," he'd apparently said. He'd also insisted that both drivers should eat with him.

"Damned selfish idiot," said Peyr as we accelerated out of the loop. "That's going to make the entire railway run an hour late for the rest of the day. I hope that either they've not told Bereg that I'll have eaten already, or he's remembered that you'll be with me and realized that you'll still want something even if I've eaten."

They hadn't told Bereg, and he had food for both Peyr and me. "Ah well, don't waste it. We'll all fatten up a bit against lean times later," he said. "They'll be annoyed at Raamba, though, a meal ready and no-one paying for it."

"Jinni will be chafing at the bit, wondering where her sister's got to, fed and ready to set off as soon as she arrives. Then she'll see it's Laar, but not want to spend time walking half a train length to meet him and find out what's going on. Tell you what — keep the chap at Raamba sweet. Here's the money for the wasted meal, you give it to him when you get there. Laar would have wanted to, but won't have been able to."

"No, you keep your money, Peyr. I'll pay him myself. Otherwise, if it turns out that Laar's managed to pay him already, or he won't take the money, I'll end up with your money in my pocket."

"Okay, if you don't mind. We ought to be able to claim it back off the company, but I think it's probably best to swallow it ourselves."

"I'm sure it is!"

Bereg helped us load up with firewood and fill the water tank, and we were off again.

The sun set while we were on the long, sloping viaduct approaching the mountains. By the time we reached the end of the viaduct, the mountains looked black against an angry red sky, and the valley below us was almost invisible.

We had to wait at a signal before we entered the tunnel where our branch line joins the main line – there was a train coming up on the main line. Far below us and about to go underneath the viaduct behind us, we could see its headlight. Behind the headlight, its two fires illuminated the clouds of smoke and steam its two engines were making. They were making a huge noise. It was a passenger train, going at a good pace despite climbing hard.

"They're late, too. They're supposed to go through just before us even when we're running on time. I wonder what happened to them? They'll be glad we were even later, or they'd be stuck behind us all the way to Laanoha."

"Wouldn't the signalmen have held us up to let them through first?"

"Not if we'd arrived before they were in sight. They wouldn't know how late the main line might be."

"I'd not thought about that before. If each signalbox is in sight of the next, how does it work through the tunnel here?"

"There are two relay boxes up on the mountain. You can't see them from the trains, but the signalman in the box down there by the main line can see the first one. The signal here is operated by a wire running over pulleys all the way from the box by the main line. It's a horrible job being signalman in the relay boxes. All the other signalmen can ride on the trains to get to and from work, or they live near their boxes. But it's a hell of a walk up to those boxes on the mountain, especially in bad weather. And lugging the wood up to them for the fire is no joke, either."

"Do they get paid extra?"

"Not really. They usually work long shifts, and they get paid extra for that, but nothing more than the standard rate for long shifts. In winter they often stay up there for a week at a time, two of them taking alternate eleven hour shifts, with two hours off when there's no trains in the small hours – except that in winter so many trains are running so late that there's often no off time at all. And they don't get paid extra for being there when they're not on duty. But a job's a job, it's better than starving."

"Someone must have to come here to look after the light in this signal, too."

"Theoretically, the signalman in the box down by the main line is supposed to keep an eye on it – clean the lens and top up the oil once a week, check the wick, things like that. He can see if it goes out from his box okay. But in practice us drivers do it. It's no trouble to us, and it'd be a real chore for the signalman, it's a hell of a climb up the path from the box. In the dark, if the signal's not lit, we stop and deal with it. Shiim got into trouble about it once – he'd got a railway official on board, and it was out. The company expect the signalman to do it, because every time a driver stops here when there isn't actually a train due on the main line it costs ten or fifteen minutes running time, and a few coins in fuel. Big deal! But they could tell we do it anyway, because the path up from the signalbox is all overgrown – well, they could tell if they ever bothered to look."

The signal changed, Peyr pulled the lever that opened the steam valve, and slowly we got moving. Setting off up that steep incline, I could understand why it cost ten or fifteen minutes of running time to stop there, although maybe that was a slight exaggeration, and nobody really seemed to take time very seriously anyway. The railway official travelling with Shiim had probably just been impatient and irritable when the train took so long to get up any speed again, and then felt the need to justify himself.

"I suppose they don't mind the main line trains stopping for signalmen going to and from their boxes, because it's not on a steep incline so it doesn't take long to get going again?"

"They don't stop, they just slow down. And not as slow as I go for you or Aila or Yaani to get on or off."

A goods train passed us going the other way just before the end of the tunnel. I wondered whether it was the next one heading onto the branch line or a main line one, but didn't ask Peyr. He seemed deep in thought.

"Poor Berraami's awfully late, to be behind that main line train. Two trains behind where she should have been anyway, with getting swapped with Laar."

We'd almost stopped at Aila's village when Aila appeared alongside the train, and clambered aboard. She had a rucksack on her back.

"Don't stop, Dad. I've got food for all three of us. I'm coming home, I've got a few days' holiday. You're awfully late, I'm freezing."

Peyr put several more lumps of wood on the fire, and drew air through the fire with a jet of steam up the chimney. The fire perked up immediately. He opened the steam valve wider and we began to pick up speed again.

"Well, that makes up a bit of our lost time, anyway. And it'll be nice to have you home for a few days. Nice for Owen to have someone more his own age around, too, not just us oldsters and young Grim."

"Subtlety isn't your style, is it, Dad?"

Peyr grinned. "I'm an engine driver, not a diplomat."

You'd make a better diplomat than most diplomats I've met, I thought, but I didn't say anything. My face felt hot. I couldn't really see Aila's expression in the firelight, so I guessed they couldn't see mine, either.

"What did you think of Briggi, Owen?"

"What I saw of it, I liked. But we didn't see all that much – we were nearly a day late arriving, because of the earthquake."

"Oh, goodness, yes. I'd forgotten about that. It was only a little tremor in Baragi, but it must've been much worse up north. Where were you, and what was it like?"

Peyr answered while I was still trying to remember the place's name. "We were at Tambuk. It wasn't too bad, but you should have seen Owen jump! He'd have run outside sharpish, but we told him Tambuk's built to stand a lot more than a little shake like that. Faahiha was there, going the other way, and we all stopped the night there, rather than crawl along in the dark looking out for landslips. So we got to Briggi about eighteen hours late. I was hoping we'd meet Graamon there – Owen's got some stories I'm sure Graamon will want to hear. Well, you will too, and everyone else, but Graamon especially. But he wasn't there, he was visiting Meyroha."

Aila laughed. "Yes, the grapevine has some interesting stories about that! But you probably know more than I do."

"I don't know. I don't know much at all – his landlady said he's often in Meyroha these days, and she wondered if he might have a girlfriend there, but it was just speculation. That was the first I'd heard at all. For all I know he could have a railway project that takes him there a lot."

"Oh, I do know a fair bit more than that, then. He's been seen going to Meyroha on passenger trains, very smart. He always used to travel on goods engines. He still does, on the branch line. If he was going to Meyroha, he used to change trains at Baragi, but now he goes right into Laanoha, smartens up, and gets the passenger train. More than that is just guesswork as far as I know, though."

"Well, it could be politics, I suppose – but it could be a girl, who knows? A good thing if it is. Fun to keep guessing, but we'll probably know one way or the other soon enough."

"Don't the passenger trains stop in Baragi?"

"Not normally, no. There's no platform there, for one thing, and for another there's only one family there who ever use passenger trains. Normally they take a carriage or a gig into Laanoha, and on the rare occasions one of them wants to go to Meyroha or Briggi, they catch the train in Laanoha. Jerem did once get the train from Meyroha to drop him off in Baragi though. They had to stop completely, he wasn't taking any chances. He even wanted them to charge him a smaller fare for the shorter journey, but they said he was lucky they weren't charging him extra for the unscheduled stop."

"Jerem's the eldest son in the house where Aila works. They're the only family in Baragi with any money to speak of. He's got a girlfriend in Kromaan, but it's a bit of a stormy relationship, I think."

"I'm not sure he still has, actually, Dad. If he has, it's a bigger storm than usual at the moment. He took the gig into Laanoha this morning. He asked me if I wanted to go with him rather than waiting for you this evening. I said I was on duty until two. Gamaara laughed after he'd gone, and said I was a sensible girl preferring to travel in the train with my old Dad!"

"You don't think Jerem's got his eye on you, do you?"

"Who knows? He wouldn't want to marry me, that's for sure, and I wouldn't want him if he did. If he tried anything else he'd learn that he'd bitten off more than he could chew, and I know his parents would take my side too."

"It's good to be with a family where you can be confident of that."

"It is, and I'll stick with it a while. But Gamaara's been teaching me to read and write, and I'm thinking to try to get a teaching job if I get good enough. They won't want a nanny in Baragi any more when the little ones get bigger, and Gamaara thinks I'm clever enough to be a good teacher."

So Aila is learning to read and write. There's an interesting snippet of information!

"That's a thing I'd been wondering about. In England, there are places – *schools* we call them in English – where children go for a few hours most days, where teachers teach them all sorts of things. I don't know whether there's anything like that here."

"Only for children with rich parents! But surely that's the same in England? The word is *adpaask* in Laana."

"Well, for bigger children, yes – thirteen and up. But there are schools for every child from seven to twelve, free for those who can't afford the fees. Not every child attends of course, but there are theoretically places for them all if they wanted to. In some areas, if they all tried to attend, there suddenly wouldn't be enough places for them, but in most areas most children go to school for at least those six years."

"Oh my goodness – so different! Here only rich people send their children to school, and not all of them, and never beyond about eleven or twelve years old. But some of them start at three or four, but that's normally more like childminding than teaching – really just a way of having your children looked after a bit cheaper than having a nanny."

Then Peyr broached a subject I'd hoped he would raise before too long. "Aila – you don't know whether Gamaara or any of them know the people at Siroha, do you?"

"I don't know. I've never heard them mention the place. Whereabouts is it? I can ask when I'm back in Baragi if you like."

"It's halfway up the road to Sirimi. It's where Owen stayed the second night after he arrived. One of the ladies from there is one of Yaana's customers, but she spotted Owen in the cab, and she's very keen for Owen to go back and visit them again. I just hoped you knew something about them, but she'll be there again on my next run so you won't be able to find out anything before that. I wonder who else might know anything about them?"

"Well, there's Gamaara's sister. She lives up near the castle. I know where, and I've met her in Baragi a few times. But I don't know her well enough to ask her about things like that. I can ask Gamaara anything, she doesn't mind at all."

"And if you can't, I certainly can't. But maybe your mother could, mothers of daughters your age can ask all kinds of things people like you and me can't."

"Dad! I don't want my employers getting to hear that my family's asking questions like that on *my* behalf, thank you. Anyway, it's for Owen's benefit, not mine."

"No, I suppose not. And your mother can only ask on Owen's behalf if it's indirectly asking on your behalf, and you don't want anyone thinking *that*, either."

"Well, no, you're right, I don't want them thinking that."

I still couldn't see Aila's expression, but I could hear the change in her tone of voice, and my heart gave a little leap. Her tone had said, *it's true, but I don't want* them *thinking that*.

Peyr had obviously heard it too. He laughed, put his arm round his daughter's shoulders and gave her a squeeze.

It really was very cramped under the floor of the cab, with even more – or bigger, I wasn't sure which – parcels under there with me. Aila was very concerned, and adjusted the parcels around me to make me as comfortable as she could. Peyr shut me in with a laugh, and I could hear him joking with Aila, "How long should we keep him in prison, then?"

"Dad! Don't be horrible!"

I tried to say, "Don't worry, I know he's joking," but I don't think they could hear me.

Then the clattering of the metal bridge under our wheels drowned out whatever else they might have been talking about above me, and I was left to my own thoughts.

Peyr knows I like Aila. Aila probably knows too. Aila likes me, and Peyr and I know that as well. How serious is she? How seriously does Peyr take it all? How serious am I? If I'm serious, what should I do now? What if she's not serious? And if I'm not serious and she is, then what?

Who can I ask about this kind of thing? Not Peyr. Judd? I don't think so.

Inspiration: Yaana. Not Yaani, definitely, but Yaana. Yes. She'll tell me straight, and won't break any confidences. And I get to spend plenty of time alone with her, making clothes.

Or did. Will I, now Aila's at home for a few days?

Ah well, who knows? What will happen, will happen.

Look at yourself, Owen – you're beginning to think like a Laanohan, and thinking in Laanohan expressions.

Nothing wrong with that – and it's probably the same as thinking like a Briggian or a Meyrohan for that matter. They all speak the same language, and it's called Laana, not Meyra. Why? What is this country called? Is it a country at all, or just an area of the world? They talk about "the border", so it must be a country. Or am I misunderstanding that word?

I am a Laanohan now, sort of. I'll be more Laanohan than English before long. And actually, I think there are differences between Laanohans and Briggians, anyway – hard to tell after just one day in Briggi, but that was definitely my first impression. I think I might actually like Briggians better – but I like Laanohans a lot, too. At least, I like this family. Shouldn't generalize from the particular!

Now there's a very English thought. Thought in English, not Laana, too.

Ah, well. How much longer stuck in here? We must be near the end of the bridge by now.

Perfect timing; at that very moment, the clattering stopped. We were coasting, steadily losing speed as we climbed the slope up into the city. The railway sloped, but the ground rose steeply, the streets zig-zagging up the hill, with staircases as short cuts for pedestrians. Even the staircases zig-zagged in places. But the railway went from a high level bridge into a cutting through the top of the hill. We rolled to a halt at the summit in the cutting, where the city guards were waiting for us.

Somehow everything seemed to go more smoothly than before – possibly something to do with there being a pretty girl in the cab with the driver. Most of the exchanges were too indistinct for me to hear what was being said, but there was no mistaking the last words of the guard who'd climbed into the cab, "Sorry to have kept you so long, Miss."

Then I heard him climb down, and we were off again. Moments later I was climbing out of my prison, and helping Peyr and Aila to get the parcels out. Yaani was already alongside, complaining about having to wait so long in the cold, but jokingly, knowing it wasn't Peyr's fault.

"Is everything good at Baragi, Aila? Are you okay?"

"Don't worry, Mum. I've just got four days' leave, that's all."

The last parcel went over the side, followed by Aila, and finally me. I didn't miss my footing this time, but Grim was there ready in case I did. Yaana had already gone with the first few parcels, but this time there were so many that Grim and Yaani had an armful each, too.

Nobody had mentioned that there was a surprise waiting for us back at the room. Grim and Yaani led the way up the stairs, and when Grim opened the door, I could see that the oil lamp, which Yaana couldn't reach and which was never left bright when everyone was out, was already bright. I guessed there was a visitor, but I'd no idea who it might be. Aila was in front of me, and she didn't say anything, but from behind I saw her put her hand to her mouth in surprise.

A rich, deep voice came from somewhere near the fireplace, "Aila! What a pleasant surprise!", then, as I entered and saw the speaker – a tall spare man of an age difficult to guess, but neither young nor old – he addressed me, "You must be Owen. I'm very pleased to meet you. I would greet you in English, but I'm afraid I know only a few words, and I've no idea how to pronounce them."

For a moment, I was dumbfounded. Then I realized that he must be Graamon, but I wasn't confident enough to say, "You must be Graamon. I'm very pleased to meet you too." I didn't know what to say for a moment, then mumbled, "Yes, I'm Owen. I'm very sorry that my knowledge of Laana is little better than your knowledge of English."

"Come, come. Your Laana is extraordinarily good, for someone who'd never even heard of the language four weeks ago. Don't be so modest! Faahiha has told me a great deal about your exploits, and the way you have mastered the language so quickly. I'm most interested to hear more about your ballooning. But you need food and drink, there is plenty of time for talk later."

"I thought you must be Graamon when you first addressed me. I wish I'd been more confident. I'm certain now. You must have met Faahiha somewhere between here and Tambuk, and decided on the spot to turn round and come back here. I'm honoured if that was to meet me."

"So you even know the names of the stations between here and Briggi already? How many times have you made the trip?"

"No, not really. They're probably all familiar by now, but I don't think I couldn't list them in order. I remember Tambuk particularly because we were there when the earthquake struck. We spent an unscheduled night there, and I heard Faahiha's story. This is the first time I've made the round trip. I'd ridden with Peyr from the Sirimi Road crossing to Laanoha before I'd learnt a word of Laana."

"And Faahiha heard your story the same night, and knew that I'd be most interested. Then there I was at Belgaam, to hear all she knew. So here I am. But food and drink!"

"A drink maybe, but couldn't we wait for Peyr to get home before we eat?"

"Of course, of course. I don't suppose he'll be long. Grim, there's a flagon of Keroo in the corner by the table. A mug for everyone!"

I'd heard of Keroo, but I'd never tasted it before. I didn't know the procedure, either, but nobody minded that I was watching everybody else for clues about what to do. At least this time I understood what people were saying – mostly! Graamon wished me a long life and a happy one, or words to that effect. Actually what he wished me was a large family, and living to see my great-grandchildren grow up, but it's a standard formula, and the real meaning is simply a long life and a happy one. I think so, anyway! I thanked him, and wished the same for everyone present, which I thought, and still think, was the right thing to do.

Yaana laughed, and said that seeing her great grandchildren grow up might be a little something I could help her out with. I didn't know where to put myself.

Aila knew. "Gran! You're worse than Dad! And he's twice as bad as a Dad should be!"

Yaana laughed again, and said, "Isn't he just! And you love him to bits, don't you, sweetheart?"

Aila looked deflated. "Yes, Gran, I do. You're right." She looked at me with a pleading look in her eyes. She wanted me to change the subject quickly, I was sure, but I didn't know how.

Graamon knew how, and was aware of the need. "I don't know how much the rest of you know about Owen's story. Probably not very much. Faahiha says that as far as she knows, he'd not really told anyone his story until the night after the earthquake – I assume everyone felt the earthquake?"

Nods all round. Everyone was still holding their mugs up a little, not drinking, and I copied them.

"Well, Peyr and Owen and Faahiha all stayed at Tambuk that night. They didn't want to run into any landslips, either by going too fast to see them in time, or in the dark if they slowed down. Very wise of them! And you all know Faahiha's story, of course, and Owen heard all that. And Owen told his story, for the first time, I believe.

"I've come here to hear it directly from him myself, because it's a very interesting story, and I think there's a lot more to hear than what he's already told Faahiha.

"Your Owen is an extraordinary young man. You're very lucky to have him, and I hope that with his permission you'll share a little of him with me.

"I'd also like to say that he's also very lucky to have you. It's not every family in Laanoha who would welcome a stranger into their midst the way you have. I shall reiterate his toast: large families and grown-up great-grandchildren in your lifetimes to all of you!"

He raised his mug high, then took a sip. The rest of us followed suit.

Keroo is a bit spicier and a bit tarter and a bit less sweet than skiir, maybe a different combination of fruit, or different proportions of each. It's red, not brown. But it's not really a lot different.

Like skiir, it's non-alcoholic. I'd not met an alcoholic drink since I left England. I thought I might have smelt alcohol at the waterside inn where we'd had our evening meal in Briggi, but I wasn't sure. It might have been the slightly disreputable atmosphere of the place that made me imagine it.

Peyr and Judd arrived just as we were sitting down.

"You might have told me we'd got a visitor, Yaani," he said, but he clearly knew already. He didn't seem surprised at all.

"And let Owen know before he got here? I knew Judd would tell you."

Yaani and Grim were already starting to serve food at the table. This was no ordinary family meal such as I'd eaten many times in this room. It was much more like the food at Siroha when I first arrived. There were plates and cutlery that I'd never seen in the room before, too.

I didn't know whether Yaani and maybe Yaana had prepared it, or whether Graamon had brought part or all of it from somewhere else. I couldn't ask, obviously. I wanted to know whether Graamon always ate like that, or whether this was a very special occasion, but I couldn't ask that, either. Maybe I'd be able to ask Yaana privately later.

Another thing was puzzling me rather. How had Yaana known so quickly that Aila and I had our eyes on each other? Was it really so immediately obvious to any observant person who knew us both? Or had the grapevine somehow got the news to her before we arrived? Or maybe she was just joking without any foreknowledge at all, in which case our reactions might have been a bit of a surprise for her.

Over the meal, there was a lot of small talk in pairs or small groups. I was between Judd and Grim, and Aila was just the other side of Grim. At one point she mentioned to Grim that she was learning to read and write, and that in England nearly all children, not just a few rich ones, went to school for about six years.

Grim turned to me, "Did you go to school, Owen? What did you learn? Did you learn to read and write, like our Aila?"

Well, it wasn't me who'd raised the question, but I couldn't avoid the subject any longer. "Yes, I can read and write English. But I can't read and write Laana, it's a complete mystery to me." I could feel everyone looking at me. I looked at Peyr, to see how he was reacting, but I don't think he'd even heard. He was deep in conversation with Graamon.

Judd had heard, though. "Would you like to learn to read Laana, Owen? I'm no expert, but I know the basics and can teach you as much as I know."

"I'd love to – but one thing I want to avoid is hurting Peyr's feelings. He can't read, can he?"

"No, Peyr can't read. But I'm sure it wouldn't hurt his feelings a bit if you learnt. You're like another son to him, he'd be proud of you. He's proud of you already. And I know how proud he is that his daughter's learning, he was telling me on the way here."

Everyone was beginning to clear their plates. There had been second helpings on many plates, and thirds on a few, and the food hadn't run out by any means, but people were definitely flagging. Graamon announced another toast, and Grim refilled everyone's mugs – not all of them had yet been emptied from the first toast, but all were topped up.

"I'll be brief this time, we've had all the proper formalities. This feast is in honour of our guest and friend, Owen from England. None of us had ever heard of England until Owen arrived, and none of us has any idea where it is. I know Judd had met a few English-speaking sailors before, but he didn't know they came from a place called England. Having heard Owen's story secondhand, I suspect but do not know that Owen also does not know where England is, or perhaps from his viewpoint, where Laanoha is. Am I right, Owen?"

"Yes, that's quite true. I'm pretty certain that it's a very long way – thousands of miles – but that's about all I really know."

I was beginning to get a little nervous about telling my story. It had been so easy with just Peyr, whom I knew quite well, and one other interested listener who kept interrupting with questions for me to answer.

"I've rambled on enough! To Owen's long life and grown-up great-grandchildren in his lifetime!"

Mugs high in the air, not including mine; everyone took a sip, then looked at me expectantly. I knew I had to begin.

"I don't have the gift of words like Graamon has, not even in my own language, much less in Laana, a language I've only been learning for four weeks.

"This meeting was a complete surprise to me. I'm honoured, of course, but I've never thought how to tell my story, where to begin, or anything. When I told Peyr and Faahiha, we were sitting at a table in the inn at Tambuk, with no particular plan to tell any stories, and it all just came tumbling out – mostly in response to questions. Please do ask questions, whatever you like. The easiest way for me to tell the story would be to answer questions."

I took a sip of keroo, then realized I should have held the mug high for a moment first, as an invitation for people to ask questions. I held it high for a moment after taking my sip instead. Several people laughed in a friendly way.

There was a short silence, then Graamon spoke.

"Perhaps I should start the questions, then, although I do have the advantage over everyone except Peyr of having heard at least a version of the story already."

"Owen, why did you want to leave England?"

Now this was a question to which everyone but Graamon *did* already know the answer, but I felt that a more measured answer was required in the circumstances.

"England is ruled by a ruthless, authoritarian regime. In some ways, it's quite similar to the regime in Laanoha – but it's much more efficient. It's very hard to avoid the authorities, or to do anything without their knowing exactly what you're doing. If they don't like it, they will very effectively thwart your activities, by whatever means they think will work."

"That sounds a bit like Meyroha," Yaana observed.

"Maybe, from what I've heard."

I suspected that the authorities in Meyroha had rather less sophisticated technology available to them than the authorities in England had, which probably made their control less complete, but I didn't say anything about that.

"The whole system exists purely for the benefit of an elite, and everyone else is treated very badly indeed. I was born into an elite family, but my parents believed in a fairer and more just society, and campaigned against the regime. They kept on campaigning, even after the authorities first told them to stop, then cut off most of their income and confiscated much of their property. Finally, they were murdered while I was away from home, studying at school. I was sixteen then."

Aila interrupted, "You were still studying at sixteen?"

"I understand you're still studying, Aila. How old are you, now?"

Yaana laughed out loud. "Owen, that is a question you're not allowed to ask a lady, certainly not in public! I'll answer for her. She's a fair bit older than sixteen!"

"I'm not studying at school, though. I'm studying privately, just one of me with someone who wants to teach me."

"Ah, okay. Schools for older people in England are a bit different from schools for children, and you gradually change from being taught by teachers, to studying more and more independently, and finally working to find out new things that nobody else could teach you because nobody knew until you find out. Then you become a teacher yourself, as well as a student."

Graamon was nodding. "We have a place a bit like that in Meyroha, but it sounds as though it's much better established in England. Do go on, anyway. What happened after your parents were murdered?"

"The headmaster knew my parents had been murdered, and he's a good man. He arranged for my school fees to be waived, and for my accommodation and food to be provided by the school. He said I was a favourite student among the teachers, doing more unusual and interesting work than many of the other students. I think he was taking a bit of a risk himself doing that, but the authorities weren't too bothered about it. They thought that getting rid of my parents was enough.

"I reached the stage where I was beginning to make the transition from student to teacher, doing a bit of each, and some independent research of my own. But I am a rebel like my parents, and as I grew older it became harder to hide the fact. I received a warning, but of course that just makes a rebel angrier.

"Luckily for me, the headmaster intervened, saying that I was a potentially valuable teacher to the school, and that the authorities should put a curb on my rebelliousness without interfering with my studies.

"Ruthless authoritarian regimes are not necessarily stupid. They listened to him. I don't think they like him much, but they recognize his value. They placed me under house arrest, but allowed me to continue my research. But I felt stifled."

"So you decided to escape. Very wise. But how could you escape, with armed guards all around the building?"

I was grateful for Graamon's prompting. He already knew the answer to that question from Faahiha, I presumed, but he was right that I needed leading.

"It wasn't just a building. I had a garden, too. I had some contact with other members of the school – but I had to give notice when I would be meeting with anyone, and there was always a guard present. Not just an average brainless guard, an intelligent guard who could generally make sense of what was going on, and who would often ask intelligent questions if he didn't understand.

"Over the four months I was under house arrest, I got to know that guard quite well. I could sympathize with his position: he had a wife and two small children to support, and his income depended on him doing his job well. I really didn't want to make life difficult for him. I hope the authorities didn't think he helped me to escape. He certainly didn't.

"My guard only monitored discussions between me and my colleagues, he didn't take any notice of what I was doing in my house or garden, or my workshop, when there was no-one but me at home. So I could do pretty much whatever I liked.

"I hope they don't think the headmaster helped me either. He didn't. I don't think there is anyone there who could have guessed I was about to escape, or who could work out afterwards where I'd gone."

Judd interrupted, "It's always hard to work out how anyone does magic. And it can only be magic, disappearing out of a place surrounded by armed guards, and re-appearing on a hillside so far away that no-one in either place knows where the other place is. A hillside miles from the coast or the border, and miles from anywhere else for that matter."

I knew that Judd was being ironical. He was a thoroughly down-to-Earth, practical man. He knew I'd got a practical method of doing it, he just didn't know what it was, and he wanted to know.

"There wasn't much point tunnelling out. It would have been an incredible amount of work, very difficult or impossible to keep secret, and where would it have got me? Still in England, and easily caught. And if I was caught, what then? I'd be lucky if the worst that happened was to be returned to house arrest. I might very possibly be killed instead.

"So I had to think of another method. Well, you know those floating lanterns, where you put a candle in a thin paper lantern with a closed top, and it floats up into the sky? Well, I worked out a way that I could do a similar thing on a much bigger scale, big enough to lift me and carry me away like a candle in a paper balloon. England often gets very foggy nights in autumn, and I chose a foggy night to float up from my garden, so no-one would see me go."

Graamon said that he wanted to know a lot more about exactly *how* I'd made a balloon capable of lifting a man, but that he was happy to hear about the details later. He was also very interested to know how confident I'd been that it was a safe thing to do.

"Oh, I wasn't confident at all. I thought there was a very real risk that I would die in any one of several ways, or that I wouldn't get far enough away, and that I'd be recaptured. Even if I got as far as some foreign country, the authorities in all the countries close to England have agreements with England about handing over people wanted by the authorities. I knew I had to get a very long way away. I thought my balloon could keep me in the air for several days, and I hoped that would be long enough to get a very long way. I was pretty sure that the wind got faster and faster the higher you went, so I wanted to float pretty high. It was certainly risky, and I thought long and hard about whether there was any other way out. I couldn't think of any other. And I couldn't face a life under permanent house arrest."

I told the story of my flight much as I'd told it to Peyr and Faahiha at Tambuk. Once I got going, I lost my nervousness, and it just flowed.

Halfway through, Grim topped everyone's keroo up, finishing the flagon.

Yaana was asleep long before I'd finished, but everyone else was still wide awake, even though it was long past midnight and most of us had been up early that morning.

"I really have to catch the first train back to Briggi tomorrow – well, today now – and I've got a few things to get ready first, so I'm going to have to get moving straight away. But I really want to hear all the details as soon as I can. Could you possibly come to Briggi with Peyr on his next trip, and stay with me at least until the trip after that? I think we have a great deal to talk about."

I hadn't mentioned my ballooning equipment at Siroha, and I didn't really want to mention it in front of everyone, I wasn't sure why. But Peyr saw an opportunity to perhaps find out about the people at Siroha.

"Before you disappear, Graamon, do you know the people at Siroha? That's the place where Owen stayed the second night after he landed. They entertained him very well, but he only stayed the one night, and was unable to communicate much at all. A lady from there met the train this morning. They're very keen for Owen to visit them again now he's learnt a bit of Laana."

"I can imagine they are. It's not often they get unexpected visitors there, especially a foreigner who's apparently somehow freshly arrived right in the middle of the country. Yes, I know them well. But they're rich people, and you know what rich people are like. They're not bad, as rural rich people go, but I wouldn't really want to be one of their tenants or their employees.

"You'll probably have to go and visit them eventually Owen, or they'll cause trouble. We'll have to work out some strategy to prevent them ensnaring you for a long stay, though."

"I rather wondered whether that might be an issue, and I said that Owen had commitments in Laanoha and might not be with me on my next trip."

"Well done Peyr, that was good thinking. I think the best ploy would be for him to hide while you pass the Sirimi road crossing. You've obviously got a pretty good hiding place somewhere on the train to have smuggled him in and out of Laanoha so neatly. Those commitments in Laanoha, whatever they are, can keep them off his back for a while yet.

"If you'll excuse me, I really must go and prepare. I don't want to miss the first train."

"Well!" said Peyr, after Graamon had disappeared into the night. "I didn't expect him to track you down quite as quickly as that! He seems as keen as I expected him to be, maybe even more so. You should definitely go to Briggi with me next time, and be ready to stay there for a while. You'll be missed here, actually, you know, and not just because Yaana's got a lot of work that she was hoping you'd help her with the cutting out for. But you can't miss a chance like this.

"Talking of Yaana's work, I've got an order for her, Judd. The Sirimi Road people. Well, they're the Siroha people, as we just discovered this morning. I still don't really know where Siroha is – somewhere between the crossing and Sirimi, that's all I know. Owen will know better."

"I think I could find it again, okay, yes, but I don't suppose I'll ever need to. If – seems like I mean when – I go there again, I guess they'll pick me up from the crossing."

"Or Graamon will take you there, I suspect. He'll want to see your ballooning stuff, and maybe take it away. And he won't want to let them hold on to you for too long, either. He's one of the few people who can probably stop them."

Peyr pulled out two little packets from his pocket and gave them to Yaana and Yaani. I remembered that I had a similar packet for Aila, and dug it out of my rucksack.

The three ladies admired their scarves, and put them on. Yaana fingered Aila's scarf admiringly, "That's a real beauty he's got you, Aila. He's got a good eye!" Aila's eyes seemed to sparkle as she thanked me.

Then she pecked me lightly on the cheek, but somehow that seemed false, a little distant, and my mood fell like a stone.

Peyr handed Judd the note the lady had given him. If I'd observed the arrival of an order before, I'd have known that Judd could read. It didn't matter, I knew now, I was going to learn, Peyr's nose wasn't going to be put out of joint a bit, and Graamon was interested in me even though he knew I couldn't – yet – read Laana.

And Aila is learning to read and write too. She and I are both going to be here for three nights and two days, but then she's going back to Baragi, and I'm going to Briggi. When will I see her again?

Hmm. Will we even still want *to see each other again by then? Maybe the attraction will wear off, who knows? It doesn't feel likely right now, but who knows?*

What are the rules of this game in this country? Peyr and Yaana seem to have made up their minds already. What if Aila doesn't agree? Or if I don't?

After Graamon had gone, we all went to sleep pretty quickly. Judd, me and Grim nearer the door, then Peyr and Yaani, and finally Aila and Yaana nearer the fire.

Chapter 6

I was the last to wake in the morning. Judd and Grim had already gone to work. Peyr and the three women were sitting at the table, talking quietly and sipping from their mugs.

Yaana saw me sit up, and said, "Owen, go and get washed and come and have some breakfast. There's still lots of good stuff from yesterday evening, and Aila will fry some of it up for you while you're washing, so don't take too long!"

I didn't need telling twice.

It was raining quite hard, and I ran from the back door over to the shelter at the pump. I slipped on the wet flagstones and fell, bashing my shoulder on the corner post of the shelter, and hurting my wrist when my outstretched hand hit the ground.

I washed, and walked sensibly back to the back door. My shoulder and wrist hurt.

As I got to the top of the stairs I could smell frying meat. Aila looked up as I opened the door, and started. She jumped up and ran over to me, "You've hurt yourself! What happened?"

Yaana got up, went over to the fire, and took over the frying.

Aila took me by the arm and led me to the bench by the table, touching my shoulder gently and examining it as we went. I hadn't realized I'd broken the skin, but there was quite a lot of blood on her hand.

"I'm a silly fellow. I tried to run to the pump to get out of the rain, and slipped. Sometimes I forget I'm not a little boy any more!"

Yaana suddenly remembered my previous accident. "How's your ankle nowadays?"

"Oh, absolutely fine. I'd pretty much forgotten about it. I don't know what that red oil is, but it really works!"

"Oh, it's just to take the pain away. It doesn't help the healing, that comes from yourself."

"Did you hurt yourself before? Oh, you poor darling!"

I hope she doesn't think I'm accident prone. It's lovely having her so tender towards me, but I mustn't wallow in it.

"I missed my footing getting off the engine in the dark the first night I arrived, and twisted my ankle. It was lucky for me Grim saw what was happening, and caught me before I fell under the wheels."

"Oh my goodness. We've all been jumping on and off moving engines since we were knee high, but doing it for the first time in the dark can't be funny. You should have realized, Dad!"

"You and Grim have been doing it since you were knee high, Aila, but your Gran and Mum haven't. But they didn't do it in the dark until they'd had a fair bit of practice, that's true. I should have realized – but what could I have done, anyway? If I'd stopped, the guards would have wondered what was going on. They can't see what we're all doing, but they'd hear the train stopping. And he couldn't stay on the train all the way into the yard, there are often people there who can't be trusted."

Aila cleaned the blood off my shoulder with a rag, and bandaged it up. Yaana brought a plate of yesterday's leftovers, fried up, for me. Leftovers? It was a good meal. I felt very spoiled.

"I feel bad, running out on you, Yaana, when you've just got some big orders in, and Peyr's brought all that cloth."

"I should think you do too!" Yaana said, but she was laughing. "If you and Peyr get ahead on the cutting and Aila helps me with the sewing in the next couple of days, I'll manage fine. Don't worry. If Graamon wants you in Briggi, that's really good news for all of us."

Aila was looking at me and nodding quite firmly. I wasn't absolutely certain what that meant, but I thought I knew. I wasn't quite sure how I felt about the rapidity with which Aila seemed to have made up her mind – it felt lovely that she seemed to feel that way, but I wasn't sure how wise it was to be so impulsive. But I had to admit to myself that I felt the same way Aila seemed to, and who cares whether it's wise or not?

"The other thing we really ought to do in the next couple of days is work on reading and writing, Owen. I don't know as much as Judd does, but he'll be at work all day, and I know enough to get you started."

"That's really much more important than the clothes, Aila. Peyr and Yaani will help me as much as they can, and you should teach Owen as much as you can. You'll need pencils and paper though, won't you? Can you get some from the railway for them, Peyr?"

"Don't worry, Dad. They gave me some in Baragi, so I could practice at home while I was on holiday. I'll have to show Gamaara some of what I've done, but I'm sure she didn't count the paper, so if Owen's used some of it it won't matter. Anyway, I can say I've left some of it here to use later."

"Better if your Dad gets you some, than risking falling out with Gamaara, Aila. But at least you can get started with what you've got."

"If Dad's going to get some, it'll be best if Owen doesn't write on any of Gamaara's paper, because the railway paper won't look the same. Or at least, it's very unlikely to. Will you be able to get some, Dad?"

"I wish we'd thought to ask Graamon for some, he'd have been able to get it easily. Folks will wonder what I want it for."

"Don't worry about me writing. I already write English, no problem. If I learn to read Laana, I'll be well pleased. It won't take me long to learn to write once I can read."

Aila and I sat at one end of the table with Aila's book and pencil and paper. Peyr stood at the other end, with the cloth and patterns and scissors. Yaana and Yaani sat by the fire, once Peyr had them supplied with cut pieces of cloth, and began to sew.

Peyr made the lunch. The cutting was well ahead of the sewing. "I won't get it all cut by the end of tomorrow, but it won't be far off. With both of you sewing, I'd be able to deliver Siroha's order on Monday – but I think it would be better to leave it a week, we don't want them thinking they can expect that kind of turnaround. Perhaps I should deliver part of the order, and keep the rest for a week's time."

'Monday' may not be the correct translation. I lost track of the days during my flight, so I don't know which day of the Laana week corresponds to which day of the English week. Judd doesn't know, either. At least they use a seven day week, like

they do in England. They think of Odama as the first day of the
week, so I translate it as Monday.

Peyr's days off rotated around the week, but everyone else's
work was on a weekly cycle. Yaani was able to sew that
Saturday (if Odibi is Saturday), but she had to go to work on the
Sunday.

Aila and I sometimes found it hard to concentrate on the
basics of written Laana. Our conversation ranged widely. Aila
wanted to know all about England, and I wanted to know all
about the country I'd landed in.

I still didn't know a name for the country as a whole. I didn't
think it had got one. Every time I'd tried to raise the issue with
anyone, I'd failed to get through at all. Aila couldn't enlighten
me, either. It was as if I was asking a nonsense question.

Maybe it was a nonsense question. What are England or
France or Spain? They're the areas controlled by the English or
French or Spanish authorities.

The Laanohan authorities more or less control Laanoha, and
the Meyrohan authorities control Meyroha pretty tightly. But
there aren't really any other significant authorities in the area,
and the writ of those two authorities doesn't extend beyond the
cities at all.

The main language in the whole area is Laana. I presume the
name Laana is cognate with Laanoha, though Meyroha is the
larger city, and as far as I know there's no distinct Meyrohan
language. There are other local languages around, which is
presumably why the language has a name. Is Laanoha an older
city than Meyroha? None of the family knew. "Laanoha years
start from longer ago than Meyroha years, but I don't think that
means anything. It's probably all mythology."

The Laana script is complicated, in ways different from the
ways in which the English script is complicated. There's a lot to
learn. But I made a start, and Aila was pleased with my progress.

My respect for Aila grew, too – she was a good teacher, and
also had a pretty good understanding of the ways of the world. I
suppose in part she had her father's job to thank for that. She'd
travelled up and down the line to Briggi with him a few times,
and been in conversations with a variety of people in the various

inns. She'd even been to Meyroha with Peyr twice, hitching a ride in the cab of a goods train with one of his fellow drivers.

Aila had one printed book for us to work from. It was obviously written for young children, but that didn't matter. It showed how the script worked, and that was what I really wanted to know.

It was also noticeable that it was produced for *rich* children. The words and pictures related to a very different world from Aila's background. Perhaps it wasn't so unlike the house where she worked.

When Aila wrote, her script looked just like the printed script, and I wondered whether that was just that she was still at an early stage of learning, or whether it was normal. I didn't want to ask, though, and I had no other handwriting to look at. I didn't feel able to ask to see the order from Siroha that Peyr had given to Judd. *Time enough*, I thought.

"We should take a break from study for bit," Aila decided in the middle of the afternoon. "There's another pair of scissors for you, Owen, you can help Dad with the cutting, and I'll join Gran and Mum at the sewing for a bit."

Yaana wasn't having that. "No, you two take a proper break. We're getting on fine here. It's stopped raining, you take him out for a look at the city for a while, Aila."

Peyr took a stool over to the window and climbed up on it to have a look outside at the weather. "Yes, it looks set to stay dry now, it'd be good for you to get out in the air for a bit."

Neither of us needed much persuading. As we reached the bottom of the stairs, Aila turned back to me. "Where would you like to go?"

"I don't know. Where do you suggest? I've been out in the bazaar and the shops a couple of time with your Gran, but I've never seen any of the rest of the city."

"We could go up round the Castle and take a look at that. Or maybe take a wander down by the docks – that might be more interesting, really. There's always a lot going on down there. Big ships from all over the world."

"There must be a lot of city guards down there, aren't there?"

"There are, but they're only really looking out for people coming off the ships. Or contraband, of course."

"But people who come off the ships must wander about a bit. I wouldn't want to get mistaken for someone off a ship, and get asked for the papers I don't have."

"You don't look like a sailor. I'm sure you've nothing to worry about. It's a good job you're wearing Dad's clothes though, not the ones you brought from England!"

"I hope you're right. I trust you!" Suddenly I felt like giving her a big hug, but I was too shy.

"I'm sure you wouldn't have anything to worry about, but maybe we shouldn't take any chances. Dad thinks you'll have papers soon. You'll be able to go anywhere you like quite safely then. The castle's perhaps not the best place either, or the river side. The best thing about the river side is the view of it from the train on the bridge, anyway, and you must've seen that. I know where we should go!"

But she didn't tell me where she was taking me.

She led the way through the muddy alleyway back to where we got on and off the train. I'd not seen it in daylight before. As far as I could see, in both directions, the railway ran in a narrow slot between high buildings, all windowless for at least a couple of storeys on the railway side. There was a bridge across the railway a couple of hundred metres away in the direction of the river, and another a little further in the other direction.

We followed the railway back towards the river a short way, then crossed over and slipped into another muddy alleyway on the other side. Like the alleyway on our side, this one turned at right angles twice, first left and then right, and emerged onto a street between high buildings. These seemed to be dwellings on the upper floors of this street too, but the ground floors weren't shops, they were workshops. I noticed a couple of places doing various sorts of woodwork, one making things out of leather, and one making candles.

Then we were slipping into another alleyway on the other side of the street. This one also turned left after ten metres, but then we were on a stone staircase between the buildings. There was a landing at the point where it turned right again, but the staircase resumed after the turn.

At the top of the stairs, we came out onto a very different street. On this side, the buildings formed a terrace broken only by the occasional alleyway, and mostly only two storeys high. On the other side there were large, detached buildings that I guessed were the houses of the rich. We turned left along the street. It sloped upwards, gently at first, then curved round slightly to the right and became steeper.

The terrace on the left ended abruptly, and we had posh houses on both sides for a short way. Finally the cobbled street, wide enough for a cart, gave way to a rough footpath over bare rock, and we left the houses behind. The footpath climbed steeply, and we had to be careful of our footing on the slippery wet rock. Aila was distinctly more surefooted than me, and at a difficult point she took my hand and helped me up.

I was puffing a bit by this time. Aila laughed and kept hold of my hand, pulling me along after her.

We reached the top, and I could see why she'd taken me there. In front of us, there was a drop of a couple of metres onto a wide rocky ledge. Beyond that, all that I could see was the sea, far below us. We were at the summit of a rocky headland between the open sea and the Aaha estuary, with Laanoha spread out behind us.

For the first time, I could see the big ships at the docks to the west, with a massive breakwater seaward of them. I could see down into the railway goods yard, just inshore of the docks, and what I took to be the engine sheds the other side of the line coming into the yard. I couldn't see the line itself, just a long straight gap in the roofs of the buildings, lined up with the bridge over the Aaha the other side of the town. Beyond the railway, the town sprawled up another hill, with the castle at the top, almost on the same level as us.

Aila gestured in the direction of the town. "Can you spot our room?"

"I've already been trying. No, not for sure. I can spot the street okay, but there's a whole lot of similar dormer windows, and I don't know which one's ours."

I suddenly realized Aila was still holding my hand. There was no-one else on the hilltop. I looked down into her face, and she looked up into mine. We kissed. I put my free arm around her shoulder, and she put hers around my back. Our other hands were still locked together.

"You didn't mean to tell me I was beautiful, that time in Baragi, did you?"

"I didn't mean to tell you, no. I meant to say you'd shown me a lovely place. But it was the truth. An accidental truth."

"You started me dreaming. I hope I've not been making a fool of myself."

I've got to make my mind up. Either we've both been making fools of ourselves, or we haven't. Or maybe making fools of ourselves is how it works, and is the best of all possible options.

"No, you've not been making a fool of yourself. It's just how things happen. Maybe I've been making a fool of myself, too. Maybe making fools of ourselves is the right thing to do."

"You're not making any sense, Owen. You always talk sense, why are you not making any sense now?"

"It's all too quick, Aila. You're lovely, I want to be with you always, but you shouldn't commit yourself to me without knowing me better. You don't know what a risk committing yourself to me might be. I don't even know that myself."

"You'll have railway papers soon, Dad thinks. I'm pretty sure he's right, I saw how Graamon reacted to you. Look at the way he turned right around and headed straight back with Faahiha, as soon as he heard your story. There's less risk committing myself to you than there'd be to almost anyone. And anyway, I don't care. I want you, Owen."

Well, that's settled then. Making fools of ourselves might be the only option. But what do we do next?

"Okay. We both want each other. You don't care if it's risky, I don't care for my own sake but I care for yours, but what can I do about it? What do we do next? Should we tell your parents, or wait a little while to let them get used to us? Or should we wait until we're a bit more certain ourselves?"

"I'm certain, aren't you?"

Am I? I don't know. I know what I want, but what is the right thing to do? I don't know how these things work here.

"I think I am, really. I just don't know what's going to happen next."

"Neither do I. We never really know what's going to happen next. Whatever it is, it's not going to kill us, so I'm not worried. It's not even going to get us into trouble, so what is there to worry about?"

"That's a very good way of looking at it. It's a very good way of looking at life altogether. Okay, I'm certain. Now what do we have to do next?"

Well, that's that. Five weeks or thereabouts after I fly out of my old life, my new life is settled. I don't know what it's settled to, but it's settled.

"I'm not sure of that myself. Gran and Dad knew before you did, maybe before I did. Certainly before I was sure. But I'm not sure what Mum thinks. Maybe she thinks it's too quick, but we're adults, it's our decision. I'd rather not upset her if it can be avoided, though."

We're adults, it's our decision. I didn't even know that.

"We can take our time telling anyone, if that'll make it easier with your Mum. But there's so much I don't know – I didn't even know we were adults in the eyes of the Laanoha authorities."

"The authorities don't care. It's nothing to do with them. Who's an adult and who's not is up to us and our parents to decide. I'm sure Mum and Dad think of me as an adult, have done for a long time. And your...oh..."

"Don't worry, you can say it. Or I'll say it for you. I got over it a long time ago. My parents died years ago. There, I've said it. I wasn't close to them, not since I was a small child. I was away at school most of the time. I still felt it badly when they were killed, but it's a long time ago now. I was much closer to the headmaster. I miss him. I hope the police in England aren't making trouble for him. It hurts a little – more than a little – to know I'll never see him again, never know whether he's okay."

Oh dear. I shouldn't have said that. I don't want to spoil things.

But Aila kissed me again. She had tears in her eyes. She wiped my cheeks – I hadn't realized it, but I had tears in my eyes, too.

"We should be getting home. It'll be getting dark before long. And it's cold up here."

It was.

"There's so much you don't know about me. There's so much I don't know about you, too."

"It doesn't matter. Plenty of time to find out, the rest of our lives. I know enough about you to know that you're my man, and I know that you've decided you know enough about me to know that I'm your woman, too. I love you, Owen."

She's right as well.

"I love you, Aila."

I never thought I'd say that. But I mean it, too.

"We won't tell Mum yet. I think she'll just realize anyway, and then she'll tell us when she's good and ready. Gran and Dad will be waiting for her to tell them."

The sun set before we reached the end of the footpath, but there was still enough light to find our footing okay. Aila held my hand tightly going down the stairs in the first alleyway. I think she might have been afraid I could fall again, which could have been more serious on those long flights of stone stairs.

She let go of my hand before we came out of the alleyway. There weren't many people on the street, although there were oil lamps in the open fronts of all the workshops.

By the time we reached the railway it was almost completely dark. I was very glad I had Aila to guide me. I'm not sure I'd have managed to find the alleyway through from the railway to our street, but Aila went straight to it without hesitation.

Yaana looked up from her sewing as we came into the room. "We rather thought you'd be home before sunset! We were about to send out a search party. Where have you been?"

"No you weren't, you old fibber, Gran! We went up on the point. I wanted to show Owen the view, it's good to see Laanoha like that. We thought about going down to the docks, or up round the Castle, but if he's going to have railway papers before too long it seemed sense to wait until he's got them before going anywhere where we might meet guards."

We might have intended to keep quiet for the moment, but Yaana wasn't going to let us. "So. What have you two decided? When's the big day?"

"Gran! We weren't going to say anything today, and we certainly haven't decided on a date yet. I'm going back to Baragi on Monday, and Owen's going to Briggi. We don't even know when we'll see each other again. We don't know when the big day is, but you're right, we have decided that there's going to be one."

I suppose that is what we've decided, yes. Okay.

Yaani got up and went to the corner. She pulled a flagon out from under the table, and put it on the table. Then she looked at the two of us still standing just inside the doorway, and smiled broadly. "I've been trying not to show my feelings. I didn't want to influence either of you either one way or the other, but I could see what was going on. Keeping your Gran and Dad quiet is impossible, of course, but whether their chatter encourages you or discourages you or has no effect, I really don't know. But now you've made up your minds, I don't mind saying I'm very, very pleased.

"And you'll be pleased to know that someone else noticed, too, and was more confident about his understanding of things than I was. He left word with his innkeeper to send this flagon round for us all to celebrate, and to apologize that he's not able to be here in person."

Graamon. I didn't know we were going to decide anything today, but Graamon knew. I felt rather as though I was being swept out to sea by the tide, but that this was a good thing.

Aila voiced the same thought, "Graamon. He knew what we didn't know ourselves then."

"He did. He wasn't the only one who knew, either."

Peyr poured out the keroo, and proposed the toast, "To Owen and Aila! A large family, and grown-up great-grandchildren in your lifetime!"

Suddenly the toast meant so much more than just a standard formula, and the implication of what we'd decided struck home in a way that it really hadn't before.

I realized it was my turn to make some kind of a speech. For a moment I was a little nervous, and then I realized what I had to say.

"I didn't have any idea when we set off for our walk today what was going to happen. I knew I liked Aila a lot, and I was pretty sure she liked me a lot, too. We talked a lot, as you can no doubt imagine. Aila said something that stuck in my mind. I'm pretty sure this is word for word what she said. 'We never really know what's going to happen next. Whatever it is, it's not going to kill us, so I'm not worried. It's not even going to get us into trouble, so what is there to worry about?' That sums it up. I don't know what's going to happen, and I'm not worried."

I turned to Aila, "Aila, I love you."

"I love you, too."

We turned to Peyr and Yaana and Yaani, "There. We've said it. In public."

We were absolutely in unison. I couldn't help laughing. It was almost as though we'd planned it.

At that moment, Grim came in. "What have you said? In public?"

Then he must have seen that Aila and I were holding hands. "Ah. Let me guess. When's the wedding? And where's my mug of keroo?"

We all laughed. I think he must have smelt the keroo, or maybe his eyes took in the whole room, and Yaani with the flagon in the corner, pretty quickly. Whatever the truth of that was, he knew what his priorities were!

Yaani poured him a mug. He lifted it high with a flourish, "I can see your great-great-grandchildren crawling all over your knees already."

Aila looked at her knees, then at mine, and laughed again. "I hope you won't say things like that when you're grown up, Grim. And preferably not outside the family even now!"

"Oh, I'm grown up enough to know when I can and when I can't make jokes, Sis, don't worry. And I know who's family and who isn't, too. Welcome into the family, brother."

And Grim surprised me with a big hug.

No-one seemed to be doing anything about supper, and Judd hadn't arrived at the time he normally had been arriving. He did have a place of his own, but he'd mostly been staying with us ever since I arrived, to talk to me in the evenings and on his days off. And he always let someone know whether to expect him for meals.

It surprised me and I think Aila as well how everyone seemed to have known what was going to happen before we did. Judd turned up three quarters of an hour later than usual, with a shoulder of salt mutton, a bagful of apples and a large round loaf of bread with a hole through the middle. "It's not quite a feast to match what Graamon brought yesterday, but I'm not Graamon."

Yaani took the mutton from Judd and handed it to Peyr. "It's much more our kind of food though, Judd. You've really done them proud. Chop up this shoulder, Peyr, while I fry some onions and slice some carrots. That mutton will make a really good stew!"

Aila went and sat by Yaana, and picked up the sewing that Yaani had been doing. "Don't leave your man feeling like a spare part, Aila," Yaana said, "While they're making supper, you and Owen get some more studying done."

"No, I'll cut some cloth while Peyr's chopping the meat. There's loads to do." I knew what patterns we were using, and could see what the next pieces to cut were. I started cutting. Yaana let me get on with it for a while, and then decided to put her foot down. "Aila, you and Owen really ought to do a bit more reading. It really could make a huge difference to how he gets on in Briggi."

"I don't think you need worry, actually, Gran," Peyr said. "I don't think there's much doubt now about Graamon wanting to take Owen on, and it's just the kind of niche Owen's looking for.

"But she's right that the sooner you learn to read the better, Owen."

"I hope you're right, Peyr. I shall need a reliable job if I'm to be a good husband to your daughter!"

"Don't you worry. I'm pretty sure Graamon wants you, but even if he doesn't, a chap of your ability can find a decent job easily enough anyway. But obviously it's good if you get a job that gets you good papers, rather than being stuck out of town permanently."

"That's something I was going to ask you about. You talked about 'good papers', and Aila called them 'railway papers'. Are your railway papers different in some way from other people's papers?"

"Oh, I don't have railway papers. I just have Laanoha papers. To visit Meyroha, I have to get a visitor's pass."

"Couldn't I have come into Laanoha on a visitor's pass?"

"Not without some kind of papers, or a big surety. While I'm in Meyroha on a pass, they hold my Laanoha papers, and I don't get them back until I leave. With railway papers, you can come and go as you please, anywhere."

"Like having both Laanoha and Meyroha papers?"

"Better than that. More like having castle papers. Not quite as good as castle papers, but nearly."

"Castle papers? What are they?"

"Castle papers are for really rich people – castle people. Without them, you can only get into the castles, either here or in Meyroha, or Barioha for that matter, as a guest of a senior Castle resident. But ordinary folks like us don't need or want to get into the castles. Castle people can demand entrance anywhere – railway offices or guard offices, anywhere. Railway papers will get you in most places – ordinary guard offices, for example, most offices of any kind. But not castles."

"Barioha? I've heard of that before."

"It's the third biggest city, halfway between here and Meyroha. Well, a bit nearer to Meyroha, really. There's a station on the main line there. It's the only stop between here and Meyroha – apart from when Jerem makes them stop in Baragi! The main line's not like our branch, with every train having to stop at every passing place."

"And it's got a castle?"

"Yes. It's not a big one like Laanoha's or Meyroha's though."

"That's four places I've heard of with names ending -oha, three of them with castles. Is that just coincidence, or does -oha have something to do with castles?"

Yaani was watching Peyr chopping the mutton – or forgetting to chop it half the time. "Peyr – is that mutton ready? The onions and carrots are ready to go in, but they'll turn to mush if the mutton doesn't go in for a while first." She knew already that it wasn't done, of course. Peyr looked at her sheepishly and finished the job quickly.

Then he turned back to me. "I don't know," he said. Then, to Judd, "Do you know, Judd?"

"Sorry, I wasn't listening. Do I know what?"

"Four places we know ending in -oha, three of them with castles. Is that just coincidence, or is there a connection?"

"I don't know. Where's the fourth place? I only know three, and they've all got castles. Might be connected, but it might just be that they're big places."

"The fourth one isn't big at all. I only heard of it the other day. It's where Owen stayed one night when he first arrived, halfway between Sirimi and the Sirimi road crossing. It's called Siroha. Just one big fancy house as far as we know, but maybe a neighbouring village as well."

"Never heard of it. You're more likely to hear about things like that than I am, stuck in the workshops here all the time."

Aila came and sat at the table, and looked up at me, patting the bench next to her. I took that as an invitation to sit beside her. She opened our childish reading book, and very quietly picked up where she'd left off teaching me the Laana script.

I tried to concentrate on the reading. I was certainly learning something, but my mind kept wandering off the subject, and I knew I was going to end up with gaps in my knowledge. There was nothing I could do about it.

I remembered Yaana, it seemed so long ago but it was only about four weeks, laughing that I couldn't earn enough to raise a family by cutting cloth for her. Had she had her eye on me as a potential grandson-in-law already, right back then?

She couldn't have. Or could she? I'd not even met Aila, didn't meet her for another three weeks. Aila didn't know I existed, unless Peyr had told her about his hitch-hiker when he picked up the meal in Baragi on my very first ride.

They're all very confident about me getting a job with Graamon. I hope they're right – and that I'll prove to be useful enough to keep the job.

"If I do get a job with Graamon, where do you think I'll be based? Will you be able to get a teaching job near to the same place? Or if I'm earning enough, will you want a job at all? There's just so much I don't know about life here."

"I don't know the answer to any of those questions. We'll find out soon enough. Don't worry. What will happen, will happen. Everything will be okay.

"Now, look at this word. That's *teymboo*. See how like *teyboo* it is?"

"Ah! That's what those little marks are. That makes sense now." *And teymboo means apple, I'd know that without the picture, but what does teyboo mean? I've forgotten.*

"So this is *kimtaa*?" The picture was a snake.

"Goodness! How did you get your tongue round that? Does English have words like that? No, it's *kintaa*."

"No, there's no *mta* in English. Not that I can think of, anyway. The nearest is *empty* with *pa* in between. But it's not hard for an English tongue to get round. Some of the sounds in Laana are awfully hard to get my tongue round, though. It took me a while to get my ear round some of them!"

But I couldn't keep my mind on the reading for long.

If I get a job with Graamon, will I be based in Briggi? Does Briggi even have a school where Aila could teach? Somehow I'd gained the impression there were few if any rich people there. But surely that impression was wrong – why else would there be shops selling the kind of luxury goods I'd seen? And why else would there be a passenger train every other day, if poor people can't afford train travel? How rich do you have to be to buy things like that, to travel by passenger train, or to send your kids to school?

"Sorry, I was daydreaming. What did you say?"

"Oh, Owen, you're hopeless. I think we should give up for today. Supper'll be ready in a moment, anyway. Maybe we'll have another go after supper – but maybe we'd better join in the general chatter, it's not fair to be too wrapped up in each other when everyone's trying to celebrate!"

She leant over and kissed me on the cheek. "I don't really think you're hopeless! You're doing really well."

I wasn't, and I knew it. But I was beginning to think that with one more day of it, I'd have enough of a start to be useful, and as long as I kept using it, my reading would improve slowly. *More lessons would undoubtedly help, though.*

But of course I've only seen this children's book – and a few street signs I've never tried to read before. I could ask to see Peyr's papers, but I'm too shy to. Oh – or Aila's. I'll ask tomorrow. Maybe.

The mutton and vegetable stew was gorgeous. We munched apples. We finished the last of the keroo.

We chatted late into the night, much of it joking about the descendants Aila and I were expected to have, how many there would be, and even elaborate fantasies about their exploits. I noticed that nobody conjured up visions of our own future – apart from the establishment of that impressive dynasty.

Well, what will happen, will happen. Everything will be okay.

Around midnight, we all snuggled down on the bedding pile in a long row. The chattering continued for some while after that, the number of participants dwindling gradually.

I went to sleep thinking, *what a whirlwind of a day*, but feeling surprisingly happy. Well, it was surprising to me, anyway. *I've found my niche. Not the kind of niche I was looking for, but a good niche. I still need the other kind of niche too, more than ever in fact, and maybe I've found that too, but that still needs confirmation. Not long before I know one way or the other, probably.*

I had turbulent dreams. I remember that they were turbulent, without remembering what actually happened in most of them.

I do remember one of them. I was in my harness, dangling from my balloons, but stationary about five metres off the ground. Below me my old headmaster was looking up at me, warning me of the dangers of girls – something he'd never done in real life, something I couldn't imagine him doing in real life. Other people, yes, but not him. Then I was rising slowly away from him, and he was disappearing gradually into the fog, waving at me and shouting something that I couldn't make out.

I woke later in the night. There was a candle alight on the table, and Peyr and Judd were sitting at the table with mugs, I guessed of skiir, talking quietly. I couldn't hear what they were saying. I didn't let them see that I was awake, and I was soon asleep again.

Chapter 7

I woke again at first light. Judd and Yaani were having their breakfast, almost ready to set off to work. Yaana was sitting by the fire, sewing. Aila was still fast asleep.

Peyr and Grim were nowhere to be seen. I guessed that Grim had already left and that maybe Peyr was outside washing himself. I thought I'd wait until he came in before I went to wash, and just lay there quietly for a while, but Peyr seemed to be gone a long time. *Maybe he's not washing himself. Maybe he's gone off somewhere already. I wonder where, and why?*

I started to get up. Aila turned over and looked at me. "I was just about to get up. I was waiting for Dad to come up from the pump, but he seems to have been gone an awful long time. Mum, has Dad gone off somewhere?"

I laughed. "That's what I was doing, too, Aila. I'd just decided he couldn't possibly still be washing. I was just going to get washed."

Yaani laughed too. "Your Dad was hoping to be back before you two woke up. Be nice to him – pretend to still be asleep!"

"I don't think I could do that, Mum. Come on Owen, we'll get washed quick. If he's not back by the time we're ready, we can pretend to be still asleep maybe."

I felt a bit shy, washing alongside Aila, and I think she felt the same a bit too. I'd got used to washing with Judd or Grim in Laanoha, and it just seemed natural to wash with Peyr at the inns on the Briggi trip. *I waited for Peyr to finish washing because I felt a bit shy to wash with him this morning. Apparently Aila did too; I wonder why.*

As we came in at the back door, Peyr was just coming up the stairs from the street, and Yaani and Judd were just coming down from the room. We all met just inside the back door.

Peyr had his rucksack on. I wondered where he'd been and what he'd been doing. He kissed Yaani on her cheek and whispered something in her ear. I couldn't make out what he said.

Yaani made a sad face, and Peyr laughed. Then Yaani laughed too, "You rotten tease!", and slapped his face, but not hard. He rubbed his face where she'd slapped it, as though it had hurt.

"Look at you two!" Judd said, "Just like two blooming teenagers in love!"

Then we all laughed. Aila turned to me and said, "Race you up the stairs!" and set off, with me in hot pursuit.

Peyr called after us, "You be careful, you two! We don't want any more accidents!" but Aila just laughed, and I called back, "Don't worry! It's not pitch dark, and it's not slippery!" Luckily neither of us tripped, and no-one came out of any of the other rooms at the wrong moment.

Yaana looked up as we came in. "He's not back yet. Are you going to pretend to be asleep?"

"Oh, bah," Aila said. "If we'd thought about it, Owen, we could have arranged with Dad to pretend we'd not bumped into him, and teased Gran instead. Too late now. He's just coming up the stairs, Gran."

Peyr came in and dumped his rucksack down in the corner by the table. "That took longer than I expected. I'd hoped to get back before you two woke up."

"Don't worry Dad. We've still no idea what it is. Obviously we can guess it's something to do with us, especially since you say you wanted to get it here without us knowing. But what? I can't even begin to guess."

"I'm not worrying, it's not a big deal. But if you can't guess, I shan't enlighten you." Big grin.

Probably it's whatever it was that Peyr and Judd were plotting in the middle of the night. But I've no idea what, either.

Aila started heating up the frying pan. "I expect you ate hours ago, Gran. Did you eat before you went out, Dad?"

"We both had some bread and apples, sweetheart, but if you're cooking something I'm sure your Dad wouldn't mind a taste."

"And neither would you, Gran! No arguments, now.

"Owen, could you slice some of the bread, thin slices? And Dad, you break half a dozen eggs into that bowl."

I don't remember there ever being eggs here before. When did they appear? Ah – they're not hens' eggs. I wonder what sort they are?

"I hope you're not going to bully your man all his life, Aila!" But Peyr was laughing.

"What? Like Mum bullies you? No, I wouldn't dream of it. Do you mind being organized, Owen?"

"Not as long as it's reasonable, like now, of course not."

What would I do if it wasn't reasonable, though? Why am I so sure it will always be reasonable? Should I be so sure?

What will happen, will happen. We'll cross that bridge when we come to it.

A promise is a promise. I take my promises seriously. Does Aila take her promises seriously? Have we actually made any promises? "Okay, I'm certain." Yes, that's a promise. Okay. Does Aila think it's a promise? Everyone's behaving as though it is. Surely it is.

"Owen? Are you all right?"

"Oh, sorry, daydreaming again. I'll get the bread done as quickly as I can."

"You really were daydreaming. Dad's done it already!"

She was laughing, I wasn't in trouble. *I think that's a good sign.*

"That's one good way not to get bullied, Owen!" Peyr was laughing, too.

"Dad! I don't think he did it on purpose. No, I don't mean that. I'm sure he didn't do it on purpose. He's got a lot to think about just now."

"So have you, but it doesn't seem to stop you thinking about getting on with ordinary things at the same time."

"Sure, but everything's strange for you all the time here. Maybe it's getting a bit familiar by now, but it's still quite a mental load, I'm sure. I think you're doing fantastically well. I'm proud of you!"

She's very aware of how unfamiliar everything is for me, considering how little she knows about how different England is. How did she figure it out? It had never occurred to me that anywhere could possibly be so different from England, until I arrived here. I thought France and Germany were different from England until I came here. Looking back now they seem almost exactly like England.

I wonder how different things are in the house where she works, and how much she knew about that environment before she went there?

I've had an instinct she had a good brain since first I met her; I get more certain of it by the minute.

"You're too kind, sweetheart!"

I hope that's the right word – it's what Yaana calls her, but I've heard Peyr use it for Yaani too, and the chap on the next floor down calls his lady that as well. If it's wrong, I'll get corrected!

"No, it's just the truth. I know what it's like being a fish out of water, and I've never been a fish out of water nearly as much as you are. It's because you're coping so well that I knew so quickly what a special man you are. There, I've said it. And I love the way you called me sweetheart, it's very sweet."

It's almost as if she can read my thoughts.

Or is it partly that I mentally translate Laana into the same words in English that I'd just thought myself, so the thoughts only need to be a bit similar to come out as the same words?

Goodness me, no, I was thinking in Laana! Well, mixed up Laana and English, anyway. It's just that my Laana vocabulary is still a bit limited, maybe, then.

Fish out of water is exactly the same as the English idiom – interesting.

I don't know what to call the food Aila made. *Parrapa*, in Laana. Thin slices of bread soaked in beaten egg, made into a sandwich filled with thin slices of apple and fried. Tasty!

Things always taste better when you know they're made with love. And a roughcast iron pan that remembers the spices of the last ten thousand meals probably helps, too. I wonder who got that pan new? Maybe Yaana, before Peyr was born? A lot more than ten thousand meals, if so. I wonder how long they've lived in this room, for that matter? I think that's something I can ask.

"A thought just occurred to me. You don't mind me asking, I hope. How long have you lived here?"

"In Laanoha? Apart from Gran, all our lives, all of us. Gran, you tell Owen how you came here!"

"I'd love to hear that story too, but I meant here in this room."

"Oh, about ten years I think. We were on the ebi floor before that, the other side of the staircase at the back. Grandad was still alive then, it was very crowded. Grim was just a tiddly little boy when we moved up here."

(I use the Laana word *ebi* because English is confused about this. Some people call it the first floor, others call it the second!)

"I hadn't thought about that – of course, there are four rooms on each floor apart from up here at the top, I've seen the doors. I suppose that is the ebi floor, even though it's ground level at the back."

"Oh, it's proper ebi floor. The shops have a cellar under there. Must be horribly wet though, the back room on the ebi floor is damp enough. But you're right – further along the street the ebi floor is straight on the ground at the back. That must be horrible, but I don't know any of the people there."

"Do you ever get trouble with water coming in through the roof? At the school where I lived in England, the ground floor was dry enough, but we always had trouble with the roof."

Peyr joined in again. "No, we don't get roof trouble. Roofs are no trouble if you look after them properly – at least Laanoha roofs aren't, I suppose some places where they don't have good slates probably have problems. But there's not a lot you can do about water at ground level if the original builders didn't get the drainage right. The shop side is dry enough, but I don't think they cared much about the back."

After breakfast, Aila and I studied and Peyr and Yaana worked on the clothes. I say we studied, and we did a bit of study, but we talked about England and Baragi and Briggi and the future as much as we studied. Aila had no more idea than I had where I was likely to be based if Graamon gave me a job, and she didn't know whether there was a school in Briggi or not.

"It might be better if there isn't one there already. There are certainly people there with a bit of money, and they must have children. I could start one! Getting a job in one that's already established might be harder there – it can't be like Laanoha or Meyroha, with big schools where there must often be vacancies."

Then Aila made lunch. I helped with peeling and cutting vegetables.

After lunch, Peyr suggested that Aila and I should go out for a walk again. Aila started to protest that we should study a bit more, but Peyr gave her a look that said, "Please go for a walk, Aila", and we did.

Aila picked a bag off the hook by the door and slung it over her shoulder as we went out.

She must have some plan in mind. That's good, better than wondering where to go.

She didn't even ask where I wanted to go, she just set off with me in tow. We went down to the railway again, but headed towards the docks rather than back to the river this time, before crossing over and slipping through a different alleyway onto the same street as the day before, but further along in the opposite direction. We followed the street for quite a way.

The street started to descend, and at the bottom of the hill I could see where the road passed through an archway under a very imposing stone building. "That's the gate to the dockyards," Aila said. "We'll go down there one day, when you've got papers."

We took a left turn, and were soon in a maze of narrow streets, little more than alleyways really, with smaller shops and the buildings more higgledy-piggledy than in the other streets. There were a lot more people on the street here, and the shopkeepers were calling out their wares, which was something I'd not heard in our part of town.

"I've not been down here before!"

"Gran didn't bring you here? She comes shopping here herself, I'm sure. That's Gran for you. Wanted to give you a more genteel impression of Laanoha!"

That didn't match up to my understanding of Yaana's personality, and I said so.

"You're right, of course, I was joking. I suspect she just didn't want to risk anyone asking awkward questions. People just don't do that sort of thing in our part of town, but it's different here. But you're much more familiar with Laana and how to behave now, and anyway, people can see that we're together in a very different way from you and Gran out shopping!"

That was true. We were holding hands, a fact I'd not really been aware of until that moment. She was dragging me along a bit at times, but that probably fitted the image she thought we were projecting too.

Then we were descending a steep little alleyway between tiny terraced houses. Most of them had two storeys, but the upper floor was in the roof, with little dormer windows that must have been almost at floor level upstairs. I'd have had to duck to get through the front doors, and I don't think the ceilings downstairs can have been much higher, or there'd have been no room upstairs at all. Several houses had open front doors, and through some of them I could see tiny children playing.

The alleyway ended at a beach of large pebbles, with a high tide mark of dry seaweed only a metre or so below the floor level of the lowest houses.

"Those houses aren't as old as they look. The bottom of that street would have been awash at high tide fifty years ago."

"Is the sea going down as fast as that? But you're right, I remember them building the bottom few houses round here when I was a little girl. But they already look as though they just grew out of the ground!"

A broad expanse of mud stretched from the foot of the beach to the sea, which was a long way out. Far out near the water I could see people working, probably collecting shellfish. We headed left along the top of the beach, away from the docks.

"With all that mud, they must have quite a job dredging a channel to the docks."

"The docks here are very old. They're planning to move them further out, onto the far side of the breakwater, and build a new breakwater further out. Already they can't bring in ships as big as they used to. They're down to solid rock in the bottom of the docks now, so there's nothing they can do about it."

There were several more alleys coming down the hill on our left, each steeper than the one before, with longer flights of

stairs and shorter slopes between them. The last row of houses
really did seem to grow out of the ground. The houses were two
low storeys high at the front, but the eaves at the back were less
than a metre above the hillside, which must have been dug away
to make space for the rooms in the houses.

The path continued between the beach on our right, and a
steep grassy slope up to the foot of a cliff on our left. Aila
pointed up to the summit of the cliff. "That's where we were
yesterday!"

"Yes, I know."

The path curved gently to the left, the grassy slope up to the
cliff foot getting narrower and narrower, until eventually the
path ran right along the foot of the cliff. At the same time, the
expanse of mud on our right became narrower and narrower.
Finally, the mud ended in a line of rocky reefs running out from
the foot of the cliff, and the path ended in a scramble up onto the
rocks. We were right at the end of the point, and I could see
round to the distant coast beyond the mouth of the Aaha river.

A few metres further on, I could see far enough up the estuary
to see the far end of the railway bridge over the river, but I
couldn't make out anything I could recognize as Kromaan on the
far bank.

"Look! There's a train on the bridge!"

There was. The train itself was barely visible, but the steam
from it was easy to make out, and the sound of its whistle
announcing its imminent arrival in Laanoha was audible above
the crashing of the waves on the rocks.

"That's today's first passenger train from Meyroha."

"You've got better eyes than I have!"

"No, silly, I can't see it that well. I know by the whistle."

"Ah, okay. I'd have known it wasn't your Dad's whistle, but
nothing more than that."

Then Aila led me out along the reef. At first there was mud on
each side, then shallow water just ebbing and flowing gently
over the mud. Far ahead of us the waves were crashing on the
rocks.

Aila bent down over a pool among the rocks of the reef, pulled
a snail shell off the rock, and showed it to me. "Do you know

these? *Ekraahi*. Really good to eat. Let's see how many we can get before the tide sends us home."

"I don't know these ones, no. They might be winkles, I'm not sure. I've never seen winkles, only heard about them. Further back, there were people out on the mud. They were collecting a different sort, I think. Those might be a kind we get in the market in England, maybe. Do you really know the tides so well that you knew it would be low tide before we'd even left the room?"

"No, not really. But I saw where the tide was yesterday, and it's just under an hour later every day."

Between us, we filled Aila's bag in about twenty minutes. Then she took off her shoes and socks and gave them and the bag to me. She tucked her skirt up into her knickers and headed out towards the waves again. "Don't you come! I won't be a minute!"

I saw her bending down right where the waves were breaking on the rocks. *She must be getting quite wet from the spray,* I thought. *I hope she's really sure footed on those rocks!*

She was. I didn't have anything to worry about on that score. She was back with me after a few moments, with several long strips of what looked like shiny greeny-brown leather. I'd never seen anything like it.

"Seaweed. The best sort. You can get this sort without a boat at the very bottom of the tide. We were lucky to be here at just the right moment."

"You use it as a vegetable?"

"Sort of. You use more than you'd use of spices, but you not as much as a vegetable. We might use half of this tonight. Dad'll hang the rest up from the rafters to dry. We used always to have some hanging up there, but since I left home Grim doesn't bother. We used to come down here together. Before that I used to come down with Gran, but she's not steady enough on her feet any more. Hasn't been for years."

"I'm surprised there's any left, so close to Laanoha."

"How many people did you see out on the point? There's only a handful of families in Laanoha who bother with it, there's nearly always plenty here. Plenty of ekraahi, too, even though they're easier to get, you don't have to catch the tide so accurately. But people don't bother."

I'm glad I've ended up in a family that does bother. I suppose it's all part of the same thing that made Peyr stop the train for me in the first place. Lucky me!

We went back the way we'd come. We didn't want to risk meeting guards on the quayside along the river. They probably wouldn't ask for our papers, but there was no point taking a chance. "Another time," Aila said. I wondered when that would be.

As we climbed the stairs, we could hear laughter and voices. I guessed it was coming from our room. The other occupants of the building seemed to be very quiet folks. We met them occasionally on the stairs, and they greeted us politely enough, but they definitely seemed to want to keep themselves to themselves.

But then, our family is usually pretty quiet, too.

The door to our room was open, and I was right. Grim spotted us coming up the stairs, and turned back into the room and shouted, "They're here!"

The laughter and voices stopped instantly. Then some kind of harplike instrument started playing, and a moment later we were greeted at the door with boisterous singing – a song Aila evidently knew, but whose words escaped me entirely.

"Oh, you absolute beasts!" she said, but she was smiling broadly. She turned to me, put her arms around my neck, pulled my face down to hers, and kissed me firmly on the mouth.

Everybody clapped, and Aila let go of me and turned to face everyone. I looked up and took in the scene properly for the first time.

The whole room was decorated with bits of coloured cloth tied on string strung across the beams. There were a dozen oil lamps, which must have been borrowed from somewhere. I'd only ever seen two before.

In the middle of the table, there was a cake – the first one I'd seen since leaving England. On the top were two figures, holding hands and clearly intended to look like Aila and me.

What they were made out of, I'd no idea. I'd no idea who'd made them in such short order either.

Grim, Judd and Yaani were home already, a couple of hours earlier than usual. In addition to the usual household, there were three other people whom I didn't know. But I guessed immediately who two of them were: they looked just like younger versions of Faahiha. They jumped up and came over to Aila and me.

Aila introduced us. "Owen, this is Jinni, and this is Berraami. And this is Owen, obviously."

"I guessed as soon as I saw you! Nice to meet you at last."

Should I have said that I guessed? They're smiling, so I guess it must have been okay.

The third stranger just sat with his instrument across his knees. He was an old man. He had two sticks leaning against his chair, which wasn't one that was normally in the room. I wondered where it had come from.

Aila led me to where he was sitting. He started to rise from his chair as I approached, but Aila gestured to him to remain seated, and he did. He offered his hand, and then spoke in a hoarse whisper, in English. "I'm Birgom. I'm delighted to meet you, young man. You've made a very good choice. You'll make a lovely couple, and no doubt you'll raise a lovely family. I'm only sad that I won't live to see them grow up. And that I can't stay for the festivities tonight. My grandson has to take out the first train for Briggi in the morning, so he's coming before long to take me and my chair and my *mizma* home, he can't stay up late. But let me play a tune for you and your lovely lady before I go."

He lifted one knee to angle the instrument towards himself a little, and began to play. It was a very different tune from the boisterous one he'd played to accompany the singing. It started as a soft, gentle, slow, almost sad piece that moved up and down the scales in modest steps; then gradually accelerated and became louder and more lively, jumping up and down in larger and larger intervals; and finally slowed and softened and returned to its gentle form before fading so gently into silence that it was hard to be sure exactly when the last note was played.

Aila clapped softly, and thanked him. "I've not heard that one for years," she said.

"I know," he replied, "I've not played it for years. But I remember how it used to be your favourite when you were a little girl. I remember how you used to tell me to play it again. And again. And again. Until everyone else was fed up with it."

"Play it again, Uncle!"

"For you, on your special day, I will, too," and he did.

"That's beautiful," I said, and I meant it. It was.

As he finished, a young man appeared at the door. He seemed a little shy to just walk in, but Aila called him over. "Viilam, come and meet Owen before you take your grandad away. Wait, I'll get you a drink. Owen, you haven't had a drink yet, either!"

"You've not had one yet, either, Sis. I'll get them." Grim fetched four drinks, and then went back to helping his mother with something at the table.

"I've had one," said Birgom in his hoarse whisper, "but I'll not refuse another."

It was keroo again.

Viilam and Birgom finished their drinks much more quickly than was normal in Laanoha, and excused themselves. Viilam carried the chair and the mizma, and Birgom walked very carefully with his two sticks as far as the top of the stairs. Then Viilam took the sticks and went down very slowly, followed by Birgom with his hands on his grandson's shoulders. This was obviously a well established procedure!

"He's not really my uncle, but we all call him Uncle. He's uncle to everyone who works on the railway, and all their families. As far as I know, Viilam's the only one who's actually related to him. Was that English he was talking with you? I've no idea how he knows English!"

"It was. He's only the third person I've met here who knows any English at all, and the first one who knows it anything like as well as that. His English is very good, you'd almost think he was a native English speaker. I wish I'd had a chance to find out more about him."

"I don't know much about him myself, other than that he's been an old man around the place playing his mizma for

everyone as long as I can remember. He used to have a
wonderful, rich voice too, but you can hear what's happened to
that – very sad. And of course that he's Viilam's grandfather,
although I'm not sure even that is really true. Neither of them
has any other family here. I'm not sure whether Birgom might
have adopted him. I don't think anyone really knows."

"Dad! I don't know what you're doing for supper, but we've
got a bag full of ekraahi and some seaweed. I'm sure it'll go
well with it, whatever it is!"

"Ah, that's where you went. Did you take the bag on the off
chance, or did you know the tide?"

"We saw it from the top yesterday, so I knew more or less.
Realized just as we were going out today. Then it was right at
the bottom while we were there, just perfect timing. Lucky."

Jinni grabbed Aila's bag. "Give us those, Aila, we'll scald
them and shell them. Your Dad's busy." Jinni and Berraami were
soon hard at work.

Aila and I didn't have a chance to do any more study, but we
weren't worried. *If this is a betrothal party – I suppose that is
what it is – what on earth is a wedding like?*

It was a magnificent feast. The ekraahi were a bit sandy – but
very tasty. There was fresh meat – the first I'd seen in Laanoha.
I asked Aila what it was, and she said she'd tell me later, which
left me somewhat puzzled. Why didn't she want to tell me there
and then? But I didn't think it right to press the question. And
lots of fruit. Someone must have spent a lot buying oranges – I'd
heard the prices being shouted out in the market.

Laughing and joking and singing and telling stories continued
well into the night. Peyr's train, with both Aila and me on board,
was due out at eight, but neither he nor Aila seemed to be
worried.

Jinni and Berraami both stayed the night. "They'd be
welcome here any time, of course, but the railway pays for them
to stay in an inn, food and all, so that's what they normally do."

"Your Gran would be here on her own to clear up tomorrow if
we weren't here," Berraami said, "Jinni's not due out until one,
and I don't go until the day after."

"Thanks very much for that," Yaana said, "it's really appreciated."

"It's nothing, Gran. We've had a wonderful evening."

Yaana wasn't their Gran any more than Birgom was Aila's uncle.

If I dreamed that night, I don't remember it. I didn't wake up until Aila shook me awake. "Time to get up, sleepy head! Dad's gone already, I've got some breakfast packed up for you to eat in the train. I'm afraid you don't even have time for a proper wash, but you'll be getting filthy under the floor soon anyway!" Laughter.

Yaana came down to the railway with us, and we were actually there in plenty of time.

Peyr's train appeared in the distance, and suddenly Yaana stiffened. "Quick – Owen, you and I must disappear!"

Yaana dragged me back into the alleyway, and Aila threw the package she'd been carrying to me.

"We'll see each other as soon as possible," Aila called. "Get Judd to sort something out, Gran!"

Then Yaana was dragging me round the corner out of sight of the railway. I heard the train pass, slowly.

"Aila will have caught the train, Owen. We'd better go back to the room."

"What happened? There was someone on the train who mustn't see me? How did Aila know?"

"Peyr doesn't need to vent steam like that when he's only just got going. If he does it, it's our private signal that we've got to get the clothes packages out of sight quickly because he's got a guard on board, or someone else we don't want to see them. Getting caught smuggling you would be even worse."

"No-one minds Aila riding with him, though?"

"No, why would they? She's got papers."

"Does that mean I won't be able to get to Briggi for another week?"

"I'm not sure. Aila seemed to think Judd might be able to get you away sooner than that somehow. You or I can't go down to the workshops to talk to him, but Jinni or Berraami can. You could go on their trains, but they don't have anywhere for you to hide, as far as I know. We'll be able to talk to them in a minute, anyway."

Jinni met us at the top of the stairs. "Oh no! I wonder who that was? That's really sad, cutting off your last couple of hours with Aila!"

"It's true there were one or two things I'd have liked to have talked to her about. But what happened, happened. She said I should ask Judd to help sort something out, but I won't be able to see him until tonight, of course."

"No, but we can. As long as there's no-one awkward in the workshops, he'll be able to make you a place on my engine – or on Berraami's, if he can't get mine done in time.

"I'll dash down there now, and talk to him. Give Yaana and Berraami a hand tidying up, Owen, and don't worry. We'll get you away today, or tomorrow at the worst. And Peyr will tell Graamon what's happened."

Jinni was as good as her word. She was back in under an hour. "Judd says no problem, nobody awkward around at all. He's putting boards across the chassis under the cab on both our engines. Then all being well, you'll be on my train at one o'clock, and if the worst comes to the worst and there's another damned guard, you can catch Berraami in the morning. It'd be incredibly unlucky for it to happen three times in a row. But you must be sure you know how to tell if we're venting steam."

"I think so. I didn't notice this morning, but I wasn't watching out for it. Just as well Yaana was!"

"Oh, she always watches for it, I'm sure. There's no point having a private signal if you don't watch for it. It's a good signal, guards or officials would never realize you couldn't possibly need to vent steam so soon after lighting up. They wouldn't even know that's what you were doing.

"Actually, I'm surprised you understood so quickly. Were you around trains in England?"

"Not much, and they're very different there anyway. But I've got a technical background, and I've ridden with Peyr all the way to Briggi and back and taken an interest in what's going on. It'd have been nice to have a chance to observe a steam venting before having to look out for one, but I'll manage. Whereabouts is the vent?"

"I'm sure he uses the one on the left cylinder. He wouldn't want to use to the top one, it'd be too obvious to anyone in the cab, and the left will be easier for you to see than the right, since you'll be on the left of the line. Don't confuse it with the regular exhaust from the cylinder, that's all!"

"That's okay, the regular exhaust comes out in spurts, I'll know all right."

"Oh, and don't worry about venting up the chimney. We're very likely to be doing that, to draw air through the fire. We have to do that a lot when we're only just getting going."

Yaana made an early lunch and we all ate with Jinni, then she set off for the yard. "I'll go a little bit early and make sure I know how to get the floor open and shut quickly before I bring the engine out."

Yaana came to the line side with me again, "Just to make sure you don't miss it if Jinni vents." I said I was confident, but Yaana wasn't having it. "No sense taking unnecessary risks!"

Berraami saw us off at the front door, "Good luck! See you in Briggi the day after tomorrow!" Then she went back inside to finish the tidying up. It was amazing how much mess we'd all made.

Then I remembered parties back in England. At least here no-one had got drunk, nothing got broken, and no-one had been sick all over the place.

Yaana had a bag over her shoulder. She'd had it in the morning too, as well as the clothes packages, which she didn't bring this time – no sense sending them with me, customers wouldn't be expecting them on Jinni's train.

Jinni didn't have to vent, and I climbed aboard no problem. Yaana walked alongside for a little way, then fished a package out of her bag and passed it up to me. "Look after her," she said. It was the little Aila that had been on top of the cake.

Yaana stood by the side of the line and waved for a while, then disappeared into the alleyway.

"You'd better get under the floor quick," Jinni said, and I did. She shut me in.

With no packages, there was plenty of room for me, but the boards weren't as neat as the ones on Peyr's train. There were gaps through which I could see the sleepers and ballast gliding past. The wood was rough, and it stuck into me in places. But it did the job, Judd had got it together in double quick time, it was only going to be used once, and I wasn't packages of cloth or clothes that needed to be kept neat and tidy.

I heard the clatter of the bridge. Looking straight down I saw the mudflats by the river through the latticework of the bridge. Then we were over the river itself, and Jinni was opening the floor panel and letting me out.

"We should remove those boards and use them in the fire – Judd got them off the firewood pile. We'll wait until we're stopped to get them out, I don't fancy doing it on the move. I'll have to be careful burning them. They're a bit long, and we've no means of cutting them."

"Don't you want to just leave them there? They could be quite useful, surely?"

"It'd be a bit of a risk. Peyr's look like they're part of the engine. They're neatly cut, and so filthy that from the underneath you can't really tell they're wooden. Nobody in the inspection pit would think twice about them. But scruffy old bits of firewood jammed across the chassis? That looks a bit odd! But of course nobody can see it except from the inspection pit, or if the floor panel's up."

"Or looking up through the bridge. But I can't imagine anyone doing that in the normal way of things, and you'd need pretty sharp eyes at that distance."

Jinni laughed. "Looking up at trains from underneath latticework bridges would be a pretty silly thing to do. You'd get all sorts of muck in your eye!

"I wouldn't be surprised if Aila's got permission to come and meet the train, in the hope that you'll be on it. I won't go through Baragi at full speed the way I usually do!"

She was there, and she had two little children with her, a girl I guessed was about eight, and a little boy of about six. They all waved at us, and we waved back, and as we passed them, she shouted, "I love you!" At least, I heard enough of her shout to be pretty sure that's what she said.

We waved to each other until they disappeared round the curve in the track. Then we were on the bridge, and I could see where we'd been standing when she showed me the view the very first time I met her. It wasn't so long ago.

"I bet she was telling those two kids, 'that's the man I'm going to marry', really proudly. If she'd been on her own, she'd have met us right at the beginning of the village, and come on board as far as the bridge. She knew I'd come through slowly if I had you on board. But they must have been relying on her to look after those two."

Jinni worked the fire up again and opened the regulator, and we put on speed. It began to rain.

We were due to stay the first night at Veglid. It had been dark for some while before we got there, and it was raining quite hard by this time. From a distance, I could see a light on the platform, and as we approached, I could see that there was a teenage boy with a large umbrella, holding a hurricane lamp.

Jinni's control was as good as Peyr's. We stopped with the cab precisely beside the boy, with barely a touch on the brakes. Jinni had already shut the fire down, leaving just enough draught to keep it smouldering until the morning.

The boy handed the umbrella to Jinni. "Hold onto this a moment while I light the other lamp." He lit another lamp, then opened another umbrella, and gave one of the lamps to her. "Two of you? Good job they're both big umbrellas! See you in a bit."

He stayed on the platform as Jinni led me down a well-worn path away from the railway. "He'll follow us down to Veglid with Preysh when he arrives. Miserable night to be hanging around waiting for trains!"

"He has to meet the trains every night? Couldn't you carry lamps on the trains?"

"We could, I suppose. And umbrellas, and waterproofs for days when it's windy as well as raining. But all the wagons are locked, and there's not a lot of room for extra clobber on the engines – the designers never thought of making space for us to carry anything much! And every engine would have to have everything, instead of just two sets here at Veglid. You don't need it anywhere else."

"Or it could be kept in a box on the platform."

"It used to be. But the lamps and umbrellas got stolen a couple of times, so they started doing it this way. It's not a big deal really anyway. It's only needed on moonless winter evenings, or wet ones."

"I've not actually met Preysh. We passed him without stopping. He and Peyr congratulated each other on a perfect passing. I remember that well."

The path became a stone staircase down the side of a steep little valley, and I could see the lighted windows of several buildings at the bottom. The stone gave way to wood as the staircase angled left down the face of what was virtually a cliff, then doubled back on itself the other way across the face, ending in an alleyway between two buildings.

A road, paved with deeply rutted flagstones and crowded with parked carts laden with firewood, was dimly illuminated by lamplight spilling from windows. We crossed the road and went into a handsome stone-built inn. There was a fire blazing, and we went and sat in front of it.

"Is that the old coaching road, with the wheel-ruts?"

"Yes. Nowadays the only traffic on it is those firewood carts supplying the railway and a few local villages. The wood carts have to go all the way round by the road to get to the station, which is much further than the way we just came. But of course that's nothing compared to the drive in from the forest before they even get to Veglid."

The innkeeper brought us our supper without a word, but with a big grin on his face. After he'd gone, Jinni turned to me. "I'd love to wipe that grin off that man's face. He thinks you're my boyfriend!"

"Tell him I'm Aila's betrothed."

"No, none of us tell him anything. He doesn't even know Peyr's got a daughter, much less what her name is."

"At least the food's good."

"Thank his wife for that. I'd worry what he might put in it if it wasn't for the fact the railway could take his living away overnight if he put a foot wrong."

"Is the railway really that important to him? Two drivers for supper, bed and breakfast every day?"

"Not even that many drivers. It's only three in two nights, the passenger trains don't stay here. But half the railway's woodcutters do. That's his main income. And there are two other inns here that would love to get more of that trade."

"Was that their son up at the station?"

"I think so, but I've never enquired too closely. I think he's okay, just not very talkative. Probably used to not saying too much anywhere near his dad."

I wondered whether Jinni actually knew anything against the innkeeper, or whether it was just an instinct, but I didn't ask. *Maybe I'll ask Peyr when I see him.*

The atmosphere in the inn certainly wasn't as congenial as the atmosphere at Briggi, Belgaam or Tambuk. In fact it was positively creepy. Whether I'd have had that feeling if Jinni hadn't said anything, I don't know – but certainly there wasn't the same cheerful chattering going on. People were talking quietly in small groups in corners.

The boy arrived with another driver. I assumed he must be Preysh. He joined Jinni and me. The innkeeper brought him his food as wordlessly as he'd brought ours. Jinni waited until he'd gone before introducing us. "Preysh, this is Owen. Owen, this is Preysh."

"I guessed that. Peyr said he thought you'd probably be on Jinni's train. Congratulations! You've caught a real prize there, Aila's a lovely girl. Look after her well!"

"You didn't pass Peyr without stopping just now, then."

"No, and I'm sorry we did that last time round. Peyr told me I'd missed meeting you at Embrouha. But there's rarely a perfect passing at Elbrouha, the down train nearly always has to wait for the up. The up train doesn't usually stop, because you don't want to lose momentum on the climb, but Graamon told me I ought to have a chat with Peyr this time. That's why I'm a bit late here. Doesn't matter on the last leg of the day, not holding anyone up."

Jinni raised an objection to that. "Apart from the innkeeper's lad, hanging about on the station in the rain."

"Oh, I don't think he minds a bit. It's a good excuse to get away from the inn for a while. Imagine what it's like actually living here."

So it's not just Jinni who has that feeling about this place, then.

I woke several times in the night.

The ceiling was just rough beams and the floorboards of the rooms above. Often there seemed to be someone moving about upstairs, the floorboards creaking as they moved and every now and then the glow of an oil lamp here and there through cracks between the boards.

When I did sleep, I had troubled dreams, haunted by a monstrous caricature of the innkeeper.

At one point he was chasing Jinni with a butcher's cleaver, and I was trying to protect her. Then Jinni became Aila, and I held her close and was about to kiss her when suddenly she was Jinni again, pushing me away and scolding me, but the innkeeper was behind her pushing her towards me.

Another time he was chasing me along an unfamiliar stony path in the dark and the rain. We reached a rickety wooden staircase down the steep side of a ravine. I could see the lights of a village ahead, but the innkeeper was close behind me, laughing horribly, and my feet kept slipping on the wet wooden steps.

Chapter 8

Things were much better in the morning. Supper had been brought in from a back kitchen somewhere, but breakfast was prepared by the innkeeper's wife at the fire we'd slept beside, in the room we'd spent the whole time in. The innkeeper himself was nowhere to be seen. "I expect he's fast asleep," Jinni said. "I don't know what he was doing, faffing about upstairs all night."

We were the second shift for breakfast. We weren't due to depart until eight, and the woodcutters had half a trainload of firewood to load onto Preysh's train before that. They had already breakfasted and set off for the station with their carts by first light.

The innkeeper hadn't made an appearance by the time we left.

The fire was still smouldering in Jinni's engine, and it didn't take long to get it going nicely. "We'll leave the boards under the floor for the moment, with all these woodcutters around. They're the other side of Preysh's train, but even so. Elbrouha's a much better place to do it."

I got my little model Aila out of my bag, and admired it. I asked Jinni, "What's she made out of?"

"Flesh and blood, of course! And bravery and humour and honesty and generosity. Like Preysh said, you've caught a real prize."

"I meant the model, silly!"

"Don't think of it as a model. It's Aila, and you're supposed to look after her, because the real Aila isn't with you for you to look after."

"Ah, okay. Will I have to make people like these for our daughter's betrothal?"

"No. I'm not sure who's job that will be. Theoretically it's your mother's, but who does it when the father's mother has already died, I'm not sure. Mum'll know, and she'll be at Raamba with us for lunch."

"So Yaana made these?"

"Yup. And Yaani will make them for Grim's daughters, and eventually it'll be Aila's turn to make them for your sons' daughters. And you're not supposed to know what they're made of. To you, they're made of flesh and blood. And most importantly, the character of the person."

The boiler pressure had got up enough to get moving. It probably wasn't quite eight o'clock yet, but it didn't matter. "We'll most likely have to wait for Laar at Elbrouha anyway. If we get there a little early, we'll wait there instead of here. Give us more time to get those boards up." So we set off.

At Elbrouha, it didn't take long at all to get all the boards out from under the floor. Jinni put them at the front of the woodpile, so they'd be the first to be used. "I don't suppose anyone who matters would notice we'd got oddly long boards to burn, but best to minimize the risk of anyone asking awkward questions. I don't know whether I'll be able to burn more than one of them at a time, though."

As it turned out, they were a serious nuisance. Jinni couldn't shut the firebox door properly, so there was too much draught. "They'd be okay on the climb, but going this way I don't need so much steam! If there's no-one else around, I'll give them to Mum to use going up the other way."

Once the end in the firebox was burnt away, Jinni pushed the rest in, and shut the door completely. Even so, she had to vent steam, and we arrived at Raamba even earlier than she'd anticipated.

Faahiha was amused by the boards. "You should have realized what would happen, Jinni! I'd have the door open anyway going up to Elbrouha, of course."

We had a good time over lunch together, but I realized as we set off again that I'd forgotten to ask her about who would make my daughter's betrothal models. Jinni had forgotten, too.

How would I have asked, anyway? How could I word the question to get round calling them models? Who knows whether we'll really have a daughter anyway? We're not even married yet. But how they all talk! It's infectious.

We'll find out things like that soon enough. It won't be the first time a grandmother wasn't around to perform her duties!

If I'd been on Peyr's train, I'd have had to hide under the floor at the Sirimi road, to avoid the lady from Siroha. We'd destroyed my hiding place, but I was sure that she wouldn't be watching for Jinni's train.

There was no-one there. "That's where Peyr originally picked me up!"

"I know. It's lucky it was Peyr. Some of the rest of them might have done the same, but most of them wouldn't. And I'm afraid that Berraami and I definitely wouldn't, even with the outlandish clothes you were wearing. Probably not Mum, either, although she's pretty relaxed about risk. I'm glad Peyr did, though." And she surprised me with a big kiss on the cheek.

I shouldn't still be surprised, I should be getting used to this by now. I like these people. Much less inhibited than the English, much more spontaneous – mostly.

I wonder what would have happened to me if Peyr hadn't picked me up? I'd have walked to Raamba, or the other way. Then what? No point speculating, really. Where does the footpath go in the other direction? Not to Elbrouha through the tunnel, that's for sure. People obviously walk that way, anyway, so it goes somewhere.

We had dinner at Belgaam. The driver and a few of the passengers off the passenger train joined us, but most of the passengers were eating on the train, or already had. Jinni knew the driver, but not very well.

Dinner was served by the same two girls who'd fed us there every time. They seemed a little surprised to see me with Jinni instead of Peyr, and slightly less attentive than before. But the meal was as good as ever, and the service was perfectly good. We parted with a friendly, "See you soon!" but again with no mention of when.

The up train was waiting at Embrouha already, and we sailed through without stopping. Just a cheerful toot on the whistles, and we were gone. It was beginning to snow.

By the time we got to Kaahes, it was snowing heavily and settling. Until we stopped, we didn't really know how much there was on the ground, but walking over to the inn we discovered there was a good fifteen centimetres – more in some places where it had drifted.

"If it keeps up like this, we'll be going nowhere tomorrow. I wonder what it's like further north now? I hope Jamaam isn't stuck anywhere between Tambuk and here already."

"What happens if a train gets stuck in the snow? How does the driver survive?"

"It's pretty horrible. But you keep the fire burning low and it doesn't get too cold in the cab, and you've got plenty of water. You can get pretty hungry if no-one gets to you for a few days, though. It's only happened to me once. I was only a couple of miles north of Tambuk, but the blizzard got so bad they didn't dare go out in it, and when it calmed down a bit there were three metre drifts across the line. It took them three days to dig through to me, and the train was stuck there for two weeks. They kept on running a few trains south of Belgaam, where there was much less snow, but not a full service."

"Can you leave a fire burning in an abandoned engine for a whole week? If you let it go out, doesn't the boiler freeze?"

"If you're in your engine, you can keep the fire going a long time, just burning low. If you're going to abandon an engine in conditions like that, you have to drain everything down. It's a real pain, because you have to tow the train out afterwards with another engine. So once they'd dug me out, we took turns to stay with the engine and keep the fire in. If the snow had lasted much longer they'd have had to start carrying more wood out to it, which is a real pain too."

Jamaam was a little late, but he made it through okay. "It's getting a bit iffy in places. If it keeps on like this, you won't be going to Tambuk tomorrow, much less on to Briggi.

"You must be Owen. Congratulations! You're a lucky man."

"You're not supposed to say that, Jamaam. Berraami would be jealous if she thought you'd have preferred Aila if you thought she'd have you!"

Jamaam laughed. "Making Berraami jealous might not be such a bad thing!"

"I don't think you mean that, really."

"No, you're right, I don't. And I do think Aila's lovely, but I'm glad I've got Berraami."

I wondered whether Jamaam and Berraami were actually married, or just betrothed, or maybe not even betrothed. But I didn't feel able to ask, and no-one volunteered the information. *Maybe I can ask Peyr. Or Aila.*

And I still have no idea how old anyone is. Jamaam and Jinni and Berraami seem quite a bit older than Aila or me – but are they? How old is Aila? Twenty-three, twenty-four? I really don't know, could easily be years less, or more.

It was interesting to contrast the character of the different inns on the railway. Kaahes was efficient, comfortable and professional feeling. It had washing facilities and latrines indoors, things I'd only seen at Siroha since leaving England. The food was good and sufficient, without being excellent or generous. The atmosphere wasn't homely like Belgaam or Tambuk, but nor was it oppressive like Veglid.

If I had dreams that night, I don't remember any of them.

The morning was bitterly cold, and the snow, which had been slightly damp when it fell, was crunchy underfoot – but no more had fallen, the sky was blue from horizon to horizon, and Jamaam and Jinni decided it was safe to proceed.

Jinni built up her fire, then while the pressure was building up in the boiler, she got me to help her adjust her snowplough right down onto the rails to scrape off anything that was actually frozen to the rail. "You don't normally want to do that, but when it's refrozen and hard like this you can even get derailed by it."

They both checked that their sandboxes were full, and we were off. "Blow my sis a kiss at Embrouha for me!" Jinni shouted to Jamaam as he climbed into his cab.

"Sorry, there'll only be time for my own!"

Laughter.

Bad matching of shifts, for a couple – at least one of them won't even stop at Embrouha. I wonder how the rest of their shifts work out – how much time do they ever get together? Sooner or later I'll find out – or not.

All the way, the pathway Jamaam's train had carved through the drifts was still visible. The further we went, the more the outline of his path had been smoothed out by additional snowfall and drifting, but the snowfall had clearly all finished not long after he arrived at Kaahes. We kept moving steadily, and didn't need to use the sand at all – never a moment's wheelslip. "I don't like using sand if I can possibly help it. It makes a horrible mud on the rails that's even worse than clean ice when it freezes. I'm pretty sure Jamaam didn't use any last night, either."

I could feel the whole engine shudder as we hit some of the drifts, but the weight of the train behind us just pushed us through, with great showers of icy snow cascading all over the engine and completely obliterating the blue sky for a moment. *Jinni's obviously done this before. She knows how big a drift she can just plough straight through!*

I think she was actually quite enjoying it, to judge by the look on her face. *Just as well we've got a tarpaulin over the woodpile, though.*

I thought of something I could ask, that might lead Jinni into volunteering some of the information I wanted. *Not that I really need any of this information, but it all helps to understand how the culture works. I think.*

"You and Berraami are Briggi people, aren't you? Is Jamaam a Briggi man, too?"

"Not originally, no, but he works Briggi-based shifts now, so as to get more time with Berraami. They both do a bit of shift swapping to get even more, but everyone wants to swap shifts here and there for different reasons, and it's not easy to get exactly the combinations you want."

The up train was already waiting for us at Tambuk. "That's good of Parruk, setting off early from Briggi so we don't have to stop here. The loop here is on quite a gradient, in ice like this it can be hard getting going again."

Jinni blew three short blasts on the whistles, two high and a low, and Parruk returned the same sequence. "I've not heard that pattern before. Does it have a special meaning?"

Jinni grinned. "Not in the rule book, no. That's blowing a kiss. He's my boyfriend."

Ah. I wondered if Jinni was attached. Actually, it's a bit of a relief that she is. Her friendliness and familiarity aren't anything more than friendliness and familiarity. That makes things easier.

I found my tongue was a little looser once I knew Jinni had a boyfriend, and felt able to ask things I was too shy to ask before. "So do railway girls always have railway boyfriends?"

I realized it was a daft question before I'd finished asking, but it didn't matter.

"There's only three of us. There's only ever been three of us. If Mum's got a boyfriend, she's keeping quiet about it, and he's not a railway man unless he's one of the very young ones, or someone cheating on his wife. I don't think she's had a boyfriend since Dad died, in fact. But Jamaam and Parruk are both drivers, yes."

Here's me being so shy about asking any questions, and people just tell me all sorts of things with no inhibitions at all without me even asking. When will I ever get used to this culture?

But I still can't ask how old anyone is. I don't even know when Aila's birthday is – or my own, in any way that makes any sense here. I don't even know how the calendar works here.

Ah. That's something I can ask!

"I know about the days of the week in Laana. In English, we divide the year into twelve *months*, as we call them, and they have names too, like the names of the days of the week. Is there anything like that in Laana?"

As we climbed out of the head of the valley, the wind got stronger, and there were big drifts that had reformed across the path Parruk had made. We were getting near the summit, and then it would be downhill or level until the viaduct just before Briggi, and we wouldn't want much steam. Jinni shut the firebox door to slow down the fire before she answered. "Well, there's four *seasons* – Cold just now, then Warming, Warm, Cooling and back to Cold. You have twelve seasons in England? Confusing!"

"No, no, we have four seasons just like you do. Months are just divisions of the year, not seasons."

"Something to do with the Moon, and the tides? Twelve and a bit?

"Hold on tight to the handrail! This is a bigger drift!"

It was, but she knew what her train could stand all right. The shock was terrific and would certainly have knocked me off my feet if I hadn't held tight, but apart from one big jerk the train just glided on as if nothing had happened. For a moment we had huge pile of snow on top of the tarpaulin over the wood, then that slid off sideways taking with it all the snow that had accumulated there already.

Jinni opened the firebox door and pulled the fire back together with a long handled rake. "All in a big pile right at the front, blocking the boiler tubes. Got to put some more wood on, too. It'd go out if I didn't, with it all in little pieces like that."

She lifted the edge of the tarpaulin and picked out a few smaller chunks of wood. *She knows just how to do all this. Learnt at her mother's knee, of course. It'd take me ages to learn all the tricks.*

"I hope everything in the wagons is well packed. There's no grab handles for the load!"

"It'll be well enough packed. The shock's much less in the wagons anyway, especially at the back end of the train. The buffers are designed to absorb a lot of shock – especially the long ones on the back of the engine.

"What were we talking about before that drift? Seasons or something?"

"I think I'd got my answer: you don't have anything between week and season. So it's just twenty-four hours in a day, seven days in a week, thirteen weeks in a season, and four seasons in a year."

"Yes, that's right. Well, sixty minutes in an hour, too, but that doesn't often matter. The railway runs by clocks at the inns for the first leg, and the passenger train has a clock to make sure it never leaves anywhere early. As if that would ever happen – they're always waiting for goods trains in the normal way of things. Apart from the first leg of the day, the goods trains always just go on as soon as they can."

Interesting that the divisions of time are mostly the same as in England. Presumably they have a common history somewhere a long way back. Written numbers are the same too, of course. I'd not thought about that before.

We talked about the counting of the years as well, and I learnt that Laanoha counts them differently from Meyroha, and Barioha differently again, but that nowadays nearly everybody uses Meyroha years, apart from a few diehard Laanoha chauvinists. "It's only fair. Everybody talks Laana. Why shouldn't we count years Meyroha fashion? They're a digit shorter, too!"

It was year 822, Meyroha style, so they were going to be a digit shorter all my life, anyway. But what the great event was that they were counted from, I didn't discover. *Most of Laanoha can't be as old as that, never mind over a thousand – most of where it is now would have been under water eight hundred years ago. Unless sea level's rate of descent has changed in that time. And that's something else I've no means of knowing.*

Lower down, the snow had drifted less since Parruk passed, and the line was pretty well clear. There was a curious peace in all the whiteness, despite the noise of the train. Somehow the snow seemed to deaden the noise, even in the cab. Of course the engine itself wasn't working hard, but even the rolling of the wheels on the rails seemed gentler somehow.

Jinni loosed a long high whistle to announce our approach to Briggi, and used the last of the boiler pressure to propel us up the final gradient into the town.

Graamon and Peyr were there to meet us. "Well done, Jinni! We knew you'd bring him if you could! What's the snow like at the top? Still drifting? As long as it doesn't snow any more, Berraami should be able to get through, if you could."

But there were angry looking clouds coming down from the north, so we weren't confident. Medaal set off as soon as we arrived, pretty much on time, but he was taking extra food in case he got stuck. Everyone wished him luck, and then the four of us went into the inn by the railway yard.

The innkeeper had warm skiir in a cauldron by the fire, which was very welcome.

"We'll stay here for lunch, then we'll go up to my workshop later on and I'll show you round. There's a lot we can talk about here, now, but the workshop will doubtless prompt a lot more."

I was a bit tongue-tied at first, but everyone was very relaxed and chatty, and gradually I found my voice. My knowledge of Laana, good enough by then for everyday conversation, was still grossly inadequate for the kind of deeper technical and scientific discussions Graamon and I wanted to have, but he was patient. "There's pencils and paper up at the worksop. When we can draw diagrams for each other it will help a great deal. And I know that your knowledge of Laana is going to improve rapidly!"

Everyone was quite at ease slipping casually back and forth between technical or personal matters or the weather, and a couple of hours passed very pleasantly – and interestingly, for me at least.

Lunch arrived, and I realized how hungry I was. The Railwayyard Inn in Briggi expects engine drivers and their friends to arrive hungry from Kaahes, and they didn't disappoint.

After lunch, it was snowing. Jinni excused herself and went home. "I'll be back at three, to meet Berraami. If she gets through – it's not snowing much down here, but who knows what it's like on the top?"

"I hope she does get through, or at worst doesn't set out from Tambuk. I don't like the idea of her being stuck up there on her own."

"Neither do I. But she'll survive even if it happens. It happened to me once, a few years ago. Nasty. You learn a lot about yourself. It's an experience, one you don't forget, but it's survivable. See you in about an hour." And she was gone.

"We'll stick around here too. The workshop will still be there this evening, or tomorrow."

"Did you ever get stuck in the snow, Peyr?"

"Not like Jinni, no. I got stuck for a couple of hours once, that's all. I was in sight of Tambuk, coming from here. I whistled and they came and dug me out. Just one big drift, and then I was moving again. There's not many of us have been stuck as long as Jinni was. But on average, it's getting worse year by year. Graamon's been working on better ploughs, haven't you?"

"Yes. There's something ready in the workshop now – not as good as it'll be by next winter, or even maybe by later this winter, but a lot better than we had last year. If Berraami doesn't arrive reasonably soon, we'll be on our way with it."

At half past four, it was decided that it was time to go in search. Three engines were coupled up, Peyr's in front, then Viilam's, and finally Jinni's, facing backwards. Jinni's engine still had its plough set at rail scraping height, for reversing out, but the other engines had their ploughs removed. Graamon's 'something' was a separate wagon in front of Peyr's engine, with a plough the full height of the engine on it.

It had special long travel buffers, to absorb even more shock than the engines' rear buffers, and it was filled with stone to make it weigh more than an engine. "The stone is fitted tight in a metal box so the whole thing is solid. It's heavy enough to stay on the rails pretty much whatever happens. It's got more inertia than an engine – it'll really hammer the drifts. And with those buffers, hammering drifts won't shock the engine much at all."

If I hadn't been able to work out a lot of what Graamon talked about for myself, I'd have been floundering trying to follow what he said. As it was, I was struggling trying to pick up all the new words. Many slipped past me, or I picked them up and then forgot them again. But I was very conscious how my learning rate had jumped back up somewhere near where it had been in the early days.

The plough was longer and sharper than the little ploughs that bolted onto the front of the engines. "The idea is that you push the snow sideways and compact it into the walls of the path you cut, rather than throwing most of it up into the air to fall where it will. If you're going through a path that's already got compacted walls, it should be able to push them back, even up the sides of cuttings. The only places I'm worried about are the three cuttings with vertical rock walls. The first and maybe second run through those should be okay, but after that I think we might have to wait for the thaw. I'm considering asking for a budget to roof them over, with the snow getting worse every year."

"That would be a really good idea anyway, even without the new plough. They're always the worst places with the old ploughs."

"Yes, but roofing over a total of nearly two miles of track is an expensive proposition. You've got to justify the expense. How often is the line shut, and for how long? Are there any other ways you can keep it open for longer? The next version of this plough will be better than this one – it's got steam rams to push the blades sideways, rather than just ramming forwards into the drifts."

"It's got its own boiler, then?"

"No, it'll be connected up to the lead engine's boiler. There'll be a couple of new controls in the cab to operate it. I don't really want to convert all the engines to connect to it, though. I'll either convert just enough of them to be sure there's always one here, or I might ask for Laar's old engine when the new one is delivered, and keep it here as a dedicated snow clearance engine, permanently coupled to the new plough."

The new plough worked very well. We found Medaal stuck in the first of the rock cuttings, unable to move forward or back. He was very pleased to see us! Well, hear us really. We were whistling like mad – three engines on both whistles, three short blasts, wait for reply, repeat – "rescue train on its way".

Having reached him, we left a team of workmen to dig away the snow around his last wagon, and returned to Briggi to detach the plough wagon. Then we went back with just an ordinary plough on the front of Peyr's engine. "If Medaal still can't get moving, we'll have to take Peyr's plough off again, couple up to the end of Medaal's train, and pull him out. Four engines have plenty of traction!"

But by the time we got back to him, Medaal was moving. We picked up the workmen, and headed back to Briggi.

"After Medaal gets to Briggi, will be going back to clear the line?"

"Not tonight, that's for sure. We'll see what tomorrow brings, tomorrow. At least we know Berraami's safe at Tambuk – as long as she's not stuck between Kaahes and Tambuk, that is. That's Tambuk and Kaahes's problem, though, there's nothing we can do about it. Trains don't often get stuck on that stretch, anyway. It's pretty wild, but not like the top."

Graamon and Jinni stayed at the inn for dinner with Peyr and Medaal and me. Conversation ranged widely again, but a lot of it was about snow and keeping the line open. "Another big advantage of the next version of the new plough is that you can open the blades at the front, and couple straight on to the train you're rescuing. You won't have to go back and detach the plough, which could be a problem if it's still snowing heavily or drifting a lot."

Graamon and Jinni headed home long after dinner. "I'll be down here first thing tomorrow, and we'll go up to the workshop."

The snow was falling heavily again. Medaal had never been stuck in snow before, and was somewhat unnerved by his experience. "I don't think anyone will be going anywhere tomorrow, even with the new plough. I think I'd want one of them on each end of three engines before I'd set out, even if it doesn't do this all night. But at least we know there's no train on the line anywhere between here and Tambuk, if Graamon does want to try."

"We'll see what conditions are like in the morning. I trust Graamon to take any decision wisely. And don't forget – as Jinni says, it's survivable, whatever happens. Although I think I'm inclined to take plenty of food!" Peyr laughed, but was failing to get Medaal to see the funny side of it.

He tried again. "Owen here has been through much scarier times than a few days stuck in a snowdrift with a nice warm fire, Medaal!"

"I heard – vaguely. Sometime I'd like to hear more of that story! I'm not sure tonight's a good time though. I'm going to have bad enough dreams as it is."

I've never thought in advance about what dreams I might have. I just take them as they come. Has Medaal planted an idea in my head? If he has, what will the consequence be? Not bad, I hope.

I lay awake for a long time after everyone else had gone to sleep – unless they were lying awake thinking quietly too. *How much snow is there in Baragi? What's Aila doing, what's she thinking about? What have I committed myself to? Is Aila lying awake, wondering what she's committed herself to? She's probably got a better idea of that than I have.*

How long will this snow last? How long will it take to get things settled, to know whether I've got a job with Graamon? When will I see Aila again? Peyr's obviously quite at ease about it all.

I remembered with utter clarity what Aila had said. "We never really know what's going to happen next. Whatever it is, it's not going to kill us, so I'm not worried. It's not even going to get us into trouble, so what is there to worry about?" My head told me she was absolutely right, but somewhere deep down inside something was gnawing away at my confidence.

When I did sleep, I dreamed that I was trying to rescue Aila from the snow. When I reached her, she was just my little model Aila, and I could still hear Aila shouting for help further away. It was almost dark, the snow was falling thick and fast, almost horizontally in the wind, and I was sinking thigh deep in drifts.

Then I was under the floor in Peyr's engine, but it was freezing cold and I knew the fire was going out for lack of fuel but I couldn't open the panel to get out and feed it.

I woke. It was dark, but by the light of the fire flickering low I could see the innkeeper sitting on a stool by the fire, just putting a couple of lumps of wood on the fire. He was wearing a thick woollen jacket over his clothes, and looked enormous. It was freezing cold. I pulled more of the bedding pile around myself and tried to go back to sleep. *Is it always as cold as this in Briggi? Are other places in Briggi warmer than this inn? Did Peyr pick up my clothes at Sirimi Road? If he did, why hasn't he mentioned them? Maybe he's got them hidden somewhere, because he didn't want someone getting ideas about them – is there someone around that he doesn't trust? I won't saying anything until there's just the two of us – he'll probably say something himself then.*

One of my feet was still cold, and I tried to reorganize the bedding a little to cover it better. The innkeeper must have heard me moving, and looked over at me. "Are you awake? Cold? Come over and warm yourself by the fire with me. I've got some hot skiir, too, it'll do you good." He spoke very softly, obviously not wanting to wake the others.

I picked an old jacket off the pile and wrapped it around my shoulders to keep my back warm, and joined the innkeeper at the fire. He ladled skiir out of the cauldron into a mug and gave it to me. We sat staring into the fire, with our hands round the warm mugs, sipping occasionally. "Is it often as cold as this here?" I whispered.

"No, not often. But the sky's cleared now, and the temperature's dropped a lot outside. There was a lot more snow after we went to sleep before it cleared, though. And it's drifting dreadfully, it's up to the eaves on the leeward side of the inn. It's not been like this since '13. That was the year Jinni was stuck up on the top."

I could hear the wind. I wasn't surprised the snow was drifting. *So Jinni's been driving engines for at least nine years. How old does that make her? I simply don't know.*

"How often do engines get stuck up there?"

"Oh, once or twice most years someone or other gets stuck for a day or two. Parruk was stuck for four days last year. There was a tremendous lot of snow on the top, but it wasn't nearly as cold as this, and it was melting as fast as it fell down here in Briggi. It got bloody cold later, but there was no more snow, and there wasn't this wind. The inn keeps toasty warm even in really cold weather, as long as there's no wind."

We lapsed into silence, sitting staring into the fire and taking occasional sips of skiir. The innkeeper put more wood on the fire at intervals, and occasionally adjusted it with a long poker and a pair of tongs.

A dim grey light gradually appeared in the sky where I could see it through the north window, but the south window was dark. I assumed it was blocked by snow.

The innkeeper built up the fire, then got up and went over to the table and fetched an oil lamp. He lit it with a taper from the fire, and took it back to the table. He started to prepare breakfast.

I went over to the north window, and looked out. This was the side away from the railway yard, and there was a wide space between the inn and another row of buildings – or what I knew to be a row of buildings from my previous visit. All I could see was a line of snowdrifts, with gaps blown clean here and there where alleyways gave the wind passage, and chimneys and the tops of roofs sticking out of the snow. Our side of the space was blown nearly clear, with just old snow half melted and refrozen, and streaks of new snow across it here and there.

The innkeeper heated a pan over the fire, then began to fry the slices of mutton he'd been preparing. The noise or the smell or the combination woke Peyr and Medaal.

The three of us went outside to relieve ourselves. We each took a pot of warm water from indoors to clean our backsides, but there was no other washing. The pump would have delivered water all right, but none of us wanted to freeze to death.

We returned to a delicious and filling breakfast of bread, fried mutton, and warm skiir.

Shortly after we'd finished, we heard someone stamping the snow off his boots in the hallway, and guessed it would be Graamon. It was. The innkeeper ladled out another mug of warm skiir for him. "I expect you've eaten?"

"Yes, yes. Viina always feeds me well, you know that. But your skiir is always welcome! Well, we're obviously not going to try clearing the line today. But you and I have a lot to talk about, Owen, and a workshop to take a look around."

But he stayed long enough to finish his skiir without hurrying, and get warm again.

I felt a little strange leaving Peyr at the inn. Somehow I felt that maybe Peyr was staying behind, either of his own volition or by prior arrangement with Graamon, to make sure that Medaal didn't come with us. I didn't know why, but I was somehow glad not to have Medaal along.

Once we were out of the inn, Graamon didn't beat about the bush. "So – how do you fancy working for the railway? We need people like you, and you need a livelihood!"

"Goodness! You scarcely know anything about me!"

"Enough. You're a young man with an independent mind, a lot of technical knowledge and understanding, and the ability to make use of it. That much I know already. What more do I need to know?"

"Well...I think it would be ideal. As you say, I need a livelihood, and the railway seems to be a good employer. In fact, I don't know anything at all about any other employer."

"Oh, there are other employers. But as you say, the railway is one of the best – it's not going to disappear overnight, that's for sure. Senior posts in the Meyroha or Laanoha guards pay better, but I'm sure you're not the kind of person who'd like working for organizations like that. Except perhaps as a fifth columnist, and that would be a perilous role. In fact, one of the advantages of working for the railway – an advantage I value highly – is the protection is gives you against the worst abuses by the guards. Possibly more important for you, the protection it gives your family."

"Well, unless you're very devious – and I'm sure Peyr doesn't think you are, and I trust his judgement – that's the best offer I could possibly want. Yes, I'd love to work for the railway."

"Good. That's settled then. I was pretty sure it would be! There's someone you need to meet. He should be at the workshops by the time we arrive. We'll talk about terms and conditions there."

"Where will I be based?"

"Oh, initially here in Briggi. You'll technically be my assistant, but I suspect you'll rapidly develop a role of your own, and we'll certainly want to visit the workshops in Laanoha and Meyroha fairly often. Between you, me and the gatepost, I've got another project in hand that's nothing to do with the railway, that I'm sure you'll be interested in, but we can't talk about that until after Baamoon goes back to Meyroha. Or at least until we get some time to ourselves."

"Baamoon?"

"He's the chap who should be waiting for us at the workshops by now. He's the head of the railway committee. We need him to sign your papers. But Baamoon's not your average committee member, he's got more sense than most of them. It's not every committee member who'd drop everything and ride on a goods train all the way to Briggi just because I send him a note saying it would probably be rather useful to have him here! And now he's stuck in Briggi until we can reopen the line. But I expect he'll forgive me."

"Ah! Was it Baamoon who rode with Peyr?"

"It was. But neither of them knew why Baamoon was coming – although Peyr very likely guessed."

Baamoon was waiting for us outside the workshop. He'd been inside, but had seen us from the window and come out to meet us. He was an elderly man, but seemingly sprightly and alert.

"You're Owen. I'm Baamoon, I'm very pleased to meet you. Graamon's been telling me about you. We're very pleased to have you on the team."

Not afraid of making assumptions, either.

"Thank you very much, I'm pleased to meet you, too. I guess you already know I said yes, then."

"Graamon said he knew you would, and I didn't see any sign of the sky falling, so I thought it was a pretty safe assumption."

I like this man. He's absolutely straightforward. Procedures here are very different from those in England, much less formal, and I like that too. Or maybe that's just the railway. Oh, and there's another idiom that's like the English one – more or less.

Graamon laughed. "I don't see any sign of the sky falling today, either. But it certainly fell yesterday."

"It certainly did! I wonder when I'll be able to get back to Meyroha? You've definitely imprisoned me here for a few days very effectively, Graamon."

"You'd enjoy a long break here, I'm sure. But I'm afraid we'll probably get you out of here quicker than you think. The expanding plough isn't ready to expand yet – we don't have an engine with a steam take-off for it yet, anyway – but we'll very soon be able use it as a back-end plough on a line-clearing train, so we can reverse out even if there's heavy drifting behind us. I think we'll probably get through to Tambuk in a couple of days time, whatever the snow does. If we have to push through to

Kaahes as well, it's all going to be a bit slow, and we'll only be taking very short trains with several engines, but as long as it doesn't snow or drift a lot more, we'll probably keep the line open. But we'll see. We can't be certain until we try. Yesterday was the first trial with the simpler one, and it was very encouraging, but it's early days yet.

"But let's get inside out of the cold, and deal with the paperwork and talk about Owen's arrangements."

Graamon's workshop was an impressive size, with two railway tracks, overhead cranes, machine tools and workbenches. The expanding plough looked small in the middle of it all. Inside, we were out of the wind, and it wasn't as cold as outside, but no-one could have called it warm. Two men in boiler suits were working on the plough, and another was doing something at a bench. They looked up as we came in, then went back to their tasks.

Graamon led the way across the end of the shop, up an open flight of stairs, and into a small room built over the workbenches. There were two windows in the outer wall, one with a desk under it and the other half obscured by a large drawing board. The opposite wall was all windows from waist height upwards, looking out over the workshop. Graamon shut the door behind us. This room was comfortably warm, and we took off our coats and gloves. Graamon slid a pot across its rack, closer to the fire, and fetched mugs. "It's worth waiting for that to warm up, I think. I've got papers ready, Baamoon, but we perhaps ought to talk some details before you sign them."

"Oh, I don't think that's necessary. You're sure you want him, he's sure he wants the job, that's good enough for me."

I wasn't quite ready. "We've not even discussed terms and conditions yet."

Graamon reassured me. "The papers are only to say you're an official of the railway company. They'll get you in and out of Laanoha and Meyroha, and pretty much any office anywhere, apart from Castle offices and upper guard offices. No more smuggling in and out of Laanoha under trains for you!"

So Graamon knows perfectly well where I was, and doesn't care that Baamoon knows, either. Well, maybe not exactly where, but more or less.

Baamoon laughed. "Really? I can't imagine how that could possibly happen. Who would have believed it? It doesn't sound very comfortable."

Graamon evidently realized that I didn't know what to say to that. "I don't suppose it is. But it's only for a few minutes, I expect. It couldn't be done without the cooperation of the engine driver, and once they're clear of Laanoha, there's no problem about carrying passengers without papers."

"Quite a trick to get out from underneath a train, and then hitch a lift in the driver's cab, without the train even stopping. But I really don't want to know how that's done. Most of the committee think I'm mad even riding in the cab. But the drivers are mostly better company than the committee."

"Too true. Here's his papers, anyway."

My papers were very different from Peyr's, the only other papers I'd ever seen. Peyr's were just a single sheet of paper, folded in four. Mine were a little booklet with a fine leather cover. Baamoon took a pen out of a pocket in his jacket, dipped it in a little pot of ink Graamon extracted from a drawer under the desk, and signed in a space amongst the printing on the first page. Then he wiped his pen clean on a rag from the drawer, and returned it to his pocket.

"Now we need your signature, Owen. Don't worry, I guess you've never written Laana before. We've got two choices. There's no theoretical reason why you shouldn't sign in English. As long as you wrote the same thing again when asked to sign, they couldn't really complain. But it would probably lead to less trouble for you if you write in Laana. I'll write it for you, and show you the proper stroke order so you can do it repeatably even when you're a fluent Laana writer, then you practice a few times before signing the papers."

"Do you have another name, Owen? I presume Owen is your personal name. Do English people have a family name too, like we do?"

"I didn't know you did, actually! I've never heard anyone use a family name. Yes, we do. Mine's Morley."

"Mor Liiauen?" Baamoon laughed. "I shouldn't laugh, but we'll have to give you a new, Laana, name. We can't have people calling you Mor Liiauen."

It took me a moment to realize that he'd put my family name first. *I oughtn't to find that difficult to get my head round. I'm used to word order being different from one language to another.* But none of the languages I knew before put family names first, and personal names last.

"No, it's Owen Morley, not Morley Owen."

Now it was their turn to get confused for a moment. Graamon got there first.

"Oh, I see. It's not that your family name is Owen, it's just that English people put their names the wrong way round. But if you call yourself Owen Morley, everyone will think Morli's your personal name, and they'll call you Morli – and that's a girl's name. But Baamoon's right – we should give you a Laana family name. Owen's okay; it's unusual, but it's a good name, and everyone who knows you knows it already."

"You laughed at Mor Liiauen, Baamoon. Well, I know what mor means, but I guess liiauen must mean something, too, by your reaction. I'd love to know what."

"I suppose that's not the kind of thing you hear often in the normal course of life – unless you spend time with butchers."

Describing the insides of animals when your foreign listener hasn't got much of the relevant vocabulary is not easy. Graamon listened to Baamoon for a few moments, and then went and got pencil and paper, and drew a picture.

"Aha! Intestines. No, I don't really want to be called Goat's Intestines, you're right!"

"You can have my name, with pleasure. Meyru Owen? Sounds good."

"I don't think that's such a good idea, Baamoon. Meyru Owen's papers, signed by Meyru Baamoon? You're not supposed to sign close relatives' papers, and Meyru's not a common name. Mine's common enough, but it's probably better if no-one thinks he's related to me, either."

"How about Riish? From what you say, Peyr seems to have pretty much adopted him."

Graamon laughed. "No, that really wouldn't do. People would think he was marrying his sister!"

I didn't even know Peyr had a family name, much less what it was. And I still don't know whether Aila gets her father's family name or her mother's, or what happens to family names, if anything, on marriage. I'll have to ask Peyr, it's not important here and now.

What about Birgom? I wonder what his family name is. I suspect that both he and Viilam would be pleased to have more family, and he speaks English, too. As if that really meant anything to anyone but us. But I need a name now, and I wouldn't want to do that without asking him. Ah – but Viilam must be here, somewhere! But I scarcely know him.

"There's an old man in Laanoha – Birgom – with whom I feel an affinity. We obviously can't ask him whether I can use his name, but his grandson is an engine driver and he's somewhere here in Briggi at the moment, I'm pretty sure. He drove the train before Peyr's coming up this time. But I don't know them well."

"I'm sure they'd be pleased really, and anyway they could scarcely object. They don't own the name. Viilam's name is Mezhab, but I don't know whether his grandfather's is the same. Maybe we should ask Peyr's advice."

Graamon slid open a window to the workshop. A cold blast hit me, and I shivered for a moment. Graamon shouted down into the workshop, "Kaasham! Pop over here a minute!"

One of the boiler-suited men came over from the plough, and must have stood just under where Graamon was leaning out of the window, but out of my sight. "Can you dash down to the Railwayyard Inn, and see if Peyr's still there? I expect he is. If he is, or you can track him down without too much trouble, can you send him up here, please? Just him, we don't want anyone else with him."

Graamon shut the window. "While we're waiting for Peyr – I expect Kaasham will find him okay – we can talk about some of the other things we need to discuss. For example, where are you going to live? The railway would be very happy to keep you in the Railwayyard Inn forever, but they'll pay for somewhere better than that, for you and your family, and it'll be better for you, and for them in the long run, if you're more comfortable."

"I'm very much in your hands, really. I don't know Briggi at all, or much about how things work here. What sort of place would you suggest?"

"I suspected you'd say something like that. For the moment, until Aila joins you, you'd probably be as happy with a room at Viina's house, where I live, as anywhere. She's a good cook, she keeps a warm, clean and tidy house, and there's plenty of table space to spread out papers or little models. And she doesn't mind residents coming and going at odd times. After that – well, it's as much up to Aila as to any of us. The railway will pay for anything reasonable."

Baamoon nodded. "Graamon's absolutely right. The railway will pay for anything reasonable. Unless you have other ideas, you move in at Viina's as soon as you like. She's got a spare room at the moment, Graamon?"

"Yes, she has. A couple at the moment, in fact, since Biiniha got married. I took the liberty of telling Viina that we'd probably want to take Biiniha's room, assuming that you'd probably want it for a while Owen, until you need a place with Aila. It's one of Briggi's very few upstairs rooms – a big room over the whole of the middle of the house, all round the chimney and with dormer windows facing each way. It's a lovely room, and always warm."

"Biiniha? She's Viina's daughter, isn't she? The one who looks like my grand-daughter Maaniya?"

"That's her. She's married Baam, a teacher from Barioha, and gone to live there with him. He's an interesting chap, been coming up here studying the glacier for years. You'll meet them before long, Owen, I'm sure. They've not visited yet since they were married. Viina's expecting them any time. Sends letters all the time, but only gets a few replies!"

"Won't they want Biiniha's room to stay in, when they come?"

"No, it's only a single room. It's a big room, but there's only a single maalba, and Viina wouldn't want to get a double just for occasional short visits. She got rid of her own double after Grim – her husband – died. They'll stay at the Briggi Inn, in the middle of town, where Baam stayed when Viina didn't have a spare room. It's the only inn with maalban in Briggi."

Maalba? I think that must mean bed. He's talking about beds. I've not slept in a bed since that night at Siroha. Luxury? I'm not sure. I've got used to piles of old clothes on the floor.

"The other question is how much we pay him, Graamon. I guess he doesn't have much idea how much anything costs, so it's really up to you to decide. The committee will accept anything reasonable if I tell them what reasonable means."

"I suggest fifty coins a week for the time being. That's more than the drivers or workshop men earn, and enough to support him and Aila in reasonable comfort, without being so much he'll make anyone jealous."

"Okay. We'll review it when we see what you're actually achieving, Owen. Does that sound okay to you?"

"If Graamon says it's enough to support Aila and me, that sounds good to me. But as you say, I don't have much idea of what things cost anyway. No doubt I'll find out."

I wonder what drivers and workshop men do earn? I wonder what Aila's earning in Baragi?

Then Peyr was knocking at the door of the office. Graamon gestured to him to come in.

"We need some advice from you, Peyr. Owen needs a family name – he's got an English one, but it really won't do in Laana. We thought about using mine, or Graamon's, or yours – but there are good arguments against all of those. Owen mentioned Birgom and Viilam, says he's got a bit of an affinity with Birgom, but we're not sure whether Birgom's family name is the same as Viilam's, and he doesn't know Viilam well enough to ask him if Birgom would mind him using his name. What do you think?"

"I'm absolutely certain that Birgom would be delighted to call Owen his grandson. Yes, Birgom's name is Mezhab, same as Viilam's. We ought at least to check what Viilam thinks, though. He's at the Briggi Inn at the moment. No problem talking to him about it, Owen, Viilam's as straight as sunbeams. I'll go and dig him out. I don't suppose he's gone walkabout in this weather."

I looked out of the window. It was snowing again, big soft flakes. *It can't be as cold as it was, big flakes like that. But it must still be damned cold up at the top. And at Tambuk, for that matter.*

And Peyr was gone. Graamon shut the door after him. "Drivers!" he muttered, "never shut doors. They forget that other people don't have fires designed to boil half a ton of water." But he was smiling.

I wonder. I never noticed Peyr forgetting to shut the door in Laanoha. But you can see by his face that Graamon is actually rather fond of Peyr.

"Well, Graamon will explain how we operate and what he expects of you. There's really only one thing left for me to deal with here. I need to know the full name you're going to use, so I can get everything set up in the paper chain. And we won't know your name until Peyr gets back, at the soonest. So I propose a wander around the workshops while we're waiting."

Graamon ladled out mugs of warm skiir from the pot. We put on our coats, and holding our mugs, we set off down the stairs into the workshop.

The expanding plough was a beautifully made thing, and the mechanical design looked as though it had been very carefully and cleverly done. The hinge pins were placed and aligned to make the two blades open in such a way that the snow was lifted slightly as it was pushed, and so that the passageway opened through the drift was actually slightly wider than the closed plough, which itself was slightly wider than the engine and wagons. The hinge pins themselves were of impressive dimensions, with bronze sleeves. "They don't need pressurized oil feeds, like the moving parts on the engine. They're not expected to operate hundreds of millions of times in their lifetime. Hand greasing is all they need."

The steam arrangements intrigued me. Where in England they'd have had flexible polymer hoses with spiral steel wire reinforcement, there were solid iron tubes with hinged joints. *Okay, fair enough, if you don't have polymer hose material. I'm sure that works. I'm sure you've done it before. But wouldn't it be better to use hydraulics, rather than running steam right out to the far end of the plough? But I won't say anything just now, not in front of Baamoon – or in front of the workshop men.*

But they could all see that I was studying the thing in detail and with an understanding eye, which I thought was probably a good thing. *But I must be careful not to give the impression that I'm deliberately trying to impress!*

Graamon showed me all the machine tools as well. There were some similarities with the machines back at the school in London, but there were some interesting differences, too. I found the little engine in the corner that provided all the power for them especially interesting, and made a mental note to ask Graamon about it later. It obviously ran extremely fast, because it had an impressive gear train between it and the main shaft down the back of the workbenches. Graamon saw me looking at it and grinned. "My own invention," he said, "it runs on flammable vapour, a by-product from charcoal production. I'll explain it to you later."

"You make your own charcoal?"

"Yes, we do. We used to buy it in from charcoal burners who made it up in the woods, but we can do it much better here – and get all the byproducts, too, instead of letting them go to waste. We've got a furnace for it in the foundry. I'll take you next door to the foundry later, but just now we'd better be here. Peyr and Viilam will probably turn up quite soon."

"I don't know about you two engineers, but I'm ready to head back to the office into the warm!"

Graamon laughed. "You're a rare committee man who takes an interest in all this stuff anyway. We could all do with a bit of warmth, and some more skiir, I'm sure."

Peyr and Viilam arrived just as we were climbing the stairs. Graamon got two more mugs, and filled all five with warm skiir.

Peyr had evidently told Viilam what it was all about already. Viilam gave me a hug in very much the way Grim had. "Welcome into the family, brother! I know for a fact that Grandad will be pleased and proud to call you Grandson! He talked about it on the way home, the night he met you – he said you'd be needing a Laana family name, and hoped you'd want his. He says he really wants a chance to have a long private chat with you as soon as you can spend some time in Laanoha, too. He hopes it will be before too long." Viilam paused for a moment, looking reflective. "He says he doesn't think he's got much longer to live. But he's been saying that for years."

"So that's settled then. You're Mezhab Owen. Now all you've got to do is learn how to write that, and fill in your signature on your papers." Graamon opened the drawer under the desk, and extracted the ink, the rag, and another pen. "This is your pen now, I'm sure you didn't have one already."

Then he turned to Baamoon. "You know, we'll have to take him up to the tailor's and get him a jacket made. He doesn't have suitable pockets for his things."

It was true. My trousers had hip pockets suitable for a rag and a wallet and a few coins, but I'd nowhere suitable for my papers or a pen. I noticed that both Baamoon's and Graamon's jackets had several pockets, very possibly with specific purposes of which I was still unaware, apart from pockets obviously specially made for papers and a pen.

"Get him a complete outfit – two in fact. He can't represent the railway in ill-fitting working men's clothes like that. It's one thing when he's riding on engines, in inns, or here in the workshop, but quite another elsewhere. He'd cause a bit of a stir in the offices, for a start – and I can imagine guards being a bit suspicious of his papers, too. But let's get this signature done."

Graamon showed me how to write my name, and I practiced a few times on a piece of paper he produced from the drawer. The pen had a tendency to flood, and make blots. Graamon took it from me, wiped it on the rag, and inspected the nib end with a little hand glass. He produced a tiny file from a pocket, adjusted the shape of the nib, and handed it back to me. "There, try that."

The pen glided smoothly instead of snatching at the paper, and the flooding had stopped. *Magic. I wish I had that kind of skill with small tools.*

"Not bad. You're doing the final downstroke upwards, though. The shape will change a little when you get that right, so you'd better get it right before you commit your signature to your papers."

Three more attempts, all looking pretty much identical. "Okay, that'll do. Here's your papers."

Somewhat nervously, I signed. Happily this one looked almost exactly the same again.

Graamon moved the papers to the far side of the desk, and put a bronze rod across the middle to hold them open while the ink dried.

"So. You exist now. I suggest we go straight to the tailor's and get you measured up before lunch, and then we'll see how they're getting on with the expanding plough. I'm hoping to take a double-ended three engine set up the line and see if we can get through this afternoon, if they've got the coupling done. No expanding yet, of course – we'll be lucky to get that done before the weather warms up anyway."

Peyr and Viilam excused themselves and headed for the Briggi Inn together. "Peyr's staying in the Railwayyard Inn, isn't he?"

"Oh, he probably wants a chat with Viilam. I think he generally prefers the Railwayyard, but I think the only reason he stayed there yesterday was because he knew Jinni would bring you there."

The three of us set off for the tailor's, wherever that was – or so I assumed. After a short way, Baamoon excused himself, "You don't need me any more, Graamon. I'll see you after lunch, and I'll probably come with you if you are going to try to clear the line. You'll be lunching at the Briggi, I imagine?"

"Yes, we'll wait for you there."

Baamoon disappeared between two snowdrifts, and into an alley between the buildings the drifts were hiding behind. The snow, now soft and damp and falling almost vertically, was beginning to cover the areas that had been blown clear, as well as giving an extra coat to the drifts of old, dry, cold, fine snow. There were a few people out on the street, but not many.

"Where will he go for lunch? He won't join us at the Briggi?"

"No, one of his sons lives here. He stays there when he's in Briggi, and he'll be going there now. I expect he's enjoying the break anyway – he's got two young grandchildren here."

The tailor's was only a hundred metres further up the street, on the south side. There was a beautifully painted sign outside, the like of which one might see outside an inn in England, but certainly not outside a tailor's. Graamon knocked at the door, but then led me inside without waiting for an answer. The tailor appeared in his shop from a backroom as we entered.

"Master Graamon! Good to see you. And what can I do for you today? You haven't worn holes in your knees and elbows again, I hope?"

Graamon laughed. "No, Lomeyr, not yet. It's nothing for me this time. This young man's just started as an assistant engineer with the railway, and we need two respectable outfits and an overcoat for him. You know the style – all the same pockets I have. Oh, and keep his measurements. He'll be wanting a wedding suit before long, too. I doubt he'll have time to put on much weight between now and then."

It was Lomeyr's turn to laugh. "Well, you certainly haven't put on any weight working for the railway, Graamon, but some of your colleagues have. You keep as active as Graamon, young man, and don't get too fond of your food, and you'll be fine. What's your name, anyway? It helps if I can put a name alongside the measurements, if I'm supposed to remember whose measurements they are."

"Owen."

Lomeyr produced a tape measure from his apron pocket, and started to measure me. "Just Owen? It's true you'll be the only Owen on my books, but I do normally put two names for everyone."

"Sorry. Mezhab Owen." I was quite proud of myself remembering not to say Owen Morley.

"You're not from anywhere around these parts, that's for sure. I can't place your accent at all, nor your clothes. And you've never been in a tailor's shop before, either, have you?"

Well, not one anything like this. But I shan't say anything about that.

Graamon realized that I didn't really know what I should or shouldn't say, and answered for me. "No, Owen's not from anywhere round these parts, you're right. He's come a very long way, and we're lucky to have him. He's only been learning Laana for a few weeks, but he's doing very well."

"This cloth is unusual. I've never seen anything like it."

He was feeling the fabric of my trousers. They were part polymer, part hemp. I'd seen hemp growing near Laanoha, but not a lot of it, and I'd not seen any sign of artificial polymers at all. Most, maybe all, of the cloth here was cotton, linen or wool. I made a non-committal gesture that I hoped said, "it's just ordinary stuff where I come from, I don't know much about it." Lomeyr seemed to accept it cheerfully enough.

"I expect you'd like one jacket as soon as possible, and the rest when it's ready? You can have one jacket by tomorrow evening, and the rest in three days' time, all being well. Okay?"

"That's absolutely fine. You're right that the first jacket is the priority."

"Okay. I'll see you tomorrow evening then. And Owen, if you can get me any of the fabric your trousers are made of, I'd be very interested."

Graamon led me out of the shop as Lomeyr disappeared into his back room. Not a word had been said about price, or payment. *He'll just bill the railway. He knows Graamon. As simple as that.*

"I don't see how I could get any of this fabric for Lomeyr. I've no contact with England, no way of establishing trade – even if I wanted contact with England, which I really don't."

"Do you know what it's made of, and how it's made? There are people here who might be able to make it, if you tell them how it's done."

"I don't know whether I know enough to make exactly this material, but I might know enough to help them make something like it – or something different from what they're making already, anyway. But things for the railway are surely what I've got to do now?"

"Certainly the railway will expect you to get on with things for them, but they don't expect you to spend every waking hour doing nothing else. I get involved in all kinds of things apart from railway work, and they don't mind at all as long as the railway work keeps progressing okay. Some of the things I do that weren't ever intended for the railway end up being very useful to the railway, and some things I do for the railway end up being useful to other people. That's life. The railway uses quite a lot of fabric, actually. Something hard wearing would be really useful in the passenger trains."

"The big difference with this fabric is that half the fibres aren't natural fibres at all, they're artificial *polymer* fibres. Polymer is the English word, I don't think there is a Laana word for it, because I don't think you have any artificial polymers here at all. We'll have to talk about how to make polymers, they're useful for all kinds of things, not just cloth. I understand the basics, but I've never seen the actual industrial processes to make them, so there'd have to be a lot of experimentation to develop methods of large scale manufacture."

"I know people who'd be very interested to learn whatever they can about things like that."

"My balloons, and the water tank I used for water ballast when I was ballooning, were made of artificial polymers."

"That's another thing we need to talk about sometime. I understand from Peyr that the people at Siroha have taken charge of all the things you left where you landed. We'll have to retrieve them somehow. He was going to pick up your clothes this last trip, he said, but with Baamoon on board he didn't stop at Sirimi road, even though the lady who was going to give them to him was waiting there. And now the timetable is all scrambled for a few days at least, so she won't know when Peyr's expected. It might be worth our while hiring a gig from Raamba to take us up there. With you in a proper senior railwayman's outfit and the two of us going together, I think they'll realize they've missed their chance to catch hold of your tail. Peyr says we'll need at least a big part of a wagon to carry your stuff in."

"I should think so. Maybe an eighth of a wagon load. Probably not even quite that much."

"Not a problem bringing them here to Briggi. It's the other direction we're usually fully loaded. We'll only take anything the other way if once we know there's a really good reason to do it."

Lunch at the Briggi was very good. I could see why Peyr preferred the Railwayyard, though. It was much more homely, and there was nothing wrong with the food there, either.

Like almost everywhere else, there was no bill to pay, nothing to sign, nothing. We were railwaymen, and the railway had a contract, end of story. I wondered whether the inns actually kept a record of how many meals they'd served, and how many railwaymen had stayed the night, or whether it was all done on an estimated long term average, or some other basis entirely. *But a couple of places, I remember Peyr paying. I don't remember which places they were. I wonder what the difference is?*

Back at the workshop, it was clear that the plough wasn't going to be ready in time for an attempt to get through to Tambuk before dark. "Don't worry, Graamon. Kaasham and I will work as long as it takes this evening, we've already decided. It'll be ready to go at daybreak tomorrow. Jinni's been in while you were out, and she's going to come down and assemble the train at first light. We guess what you want is the old new plough on the front, three engines, then four or five ordinary wagons, and the new new plough on the back? You won't want more than four or five wagons, I don't think, or you'll start cutting into your traction, but you'll want a few if you're going to go right through to Laanoha with it, and I guess you'll do that?"

"I'm not sure about that. For one thing, I'd like the ploughs to come back with Berraami, assuming she's at Tambuk. If she's still at Kaahes, or worse still somewhere on the line in between, we'll be clearing that stretch as well. We'll definitely want the ploughs on her train, when I think about it. And probably extra engines, too, just in case. I think we'll take all five engines."

"With five engines, you can take as many wagons as will fit in a loop. You don't want more than that if you're going to have to shuffle at Tambuk to get the ploughs onto Berraami's train. Oh, and I'll put an old plough in a wagon for you – you might need it in the mountains down south."

"Hopefully we won't need ploughs in the mountains down south – we don't get drifts on the viaduct at the end of the branch, and the main line should be clear enough. But you're right, best not to take a chance. Of course if it's actually blocked, that's another matter!"

"That's never happened, has it?"

"Not yet, no. But it's getting worse, year by year, and this looks like it's a particularly bad one. If these ploughs really work, I can see us wanting some down there before long. Or we'll work out how to make better ones, and they can have these ones."

We left the three workshop men busy at the plough, and headed for Graamon's lodgings. *Viina's place – **my** lodgings!* I'd been there once before, with Peyr, looking for Graamon.

We had to go round to the back door, because there was a snowdrift half way up the roof at the front of the house.

Viina remembered me, and welcomed me like a long-lost son. I wasn't sure whether it was moving or funny or both.

"So you're Owen. Peyr never introduced us, when you were here before. I'd better show you the room, see if you like it. There's actually a choice of two, but I think I know which one you'll want."

She showed me the downstairs room first. It had a big window, but that was blocked by snow, and she lit an oil lamp. The room was perfectly lovely, there was nothing wrong with it at all. It was a very good size, with a substantial table, three chairs, a bed, a cupboard, and a chest of drawers. It was spotlessly clean, dry and reasonably warm despite the snow drifted against the outside wall and window.

Furnished like Siroha. Not like Peyr's place at all. I hope I don't get above myself – Peyr's still my best friend here.

Graamon seemed quite at ease at Peyr's place, and everyone seemed at ease with him there. Everything will be fine.

"It's a lovely room!"

"Thank you. But I think you'll like upstairs better."

We crossed a large living room cum kitchen. There was a blazing fire in a large fireplace. Our way was opposite the

fireplace, up a flight of very solid stone stairs with one side open
to the room. At the top, a door led into my room.

My room. Viina was right – this was the room I wanted. I felt
incredibly lucky to have it. It was bigger than the one
downstairs, probably twice the size or a little more. It ran the
length of the house, down the middle of the space under the
roof. One dormer window had snow halfway up it, but the
opposite one was clear, and the room was quite light. The
furnishing was similar to that downstairs, but the table was
larger and there were two benches rather than chairs. It wasn't
nearly as big as Peyr's family's room in Laanoha, but it was
more than generous for one of me. The chimney was about
halfway along, and extended from one wall almost halfway to
the other, almost cutting the room in two.

*There's plenty of room for both me and Aila here, until we
have children. Except that she'll probably want to have our own
place, rather than being lodgers, with Viina running the house.
Or will she? Yaani seems perfectly happy sharing a home with
Yaana. I just don't know until we talk about it – maybe not even
then, until we've tried it.*

*Graamon said Viina didn't want to get a double maalba just
for short visits – but it might be quite okay to have one for
permanent residents. Or maybe Aila would prefer us to sleep on
the floor anyway.*

"This is perfectly wonderful, Viina! The rent must be a lot
more for this room. Are you sure the railway's okay about it,
Graamon?"

"Absolutely. Remember, they expect eventually to have to
provide not only for you but for your wife and children, too.
This is no problem."

"So you'll take this one then?"

I was speechless. Graamon answered for me, "Yes, please."

And that was that. Settled.

We went back downstairs, and Viina busied herself with
something at the fire. Graamon took me through the back hall,
and showed me the washing and lavatory facilities – all indoors,
and with warm water on tap. "There's a tank built into the side
of the chimney, the side away from your room under the edge of

the roof. There's a little door from your room to get at it, but there's never any need. Everything works fine – as long as someone goes outside and works the pump every now and then! If you work the pump until the tank just starts overflowing, that usually keeps us in water for two or three days."

He took me out of the back door and showed me a long handled pump that I hadn't noticed as we arrived, and the little pipe under the eaves where the water came out when the tank overflowed.

Then Graamon said there was some paperwork he ought to deal with while we were waiting for the plough to be ready. "I know how good your spoken Laana is, but how's your reading and writing coming along?"

How did he know I was learning?

"It's coming along, but I've only just begun. Aila's been teaching me for a couple of days, but that's all. And she's really only a beginner herself."

"Ah, okay. I don't think you'll be able to help much with the paperwork yet then. I'm sure Viina would be very happy to teach you, though."

She was, she was delighted. "We can work on it for about an hour now, before I start preparing dinner, then again as long as you like when I've cleaned up after dinner."

Viina was a very good teacher, and we got on very well. The hour seemed to be gone very quickly, and Viina went to start preparing dinner. I sat at a table in the living room with a pile of paper and a pencil, and practiced cursive writing. I'd only written printed-style writing with Aila. I assumed she'd been going to go on to cursive writing later, but didn't know for sure whether she'd actually got that far herself yet. I knew I still had a lot more to learn about the printed style, anyway.

I wonder how good a teacher Gamaara is? I hope I don't end up ahead of Aila. I don't want to upset her.

There were two other lodgers, two young men from outlying villages who'd got work in Briggi. They joined us for dinner. They introduced themselves, but said very little thereafter.

Dinner was very good – something midway between the kind of food at Peyr's home or in the inns, and the food at Siroha. Not as elaborately presented as at Siroha, but with more expensive ingredients than Peyr's family usually had. *Shopping with Yaana taught me a lot about the prices of different things – but of course prices here in Briggi could well be very different from those in Laanoha.*

Viina and I worked at reading and writing again for a couple of hours after dinner, as well. After a while, Graamon joined us. "I've had enough of that damned paperwork. It'll keep a bit longer."

He sat the opposite side from the table from us, and watched me writing for a time. "Write your name again, Owen."

I did. I even remembered the Mezhab bit, and to put it first. "Now let's have a look at your papers."

"Good, good – looks like the same handwriting, but not so identical as to be suspicious. Excellent! Not that you'll have to sign to prove it's really you very often. Now all you need is that jacket to keep your papers and pen safe."

We carried on doing a bit of reading and writing, but got chatting a lot more, too. Viina wanted to see my model Aila, so I got her out of my bag. Viina admired her, "Your grandmother-in-law to be is a fine craftswoman! Has she got many grand-daughters married already?"

"No, Aila's her only granddaughter."

"She's been practising a lot, then. Or she had help – but I shouldn't say that, no-one ever gets help."

Graamon laughed. "Officially," he said, but Viina gave him a look that said "Stop!" and he did.

"You know you've got to keep her safe until you can keep the real Aila safe, don't you?"

"Yes, I know that. Will she be safe in my room?"

"For a little while, but if you go far you have to take her with you."

"Oh, I would anyway. I wouldn't want to be far away from her."

"I'm sure you don't want to be far away from the real Aila, either, but that can't be helped for the moment, I imagine. Is she with her mother?"

"No, she's working as a nanny in a village two hours' train ride from home. But the children are nearly ready for school – one of them could go already, and the other one will be ready soon. Her employer is teaching her reading and writing, and she was thinking to try to get a nursery teaching job when she's not needed there any more."

"Will she be looking for a job like that here? There's plenty of families who'd be pleased to employ her if she is. I'd have room to run a kindergarten here, in fact. I'd love that."

"I'll have to discuss it with her, of course, but that sounds ideal to me!"

"And of course there's plenty of room for her to share your room, at least until you have a flock of your own children!"

People here aren't shy about things like that, are they! But how can I question whether Aila will want to be in lodgings? Maybe I don't need to, at least until Aila's here. Well, I can't, so the question doesn't arise.

But Graamon knew how to handle that. "You can't ask Owen to speak for his fiancée about things like that, Viina. I'm afraid you'll have to wait for Aila's own opinion."

Viina put on a sour face, but couldn't hold it, and burst into laughter. "You're right, of course, Graamon. But you can't blame me for trying."

Graamon knows Viina well, of course. I'll get to know her, too. She seems like a lovely landlady.

It felt strange to be in a bed again after so long, and all alone in the room. The clouds had cleared, and the moon was shining in through the top half of the window whose lower half was covered with snow, filling the room with a silvery light. It was so quiet that I could hear the tiny sounds made by the fire in the room downstairs. There wasn't even a breath of wind.

I woke to the sound of wind. The sky had clouded over again. I could just make out the windows, a slightly paler shade of black against an utterly black background.

Chapter 9

I woke again. Someone was knocking at the door of my room. "Hello?" I said.

"Breakfast time, Owen. Graamon said he wants to be at the yard at first light." It was Viina.

There was just the faintest hint of light in the sky, and I could see lamplight under the door of my room. I guessed that Viina had left an oil lamp outside my room for me, and went and opened the door. She had.

Graamon was already in the washroom. I joined him.

Breakfast was porridge made with milk, something I'd not seen since I left England, and boiled eggs. Graamon and I were the only ones eating. "I'll have mine later, with the lads," Viina said, "There's packed meals for you on the table in the hall. I'll expect you if I see you for dinner, to judge by what you were saying, Graamon, so there's enough in your lunch packs to keep you going all night if need be."

"Thanks, Viina. I hope we'll be back in time to pick up Owen's jacket from Lomeyr, though. I think with a bit of luck we might be."

It was bitterly cold as we walked down to the yard. *It'll be okay on the engines, though.*

Jinni had already built up the fires in all five engines and put the train together. Peyr and the other drivers arrived just as Graamon and I did. We all gathered to discuss plans, and agree communication. "We can't just use the standard whistles for communication between two or three engines working together, it'd get too confusing." I didn't manage to follow the whole discussion, but I knew they'd worked out a system.

Baamoon arrived just as we were ready to set off.

"We can't all three crowd into Jinni's engine at the front," Graamon said. "I'd better be with Jinni, but you and Owen go with Peyr, Baamoon." Peyr's engine was second in line.

It began to rain as we set off. "It's rain down here in Briggi, but it'll be more snow on the top," Peyr said. He was right; the rain changed to snow far below the top.

The snow had drifted again since we'd ploughed our way through before, and the path we'd cut had been completely obliterated. But with five engines and the big heavy plough we cut straight through the snow as if it wasn't there – until we got to the first rock cutting. Here, we'd already packed snow against the cutting walls from our earlier passing. More snow had drifted, and filled in the passageway we'd cut. It was snowing heavily by this time, too. Even with five engines, we'd only gone twenty metres into the cutting before we'd lost all our momentum.

Jinni whistled the code for reverse, and we backed out of the cutting, then "Forward!", and we charged the snow again. What the jarring was like in Jinni's engine, I don't know, but it wasn't too bad in ours, with two more pairs of buffers in between to absorb the shock. *Still, they've got the long travel buffers on the back of the plough, which are worth several sets of ordinary buffers. It won't be too bad.*

We'd gained another twenty metres. Gradually we hammered our way through the cutting – then suddenly we were free, and heading through easy drifts to the next cutting. Baamoon observed drily that it took eleven charges to travel just under half a mile. "Well worth having a roof over that cutting. I don't know what this is doing to the engines, never mind the fuel we're using, or even what we're doing to the cutting walls. And if we can't get all the way through, we might yet have to hammer our way back out through that lot. It's beginning to fill up again already."

That's probably true too, looking at the way this is falling, and how it's blowing about.

Half way through the next cutting, after the eighth charge, Jinni whistled the reverse code again. All five engines went into reverse – and went nowhere. Thirty driving wheels spun uselessly on the track. The plough refused to budge.

Jinni whistled the stop code, then "creep forward". "If we can," Peyr muttered under his breath, "Graamon wants to take the tension off the coupling, so he can uncouple the plough," he explained. "We're going back to Briggi without it. It's wedged in solid."

Peyr was right. It took Graamon some time to get the plough uncoupled, but eventually the "Head for home" whistle came, and then an answering, "Okay, I'm the lead engine now" from the other end of the train.

With the plough detached, we got moving again without difficulty. But Baamoon was right as well – we had to hammer our way back out through the first cutting, because it had filled in again quite a lot. "I hope we don't get stuck in this cutting now. I don't fancy being here until they dig us out. But I think we should be okay, I doubt if it's filled in that much yet."

It only took five charges to get back through the first cutting. We were back in Briggi in time for a late lunch.

It was raining hard in Briggi. Huge snowdrifts were visibly shrinking, turning into rivers of grey slush that blocked the gutters and made great slushy ponds everywhere. We were all glad of our long boots and thick socks – I was wearing some of Graamon's, which were several sizes too big for me, but we weren't going far or fast.

"We'll keep the packed lunches for later. Let's all go to the Briggi." No-one disagreed with Baamoon's suggestion.

"Disappointing" was Graamon's verdict on the morning. "I'd hoped we'd get through, especially after getting through the first cutting relatively easily. But I wasn't originally thinking of using five engines, and it's clear that we'd have been struggling even sooner with any less."

Baamoon wasn't sure about that. "I think all it would have meant would have been a longer run-up for each charge. It was the momentum of the plough itself that did the work, not engines pushing."

"Okay, but it would still have meant the whole process would have been much slower. You don't want to be taking all day just getting through the cuttings. I'm beginning to wonder about the expanding plough idea, too, now – it might have got us through where we got stuck today, but it wouldn't be a quick process. I think I want those roofs. What do you think, Baamoon?"

"I was saying the same thing to Owen and Peyr when we were out there. But we'll talk about that later, Graamon." Baamoon gave Graamon a look that I read as, "there's an issue

here that I don't want to talk about in front of all these drivers."
Umm, I thought.

"Apart from being slower with less engines, the plough might have got stuck sooner, with less engines to pull it back out."

"That's true, Owen. The expanding plough might solve that problem anyway, but we obviously need two of them in case we still need to back out. If we'd spent much longer in the second cutting, or even got through to the third before we got stuck, the infilling behind us could have trapped us completely. And this is a bigger snow than anyone's ever dug through to rescue drivers yet, I think. We're obviously going to have to sit it out until the thaw now. I just hope Berraami's safe at Tambuk or Kaahes, that's all."

"The more I think about it, the more I want those roofs. And two expanding ploughs. If the snows get any worse than this, we're going to need them all the way, not just in the cuttings."

"It's not *if,* it's *when,* Baamoon. Unless the weather changes the habits of the last few hundred years, anyway. Hell, when my Dad was a boy, there was never more than a few centimetres of snow in Briggi, and my Grandad remembered keeping goats in Liimiha. It's always been bad on the top, but never like this before."

Baamoon gave Graamon that look again, and Graamon changed the subject. A discussion ensued about things that could usefully get done in the yard while we waited for the thaw.

It was still pouring with rain when we'd finished lunch. Baamoon, Graamon and I headed for the workshops, and the drivers headed for the yard. "I'll bring the expandable up to the workshops in a minute," Medaal said as we parted.

"Thanks." Graamon was deep in thought.

We left our boots and thick socks at the foot of the stairs up to the office.

In the office, Graamon slid the pot of skiir closer to the fire, and we all sat down. Nobody spoke for a few moments, then Graamon began.

"The question has to be raised. Whatever we do, sooner or later Briggi is going to be cut off for weeks at a time every winter. We can keep fighting to keep the line open in all weathers, but that's just going to cost more and more every year, and we'll always be a step behind anyway, like we are now. Who knows how long it'll be before we can get through again? My guess is a couple of weeks, but it could be less – or it could be more. Roofing the cuttings, and routinely putting big ploughs on both ends of every train between Kaahes and Briggi at the first sign of snow, will obviously help, but it only delays the evil day. If we carry on like this, sooner or later we're going to have a driver frozen to death, and nobody wants that. We're going to have to work out a procedure for deciding when to close the line *before* we get a stuck train, not after – and just accept that it's closed for as long as it has to be."

Baamoon raised another option. "We could build a complete new line down the valley instead of over the top, and then tunnel through under the pass between Maaram and Belgaam, or even just carry on down the valley all the way to Barioha. There's other towns we could connect if we did that. But that's a huge project, and I doubt whether the committee would be prepared to raise the coins. In the long run, it could be worth it – but how long is the long run, for Briggi?"

"That's another question that has to be raised, painful as it is. I can guess, but the man who can really give you an answer is in Barioha – Baam, Biiniha's husband, who's been studying the glacier for years. Of course when Briggi finally is abandoned, somewhere further south will grow a lot, but second guessing where that will be could be hard. Except that the railway itself will be a big influence on where people choose to resettle, of course. Is the committee bright enough to realize that?"

"Some of them are. Between us, we can probably persuade the others. But it'll take time."

"There's another problem with the route down the valley, of course, which is why it was never routed that way in the first place. Landslides, especially at the narrows, but also for the next twenty-five miles downstream. The valley sides are steep and unstable. It would be possible to engineer a route, but it'd be awfully expensive to make it safe, and there'd be a lot of repairs to do after every earthquake. It would probably be cheaper to roof the line all the way to Kaahes."

"We'll push for roofing the rock cuttings, and plenty of big ploughs. Then probably the best rule is to give up the first time you're stopped, on the basis you can always hammer your way out backwards."

"It's not as simple as that, Baamoon. It's one thing to hammer your way backwards when you've got an engine at each end of a short train. I don't fancy hammering backwards with a single engine at the front of a full length train. Sounds like a recipe for a derailment, to me."

"I suppose so. So what's the solution? Put an engine on both ends of every train at the first sign of snow?"

"It might sound expensive, but it's probably cheaper than playing the kind of game we played this morning several times a year. And with the rock cuttings roofed, trains like that could probably get through anyway – it was only in those cuttings we had any trouble. Everywhere else, we barely noticed the snow at all, even drifts practically the height of the engine. Okay, that was five engines, but even so. I wish I'd had a gauge on those long buffers, so I knew what force we'd used and where. Before we do another run, I'll get Roonim to put one on, with a dial in the cab. Means a link to connect every time you put the plough on, which is a pain, but worth it I think."

Roonim must be the senior workshop man, I suppose.

For the first time, I felt I had something to contribute. "Surely a gauge on the engine's own buffers would give you the same information?"

"That's true. Good thinking, Owen. In fact, it's something that would be useful on all the engines, front and back, for normal operations as well as for snow clearing. Coupling tension as well as buffer pressure. Excellent! No special gauge needed on the plough at all, then."

Baamoon decided there was nothing much he could do around the railway for a while. "I can see it being a while before we venture up the line again. I'll pop in every now and then, and see what's going on, but I'll go and play with my grandchildren for the moment, I think. Send word if anything comes up."

Graamon was quite glad to see him go. "Baamoon's a good chap, as committee members go fantastically good, but I can only take so much of him. It's quite nice to have the office to ourselves!"

"You'd think committee members would have more idea of the relative costs of things."

"You certainly would. Especially the head of the committee. He's actually pretty good at it, when he thinks about it – but it's not instinctive for him, he has to work it out. In some ways that's good, it means he's prepared to listen to ideas that sound crazy at first but actually work out well. For example, I don't think a line down the valley between here and Maaram would be a good idea at all, but it really might be worth thinking about a tunnel through from Belgaam to Maaram, and a line from Maaram down to Barioha. I don't think there'd be any engineering problems about any of that, and we'd serve quite a few sizeable villages, one or more of which might well develop strongly if they had a railway. It's more fertile land than the Belgaam side of the ridge, but mostly wilderness because it's so inaccessible at the moment."

"I really don't have much idea of the geography around here yet. I'd never even heard of Maaram before. But one thing has been puzzling me. As far as I can make out, I must have crossed the main line somewhere between the coast and Sirimi, yet I didn't see it from the air. It seemed to be unbroken forest from the coast almost until Sirimi."

"I think I know pretty much the route you must have followed, then. There's a four mile stretch of cut-and-cover tunnel along the foot of the escarpment south of Sirimi. You probably saw a line of tall cliffs with scree at the foot of them in the middle of the forest. The line is underneath that scree. One of the nastiest bits of engineering on the entire railway, but the best option of a bad lot.

"Baam reckons it's old sea cliffs, from the time of the ancients when sea level was stable for a long time. That's why they're much taller and steeper than most sea cliffs nowadays. And why there's such a huge flat area to the south of them."

"I might have seen it at the time, but I don't remember. I'd seen a lot of natural landforms by then, and what I was looking for was signs of human activity. If I did see it, I didn't take any notice of it."

"I can understand that. Sometime before too long you'll have to come to Meyroha, but of course unless we get off the train and go walkabout, all you'll see of that area is two tunnel entrances."

Will Aila get to go here and there with me? I don't know how often any of the family go anywhere much with Peyr – but then it's probably different for drivers and assistant engineers anyway. Time enough to find things like that out later.

Aha! I do know that Faahiha travelled with Berraam – and they weren't even married. That was a long time ago; things could have changed. But I also know Aila's travelled with Peyr quite a bit, and not just back and forth to Baragi, either.

"Sometime we'll want to do drawings for those buffer and coupling gauges for Roonim, but he's up to his eyes with the expanding plough at the moment, so there's no hurry with that. We might as well go home too. Viina will probably be only too happy to carry on teaching you reading and writing, and I can finish that paperwork. And we mustn't forget to pick up your jacket."

At the bottom of the stairs, we put on our – well, Graamon's – boots and socks. "We ought to get you some of your own. I've got plenty, that's not the problem, but they're too big for you, I think! We'll go there on the way home. We'll get you some shoes that don't look so outlandish while we're at it. Anything goes in Laanoha, but in most other places they do stand out a bit."

The cobbler laughed at Graamon's big boots on my small feet. He measured my feet in more places than any cobbler in England ever had, and round my legs in several places almost up to the knee. "They'll be ready in five days' time. I've got socks the right size for you in stock, though. Three pairs enough?"

"Give him five pairs if you've got them. He's going to be away from home for a couple of weeks at a time quite often."

"You can have the other two when you pick up the boots and shoes, they're not made yet."

Viina was very happy to continue my lessons. After about an hour, she said, "You and Graamon ought to go and get your jacket, and I'll get started making dinner. I'll dig out some books for you later on, you ought to start practising reading – and probably copying out, and rewriting things from books in cursive script. You'll have the occasional question for me or for Graamon when something's not clear to you, but basically practice is really all you need now."

She'd gone and called Graamon before I'd had a chance to react. Graamon and I set off through the rain to Lomeyr's shop.

My jacket was ready, and was a perfect fit. I'd never had such beautifully made clothing before.

After dinner, Viina found me a book to read and copy from. Graamon went to finish his paperwork. I sat by the fire and tried to read. Viina sat knitting in another chair near the fire.

Even when you're beginning to get fluent conversing in a foreign language, and have learnt more or less how the script works, reading is hard at first. I could convert the text into the sounds of the words in my head, but the meaning didn't come immediately, even when I actually knew the words. I had to repeat the sounds to myself to hear the meaning. And Viina's book contained a lot of words I didn't know anyway – many more than I was used to encountering in conversation. But Viina was quite happy to explain them to me.

At first I wasn't sure whether the book was fiction or an account of someone's actual experiences, but it didn't actually matter one way or the other. It was mainly just reading practice for me. Of course I was also learning about the culture, without really realizing it. Gradually I realized that it was at least basically an account, possibly with fictional embellishments, of a life in Liimiha maybe a hundred or a hundred and fifty years earlier, before the railway was built. The culture had evidently been a little different then, but seeing the changes made me more aware of the present reality. Noticing that effect was an interesting and enlightening experience. *I wonder to what extent Viina chose this particular book deliberately? Surely she didn't actually anticipate that effect? She's clearly an intelligent and perceptive lady, but for her to be so aware of the way having a different cultural background affects one's perceptions is surely too much to believe. Maybe subconsciously? Possible, I suppose.*

After a while, Graamon emerged from his room. "Finished! There's nothing more I can do with that until I can talk to the committee, and I can't do that until we can get down to Meyroha. How's he getting on, Viina?"

"Oh, he's doing fine. He needs some more writing practice, but look at him reading! He's getting well into my great-grandfather's book, and I know he's taking it in by the questions he asks."

"Oh, I love that book. But the language is a bit archaic, if I remember correctly, isn't it?"

"I suppose it is, I hadn't thought of that. Most of my books are probably like that, I'm afraid – maybe not quite as much so as that one, that's true. But archaic is just more formal, really, nothing wrong with it – and learning to write formal Laana is probably better than writing the modern slipshod way, anyway!" Viina laughed.

"You might laugh, Viina, but you've got a point, really. I remember your grandfather addressing a public meeting here in Briggi when I was a tiny boy. I laughed at his way of speaking at the time, but I realized later how much respect he commanded amongst the adults – and part of that was the way he spoke. Formal language carries weight, whether people are consciously aware of it or not."

"This is your great-grandfather's book, Viina? Is it all true, or is it partly fictional?" I realized too late that this might be a rude question to ask, but Viina was unperturbed.

"I think it's mostly true. I can't be sure about some of the stories, and he certainly changed a lot of the names. I don't really remember my great-grandfather, he died when I was very little, but my grandfather said it was all true. But however much weight his speeches might have had, in the family we all knew that grandfather was fond of telling fairytales. If you knew him, you could tell when he was telling the truth and when he wasn't by a little twinkle in his eye, but people who didn't know him ended up believing all kinds of crazy things. He didn't have that twinkle when he said his father's book was all true – but that could just be that he believed it himself, not necessarily that it was actually true. And there's no checking any of it now, with Liimiha ground to powder under the ice, and all the people long dead and gone."

Graamon was thoughtful. "What is truth, anyway? What is the difference between truth and fiction, when there's absolutely no possible way of knowing which is which?"

"I remember my headmaster asking questions like that. We had long discussions about them, interesting discussions at the time, but I'm not sure they were really very productive."

"I almost wonder whether it's more about the limitations of the meanings of the words, than about any real substantive issue. Maybe we need a word for 'possible as far as we know at present, might prove to be true or might prove to be false eventually, or we might never know'. And it's a continuous range from black to white with every grey in between, not just three words. And we've only got two in Laana."

"Same two in English! But you're right to mention the language. I've been noticing more and more how words in Laana and words in English don't match up one to one – sometimes there are five or six words in Laana covering a range of related meanings that we have to cover with just two or three words in English, and sometimes it's the other way round. You get the same effect between English and French or German, but not to the same extent. And then there's the sounds the language is made up of, and they don't match up one for one either. Learning to read and write is helping a lot with this, actually. It's cleared up the way you have five different consonants in the err, eyr, er, el, and ell area – we only have two in that area, although people in different parts of England do say them a bit differently. And I expect you'd have trouble with vee and wee, because we have two sounds there where you only have one sort of halfway between our two – one of ours is almost into the end of your el and ell area. Those aren't the only examples, either."

"Without knowing English, that's an idea that's quite hard to get my head round. Oh, with words it's easy enough. I grew up bilingual in Liimi and Laana, and you get that effect there. Maybe not as much, but enough to be conscious of it. But Liimi and Laana use the same script, and the pronunciation works pretty much the same way. What does English writing look like?"

But her great grandfather, from Liimiha, wrote in Laana, not Liimi. I wonder why? I'll have to ask her later.

"Oh, I can show you. We've got an alphabet of twenty-two letters, but each of them can be written in two or three different ways. One of the differences is a bit like your printing and cursive forms – it's the difference between a printed book and handwriting. The other is something Laana doesn't have at all. It's called capitals and lower case. You can write in all capitals, but writing is usually mostly in lower case, with capital letters just at the beginning of some words, or for emphasis. Most capital letters are the same in printing and handwriting, but lots of the lower case letters look different. I'll draw them all for you."

The handwritten forms were easy enough of course, but I found drawing the printed forms quite difficult, which took me by surprise.

"Goodness me! Complicated. But I suppose Laana writing seems just as complicated to you."

"Well, at first it didn't seem to make any sense at all, but it didn't take Aila long to explain it enough that I could see the patterns. And I think I'm beginning to get the hang of it. But every time I think I've got it all into my head, something new turns up! And of course I need lots of practice, or it will slip away from me again."

"If once you learn the twenty-two letters of English in all their forms, is that it? Or do new things keep turning up in English, too?"

"Well, no new letters turn up. But there are punctuation marks – a lot more than Laana seems to have, unless your great-grandfather didn't use them all. And English uses combinations of letters in weird ways, so although you can learn all the letters and punctuation quite quickly, you have to learn how to write every word individually – you can't tell from the pronunciation, although you can often make a reasonable guess. The other way round isn't so bad. If you see a word written you can usually guess what it is – if you know the word. If you don't know the word, you can make a guess at the pronunciation, but it might be a bit wrong. At least with Laana, if you can read a word you know how it's pronounced."

"Well, you know how well-spoken people will pronounce it, and if you pronounce it that way, people will think you're well spoken. Not everyone speaks like that."

"Aha! Last time I was in Briggi, Peyr took me to an inn down by the river for a meal, and I couldn't understand what they were saying."

"That probably wasn't Laana at all, though. Mostly the river men talk Maara."

"Peyr seemed to understand them okay, and he was talking back in plain Laana."

"Well, they'd understand Laana okay, of course. But how Peyr comes to understand Maara, if he does, I don't know. But he's a one, that Peyr, full of surprises. Good brain. Pity he never got an education."

"How's a man from a poor family going to get an education, Graamon?"

"That's a good question, Viina. One we could do with an answer to, but I don't have one. But look at all the wasted effort trying to educate rich children with no brains, and all the wasted brainpower of poor people with no money."

"There's something in that, Graamon, but it's not that simple. In England, some poor people do get an education. Well, they all do up to twelve, but those who do particularly well sometimes get sponsored to continue beyond that. But usually those people either end up rich and leave their roots behind completely, or they end up frustrated because despite their good education, rich people don't take them seriously and they feel they can't achieve much without money. And poor communities need some clever people to deal with the poor communities' issues just as much as rich communities need them – maybe more."

"That's an interesting thought. In fact, that could be a perspective changing thought. Hmm. I shall think about that."

I already had a high opinion of Graamon, but that raised it higher still. *A willingness to reconsider things like that is not common.*

"Owen...you're nodding off. You should go to bed. Breakfast back to your normal time in the morning, Graamon?"

"That'll be fine, Viina. He's had a long day, look at him!"

"Same length as yours, Graamon, near enough."

"Yes, but it's all new to you. I know how much more tiring that is. See you in the morning!"

Chapter 10

I woke about dawn. The smell of cooking was coming up the cracks in the floor. I could hear voices downstairs, but I couldn't hear what they were saying. I recognized Viina's voice, and I guessed the other voices were the two lads who had the other room downstairs.

I was wrong. When I went downstairs, I found Viina sitting at the table with Roonim and Medaal, sipping skiir. "Graamon's in the washroom, Owen. Breakfast's ready when you are."

I joined Graamon in the washroom, and then we both joined the others at the table.

Roonim began. "Medaal's come up with an idea, Graamon. I think we could do it, but obviously it's your decision – and up to you to design the details if you think it's a good idea."

Graamon got Medaal to explain it. The idea was a method of releasing a plough that had got stuck the way ours had the previous day, by blowing steam out of holes in the plough blades.

"Hmm. Might work, but I don't think so. I can see problems. Unless you blow a little steam all the time, the holes are going to get blocked as you plough. You'd have to blow enough steam to keep the pipes warm enough not to get filled with condensation, which would block the pipes as soon as it freezes. The pipes are going to be being chilled by contact with the metal of the plough blade, which is being chilled by contact with lots of snow. Effectively, you're trying to keep the plough blade warm – practically melting your way through the snow. Much too much energy needed. An expensive thing, in time and materials, to try out with not much prospect of success, I'm afraid."

Medaal looked crestfallen, but Roonim seemed satisfied. I had the distinct feeling that Roonim hadn't really believed in it from the beginning.

"But don't be discouraged, Medaal," Graamon went on. "If you have more ideas, don't be afraid to tell me. I'm always willing to think about them and discuss them, and you'll learn from the discussions and get more likely to have usable ideas.

I'm glad you're thinking about these things – the more people did that, the better things would be all round. And not all my ideas work out, either – as you saw yesterday!"

Roonim and Medaal let themselves out, and Viina put our breakfast in front of us. "Sorry it's a bit overdone! But better that than cold."

"Not your fault, Viina. Anyway, it's absolutely fine."

"What are your plans for today? It's been raining all night, and the snow's almost completely gone. We'll be using the front door again soon."

"If it's been raining all night here, it's almost certainly been snowing all night on the top. We won't even be able to get to the stuck plough, and if we try without a rear end plough, we'll end up getting stuck ourselves. But we ought at least to go and see what the weather's like up there. We'll keep the big plough on the back of the train, and come back as soon as we get to dry snow, or when the little plough on the front won't take us any further. We'll most likely be back for lunch, but we've still got yesterday's packed lunch if not."

"You're a one, Graamon. It'll be completely stale."

"Yes, but perfectly eatable. I'm not one for feeding perfectly good food to the goats or the pigs and turning ten meals into one."

Viina laughed. "I should be used to you by now. Well, to tell the truth I am used to you. Owen will get used to you in the end, too."

"I'm sure I will. But I've always felt the way he does about food, anyway."

"You must have eaten some pretty stale stuff on your balloon ride!"

"I certainly did. But that was the least of my worries, really."

All the drivers were already in the Railwayyard inn. They'd tended their fires, which they were keeping going low to stop the engines freezing up. "If we were confident the cold weather wasn't about to come back, we'd let the fires out in most of them for the moment, just keep a couple ready to fire up and go. But it could so easily freeze hard again tonight."

"We'll go up the line to take a look at the weather on the top. Big plough on the back, little plough on the front. I don't expect to get anywhere near as far as the stuck plough, but I want at least to take a look. No need to take more than two engines – worth taking two rather than just one, I think. Jinni and Viilam, we'll take your engines. You're on each end of the train as it is just now, facing the right ways and already coupled to the plough. That way we don't need to move the other engines at all. If anyone else wants to come for the ride, you'd be more than welcome."

If all the drivers come, that'll be seven of us altogether – four in one of the cabs. Graamon didn't want four of us in Jinni's cab yesterday – but one of the four would have been Baamoon. Graamon thinks Baamoon needs more personal space, I think, even though he's no bigger than me. But it fits with my understanding of the way people are. Baamoon's presumably playing with his grandchildren today.

In the end, only Peyr came for the ride. "I'll come in Jinni's engine. I feel a bit mean leaving Viilam on his own, but you see better from the front engine, obviously."

Viilam laughed. "Don't worry, Peyr. It'll be Jinni's turn to be on her own on the way back!"

"On the way back it won't make much difference which engine anyone's in. You can't see through the big plough!"

"That's a bit of an issue, actually. You can see past it by leaning out of the cab, but not easily and not very well. I wonder about making one just over half the height, with extra blades you can slide up when you need them. Using steam rams, obviously – you don't want to have to put them up and down manually."

I must remember to mention using hydraulics, rather than running steam out to the plough. But this isn't the time, in front of all the drivers.

We didn't even get as far as the first rock cutting. "We could obviously have got a lot further with a big plough on the front, but what's the point? We know it's not thawing up here, and that's all we need to know. I just wish there was some way of knowing when the thaw gets under way without having to come up here every day for a look."

Well, in England I'd know how to do that – or at least, how to know what the temperature was in a selection of locations. But can I think of a way to do it with things we can get here? Doubtful. But we'll talk about it.

We didn't have any trouble backing out. Even though we'd been slipping trying to go forwards, we set off smoothly enough backwards with no sign of slipping. "It's the shape of the plough," Graamon explained. "These little ploughs only have a very blunt angle at the front, so they don't wedge themselves into the drift like the big one. It means they get stuck sooner going forward because they're piling up snow in front, but can pull back easily."

I'd realized that anyway, but didn't say anything.

We were back by mid-morning. "We'll do the same thing tomorrow. I don't suppose things will change much for a while, but we've got to know as soon they do."

In Briggi, the snow was completely gone. Even the slushy ponds had drained away.

We popped into the workshops on the way home – *home! Viina's place. My own room, my home. Will Aila want to stay there, for a while at least? We'll see. I wonder what kind of place we'll get when we have a place of our own, and when will that be?*

Roonim showed us the progress on the expandable plough. "I did right to bring Medaal round this morning, I hope?"

"Oh, yes, certainly. You know I like to encourage anybody to come forward with ideas. You did a good job of not showing your doubts! I could see what your reaction was, but only because I know you very well. I don't think Medaal could possibly have seen anything but encouragement from you. And much better that he came to me at home rather than embarrassing himself in front of the other drivers."

Graamon explained his idea about the two-tier version of the expandable plough to Roonim. "It's not fully worked out yet by any means, and there are obvious problems. It's even more complicated than this one, of course, harder to make it strong enough, and harder to build as much weight into it. I'm not certain yet that I even want to try it, it'll take some cogitation. But you know I value your thoughts."

"Well, my immediate reaction is exactly those obvious problems. But the fixed blades at the bottom could be a lot more than half height without obstructing the view, and that would help with the strength and the weight. I'll think about it too, and let you know if I come up with anything. It'll be a few days before you're ready to do any detailed planning, if I know you."

Graamon laughed. "Which you do, of course."

I get the feeling that before long I'll feel perfectly comfortable talking about ideas in front of Roonim. I like him. He's obviously a very good workshop man, too.

We were stuck in Briggi for four weeks. The temperature in Briggi remained above freezing for several days, and we made daily trips up the line towards Tambuk, but each time we failed to get as far as we had the day before because more snow had fallen in the meantime. Then the temperature dropped below freezing in Briggi again, and we didn't even bother to venture up the line for another two weeks. We didn't get much snow in Briggi, but it obviously wasn't going to be thawing on the top.

We picked up my second jacket and two pairs of trousers. Lomeyr asked when the wedding would be, and we told him we didn't know yet, and that my fiancée wasn't in Briggi – we were stuck one each side of all the snow. He made a sad face and expressed his sympathy.

Back at home, I tried on the trousers and overcoat. Like the jackets, they were the best I'd ever had.

My new boots and shoes were the best I'd ever had, too – a perfect fit. "Keep them well oiled, and they'll last you a lifetime," Graamon said as we left the cobblers. "He'll put new soles and heels on them for you once a year – don't wait until they're worn out, or you'll damage the body of the shoe."

He's been looking at my English shoes!

Graamon was desperate to make a trip to Siroha and pick up my things. Of course I wanted to see Aila, tell her about my job and my room and everything, and work out with her what we'd do. *Ah well, what happened, happened. You can't change the past.*

We spent a lot of our time just talking, and drawing diagrams for each other to help explain what we were talking about. Graamon showed me around the workshops, and we went into a lot more detail than when Baamoon had been with us. I got to know, and appreciate, Roonim.

"You couldn't ask for a better workshop man," Graamon said. "With a better education, he could have been a good engineer. But I'm still thinking about what you said the other day. A lot of our best workshop men in Laanoha and Meyroha could have been good engineers. And then how would we run the workshops?"

Well, I know one Laanoha workshop man. Judd could probably have been an engineer, with the right education. Or Peyr, for that matter – and he's not even a workshop man. Being out on the line instead of shut up in a workshop probably suits Peyr better, though. I'm sure it would suit Judd better, too, come to that. We can't all have our ideal life.

"Well, good engineers can still do workshop work. I'm sure you can operate all the machinery in the workshop, for example."

"Oh, certainly I can. But truth to tell I'm not as good at it as Roonim. I'm not even as good as Kaasham, who's only been learning for a few months."

"I wonder. I bet they're very good at doing things they've done twenty-five times before, but I bet you're at least as good as them, probably better, at doing anything new."

"Yes, you're right. That's certainly true."

"It's a matter of what they – and you – are practised at. They've had much more practice doing repetitive work on the machines, and you've had much more practice thinking about engineering problems."

Graamon showed me around the foundry, introduced me to the foundry workers, and showed me the charcoal plant. I knew about charcoal plants in England, similar in principle but on an industrial scale. Graamon wanted to know anything I could tell him about them.

"This little plant of mine is useful in itself, but I'm mainly trying to develop the process for Barioha. Our iron smelters there use a lot of charcoal, all made in the forest by traditional charcoal burners. Some of the charcoal burners make tar as well as charcoal, but all the gas and liquid products just go to waste – and all the heat. Most of the charcoal burners don't even make tar, they say it's too much trouble making the tar traps."

"I know that in England they separate a lot of different products, but that's only feasible because they're doing it on a much bigger scale. But I've never actually seen them, I only know about them from my teachers. As far as I can remember, they work pretty much exactly the same way yours does."

I tried to tell him that I didn't know much about the chemistry of the products, but couldn't find the words to get my meaning across. I wasn't sure whether chemistry was a subject about which anyone here really knew anything.

We discussed at length how the ancients must have known far more about this kind of thing than anyone did in our time. I told Graamon about Godfrey, his theories about some of the things the ancients did, and how he was pretty sure that they had many materials and resources that we simply didn't have any more. "The amount of iron they had, they must have been able to make iron without charcoal. The world couldn't have had enough trees to make all that charcoal."

"Did they have a huge amount of iron in England, and the countries around there? They had some around here, but I don't know that they had all that much. What we do know is that they chopped down pretty much every tree in these parts. The general opinion around here is that what finished them was running out of trees – but the evidence is pretty skimpy and I'm skeptical, and there are some other theories floating about. It's one of the things we want to investigate."

"Does the railway really care?"

Graamon laughed. "No, the railway doesn't care a bit. This is part of that other project I mentioned. You remember when you were telling us about schools in England, how people gradually move from being students to being researchers and then to teaching what they've discovered in their research? Well, there's a certain amount of that going on in some of the bigger schools in Meyroha. I know a lot of the people involved. They find Meyroha very stifling – the authorities want complete control of everything that goes on there. We're thinking to set up a new institute somewhere other than Meyroha – and not Laanoha or Barioha, either. Laanoha's almost as bad as Meyroha, and Barioha could easily get that way too, it shows all the signs."

"Briggi?"

"I don't think so, although that's been strongly suggested in some quarters. The trouble with Briggi is exactly what's going on now: it's liable to be cut off in winter. Worse than that, in fact – and of course this is something that touches me especially hard – it's only a matter of time before we have to abandon Briggi altogether. A few years ago Baam gave Briggi sixty or seventy years, but I know he's been revising his estimates, and I'm pretty sure it's downwards. By how much, I'm still waiting to hear. Even if it's that far away, that's soon enough that we don't really want to be setting up a major institute here."

"Where else is there? It would surely be difficult to set it up in a really small place. Of course I only know the places on this line, and have heard of Meyroha and Barioha. Oh, and Maaram, but my impression was that's small, too."

"Well, there are a couple of other places, but the main candidate so far as I'm concerned is Kiizhiha. It's quite big. It's an old place, and used to be pretty important – and it's got some very well built, big old buildings that aren't being used, beautiful big old stone places. Aha! You might even have noticed it – you can see it in the distance from the Sirimi road, as you come down from Siroha. I'd not thought of Maaram, though. It's true it's small, but it's not all that small – a lot bigger than Belgaam, which is the biggest place between Briggi and Kromaan. It's a bit off the beaten track, like Kiizhiha, but it wouldn't be if we built that line from Belgaam to Barioha that way. I could easily see it becoming the new north outpost, like Briggi is now and like Liimiha was before Briggi. Kiizhiha will always be a bit off the beaten track – there's nothing else over that way at all."

"You say Kiizhiha used to be important – what happened to it?"

"Oh, the railway is what happened to Kiizhiha. It was important in the days when the main traffic was coaches and the river. But the engineers who designed the line reckoned the cost of constructing the railway that way was more than it was worth – they thought Kiizhiha could manage with a coach service from Raamba or Veglid. Well, it does – but it's dying on its feet now."

"Would it have been so much further via Kiizhiha?"

"No, slightly shorter in fact – but it would have been on soft ground for a long, long way. Building railways on soft ground is expensive. Kiizhiha itself is on bedrock, but it's an island of it in the middle of a sea of deep mud. We've got the same problem all the way from Laanoha to the foot of the mountains, but Laanoha is a much more important place. The first railway was Meyroha to Barioha, but then it was obvious it had to extend to Laanoha. Or at least, to Kromaan – it didn't go through to Laanoha until 770, there was a ferry before that. Well, there still is a ferry, of course, but it's nothing like as important as it was."

"You say Kiizhiha is dying on its feet without the railway – but it seems Maaram is doing okay with just a coach service, isn't it?"

"There's two reasons for that. One is that Kiizhiha is on its own, there's nothing else anywhere near it, whereas Maaram is a centre for quite a lot of villages. All small, but a lot of them. The other is that Maaram has much better river access – it goes directly to Barioha in one direction, and Briggi in the other. There's nothing else of any significance on Kiizhiha's river, you have to go all the way down to the sea and then along the coast to Laanoha. On the Maaram side, firewood and timber – and charcoal – go straight down the river to Barioha."

"Could a railway compete with the river on the Maaram side?"

"If it was just firewood, no, pretty certainly not. But for fresh produce we would, the river's too slow. And we're better than coaches for passengers, too. It wouldn't justify as many trains as we have on this line, though, so there'd probably only be one passing loop between Barioha and Maaram. Mind you, there was only the one at Belgaam when the Briggi line first opened. Even the main line was single track at first."

Another time, we got talking about the advance of the ice, and the history of sea level changes. I'd learnt something from Godfrey, but sadly didn't know all he knew by any means. Graamon was in a similar position, with Baam and another friend, Kerrim, as his experts. The difference of course was that we'd be able to talk to Baam and Kerrim about it later, whereas all we could ever get from Godfrey was what was already in my head.

"Nonetheless, that's potentially valuable – it may not be all that's known in England, but it's still more than we here knew about the other side of the world."

Within the limits of our knowledge, history in the two regions did seem roughly to match, which inspired some confidence that our understanding was probably broadly speaking correct. In both regions, sea level was currently descending by about seven centimetres a year, which it obviously couldn't have been doing forever. It had certainly being descending for the whole of recorded history, and at roughly the same rate for at least several decades. In both places, about forty-five metres above current sea level, there was a line that appeared to have been a coast for a protracted period.

In both regions, that line had been noticeable but hard to interpret. It had only gradually dawned on researchers what the sea could do when it remained at the same level for a long time: cutting away the rock like people quarrying at it, and making huge flat areas of rock, boulders, gravel, sand or mud at or just below sea level. We could still see similar processes going on in our time, but on a tiny scale by comparison. Godfrey reckoned that sea level must have been within a metre or so of a constant level for thousands of years, and Kerrim had apparently come to exactly the same conclusion.

That also explained why the ancients' activities had apparently been particularly concentrated along that line. They had built elaborate structures there, seemingly dock facilities and the like. They appeared to have been intended to be permanent, but had evidently subsequently been submerged by a rising sea level. Sea level appeared to have risen to a peak about ninety metres above its present level before beginning its descent.

In both regions, ice was advancing southwards, but the rate of advance was so variable from place to place even within the same region that we couldn't put any useful figure on it. "I don't know whether Baam could work out some kind of average value, but I think it would be very hard – we don't know how much snow is falling on the ice, or how thick it is. But it's pretty obvious that the descent of sea level is a direct result of the accumulation of snow on land."

"And presumably, the prehistoric rise of sea level was a result of a general melting of ice. The only thing that's a bit hard to explain is the apparent stability of the coastline in the time of the ancients. Perhaps they knew how to stabilize the ice, to prevent more ice accumulating or melting?"

"If so, they seem to have done it for thousands of years. But it's hard to imagine that they could have stabilized the ice until they'd developed some pretty clever technology, and the general consensus is that their technological heyday was quite short-lived. I think it's more likely that it was something the ancients did in their heyday, presumably unintentionally, that destabilized a system that had been naturally stable for a long time. We're pretty sure the population peaked at many times today's, and they seem to have been using resources at a rate that makes it hard to imagine where they got them from."

"That's almost exactly what Godfrey says. I remember his words, 'They were using resources like there was no tomorrow. And for them, there was no tomorrow.' It made me laugh at the time, but we went on to realize that in the last few generations we'd embarked on the same road again. In England, they're cutting the forests faster than they can grow."

"Here too. At the present rate there's a few hundred years' worth left, but the rate is increasing. That's one of the reasons I'm so keen to improve the efficiency of engines, and charcoal production."

"Godfrey was convinced the ancients had some other source of energy, other than muscles and burning wood. He couldn't see how they could possibly have powered all the machinery they seem to have had without using all the world's trees in just a few years. Perhaps we should be trying to find out what it was."

"Well, we know they did consume pretty much all the world's trees, in these parts at least, and from what you say, in England too – but we're going round in circles now."

But we carried on going round in circles. There wasn't much else we could do until we could get together with some of Graamon's friends. I was really looking forward to that.

When will this snow thaw? When will I see Aila again?

The expanding plough was finished, but Graamon didn't want to try it while the other big plough was stuck. "We might even get through to the other plough. And then what? We very possibly wouldn't be able to get home again. With a big plough on the back, we could pretty certainly reverse out okay, but with just a small plough on the back, I'm far from sure of it. And until the thaw, I don't see much prospect of getting that stuck plough out now. No, we've got to wait until the thaw."

Roonim suggested he spend the time building another non-expandable plough, but Graamon thought it would be better to wait to see how the expanding plough performed. "If the expanding plough works well, we'll want at least one more of those, possibly one with a movable top, but we won't want any more plain ones. We'll only want more plain ones if the expanding one is a failure for some reason."

I eventually got round to suggesting hydraulics. I had to explain what I meant. "Use the steam to push a piston, then use that to push a liquid, then drive the rams with that liquid, rather than directly with the steam. That way the volume of steam used is only what's needed to push the ram, rather than a lot being wasted when it condenses in all the pipework."

Graamon was interested, and thought it might have applications elsewhere, but wasn't sure about it for the plough. "What kind of fluid are you thinking of? You need something that won't freeze solid at the temperatures the plough gets down to. Steam's a bit annoying, it's true, because you spend a lot of energy just warming up cylinders and pistons to the point where it stops condensing, but at least you're delivering heat to do that."

"Even oil freezes, or gets too viscous for the system to work properly, when it gets too cold. But you could deliver heat with a recirculating system, and you wouldn't need to keep it anywhere near as hot as a steam system. With the intermediate fluid at a higher pressure, using smaller pistons, everything's smaller, too, so it needs less heat to keep it warm for that reason as well."

"Ah, now that makes it something worth exploring. I hadn't thought about using very high pressures in your intermediate fluid. That makes it much more interesting. What do you think, Roonim?"

"Well, even though it's more complicated, it's using less metal – smaller parts are quicker to make, so even with more of them, the complication doesn't worry me. Definitely interesting, but I think we should do some preliminary experimental work on it first."

"Well, there's something useful we can be doing while we're stuck here, anyway. I'll get some designs drawn up."

It was actually me who did most of the drawing, with some guidance about local drawing conventions from Graamon. At last I felt as though I was doing something useful for my actual job with the railway. Roonim and Kaasham built the experimental set up, which worked with only a little tinkering.

"Now we need to try something with recirculating fluid, and take it somewhere cold. That's actually a bit of a problem – I don't want to risk getting stuck, going up the line, and how else are we going to get anywhere much colder than about freezing?"

"Can we get hold of a lot of salt in Briggi?"

"How much is a lot? We can certainly get hold of a few hundred hefts of it it. Why?"

"Well, there's plenty of snow about. We can make a cold room. Build an insulated room, put a load of snow in it, and mix the snow with salt – you can take the temperature down really low like that."

"Well, if that works, that's a really useful trick. I never knew that."

Building the cold room kept us all busy for several more days. Then I designed a heating system for the hydraulics. In the end it was a simple vented steam system, rather than a recirculating fluid. "More trouble than it's worth, recirculating. Twice the pipework and a pump? Not worth it. You'd save no fuel at all, and water isn't a problem. In fact, you'd waste fuel, keeping the extra pipework warm."

We found that insulating the pipework was really worthwhile, but we didn't try to insulate the joints. I told Graamon about flexible polymer hoses, but we agreed that if that was possible for us at all, it was a long term project to be undertaken in collaboration with others. I didn't even know the chemistry well enough, all I could do would be to provide some pointers for others about lines of experimentation worth following.

We talked about electricity. Graamon did know something about it – his little engine used electric ignition, for example – but not very much, and the idea of a public electricity supply astonished him. He thought it sounded like a frightful waste of energy, and I agreed that it probably was. "Yet the ancients seem to have managed it on a vastly greater scale. And Godfrey thinks they had connections between towns, not just within towns. I don't think Godfrey himself has seen the evidence, but he knew people who had, and they'd regarded the evidence as pretty convincing. They seem to have had electrical connections pretty much all the way along their railways, although those could have just been telephone wires."

Then I had to explain telephones to him. He was amazed. "So if we had telephones between here and Tambuk, we'd only have to dig through from one direction when someone got stuck in between? Or at least, we'd presumably start digging from both, but then one end would give up as soon as the other said they found the train?"

"Better than that. They could carry a telephone on the train, and clip it to wires by the lineside. Then the driver could tell us where he – or she – was stuck, and we'd only dig from the nearer end. The other thing I was going to mention is that there's a method of making a thermometer that can be read from the other end of a pair of wires, so we could know in Briggi what the temperature is at several points along the line, without having to go up the line ourselves. You'd need a lot of wire though – two for each thermometer, and two for the phone. Well, no, they could all share one of the wires, so it's only one more than one each."

"I'm not sure I could do a single wire all the way to Tambuk, never mind a whole bundle of them. Imagine the work winding the insulation onto them! I suppose we could design a machine to do the winding."

"I'm sure we could. There must be machines for that in England. You can buy reels of ready insulated wire there, reasonably cheap for the quantity you need to wire a few lamps in a house – although for a fifty mile telephone run it would work out pretty expensive. Apart from the length, you'd need thicker wire, because there's too much loss in thin wires over long distances. What's the price of copper like here?"

"It's expensive. About eight hundred coins a heft, and always rising. Almost all of what's on the market is recycled scrap. Sometimes a ship arrives from here or there with a bit to sell, but they never undercut the local price. There's none left in any of the ancient sites – at least, not in any of the known sites. Where the ancients got it from, who knows? Or maybe they made it somehow."

"It's not cheap in England, either, but I don't think it's as expensive as that. It's hard to make comparisons between prices, though. How much is a coin worth in eksyus? The only way to compare is to decide that some particular item should be the same value in both places – and then everything else is different. Eight hundred coins is sixteen weeks' of my income, which sounds like a lot. Sixteen weeks' of an assistant engineer's income in England would buy a lot more than a heft of copper there, but here I'm getting accommodation, clothing and food supplied by my employer, which an assistant engineer in England would have to pay for himself. I don't think an assistant engineer in England could afford accommodation like mine at all, before you start on food and clothing."

"Don't forget this is Briggi. Accommodation here is much cheaper than it is in Laanoha or Meyroha. You wouldn't get a room like yours there until you'd been with the railway a couple of years. Well, never, really – they just don't exist, or at least, nothing like it ever seems to become available."

"Peyr's place isn't bad. I've never seen Judd's, though."

"Grim and Yaani are both working – and I dare say Yaana's earning a fair bit on the quiet. And of course the railway doesn't feed Peyr at home. It won't feed you at home when you and Aila get a place of your own, but your income will have increased by then. I don't know Judd's place, either. I know where it is, but I've never been inside. I do know it's not very big."

'When you and Aila get a place of your own.' Aila! We had so little time together, and it seems so long ago now. It's almost like a dream. I hope it's really going to work out, and that it really is right for both of us.

Graamon clearly takes it for granted. So does Peyr.

Eventually the temperature rose above freezing again in Briggi, and it began to rain. We took an engine up the line towards Tambuk. We only took one engine, not intending to push beyond the point where the rain turned to snow. "There's no point until there's a chance of getting through. We're only going up there to take a look."

We'd only gone five miles and climbed about a hundred and fifty metres when we reached the snow and headed back. "We won't get through tomorrow, either, but we'll come and take another look if it's still above freezing in Briggi."

It was, and we did. We got a bit further before the rain turned to snow, but by then we'd been splashing through slush for some way, and in places there was still enough wet snow on the rails to make our wheels spin for a moment. "Don't worry, though. It's downhill on the way back, and there won't be any more muck on the line going back than there was coming up."

Peyr was right. The return journey was no trouble at all. "It's just another run up for a look again tomorrow, one engine. There's no way we'll be able to get through tomorrow."

On the fifth day, Graamon and Peyr agreed that we'd attempt to reach the stuck plough the next day.

"Even if we manage to reach the plough, we may not be able to get through, of course. But I'd like to be ready just to head south straight away if we do. I know you'd like to get to see Aila as soon as possible, Owen, but do you think we could make a detour via Siroha, to make arrangements to pick up your stuff? I think it'll inevitably cost us a day or even two, and we won't be able to take the things ourselves – apart from your clothes. We should be able to take those okay. We'll hire a gig from Raamba."

"Of course that's okay. If we don't do that now, it could be a while before we get the chance again, I suspect."

"Well, yes. Then I ought to visit the workshops in Laanoha, arrange a wagon on the next train to take your stuff to Briggi, see what's been going on in the workshops, and then head for Meyroha as quick as I can. I'll get Judd to bring you along as soon as you've sorted things out with Aila, and we'll get you introduced in Meyroha. I've not asked you before, have you and Aila actually fixed a date yet?"

"No, not yet. She had to talk with Gamaara, and I really don't know the proper procedure at all. I need advice!"

"I suppose you do. You've settled in so well in general I forget how new it all is for you. Do you have any idea what Aila's thinking, Peyr? Or do you have any ideas yourself?"

"Oh, that's a hard question for a man to answer! My mother would be the one to ask that. But I guess we'll be seeing Aila before we see my mother, and she might well tell us herself. But the only option is to wait and see. Anything else is guessing. I'll be taking the first train down, so if you and Owen go up to Siroha, Graamon, I'll see Aila before either of you do – but I don't see how I'll know which train you'll be on, to make sure she meets your train. Can you find your way to Gamaara's house, Owen?"

"Well, I can find my way to the big gates. Will I be able to open them, or do you need a key, or any special trick? And once I'm through the gates, is the way easy to find?"

"There's no problem once you're through the gates, you just follow the track and there's the house. They normally lock the gates at night, but they leave them open when my train's due if I'm on one of the late trains, and I can get them to leave them open for you, too."

"The only problem about that is that we really don't know which train we'll be on. Who knows how long it's going to take us to get to Siroha, how long they'll keep us there before we can decently get away, and how long it's going to take to get back to Raamba? And the timetable's going to be all shot to pieces for days anyway."

"That's very true. They'll have been running a shuttle service between Laanoha and Kaahes, or even all the way up to Tambuk if that stretch is open."

"Jinni will be bringing the next train after mine down. All being well, I can tell Aila to catch Jinni's train and come home straight away, then she'll be at home when you arrive, Owen. I'm sure she'll have sorted things out with Gamaara by now. She might even be at home already, desperately waiting for you to get through."

"That's a better solution, Peyr."

I was beginning to feel a bit nervous about seeing Aila again – but looking forward to it, too.

The five engine train, with the expandable plough on the front, was ready not long after dawn, but Graamon waited until about eleven before deciding to set off. "We'll give the day a chance to warm up a little. I dare say it froze again overnight near the top. We'll probably get a chance to try the expandable in the cutting. Even if it's raining right at the top, I doubt if it's washed all the snow out of the cut yet. But I don't think there's much risk of getting stuck, even with only a small plough on the back end, as long as we give up if it starts to look risky."

Graamon was with Jinni in the front engine again, then me and Baamoon in the second with Peyr. It was sunny as we set

off, the first morning we'd seen the sun for weeks, but the
clouds closed in again as we climbed, and it began to rain – not
heavily, just a little more than a steady drizzle.

Even the slush had mainly washed away at first, but by the
time we reached the first rock cutting we were splashing along
through deep slush flowing sluggishly along or across the line in
many places. In a few places there were faster moving rivers of
more or less ice-free water.

The first cutting was a sight to behold. It was half filled with
a bank of wet snow probably twice the height of the engines,
with a river of slush pouring out of a cave underneath it. Jinni
brought the train to a halt, and we all climbed down for a better
look.

"Well! We don't want to go charging into that. We'd end up
buried in soggy snow."

"I suspect you're right, Peyr. No, we'll creep up to it gently
and nudge it. I suspect it'll all collapse of its own accord with
only a few gentle nudges. It'll probably be easiest if we
uncouple just behind Jinni's engine, and the rest of you back off
a bit. Jinni'll have more control like that."

I could see the relief in Jinni's face. *Controlling a whole train
by remote control, whistling to four other drivers what to do,
can't be easy.*

Peyr uncoupled his engine from Jinni's, and the bulk of the
train backed off a few metres. Jinni and Graamon hung out one
each side of the cab to see around the big plough, and crept
forward. As Graamon had predicted, the first touch of the
plough on the near edge of the mound released an avalanche of
wet snow that cascaded down each side of the plough, and
sloshed alongside the engine halfway up its wheels. Jinni rapidly
reversed the engine back out of the cut.

It didn't take long for the avalanche to stop. When it had,
there was no cave underneath the pile of snow, and only a trickle
of slush running from the bottom. We all got out for a look
again.

Graamon almost got the slush over the top of his boots before
he turned back. "I think if we just push into the pile and pull
back, then push in again, it'll gradually all pour out. We

shouldn't leave it too long between pushes, either – the river that was coming out before must be ponding up behind that snow that's fallen at the front, and it'll coming gushing out. We don't want to be completely flooded."

After the fifth push, we could see right over the top of what was left of the pile, and Graamon decided we should just couple up again and push straight through. "We might get a bit wet in Jinni's and Peyr's cabs, but we don't want to spend all day here. If the worst comes to the worst and it puts our fires out, the other three engines will be able to push us through easily enough."

Jinni had a better idea. "If Peyr and I shut our firebox doors before we go through, there's not much risk of that. We'll just put our valve gear in neutral and let the other three push us through from the beginning."

In the event, we got through with only a modest amount of wet snow falling into the cabs of any of the engines, and we pushed it out again as soon as we came out of the other end of the cutting. Baamoon was clearly relieved. "Let's hope the other cuttings are as easy!"

The second cutting looked much the same as the first had. Again, Peyr uncoupled and Jinni and Graamon edged up to the snow and released an avalanche, then pushed in and out until the other big plough appeared out of the pile. Then they opened the front of the expandable plough right up and coupled on.

The stuck plough pulled out of the pile with no trouble at all. They didn't even need the other engines. But at that point the pile didn't collapse completely. Some snow fell down where the plough had been, but the wall of ice that the plough had been stuck in stood firm.

Jinni backed out, and Peyr coupled up. Jinni and Peyr shut their fireboxes and put their valve gear in neutral again. Then we charged the pile – and just kept on going. We popped out the other end of the cutting, pushing a huge lump of ice in front of the plough. Jinni – I assumed on instruction from Graamon – whistled to us all to stop, and we did.

"We'll have to smash that up somehow before we reach the next cutting. We've got pickaxes in the first wagon, but that looks like a bit of a big job for eight of us with pickaxes!"

"It'd be quicker to go back to Briggi, take the first plough off the front, bring the expandable plough up to it, and split it in half!"

"If it did split in half. I think we might just break the two wedges off this end of it, and leave the rest unaffected."

I suggested that if we simply backed off and charged it a couple of times it would probably fall to bits, now it was out of the cutting, and that's what we did. And it did.

The third cutting was only a little more trouble than the first. Jinni's cab did get flooded, but with the firebox door shut it didn't put the fire out. She and Graamon got wet and cold, but as soon as we were through they swept the slush out of the cab, got the fire going well and warmed up.

We whistled a five engine, ten whistle chorus as we steamed down to Tambuk. Tambuk's whole family, and Berraami, were there to greet us.

"Five engines? Eight mouths to feed? We'll get some more food cooking as quick as we can!" Tambuk and his wife disappeared into the inn at a run.

Berraami came over to me and Peyr, and gestured to Graamon to join us. She was looking very serious. "I'm glad I was still here when you got through, Owen, not any of the others. I have bad news. Come in and sit down, you three."

Me, particularly, and Peyr and Graamon? I hope Aila's all right!

We sat at a table in a corner. Berraami poured us each a mug of warm skiir, then began her story.

"Fortunately, mine was the first train going north the morning after you came north. I was going full speed approaching Baragi, not expecting to stop there, but right at the beginning of the village I saw Aila, waving like mad, obviously wanting me to stop. I put the brakes on hard, and Aila began to run alongside the train. She caught up with the cab before I'd had really got down to the right speed for anyone to jump on board, but she jumped and managed to grab the rail and pull herself in. She told me to get going again, so I did.

"She was shivering cold – it was only seven in the morning, and she was only wearing her indoor clothes. She'd got nothing else with her but what she stood up in.

"Well, I'll cut a long story short. The night before, Jerem had got into a real rage when he heard about Aila and you. He smashed her little Owen, and tried to rape Aila. That was a big mistake for him – she isn't a girl to mess with. She whacked him on the head good and proper with one of the children's toys, a really heavy one, and then ran out of the house. She wasn't sure whether she'd killed him, in fact. She hid up until she heard my whistle as I approached Baragi."

Bloody hell! I hope she's all right! I thought, but I couldn't say anything. I could see in his face that Peyr was thinking much the same thing.

Berraami went on, "Well, she came with me as far as Elbrouha, where I was due to wait for Mum, but she wanted to go back to Laanoha with Mum, so I stopped short of the loop to make sure Mum didn't steam straight past, and then slid in and stopped cab to cab. Aila went with Mum, and that's the last I know. My train's stuck between here and Kaahes. Tambuk's men got to my train first, so here I am."

Peyr looked relieved. "Well, at least we know Aila's all right. And you don't know any more than we do about whether Jerem's okay. I don't think his family would make trouble for Aila anyway, whether he is or isn't."

Peyr didn't say it, but I could see what he was thinking. *Nobody would miss Jerem much, apart from his parents, and maybe his on-off girlfriend in Kromaan. And even his parents would understand Aila's point of view.*

"Aila's all right physically, certainly, and of course she's a tough cookie mentally, too. But she was pretty upset, naturally. I think she was more upset about Jerem smashing you to bits than anything else, Owen. The sooner she sees you whole and well, the better!"

Graamon was thoughtful. "I'm sure she doesn't believe that stuff – in her head. But it's one thing not to believe something in your head, it's quite another what you feel. She'll really be hurting, Owen. We'll cancel our trip to Siroha, they can wait.

My curiosity about your ballooning stuff can wait, too. It's too late to dig Berraami's train out today, but we'll do it first thing tomorrow, and then we'll get down to Laanoha as fast as we possibly can. They'll be running a shuttle between Kaahes and Laanoha, and that should mean only one overnight, even if it takes us a while digging Berraami's train out."

"I'm afraid my engine's drained down, Graamon. I kept the fire in for a week, but they don't have a lot of extra wood here in Tambuk, and my train's too far from Kaahes for them to carry it from there. They only visited once, just to check that I wasn't still waiting to be rescued. If I'd had a plough like that one you've got, Graamon, I don't think I'd have been stuck at all. It's amazing."

It was only later she realized that it was actually two ploughs, one in front of the other.

They shuffled the train around straight after we'd all eaten, so as to be ready to go at dawn the following day. There was no way to turn anything round, so the first new plough was left, still facing south, in the loop ready for Berraami to take it down to Briggi on the back of her train. It was quite a shuffle to leave it in the south loop, so that we wouldn't crash into its coupling-less pointy end when we came back up the line pulling Berraami's train.

I scarcely slept that night. Every time I got to sleep, I had nightmares, and woke up again. For some reason it was usually the innkeeper from Veglid I was trying to protect Aila from, but sometimes she was lost in the snow, or drowning in slush, and once I was holding the little Aila and she was breaking into matchwood and bits of painted plaster in my hand. I didn't even know for sure that's how she was made, but I suspected it.

Sometime in the small hours, I woke and saw a candle alight on the table. Jinni and Berraami were sitting at the table, sipping skiir and talking quietly. I wondered whether to let them know I was awake, and join them at the table, but decided against.

The next time I woke it was pitch dark, apart from the glow of the fire on the beams of the ceiling. I wondered what they'd been talking about.

Chapter 11

In the morning, everyone else was awake before me. Peyr woke me, and we went out to get washed.

"How did you sleep?"

"Not very well. How about you?"

"Okay. Don't worry about Aila – she's fine. Like Berraami said, she's a tough cookie. She'll be looking forward to you coming – and hoping every day that it's the day you'll arrive. Not long now!"

"I hope you're right!"

"I'm sure I am."

After breakfast, the expanding plough pushed through to Berraami's train without problems. They opened the front again, took Berraami's little plough off, and coupled up. Pulling Berraami's loaded train was no problem for five engines, either. "I thought we wouldn't need all five," Graamon said, "but better to have them and not need them, than to find we had to go back for more."

Back at Tambuk there was a fairly simple shuffle to get the two trains in shape, then Medaal set off for Briggi towing Berraami's train with the first new plough on the back. The rest of us had an early lunch at Tambuk before we set off for Kaahes.

Berraami came with us, even though her train was going to Briggi. "Until I'm back in Briggi, someone else will have to take the trains south. Nobody will mind getting out of Briggi sooner while there's a risk of getting stuck there, and it'll be days before we're operating a normal schedule anyway."

At Kaahes, we found one of the Laars just arriving from the south with a short train. He was very pleased to see us coming through, and laughed at the number of engines. We told him we'd had five as far as Tambuk, and he laughed again – until we told him about the plough getting stuck, even with five engines behind it.

Peyr asked him if he had any news about Aila, but he said he didn't know anything. I saw Berraami catch Peyr's eye. She took him on one side. Then Peyr was nodding, apparently agreeing with something she'd said.

There was a bigger shuffle to get the trains sorted out this time, and then Laar's train with the expanding plough and all the engines except Jinni's headed back towards Tambuk. Jinni, Berraami, Graamon and I headed south.

Baamoon went back with Peyr. "I'll come down with Peyr. An extra half day isn't going to make any difference." *He doesn't want to be in too crowded a cab, that's why.*

As soon as we were under way, Berraami told me what she'd been saying to Peyr. "Don't ask the drivers about Aila. They'll wonder what's up. She only told me and Mum. She won't want everyone to know. Obviously you and Peyr and Graamon needed to know, and I'm perfectly certain she won't mind Jinni knowing, but otherwise keep it quiet."

"Yes, of course."

"If anyone does know anything, I'm sure they'll volunteer it without having to be asked. I think Jerem must have survived, or the news would be everywhere by now. Well, everywhere south of the snow, anyway. Unless his parents are keeping quiet, of course, which from what I hear about them isn't beyond the realms of possibility."

We stopped that night at Belgaam. I was a little apprehensive about the two girls there, but Jinni and Berraami understood the situation very well without anybody saying anything. They sat one each side of me all evening, which was wonderfully effective.

I slept better that night. I had nightmares, but only woke up a couple of times. Once, Jinni and Berraami were up and talking; the other time the two Belgaam girls were. I could just hear the murmur of their voices, but I couldn't make out what they were saying at all, not a single word.

It's quite the normal thing to do here, it seems. I suppose it's something to do with all sleeping in the same room like this. One's aware when others are awake, and you can't talk lying where you are without disturbing others. What a different world from England – but I like it. But of course it's not like this everywhere – not at Viina's, anyway.

One of the two girls cornered me coming back from getting washed in the morning. *Damn! I should have waited for Graamon!*

"You're quite the one!" she said. "You know that Jinni and Berraami are both attached, don't you?"

"Yes, I know that. I know both their boyfriends, too." This wasn't quite true – I knew *about* them, and I'd met one of them briefly.

"I like your new outfit. Quite a change from the first time we met! You've certainly moved up in the world quickly."

"I suppose I have. I've never thought about how long it normally takes."

"It doesn't normally happen at all. Most people don't move up in the world, they stay where they are. Do you like me, or Biishi?"

Bloody hell! Talk about direct!

"I like you both, you're both lovely. I didn't know her name before, and I don't know yours now. But you know I'm attached, don't you?"

Two can play direct.

"I'm Maashi. People think we're twins, but we're not even sisters, we're double cousins. My Dad's her Mum's big brother, and my Mum's her Dad's little sister." She looked crestfallen, and I felt terrible.

Better to know now, Maashi, than to stay hopeful now and find out later, I thought, but I still felt terrible. "We'd better get inside. It's cold out here."

We met Graamon coming out as we went in. He looked a bit surprised, but I gave him a grin which I hoped said all was well.

Jinni and Berraami sat one each side of me again at breakfast. Biishi and Maashi were as attentive, to everyone, as ever – seemingly more so than the previous evening, or when Jinni and I had stopped for dinner on the way north.

I wonder how long they'll take to latch onto somebody else? Is there anyone else to latch onto? Is there something wrong with Diraan? He seems like a good chap, but they don't seem interested in him at all. Not that I'm a good judge of a man's marriage-worthiness – especially here, where I don't really understand the culture very well yet.

Latch onto? That's a mean thought.

I'm not sure how else to think of it, though.

After breakfast, Berraami headed back north with Diraan. Jinni, Graamon and I headed south.

I'm going to see Aila soon! I was half excited, and half a bit nervous.

We were pretty much on time coming into Laanoha at ten o'clock that evening. It was strange not to have to hide under the floor as we approached the city. The guards barely even glanced at my papers. My clothes seemed to tell them I was Railway, with a capital R. *Perhaps if I hadn't been with Graamon they'd have been more diligent – anyone could get clothes like these made, I suppose. Maybe not all that easily, but surely possible.*

Graamon and I stayed on the engine all the way into the yard. Jinni was welcomed like a conquering hero. "So! You've made it at last! Who was stuck? How long were they stuck for?"

"Medaal was stuck for a few hours. We got through to him from Briggi with Graamon's new plough and four engines. Berraami was stuck for a day and a half before the Tambuk men got through to her with shovels. Luckily she was within whistling distance of Tambuk, so they started as soon as she got stuck. We tried to get through all the way with Graamon's new plough, but the plough got stuck, and we had to leave it and go back to Briggi while we still could."

Jinni knew how desperate I was to see Aila, and we didn't hang around at the yard any longer than we had to. Jinni headed for Parruk's place.

Graamon and I made very good time walking up to the room. We knew no-one knew we were on the way, so we weren't surprised that all was quiet as we climbed the stairs in the pitch dark. "You go in first, Owen. They're probably all asleep, but they'll be so pleased to see you!"

I opened the door quietly and crept in. They were indeed all asleep. In the flickering light of a low fire I could see my way just well enough to go to the shelves and get a taper to light the oil lamps. Grim stirred as I tiptoed past his feet. He leapt up. "Owen! And Graamon! You've made it!"

Two more bodies stirred and sat up. *Not three. Who's missing?*

It was Yaani and Yaana. There was no sign of Aila.

"Where's Aila?" I'd said it before I'd thought whether I should or not.

Grim had both lanterns alight before I'd got anywhere. There were tears in his eyes. I looked at Yaani and Yaana, and there were tears in their eyes, too. *What's wrong? It's not tears of joy, I can tell by their faces.* "We don't know. You must have seen Berraami, so you know what happened?"

"Yes. Berraami said Aila was coming here."

"She did come here. Get them some skiir, Grim. And sit down, all of you. I'll get some food going. She stayed three days, but then she went, and we don't know where to. She left you a letter. Here it is."

Oh God. Where is she? What is she doing? I hope she's okay. My world was falling apart. *The letter. Read the letter.*

It was a single sheet of paper, folded in four and stuck together along two edges with wax. I carefully tore off the waxed edges and opened it up. This is what she'd written, in a childish print:

Owen my love,

Berraami must have told you what happened by now. If I can't even look after my little Owen properly, how can I possibly look after my big Owen? I will love you forever, but I can't marry you. You must find somebody else who will look after you better. All my love, Aila. Oh, and Birgom wants to talk to you.

Birgom wants to talk to me? I did want to talk to Birgom, but I want Aila! What does anything or anybody else matter if I've lost my Aila? Will Yaana know what to do? Do they know what Aila's written? Should I show them?

They can't read. I'll have to read it to them. Should I show Graamon? Should I get him to read it to them?

No. It's my job. Should Grim hear it, or should I keep quiet until a better opportunity?

Yaana didn't let me worry about that. "What does she say?"

I started to read it aloud, but after a couple of words my voice wouldn't work. Graamon put his hand on my arm and I looked round at him. "Shall I read it for you?"

I nodded, and he took the letter, and read it out. His voice was shaking, too.

I had my voice back. "What should I do?"

Yaana looked at me with big tearful eyes. "What can you do? What can anyone do?"

Graamon had a different question. "What do you *want* to do?"

That was easier to answer. "Well, obviously I want to find her, and tell her not to be silly. Just because some stupid boy tries to spoil things doesn't mean she can't look after me perfectly well. Hell, I'd have a hard time finding anyone who can look after me better than that. How many young women could have fought him off like that?"

Wanting to find her and being able to find her might be very different, of course. Does she want to be found, or does she really mean it's over for good? How can I tell? Does anyone know? How can I ask them?

Graamon had much the same thoughts. "That's the spirit! Finding her might be harder than saying it, especially if she doesn't want to be found. Persuading her to change her mind may not be easy, either. I'm sure she knows in her head that you're still her man and she's still your woman, but it's one thing to know something in your head, it's quite another what you feel."

Yaana was looking more hopeful. "It's not just that a girl who's had her little man smashed feels useless, it's how the boy feels, too. You're different – you're angry with Jerem, not with Aila, and if you manage to find her she'll know that, without you even having to say. If she even hears that you're seriously trying to find her, she'll know it. It still won't be easy for her. It's one thing to know something in your head, it's quite another what you feel."

"Will I be able to persuade her, do you think?"

Yaani was thoughtful. "If anyone could, you can, Owen. But how on earth will you find her? She could be anywhere. There are a million pebbles on the hill."

Graamon was thoughtful, too. "There's one question that's not easy to ask, but it has to be asked. Does anyone know how Jerem is? Be that as it may, how are his family reacting?"

"That's easy to answer. Gamaara's sister Mashaari came here the day Aila went missing. It's a pity she didn't come sooner, but she didn't hear the story for a couple of days, and then she had to find out where we lived. Jerem's survived, but he won't try to rape anyone ever again. She smashed his knees so thoroughly he'll be on crutches for the rest of his life if he can ever walk again at all, and serve him right. He's not right in the head, either – never was, really, from what I've heard, but he can't even talk straight any more. But the family are very good, they're not angry with Aila at all. Mashaari was all apologies and wanting to know what they could do to help."

Yaani had made a huge omelette with about twenty auk eggs and some onions. We ate in silence, all of us deep in thought.

How on earth do I even begin to look for her? Will she still be in Laanoha, or will she have gone to Meyroha, or Barioha, or somewhere else entirely? How will she be living? Will she have found another nannying job somewhere? How will I live while I'm looking for her? If I give up my job to go looking, will I have to give up my railway papers? Will anyone be able to help me? Or at least give me some idea of where and how to look?

Graamon realized I'd be having some of those thoughts. "Don't worry about your job, Owen. It'll still be there for you when you've found Aila. In fact, you won't stop being a railway man for a moment. Your papers are valid for life – once a railway man, always a railway man, even after you retire. Nobody will ask where you are, that's entirely my business. You're my assistant. You won't stop thinking about railway matters anyway – or research institute matters, and that's just as important to me really. Get a notebook and pencils at the railway office tomorrow, then you can take notes of whatever you've been thinking about. But don't worry about it. Worry about finding Aila. And don't worry about money, either. You're a railway man. Any major business will bill the railway for whatever you need, and you can pick up your weekly coins for little things at any railway office, or even have an advance if you need one."

"I don't even know where the railway offices are. There isn't one in Briggi, is there?"

"Oh, goodness, that's something I should have explained before. The Railwayyard inn is the railway office in Briggi. I can get coins there when I need them, but I don't often because everyone in Briggi just bills the railway anyway. The inn at Belgaam is a railway office, too. Here in Laanoha we've got our own office in the guards' building at the docks, just beside the line that runs down to the dockside. You know where it is, don't you, Grim? Could you show him tomorrow? I really ought to go and make my presence felt in Meyroha. The yard here seems to be on top of things very nicely. I'll catch the first Meyroha train in the morning. I'll keep in touch here through Peyr or any of the drivers so you can catch my tail when you're ready, Owen, or any time you need me. I'll be back here in about a week's time, most probably. The best way to learn where the offices are in Barioha and Meyroha would be to get Peyr to introduce you to one of the mainline drivers, and get them to show you."

Grim wanted to know when his Dad was coming.

"He's expected first train tomorrow – he was going to be the next one after us. So about three tomorrow afternoon."

"Couldn't he show Owen the offices? I really ought to be at work tomorrow."

Yaana said that there were times when she really wished she had papers. "I know my way down to the guards' office at the docks, but I don't know the way from there on, I've never been. I couldn't go if I did know the way. I'm pretty sure Owen already knows the way that far."

I did. I realized for the first time that Yaana could only get in and out of Laanoha the same way I used to, under the cab floor. *What a way to treat an old lady. I wonder how often she does that, whether she's done it in recent years at all?*

Yaani had a solution. "You take him to the railway yard, Mum. He could probably find his own way there, but better if you take him and help him find Judd's hidey hole. Judd'll take him down to the offices. It'll be better Judd taking him than Grim, anyway. And he doesn't want to have to wait for Peyr."

"Does Judd know Aila's missing?"

"How could he not? He's been helping us out a lot, with Peyr away. It's Judd who's been bringing us all these auk eggs, and Peyr's coins. It'd be difficult for us without him, he's a real friend."

"How many people do know?"

"Not many. We didn't want to tell people, they'd want to know the whole story, and that could make trouble for her, wherever she is. Jerem's family wouldn't like it much if the story was widely known, either, and they've got influence. But you have got one new clue that we didn't have before. She must have been talking to Birgom, or she wouldn't have mentioned him in your letter. That could even be a deliberate hint. She surely knows you're the kind of man who might come looking for her, and maybe she wants you to, or isn't sure whether she wants you to or not. You should go round to Birgom's tomorrow, I reckon."

"You should talk to Judd, too. He won't have said anything to anybody, but he'll be keeping his ear to the ground. He gets more opportunity to hear gossip than most of us do."

Graamon excused himself, and headed off for his Laanoha lodgings to sort things out for the following day.

"We should all get some sleep. You've got a mountain to climb, Owen. Thank goodness you've got Graamon's wholehearted backing, anyway. And thank goodness Aila's got you!"

"She's got me if I can find her. I wish I was more confident of that than I am. And none of this would have happened if it wasn't for me, it's all my fault."

"No it's not! If it hadn't been you, it would have been someone else eventually, unless she stayed single forever. It's not your fault at all, it's entirely Jerem's fault. We all know that – even Jerem's family knows that for goodness sakes."

It's one thing to know something in your head, it's quite another what you feel.

Grim found my hand as we lay there in the darkness, and held it tight. "You're the best brother I could possibly have. You'll find her. She needs you," he whispered.

"I need her, too."

I'd never seen Jerem, of course. But I knew that the man I saw in my dreams was Jerem, even though he was the Veglid innkeeper. He was stomping along on his crutches at an impossible speed, and I was desperately trying to keep ahead of him. Then I was lying on the bedding pile in the inn in Veglid, and I could hear him stomping about upstairs, the glimmer of his lantern flickering here and there through the cracks in the ceiling.

I knew I was searching for Aila, and I kept thinking I'd found her, but every time when I got close enough she was Maashi. Then she was hitting me over the head with a heavy wooden toy, and I was trying to tell her it was me, it was okay, but my voice wouldn't come.

Grim was shaking me. "Are you okay? You were shouting!"

"Oh, goodness, I'm sorry. I was dreaming. I'm sorry, I must have woken all three of you."

Yaani said, "Well, Gran's still asleep, I think. Don't worry, Owen, we understand. It's a big worry for all of us, but it's only just hit you."

I didn't manage to get back to sleep. I just lay there thinking, wondering how in the world one goes about searching for someone – preferably without telling too many people who or why. How long it would take, and how long I could really just go on being a railway man who wasn't doing anything to do with the railway. *Surely this could take months? Even years? I hope Birgom or Judd have some kind of clue to get me started.*

Gradually the light coming in at the windows overpowered the flickering light of the remains of the fire. Yaana stirred and sat up. I propped myself up on one elbow. "I hope I didn't wake you in the middle of the night," I whispered.

"No, I sleep like old clothes. Peyr says he could drive an engine over me without waking me up. What were you doing?"

"I was shouting in my sleep, dreaming. I hope I don't start doing that a lot, it could be a nuisance. Especially if I say anything I don't want people to know."

Grim snorted. I hadn't realized he was awake. "There's not many people around who know English. I assume that was English."

So I don't dream in Laana. Yet. I've caught myself thinking in Laana more and more lately. I hope I don't start shouting in Laana in my sleep. I hope I don't carry on shouting in my sleep at all.

Yaana got up and started building the fire up. Grim and I got up and went downstairs to get washed. We met Yaani on the stairs as we came back up. "You should have woken me up! It's going to be a rush getting to work!"

"We only woke up a couple of moments ago ourselves, Mum."

I'd actually been awake for hours, but I didn't have a clue what the time was. How they knew, I didn't know.

Grim and Yaani went off to work. Yaana and I set off for the railway yard.

"They don't feel like going to work with Aila missing, but life has to go on. If Aila comes back, it's no use to her if everything's falling to bits back at home as well. Having you, with Graamon's backing, to go looking for her is a miracle for us."

"If I can find her. There's a million pebbles on the hill. And I don't even know which hill to search. She'd never have gone missing if it wasn't for me."

"There's a million pebbles, but they're all different. There's only one Aila. Well, only one Riish Aila."

That answers one of the questions I've never asked. "That's something I was going to ask you about. How do family names work here? Are you and Yaani Riish, too?"

"Yes, of course we are. Ever since we married, both of us. And Aila will be – oh! I don't know what your family name is!"

"That's a long story. It's Mezhab – now. It was Morley, back in England, but we changed it. Baamoon said it wasn't a good idea to be called Mor Liiauen, and I rather agreed. In England I was Owen Morley, but that's even more confusing here."

It took Yaana a few moments to get her head round that, but not long. "Oh! I see. You put your names the wrong way round."

There's nothing wrong with the brains in this Riish family! And thank goodness for that.

"But you're Mezhab Owen now. I like that. How did you choose Mezhab? Did you know it's Birgom's name – and Viilam's?"

"Yes, that's how I chose it. There's something about Birgom, I felt it the once I met him. It's not just that he knows English, I don't think. And then Viilam was stuck in Briggi at the same time I was, so we asked him what he thought Birgom would think, and he said they'd both be pleased to have me in the family. I was touched. I hope Aila will be happy with it!"

"I'm sure she will. There's something about Birgom, you're right. And Aila's always had a soft spot for him – maybe because he's always had a soft spot for Aila, ever since she was a baby. I'll take you up to Birgom's place when you get back from the railway office. I'll be back in the room, I'll go straight back once you're with Judd."

But Judd wasn't in his workshop, and we couldn't see him working on any of the engines. "That's odd. It's not his day off."

Yaana was about to ask one of the other workshopmen where he was, when Jinni appeared. "Jinni! You don't know where Judd is, do you?"

"No. I was just coming to look for him myself. He wants to talk to me, Parruk told me. He must have popped out somewhere for some reason, I expect he'll be back soon."

"Actually, are you busy? You'll do just as well as Judd anyway." Yaana continued softly, "Could you take Owen down and show him where the railway office is? You know I can't."

"Of course, it's no trouble. I'm sure whatever Judd wanted me for will wait."

Then Yaana realized, "Of course! You only got here last night. It was your train Graamon and Owen were on. I expect you were at Parruk's last night, I don't suppose you saw your mother. I think we know what Judd wanted you for. You tell her on your way, Owen."

Yaana headed out of the yard in the direction of home. Jinni and I met Judd coming in as we were going out of the other gate. "Oh! Are you just going somewhere? I wanted to talk to you, Jinni. Well, both of you really, but you'll know the main thing now."

"I've not told Jinni yet. We've only just bumped into each other."

"Where are you headed? Should I come with you? There's nothing much I'm needed for here just now, the others are doing your engine, Jinni."

"I know, I saw. It needs it. Five weeks is a long time, and it's not even been sitting idle. We're just off to the office, to introduce Owen. He's a proper Railway man now."

"I can see that. Congratulations! I knew you would be, though. I'll come with you."

"Anyway, Owen, how's Aila? She must be very pleased to see you."

"That's what I – we – have to tell you, Jinni. We don't know where she is. She's missing. She only stayed at home for three days, then just disappeared. She left me a letter."

"Oh Owen! That's terrible. What are you going to do? What did she say in the letter?"

"I was going to ask you that, too. Yaana showed me the letter, but obviously I didn't want to open it, since it was addressed to you."

"She said she can't marry me – if she can't even look after the little me, how can she look after the big me? She said she'll love me forever, but that I must look for someone else who can look after me better."

"Well, that is the tradition. The idea of the little people is that you have to look after them like you'd look after the big person. But I'd have thought Aila would be more independent minded than that."

"It's one thing to know something in your head, it's quite another what you feel. So what are you going to do?"

"Try and find her, of course, and try to persuade her to change her mind. From what I've heard, she can look after me better than anyone else could. But whether she could or not, I love her, which is what really matters."

"It is, it is. And she says she'll love you forever, and I'm sure she means it, too. But where will she have gone to? Who knows?"

"I was hoping you two might have some ideas. I really don't have much clue at all. The only thing I've got to go on at all is that she said Birgom wanted to talk to me. I knew Birgom wanted to talk to me anyway, and I wanted to talk to him, too – but Aila made a point of it at the end of her letter. She must have talked to him during the three days she was at home. I want to go round there today. Maybe he'll have some ideas. I don't know where he lives, but Yaana says she'll take me round there when I get back from the office."

"It'd be quicker if I take you straight there from the office, then I'll go and let Yaana know what's going on. We mustn't forget that Peyr's arriving this afternoon, and he won't know what's happened yet. It'd be good if you and I were at his place, or maybe at the railway yard to meet him."

Judd thought it would be better if Jinni and I were at the room, and Judd met him at the railway yard. "I'll tell him quietly on the way up."

To get to the railway office, we had to go through the dockyard gate. The guard looked me up and down. "You're a railway man? You're new. Let's see your papers."

I got the distinct impression that he couldn't read, but he knew what railway papers should look like. Mine clearly looked right. He didn't even look at Jinni's or Judd's papers. *They're familiar faces.*

In the railway office, Judd introduced me. "Maarim, this is Owen. He's Graamon's new assistant." He turned to me. "Show Maarim your papers, Owen."

"Mezhab Owen? You a relation of Viilam's? I didn't know he had any relatives other than his grandad."

Graamon had prepared me for this. "No, it's just a coincidence. I'm not from round here at all."

Maarim laughed. "Nor is Viilam's grandad, I don't think! I don't know where he is from though, and I don't suppose it would mean much to me if I did. Are you from the same place?"

"I don't know. I don't know where he's from."

"I daresay you'll be wanting your coins from me while you're in Laanoha. How much do you get?"

What a difference from England. Here, he trusts me to tell him what my pay should be – he knows there's no sense me lying, I'd get found out, and then not only would it get corrected, I'd get into trouble, too. In England, I'd have to manage without any money until the paperwork came through.

"Fifty a week."

Maarim wrote it down in a big book he pulled out from a shelf under the desk. "You want some now?"

"Yes, please."

More scribbling, and a handful of coins.

"Oh, and could I have a pocket notebook and a couple of pencils, too, please."

Maarim went to a cupboard at the back of the office. "Have you got a sharpener?"

"Oh, no. That would be useful!"

The sharpener was a tiny pen-knife with a concave blade. *So that's what that pocket is for.* It fitted perfectly, as did the notebook and pencils. *A pocket for everything. I wonder what the others are for? No doubt I'll find out eventually.*

"Nice to meet you, anyway, Owen. You staying at the Railwayyard inn while you're in Laanoha?"

"No, I'm staying with Peyr's family. We're old friends."

"Oh, okay. I should give you another ten coins to give them, then. And don't forget there's meals and drinks for you at the Railwayyard inn whenever you want them."

Maarim handed me another two five coin pieces. *I suppose I'll learn how all these things work in the end. Everything is so relaxed compared with England.*

Umm. If you've got papers. Not so good if you haven't, of course.

I thanked Maarim, and we left. Judd headed back to the railway yard, and Jinni led me through the back lanes to where

Birgom lived, not far from where Aila had taken me down to the shore when we went out to the point. "I'll just say hello, then I'll leg it back to tell Yaana what's going on."

Birgom was visibly pleased to see me. "Come in, come in. You too, Jinni. I've skiir by the fire."

"I can't stay, Birgom, I've got to go and talk to Yaana. I just came to show Owen where you live."

"Well, you come another time, when you can. I'd like to talk to you sometime, too!"

Birgom's house was tiny. It had a single small room downstairs, with just enough headroom for Birgom to stand up. Birgom told me that upstairs was Viilam's room, but I never saw it. Judging by what the house looked like from outside, if there was standing room upstairs at all, it was only right in the middle of the room.

But it was cosy in that downstairs room. Birgom sat me down in one of the two chairs by the fire, and lowered himself carefully into the other. Then he leant forward and poured two mugs of warm skiir.

"It's been a long time. You must have been snowed in in Briggi. Viilam too, obviously."

"How do you manage without Viilam?"

"Oh, I manage. I can get up to the market all right, and that's the only thing I actually have to do. It's nice when he can help me on stairs so I can go visiting, but I can live without. It's nice when people visit me, too. I wish it was better business you were here for, but what happened, happened. You can't change the past. How much do you know?"

"About Aila? I know about what Jerem did, and how Aila went north with Berraami and then back home with Faahiha, and was at home for three days and then went missing. That's pretty much all I know."

"Aila doesn't know whether Jerem's alive or dead, unless she's found out since she went. And she doesn't know his knees are smashed and that they're saying she did it, either."

"That's something that puzzled me, too. Berraami said Aila had told her she'd hit him round the head with one of the children's toys, a heavy one, and knocked him out and maybe killed him, but she didn't mention smashing the knees. The first time I heard that was from Yaana, I think, or maybe Yaani, I don't remember. Here, anyway."

"They heard it from Mashaari, after Aila had left. Aila described the whole fight to me though, in detail. I'm perfectly certain she'd have told me if she'd broken his knees. I've not said anything to Yaani and Yaana, because it'd just make things worse for them, but you need to know – assuming you're going to try to find Aila. I just know you are, you're not tied by traditions you didn't even grow up with. I was a bit surprised that Aila felt as bad as she seemed to, but it's one thing to know something in your head, it's quite another what you feel."

"So who did smash Jerem's knees? And why would Mashaari lie about it? Yaani says that the family aren't blaming Aila at all."

"I'm sure Mashaari believes what she said. Probably Gamaara believes it too. From what I hear, they're both as straight as sunbeams. I'm pretty sure it must have been Jerem's father who smashed his knees for him. That man is notorious for his temper, and he'd have been pretty angry with Jerem for messing with Aila. Then he wouldn't want to admit that he'd done it, and it would be awfully convenient for him to say Aila had, with Jerem himself a gibbering idiot now anyway. But I think it's true that no-one's blaming Aila. Everyone says it was entirely self defence – although how you can bash someone that hard round the head and smash both their knees as well, all in self-defence, I'm not sure."

"Everyone? I thought not many people knew at all."

"Oh, I mean everyone who knows. It's all been kept pretty quiet, yes. If it could be proved, I'd love to see Jerem's father in boiling oil for what he did. I really am sure it must have been him. But for Aila's sake I'd rather it was all kept as quiet as possible, and if that means letting him get away with it, so be it."

"Do you have any idea where Aila might have got to? I'm really at a loss to know where to look."

"I can imagine. I remember what it was like when I first arrived here myself. But yes, I've got some ideas about how you can start. But Aila won't want you to look for her – or she'll be in two minds about it, anyway. Even if she doesn't want you to look for her, I'm pretty sure she'll be glad that you did if you find her, although she might not realize it herself at first. It's one of those 'it's one thing to know something in your head, it's quite another what you feel' things, I suspect – and I don't even know which is which."

'I remember what it was like when I first arrived here myself.' What is Birgom's history? But I don't want to ask him just now.

Birgom told me that Mashaari had offered to help find Aila another job as a nanny somewhere else. "But Aila doesn't know about that, because she'd already gone before Mashaari came. Yaani and Yaana didn't know she'd gone. She'd only been gone a few hours and they thought she'd be back soon. They hadn't found the letter then, and anyway they didn't know it was a letter for you until they showed it to Judd and he read your name on the outside.

"I don't think Aila would want Mashaari's help anyway. I think she'd trust Mashaari to be on her side, but she'd rather go somewhere where Jerem's family wouldn't know where she was. She presumably doesn't know how disabled Jerem is, so she'd be worried about him finding her – and if she does somehow know the whole story, she'll be worried about Jerem's father. He wouldn't do anything to her himself, but he's a wealthy man. He can afford to pay someone else to do his dirty work for him."

"So it's not just me she's run away from, then – it's Jerem's family, too, whatever they say about not blaming Aila."

"Oh, I'm sure Jerem's father doesn't blame Aila either. But he might well be afraid of her telling people she never smashed Jerem's legs. And she'll realize that as soon as she knows his legs are smashed."

"So he must be trying to keep Jerem's smashed legs a secret, then. That's surely his first line of defence."

"Difficult for him, without telling his wife why, and he won't want to do that. But he knows that none of the family will want to make too much noise about it, the whole story is quite embarrassing for them. But they can't hide Jerem's condition from other people in their social circle."

I suddenly realized that we were talking Laana, although his English was much better than my Laana, and he'd seemed so keen to talk English with me before. I wondered why, but this wasn't the time to talk about that.

"If I've got a chance of finding her, then surely Jerem's father's man will be able to find her more easily than I can. That's a bit scary."

"It is, a bit, but maybe not as scary as you think. For one thing, you'll recognize her more easily. Jerem's father would know her himself, of course, but anyone he hires will only have a description and a name."

"I hadn't thought about that. You think she'll use a false name? What about her papers?"

"I'm sure she'll use a false name. There are lots of people here without papers – Yaana, just for example. She talks like a local, nobody will ask any questions as long as she doesn't go anywhere you might have to show papers. But of course people know Aila around Laanoha, so unless she's somehow changed her appearance, someone somewhere might give her whereabouts away. But it's only in Laanoha and Meyroha you need papers anyway. She won't be in Meyroha, you can't slip down the cracks there. My best guess is Barioha, but she might think that's too obvious. She could be in any of the smaller towns."

"And calling herself anything. That makes it pretty hard!"

"It makes it even harder for Jerem's father's man, if he exists."

"I'm beginning to really hope he doesn't exist. Or worse still, more than one of them."

"I think there's a very good chance he doesn't exist, but you need to be wise to the possibility. But how can you afford to spend time looking for her? I can see by your outfit that Peyr was right, and that Graamon's taken you on to work for the railway."

"Graamon knows what's happened, and says I just have to get on and find Aila, and not to worry about the job. He's right behind me. In England they'd call it 'indefinite paid leave', and it would be a miracle, especially for someone as new in the job as me."

"It's not much short of a miracle here. Graamon must have a very high opinion of you. He's a bit of a law unto himself, they can't afford to upset him and he knows they know it."

Birgom suddenly switched into English. "You know, I'd forgotten you were English. It's amazing how much your Laana has improved. I was sort of conscious you were a foreigner in the back of my mind, but I'd quite forgotten about the language issue."

"I hadn't thought about it at first, then a little while ago I realized we were talking Laana, but didn't want to say anything about it, other things seemed much more important."

"Other things are much more important. We've got lots to talk about sometime, but now's not the time."

He switched back into Laana. "It's probably best if we stick with Laana for the moment anyway. Even though your Laana is pretty good now, you need all the practice you can get – and in particular, there could be words or expressions related to your search that you don't know and might need, that we'd not think of if we talk English."

"I'm still wondering how I start looking, even if I've decided to look in a particular place. Just wandering the streets hoping to see her seems pretty hopeless."

"Of course. There'll obviously be some wandering the streets involved, but not just hoping to see her. You've got to try to work out how the place ticks, think where a young woman trying to earn a decent living would find herself, then watch there. Find out what time people come and go. And you're going to have to do some asking, there's no avoiding that. People will wonder what you're doing, anyway. But you may want to be less conspicuous. You need some less fancy clothes and shoes. Your papers are enough to get you everywhere, you don't want to look the part too. Get Judd to take you to the tailors, he'll know what to ask for. Or Peyr."

There was a soft knocking at the door. Birgom started to get up, then sat down again. "That sounds like Yaana's knock to me. You let her in, Owen."

It was Yaana, and Jinni too. Yaana started to get down onto the floor by the fire, but Birgom stopped her. "You sit in the chair, Yaana. The youngsters can sit on the floor! Get them a mug of skiir, Owen."

I found some mugs on a shelf in the corner, and did as I was told.

Yaana had tears in her eyes. She started to try to say something, then gave up. Jinni took hold of her hand, and took over. "So. What's the plan of action?"

"Did Gran tell you that Graamon's given me paid leave for as long as it takes to find Aila? I'm going in search."

"Yes, she told me. That's one piece of very good news. But what's the plan for the search?"

"We've barely begun to think about it. You can probably help us quite a lot. What would a young woman needing to earn a decent living in a strange place do? And how will she choose where to go?"

"The key word there is 'decent'. She's a pretty girl of a certain age. If she's not careful, as soon as she appears the least bit lost in a strange place, there'll be pimps watching her, ready to pounce. But she's no fool, she knows that. She'd only have to beat one of them up to get them to leave her alone, and we know she can do that if she has to, but it would draw attention to her. She'll do her level best never to appear lost. The easy way to do that would be to go straight to the fanciest house she could find and try to get a nannying job. If they didn't need a nanny themselves, there's a good chance they'd know who did. And she's got a good reputation as a nanny."

We'll have to tell Jinni about Birgom's worries about Jerem's father. But we don't want to say anything in front of Yaana. What to do?

Birgom was obviously having the same thought. "She doesn't know the family aren't blaming her. We think she'll probably be using a false name, so she won't be showing anyone her papers in the normal way of things."

That'll do for the moment. Jinni needs to know more when we get a chance, though. I think.

"If that's true, that'll make it much harder for her. Outside Laanoha and Meyroha, nobody would think about papers, but getting a nannying job under a false name would be hard, with no history and no connections. And anyway, you never know who knows whom or who visits whom among the rich. She'd be spotted by someone. She might still go straight to a fancy house, but she'd be looking for a cleaning or cooking job, not nannying. Or she might try to get a labouring or sweatshop job. But whatever she does, she's got to find her way to the right place without looking lost while she's finding her way, and that means asking someone. She'd ask the first reliable person she could find. If she arrived by railway, the innkeeper at the railway inn – but we'd soon know if she caught a lift with an engine driver, and she wouldn't for that reason. Gran reckons she didn't have enough money on her to get a coach or a passenger train, so unless she earnt some in Laanoha before she left, she either walked or got a cooking job on a boat. Unless she's still somewhere in Laanoha, of course."

"If she's left Laanoha, she'll have had to show her papers to a guard somewhere, won't she?"

"Not necessarily. She wouldn't be worried about us finding her that way – she knows we wouldn't go asking the guards. But if she's worried about Jerem or his family looking for her, and I think she would be, she'd know they'd be quite capable of asking guards. It's not so hard to get in and out of Laanoha without, though. Under the floor of an engine isn't the only way!"

"So you think it's likely she got a job on a boat?"

"I'd say it's about equally likely she did that, or got a job in Laanoha for a little while, and then got a coach. But I think if she got a coach, she probably caught it in Kromaan, not Laanoha. There have been a couple of foggy days recently, and on a foggy day at low tide you can walk round the point and along the riverside below the quays to get to the ferry without the guards even seeing you."

Birgom seized on that quickly. "That's an idea worth following up, Jinni. Good thinking. The coach drivers would probably remember an unfamiliar girl catching a coach in Kromaan on a foggy morning. Especially one with muddy boots. And there's no harm asking the coach drivers, it's not like asking guards."

"She wouldn't have muddy boots, Birgom! She'd wash it off before she even got to the ferry. I bet you would, Owen, wouldn't you!"

"If I thought of it, certainly. But I might not think. I guess you're right that Aila would, though."

Up to this time, Yaana had said not a word, but had gradually been looking a little brighter. "You're sure she's okay, Birgom?"

"Oh, we'd have heard by now if she'd beaten up a pimp, Yaana!"

I hope Jinni's right about that. I can imagine pimps being less easy to beat up than Jerem – and quite likely to be carrying knives, too. But Jinni's probably right that Aila would try very hard to avoid situations like that. Even when running away in a state of desperation.

"If she went by coach after earning some money, she's likely to have gone very recently. It was foggy three days ago, and before that the last foggy day was probably too soon after she went missing. I'd say it's worth chasing that one as soon as you can. Tomorrow morning first thing, get the first train to Kromaan. If she got a job on a boat, she went more than three weeks ago, it won't make any difference leaving that a few more days."

"I'll do that. If she went by boat, what can I possibly do to trace her?"

"I'm pretty sure she won't have wanted to go far. She won't have wanted to go anywhere where she doesn't know the language. So it would only be a coaster or a riverboat – and there's not a lot of casual work on riverboats, so it's really just a coaster. I don't think there'd be much point asking on the boats themselves, but she'd have landed at one of the ports. She'd have enquired about work in the town at the port office."

I was beginning to feel this wasn't an impossible quest after all. We talked things over for another hour or so, and then Birgom suggested that I should go and get Judd help me to get some different clothes.

"They won't be ready for a few days though, will they? I can't get a tailor to make me things in an afternoon!"

"Oh, goodness. People like Judd, or the man you're trying to look like, don't get things tailored to fit – not in Laanoha. It'll be ready made, you'll pick it up on the spot."

"Gran and I'll come with you to the railway yard, Owen. Then we'll go home and you follow as soon as you've got an outfit."

"Thank you so much for your help, Birgom. You can't imagine how much I appreciate it."

"Yaana knows I'd do anything for Aila. I wish there was more I could do."

Judd started to take me to the place where he got his own clothes, and then stopped. "You don't want to look like a workshop man on a day off, or a driver. It's probably best if you don't look like a railway man at all. You need to look so ordinary that no-one will wonder who you are and what you're doing – not rich, but not the kind of person who's tied to a rota that you're obviously missing. I know where we should go. I think they'll bill the railway okay if you show them your papers."

We headed up towards the Castle, an area of town I'd never been in before, although I roughly remembered the layout I'd seen looking back from the top of the headland when I went up there with Aila, the day we'd realized we belonged to each other. It seemed so long ago.

There was a street of shops unlike any in the parts of town I knew. They didn't have open fronts, they had rows of glass windows, many of them bow-fronted, and glazed double doors. Judd took me into one of them. Inside the front doors there was a small lobby with a matting floor, then another pair of double doors before we got into the shop. It was warm inside, more like a home than a business. A smartly dressed young woman took our coats, and disappeared with them into a door marked PRIVATE. She returned a moment later and stood beside the door where she'd been when we arrived.

I realized Judd was as lost as I was. The young woman obviously realized the same thing at the same moment. She approached us again. "Can I help? You don't seem to know where to go."

"We need smart casual clothes for Owen here. Nothing too smart, he doesn't want to look out of place anywhere, really."

"Ebi floor. Just ring the bell on the counter when you get there if there's no-one around. There are the stairs." She pointed to the stairs, which were plainly visible anyway. They were carpeted – the first carpets I'd seen since I left England. It wasn't until I noticed the carpets than I noticed the rest of the floor in the shop – the same unslippery shiny smooth finish I'd seen at Siroha.

There were more oil lamps than I'd ever seen in one place before. Each had its own glass chimney that disappeared into a hole in the ceiling.

A man met us at the top of the stairs. He was wearing a collarless grey suit that wouldn't have looked out of place on a teacher in an expensive school in London. He had a tape measure round the back of his neck, dangling down the front of his jacket. "For you, young man? I heard what you wanted. You're a Railway man, by the look of you, but I don't know you, so I hope you won't be offended if I ask to see your papers?"

"Of course, no problem." I showed them to him.

"Mezhab Owen? You're not related to Birgom, are you?"

"No, it's a coincidence. But I do know him."

"I should think everybody on the railway knows him – all the Laanoha railwaymen, anyway. You're not from Laanoha, though, I can tell that. But let's see what you need, anyway."

An hour later when we came out of the shop, I was wearing a new outfit – plain loose-legged trousers, a loose shirt that covered me halfway down my thighs, and a long warm overcoat buttoned up to my throat. I had a new rucksack, bigger then the one Judd had lent me but not as big as my English one, with my railway outfit, two spare shirts and a spare pair of trousers in it.

Halfway down the hill, Judd suddenly laughed. "Blimey. I wish I had papers like those. He didn't even ask you how many of everything you wanted! And he's done exactly what's needed. You could be any middle-class gent on holiday. A teacher, a middle-ranking bureaucrat – almost anything. But not rich, not Railway, and not a working man who'd attract attention if he seemed to be away from his work too much. Spot on."

"I wonder how he knows Birgom?"

"I've seen him before. I think he lives somewhere down near Birgom."

"It's odd to think of someone like him living down there. Somehow I'd imagined he'd live somewhere round here."

"Oh, in a job like his he couldn't afford to live round here. These shops aren't like the shops in our part of town, where the shopkeeper is the owner and lives over his shop. The people who work in these shops don't get paid very well at all, and the owners are rich. They live in posh houses, some further up right under the Castle, maybe some over on the point. You'll have seen the posh houses over there?"

"Yes, Aila took me up there. Ages ago. How much of the railway's money do you think we just spent?"

"I really don't know. Maybe two hundred and fifty coins, maybe three hundred, but I've never bought that kind of clothes. A lot less than your proper railway clothes, anyway."

"Do you have to buy your own clothes?"

"Well, I'd have to if I wanted to wear anything other than workshop clothes. But I just wear work clothes all the time, like most people do, so the railway buys them for me. But I know what they cost."

We walked together as far as my street, then Judd went down towards the railway yard, and I turned the other way to go home. *Home? Is this home, or is Viina's place home? Both. But I'm a paying guest here now. That's good in some ways, but I think I preferred it when I paid my way by helping Yaana. No time for that now, though.*

Yaana and Jinni had already had a late lunch by the time I arrived. "Yours is cold, I'm afraid. I'll reheat it. Peyr won't be long now. I wish we could hear the whistles from here, but we can't. Well, you can if you open the south window, but in this weather you don't want to have that open all the time."

I looked out of the window. It had started to snow. Jinni had noticed, too. "Did it snow down here while we were stuck up in Briggi, Gran?"

"A bit, but it only settled overnight a couple of times. It was raining a lot. They said the line was a bit iffy through the mountains for a day or two. They were running short trains and triple heading up the escarpment for a couple of days, but no-one got stuck."

I gave Yaana the two fives Maarim had said were for my accommodation. I felt a bit mean. I knew it was much less than the railway would pay the inn if I stayed there, but Yaana seemed pleased enough. "We don't really expect anything, you're family. But if they give you this for us, we'll not refuse it!"

If I'm family, I should pay my share of the rent and the housekeeping like everybody else. But they won't want to take it, and I don't want to argue with anyone over it. Difficult. But I won't be here all that long or all that often any more.

It was probably about an hour later that Peyr and Judd arrived. I could tell by Peyr's face that Judd had already told him. "What can I say?" he said as they sat down.

Jinni gave them each a mug of warm skiir without a word. We all sat in silence for some time, then Jinni reached out, put her hand on Peyr's forearm, and squeezed gently. "She'll be fine. Owen'll find her, and all will be well."

"I hope you're right, Jinni. I hope you're right."

I hope she's right, too, I thought, but I didn't say anything.

After a while Peyr pulled himself upright in his chair resolutely. "Well, Owen, unless your plans have changed since what Judd told me, you want to catch Faahiha's train at four tomorrow morning. It's a bit early, you'll be hanging around freezing in Kromaan for a couple of hours, but the next train misses the first coaches, and you'll want to talk to as many coach drivers as you can. I'm free for the next couple of days, of course, I could come with you, but it's probably better if you're on your own really. Nobody will know it's Aila you're looking for, whereas someone might put two and two together if I'm with you. And don't forget, you'll be catching Faahiha's train in the yard, not by the line side, and you won't have to hide under the floor!"

Everybody laughed, but it didn't last long.

He went on, "And coming back, it's best if you get the coach into Laanoha from wherever you end up, unless you're actually at a station. It's one thing stopping a train to drop someone off, or picking someone up who you know is going to be there. It's another stopping for someone you weren't expecting. Some drivers might stop, some won't, and nobody will be impressed if they think you stopped them for no good reason. You won't know when you want to come back until you're on your way, so they can't be expecting you. You'll have to pay for coaches, the railway doesn't have arrangements with the coach drivers."

I felt a little hurt for a moment, but realized Peyr knew I needed to know.

Yaana asked me how much money I'd got, then gave me the two fives back. "We don't need these, and you might. That's my grand-daughter you're rescuing."

And my fiancée, but she's right. I might need more than fifty coins, I've no idea.

Grim and Yaani arrived just as it was getting dark. Judd filled them in on the day's events while Jinni and Yaana served out steaming bowls of fish and vegetable stew. I'd scarcely even been aware that they'd been making it.

Peyr was nodding as Judd spoke, then he turned to me. "Graamon must have told you about Baam, since it's Biiniha's old room you've got. You could go and introduce yourself to Baam, if you need any help in Barioha any time. You might never go there, and if you do, it seems quite likely you'll be back here at least once first, but in case you're not, I'll describe how to get to his place for you."

It wasn't straightforward, so I got my notebook and pencil out of my rucksack, and got him to repeat it while I took notes. I realized later that I'd written them in a mixture of Laana and English – Laana for things Peyr had actually said, such as street names, and English for my own explanations.

"Are you sure he wouldn't mind? Do you know him, or just know about him from Graamon?"

"Oh, we all know Baam quite well. He's been going up to Briggi three or four times a year for years. He nearly always goes by goods train – Graamon's best friends mostly do. You can tell him everything, and he'll be very willing to help. If Aila's in Barioha, Biiniha could be very useful too. She could go places you couldn't."

As soon as we'd finished eating, Jinni excused herself. "I really ought to go and see Mum. She'll have heard I'm back. She'd understand me spending last night at Parruk's, of course, but she'll be wondering where I've got to by now. I might see you in the morning, Owen, but in case I don't – good luck!"

She gave me a kiss on the cheek, pressed something into my hand, and was gone.

It was a little packet with five fives in it.

We didn't talk late into the night. Everyone was tired and I had to be off to the railway yard not long after three in the morning. I didn't get to sleep very quickly though, thinking about all the things I didn't know but probably needed to. *I know a lot more now than I did when I landed at Sirimi.* But that thought didn't help much.

Chapter 12

Faahiha dropped me off at Kromaan at about half past four in the morning. I knew the first coaches weren't due to leave until seven, but that then there were four due to leave in different directions. There were three coaches parked outside an inn – I guessed probably Kromaan's only inn – a stone's throw from where Faahiha left me. I guessed the fourth coach would be arriving from somewhere – presumably somewhere not far away, unless it was an overnight service. I didn't even know whether such services existed.

At least I didn't have to hang around freezing. The innkeeper had heard the train stop and start again, and came out to see what was going on. He saw me walking up the street, and called softly, "You catching a coach somewhere later on? Come into the warm to wait. Have you had breakfast? I've just started making it."

I had, but that was nearly two hours earlier, and I'd got cold walking down to the railway yard. Faahiha's fire had helped a lot, but my feet were still cold.

"I have, but that was hours ago and I'm cold and another one sounds wonderful."

"Okay. I'll do you a small one then. You don't want to be too full riding in a coach. Have some hot skiir while you're waiting, anyway."

I assumed that this inn would be a place I'd have to pay in coins, and wondered how much the bill would be. *I've got to learn these things, and it's not going to break the bank.*

Breakfast was in two sittings. I ate my half breakfast with the coach drivers and the innkeeper and his family.

One of the coach drivers turned to me, "Where are you headed, then, young man?"

"Maybe back into Laanoha, I don't actually know yet. I'm trying to find a young lady..."

I was interrupted before I could go on. "Aren't we all!"

Laughter, but the innkeeper's wife looked daggers at the men. "Gentlemen – if I can call you that! The children are here! I

think he probably meant a *particular* young lady, didn't you,
young man?"

I mentally translated the word she used as 'particular', and
was glad that it didn't have the same double meaning as in
English.

"Indeed I did, Madam, and thank you. She's quite small, not
much bigger than your daughter, and quite slender, and of course
she'd be a stranger around here. She'd most likely have come
four days ago, the morning it was very foggy. I don't know
whether she came this way at all, but if she did, I'd be most
grateful if you could tell me. I'd like a ride to wherever she
went."

The three coach drivers agreed that none of them had had
such a passenger that day, or indeed recently at all. "Preysh will
be here with the Karrem coach from Laanoha soon. She could
have been one of his. Seems fairly likely, in fact. That was four
days ago, so it was Preysh that morning. From what you said, I
guess she probably used the foggy morning to evade the guards
coming out of Laanoha, then she might have caught Preysh on
the ferry.

"I can see by your face I'm right. I can read you like a book,
mister."

Laughter again, this time more from the innkeeper's wife than
anybody else. "That's good coming from you, Boorman. Read a
book? If only."

Boorman himself was laughing too. "You want to be glad
we're honest men around here, mister. Any of us could've said
we'd taken her, and taken you for a ride anywhere."

Now it was the innkeeper's turn to laugh. "Honest? I don't
know about that. But you know very well that you'd go hungry
and cold here and probably everywhere else if you were caught
out."

The coach drivers finished their breakfasts and went out to
tend their horses. The innkeeper moved me to a chair by the fire,
and began to set out the passengers' breakfasts.

I stared into the fire for a while. *I wonder if Preysh – this
other Preysh – did pick Aila up? Where is this Karrem place?
How far? How long does it take? How big is it? What would she*

do there? Or does the coach stop anywhere else on the way, or is there anywhere to go on to from there?

The bill was a half coin for a half breakfast, and an eighth for a skiir. *I see. That seems pretty reasonable. I wonder how much coach rides are?*

The innkeeper alerted me to the sound of the Karrem coach arriving. "He'll probably come in here for a skiir, but you'd better go out and meet him in case he doesn't."

It seemed that Aila hadn't caught the Karrem coach, either. The four coaches went their four ways, and I returned to the inn. "Don't worry, son. You'll find her. How likely do you think it is she'd have to got to the ferry by six in the morning, at this time of year? If she really did have to avoid the guards, she must have walked all the way round the foot of the point and along the riverside in the mud under the edge of the quays. In the dark? I think the eleven o'clock coaches are much more likely. There's three of them, and two of them come from Laanoha as well."

The innkeeper started to pour out another skiir. I gestured not to, but he carried on. "On the house. The missus says you're a good man to go after her like this, and I'm to look after you."

They think I'm less well off than I am. I'll accept their generosity for the moment, but I'll remember them. I made a mental note to put a written note in my notebook later.

"You're not from round here at all, are you? Your Laana is pretty good, but it's not your own language."

"True. I'm a very long way from where I come from, but my home's here now. But I don't know my way around very well yet. I'd never heard of Karrem before, for example."

"Oh, Karrem's only a little place. Bigger than Kromaan, but not big. It's about a third of the way to Barioha, just at the foot of the mountains. I guess from the way you arrived that you must have railway friends. Do you know the places on the railway?"

"Between here and Briggi, yes. But I've never been to Barioha or Meyroha."

"Ah, okay. I've never been beyond Belgaam, but I've got relatives there and we've been a few times for family occasions.

Karrem's bigger than Belgaam, but nowhere near as big as Briggi, judging by what people say."

"Where do the other coaches go?"

"Boorman goes into Laanoha, and then goes on west to Iimoni. Juk goes north to Imblim, and then tomorrow goes along the foot of the mountains to Gorb, so his round trip is four days. Emon goes to Baragi and back."

"Does he do that every day?"

"Well, four days out of five, yes. Has done for fifteen years now, apart from three weeks when he was ill a few years ago. The others reduced their services a bit so they could take turns at doing a couple of his. It wasn't too bad, but people got confused about which coaches went where, and when. We ended up with people sleeping all over the place. It was lucky it was summer. If it had been winter we'd have run out of bedding."

"What about the eleven o'clock ones?"

"One of them's Baragi to Laanoha, the others are Laanoha to Griishi and Laanoha to Imblim."

"Then there's more later in the day?"

"Yes, but I think it's most likely your young lady got here in the morning if she used the fog to evade the guards. Of course if she wanted to catch a particular coach later in the day, she could have stayed somewhere else for a few hours, who knows? But she didn't come into the inn. We'll see what the eleven o'clock drivers say."

Aila – or someone matching her description – had caught the Griishi coach at the ferry, but not just four days ago. "That was about three weeks ago, mister. But I noticed her especially, because she was wearing house shoes, and she was freezing. And none of the Griishi regulars seemed to know her at all. I was a bit worried about her, to be honest, but what could I do? She said she wanted to go to Griishi, and she paid for her ride. I got her a hot water bottle from the inn. You probably remember her, Kemmina? I think you were on the coach that day."

"I was. I noticed her especially, too. None of us did know her, you're right, and she obviously didn't know Griishi at all. She was listening intently to all the conversation in the coach, but scarcely said anything herself. She did ask one or two questions, and they seemed to have been carefully thought out first. When we got there, she looked all round, then headed straight for the inn. I've not seen her around Griishi since, and nobody's mentioned her to me."

Two of the six seats in the coach were vacant. "Three and a half coins. One and a half with me in the box, but you don't want to be up there in this weather." I took a seat inside, and Kemmina climbed in and sat opposite me in the other vacant seat. The other passengers had never got out.

I'd no idea what I'd do when I got to Griishi. *I'm sure that was her. I'll listen intently to all the conversation in the coach too, and ask one or two carefully thought out questions. But what happened to her boots? And how did she get enough money for the coach, without working somewhere for a bit first? Berraami was sure she'd run out at Baragi without anything. Sold her boots? It's possible, I suppose – I don't know what's possible in Laanoha. Then tucked her skirt into her knickers, went barefoot through the mud, then washed her feet in the river by the ferry. No wonder she was freezing.* I was pretty sure I'd solved the conundrum, and it wasn't a happy thought.

Despite the big curved springs supporting the coach, it jerked and jolted the whole time.

Kemmina was sitting opposite me, and tried to grill me about Aila, but I pretended to understand Laana less well than I really did, and she accepted that. I didn't glean much from other conversations in the coach. None of the other passengers had been on the coach the day Aila was, and their talk meant nothing to me. I wondered how much more it might have meant to someone who had more context to put it into.

At about two, we stopped for lunch at an inn in a village whose name I forget. Lunch was a good sized piece of fried fish, with vegetables and skiir, and it cost me one and three eighths. *I'll slowly get the hang of money here.* I already knew the price of raw food in the market in Laanoha, from going shopping with Yaana, but that hadn't given me much idea of the prices of things in general.

There was less talk after lunch. Some of the passengers went to sleep. We lurched on.

I tried to watch the countryside, but found the movement of the coach made it very difficult, and it seemed to make my headache worse. *That's annoying. It would be good to get to know what the area is like. I like riding on engines – you can see much better. It's noisy, but the ride is lovely and smooth. Maybe it's better on the roof of a coach. At least I'd be able to see in all directions, and the air would be better. But the driver's right that it would be cold. And the movement would be even more erratic.*

We arrived somewhere just before sunset. Kemmina told me it was Griishi. We seemed to be in the middle of nowhere. All I could see was just an inn and couple of houses, but when I got out I could see that the road became a narrow track between rocks only a few metres beyond the houses. Beyond that the land dropped away, but I could see chimneys sticking up, and beyond them the sea thirty metres or more below us.

The passengers who were awake woke the others, and everybody clambered out. Kemmina grabbed my arm with a gloved hand, and whispered in my ear, "Good luck, young man. I'll come up to the inn later."

I wondered for a moment why on earth she would do that. *She must know more than she wanted to reveal in front of the other passengers, it's the only thing I can think of.* She followed the other passengers over the edge towards the village before I could thank her.

Two lads came out of the inn, and started carrying packages into the inn from the box on the rear of the coach. The driver and I went into the inn.

The innkeeper fed us and skiired us, and then sat by the fire with us. For a short while I just stared into the fire, wondering what on earth to do next. Then the innkeeper spoke.

"Well, it's not often we get strangers here. Do you mind if I ask you who you are, and why you're here?"

"No, I don't mind. In fact, you can probably help me. I'm Owen, and I'm trying to find my young lady. I believe she may have arrived here about three weeks ago, probably looking for work." *I've got to trust someone, risky as it is, and he's surely as good a person to trust as anyone. And I know she came in here – if she was Aila. Surely she was?*

"Does your young lady have a name?"

"She does, but I don't think she'd be using it. I don't know what she'd be calling herself."

Out of the corner of my eye, I saw the driver nodding gently to himself – or maybe to me. I didn't think the innkeeper could see it, and I think the driver would have known that too.

"She didn't come in here, as far as I know. I'll ask my wife if she saw her."

The driver was shaking his head gently. Now I knew it was for my benefit, but what it meant, I wasn't sure.

The innkeeper disappeared into another room. Moments later a young woman appeared with a bowl. Without a word, she sat at a table near us, and started to peel vegetables. I waited for her to say something, but she just sat and worked in silence. *Peeling vegetables after the evening meal? Are they expecting more guests, wanting a late supper? Or will she leave them in water overnight? Seems strange.*

I wanted to ask her if she was the innkeeper's wife, but something held me back. *She can't be. She's less than half his age.*

She finished her peeling, and took the bowl back into what I assumed was a separate kitchen. After a short while an older woman came out. *Ah, now. She **is** the innkeeper's wife. That'll have been their daughter, I expect.*

She came and sat by the fire, and looked at me intently. Then she smiled. "Okay, you really are Owen. I'm pleased to meet you. I'm Kammeni. Your young lady was here. I'm afraid she's not here any more, though, and I don't know where she is. She's a very frightened young lady, you know. She was here for three days, then I think she must have taken a fright. She never said a word about going, but I saw her catch the coach to Karrem. She was calling herself Griima, but I was sure that wasn't her real name. It's not, is it?"

So it really was Aila. There's no reasonable doubt. So I've got to go to Karrem – tomorrow. Kammeni – Kemmina? Sisters? She looks like her.

"No, it's not. But I know how she chose that name."

"Don't worry, I don't want to know her real name. The fewer people know that, the better, I'm sure. It would be good if you could use a false name too, or at least not be too open about it."

"Are you sure she took a fright? Could she simply have been looking for work, and not found any here?"

"It's possible, but I don't think so. The very first day, she came back in the afternoon with a whole bag full of ekraahi and wanted to know if I wanted them. I gave her five coins for them, and they were very popular with the diners. Then she asked me if I'd like some bird's eggs or bird meat or seaweed, and could she borrow a rope? She's a tough one, your young lady – she's a better auker than any of the lads here. Most of them don't even bother these days. She was out on the cliffs all the next day, all on her own, then the day after that she plucked and gutted the lot, about sixty of them. They're drying round the chimney upstairs now, and we've got enough eggs to last us weeks as well. She got on well with our niece, too – and our sons. I was sorry to see her go, but what can you do?"

What can I do indeed? I wonder how far she'll have gone in three weeks? And she's afraid. She really does think Jerem – or his family – could be after her. I wonder if they are?

"Has anyone else been asking about her?"

"Not as far as I know. Have you heard anything, Gobiir?"

"No, I haven't. I've had no strangers in the coach recently apart from her and Owen. And I shan't mention your name, or indeed the fact that I've had strangers on the coach at all, to a soul, Owen. I can tell whose side right is on! I'll mention it quietly to Skiimon to keep quiet, too."

"Skiimon?"

"Oh, of course, you don't know his name. He's the innkeeper at Kromaan. He knows you were looking. He'll have guessed I must have taken your young lady, too, when you caught my coach."

I heard someone in the hallway, and Kemmina came in. She looked all around the room, then came and sat with us by the fire. "I'm sorry. I said too much in the coach. I don't think it'll matter, but I'm not completely certain. I hope it won't."

She turned to Kammeni. "You've realized he's really Owen, too?"

"Yes. Biilam wasn't sure, and sent Kiimi out for her opinion. She was pretty sure, but told me to make absolutely sure. And I am, yes."

"Do you have any idea what she's so scared of?"

"No, but I'm sure you do. She's afraid of someone following her, for whatever reason. She's not scared of you, but she's scared what might happen to you if you follow her, you know that? And she's not one to be easily frightened, I can tell. I saw her on the cliffs. She's no daredevil, she's very careful. But not many boys have the courage to do what she was doing."

"And she doesn't want the rich folks to see her, I've noticed that. That's why I said I hadn't seen her, when of course I had – I suddenly realized who else we'd got in the coach. But she'd left Griishi within a few days. I doubt if either of those two boys know much about anything, but who knows? And I don't remember who was in the coach when she came, do you, Gobiir?"

"No, not really. I only remembered that you were there that day because I remembered you trying to talk to her on the ferry, after she'd asked me where I was going. I don't think there can have been anyone there who made her particularly nervous, though. I remember she put her hood down after Kromaan. I think she was very nervous about the possibility of anyone seeing her at Kromaan."

That figures. But don't say anything!

Kammeni got up. "There'll be diners here soon. I think you should come into the kitchen, Owen. Let them think you're family, if they know you're here at all."

Kemmina came into the kitchen too, leaving Gobiir alone by the fire. He seemed reflective.

Biilam was working at the range, frying meat – bird meat of some sort, by the look of it. He looked round as we came in. "Has anyone arrived yet?"

"No, that was just Kemmina, no-one else. There's only Gobiir out there just now."

Biilam turned to me. "I'm sorry I was so distrusting, but I'm sure you understand."

"I certainly do. Thank you very much for being so careful! I'll be following her tomorrow, of course. Does the Karrem coach leave from here? What time?"

"There's no coach for Karrem tomorrow, it only goes alternate days. One day Karrem to here, next day back again, same as Gobiir from Laanoha, but the alternate days. They never meet each other at all!"

We all laughed for a moment, but not for long. "That has one unfortunate consequence. Falbaash scarcely knows Gobiir at all, and we've not talked about Griima with him. He might have realized he ought to keep quiet about her, but he probably hasn't."

"We'd not said anything to Gobiir, either, and he hadn't realized. Why would they? It's lucky Owen's come before anyone else."

"If anyone else is coming. I think there's a pretty good chance there isn't, but she's right to be worried. They might be."

"If you wait here a whole day, and then catch the Karrem coach, if anyone's suspects that you're looking for her, they'll know you've got reason to think she's gone to Karrem. You could get there just as soon by going back to Kromaan with Gobiir, and then getting the coach to Karrem from Kromaan. Throw them off the trail."

"Yes, but lose his chance to find out if Falbaash knows anything. If anyone here's watching, they've already worked out that's the way she went, surely?"

"Hmm. We know there haven't been any strangers arrived from Kromaan since she did, but they could have come the other way. And the other thing we don't know is whether anyone who isn't a stranger might be involved. To judge by the way it's the rich folks she's wary of, whoever's after her is rich. And you know what the rich are like – all connected. It is someone rich she's scared of, isn't it, Owen?"

There's no point trying to hide it, they know already. "Yes."

"It's likely the Borjiis don't know anything. But they come and go without anyone taking any notice, so they might have heard something without anyone visiting at all. Two of their boys were on your coach just now, Owen."

"What are the Borjiis like?"

"Oh, they're decent people, as rich folks go. They wouldn't touch you themselves, or even pay anyone else to. But they'll tell their rich friends about your movements if they know they're interested and don't realize they're dangerous. Rich folks can be remarkably naïve about how dangerous their friends might be."

"I suppose that's because they're not dangerous to each other, only to little people. And they don't notice when little people disappear."

"Something like that. But let's not dwell on it."

"Sounds as though the Borjiis aren't really a problem in themselves, really. They won't be following me, just leaking information – and that'll take time, and I'll have disappeared again before anyone more dangerous catches hold of my tail. No-one's going to hurt me, as long as I'm on the trail – it's her they want to find. I want to avoid anyone tailing me. Kromaan might be a bad place to go a second time – and I can find out from the driver whether there are any strangers on the Karrem coach, do you think?"

"Whatever you do has its risks. It depends partly how determined they are – rich folks don't have to use the coaches, although they mostly do if they're going far. But they've got their own horses and carriages anyway."

There was a sudden eruption of chattering in the hallway, and Biilam and Kammeni went through into the lounge to greet the diners. The rest of us stayed in the kitchen, and kept our voices down. The diners had no such inhibitions, and were chattering so loudly that they couldn't possibly have caught a word from the kitchen.

"That's rich folks for you. We could listen in to their conversations, no trouble, if it was worth it. Sometimes it's fun, just to hear the gossip."

"They're pretty irritating sometimes, but the money's worth it. Biilam couldn't keep the inn going without them coming for meals. And at least they always book in advance if there's more than two or three of them. They think they're doing the family a big favour – well I suppose they are, but they need the inn here too, and Biilam's not getting rich."

"Griima was amazing. I really miss her, even though she was only here three days. She promised to show me how to go auking – and then she was gone, just like that."

I grinned to myself. *Teenage boy, capable young woman. Griima. Must remember to call her Griima – here, anyway. I've got so used to these people already, I could so easily end up using her real name. Careful!*

"I'd have liked to go auking, too."

"Yes, but you're a girl."

"So's Griima."

"Oh! Yes, that's true. I hadn't thought about that."

Somehow I couldn't see Kiimi clambering around cliffs with nothing but a rope tied at the top to hang onto with one hand while she caught birds and collected eggs with the other. She wasn't built right for that kind of thing. I hadn't known that Aila did it, but somehow it didn't surprise me.

We eventually decided that as good a plan as any for me was to catch the Karrem coach. I was going to spend the day playing the casual visitor part, wandering around the village, taking a look in the shops and down at the harbour, and then in the evening they'd introduce me to the Karrem coach driver. *Falbaash. Remember that, Owen. Even, write it down. Oh, and write down how good Skiimon was – and Gobiir, and this family.*

Falbaash will probably remember if he's carried any strangers recently. He might even know where Aila – Griima – had been heading for after Karrem, if she hadn't stayed there. Then in the morning he can let me know by a private signal if there was anyone suspicious on the coach.

With Kemmina's help, I drew a sketch map of all the towns and villages in the area, and the coach routes. *I wish I'd thought to do that earlier – but when? I don't know who else actually has all this information in their heads. And I've managed well enough without so far. But I think this'll be useful.*

After the diners had left, Biilam and Kammeni came and sat with us with a skiir for a while. I could see they were exhausted. "Well, it's good to get the coins," Biilam said. "But I'm glad they don't come every night."

"Was that the Borjiis?"

"Who else would it be? Six Borjiis and four friends. But don't worry, they're local friends, just people from the next village. But they're staying at the Borjii place tonight. Didn't hear anything to suggest they're even aware of Griima's existence or yours, Owen. They were gossiping enough about everybody else in the village. It's as if we're not there, the way they talk."

That's reassuring. It would just be paranoia to think they'd planned that on purpose. I wonder how to say paranoia *in Laana?*

Kemmina disappeared into the night, Gobiir and I bedded down in the lounge, and the rest of them went off somewhere else in the inn.

In the morning it was sunny, and I was ready to go and explore after breakfast. "Lunch at about one if you want it, or there's a place down by the harbour where you can get lunch if you're down that way and don't feel like walking back up the hill."

One of the boys offered to come with me and show me around, but Kammeni thought it would be better if they didn't seem too familiar with me. She thought it would give them a better chance of overhearing anything the Borjiis might let slip in the future. I didn't think I'd be around long to get any such reports, but she said the coach drivers would happily pass on messages, and they'd know who else could be relied upon, too. "It's probably best if you do have lunch down at the harbour, too, for the same reason. More like what a casual visitor would do."

*I see what Peyr meant about the grapevine – although
Kammeni's talking about a coach drivers' grapevine, and that'll
be quite different from the rich folks' grapevine that spreads
word of Yaana's tailoring skills.*

It was cold outside, despite the sunshine. Griishi seemed like
a lovely little place, but then anywhere looks much nicer in
sunshine, even if it's cold. But I knew Aila wasn't there, and I
wanted to be wherever she was. *As soon as possible. But today I
have to be a casual visitor, just exploring and taking a look at a
picturesque place. And getting the feel of the whole of this
country. Now that is useful – this isn't like anywhere I've been
before.*

There were just four shops: a fishmonger who was also a
butcher, made candles, and sold cheese, eggs and cheap smelly
fish oil for lamps; a greengrocer who was also a baker, and sold
more expensive vegetable oil for lamps and cooking; a cobbler
who also did other leatherwork and some woodwork; and a
general merchant who sold everything from ironmongery to
haberdashery, and would do minor clothing repairs for you. The
fishmonger was not far above the harbour, right alongside
Griishi's only other inn, but the other shops were further up the
hill.

There was no dock or quay big enough for coasters. If they
called here at all, they must have used a small boat between the
ship and the shore. There were a couple of fishing boats in the
harbour, with people doing repairs to rigging and nets, but it was
obvious that there were several more boats already out for the
day, or on longer trips – there was room in the harbour for six or
seven boats.

The cliffs began as a rocky hillside behind the harbour end of
the village, then got steeper and taller out towards a point that
looked like a slightly smaller version of the point at Laanoha.
There were innumerable seabirds wheeling around in the sky
over the harbour, and all along the cliffs. I wandered along the
foot of the cliffs, looking up at them and trying to imagine Aila
scrambling around up there. It was a rather scary thought. *But
she clearly knew what she was doing.*

Walking along the foot of the cliffs, I was careful not to get below the high tide line, so as to be sure to be able to return safely.

At the point, I noticed the tide was actually quite far out. I clambered out along the rocks. On a whim, I began to collect ekraahi, and then found myself within reach of the same seaweed Aila had been collecting. I filled my bag, and then realized the sea was coming up. I had to hurry to get back to the foot of the cliffs before I was cut off, but made it safely. *That's a lesson to remember – think more about the tide, and watch it. That could have been very nasty – the death of me, even. And I'd be no good to Aila then. Am I any good to her anyway?*

I'd scarcely ever been by the sea, and never before alone – just that one day with Aila. As a child, I'd spent happy hours with my grandmother by the mudflats of the Thames estuary, gazing over at the French bank, but does that count? We'd never strayed below the high water mark – too muddy.

I headed back to the village. By the time I got there, I was ready for lunch, and headed to the harbour inn. They were very friendly, and served me a good lunch.

This was clearly Griishi's equivalent of the waterside inn in Briggi. Some of the talk was in plain Laana that I understood well enough, but some was in a language or dialect in which I could only recognize the odd word. I didn't feel at all threatened, but I was glad I wasn't wearing my Railway clothes. I felt my boots marked me out rather, but nobody seemed to take any notice.

Nobody seemed *to.* As I left, two men who'd been talking the other language got up and followed me out. *Coincidence. If anyone's following me, they want to follow me to Aila, they're not going to let me know they're following me.*

They followed me at a distance, which I still thought could have been coincidence. But it wasn't. I wandered randomly in the village for a little while, to see what they did, and they were still following me. Eventually I found myself in a dead-end street, with a rock face at the end, the last two houses butting right up against it. I turned round, and they confronted me.

"You were collecting sea-weed and ekraahi, weren't you?"

Ah. Nothing to do with Aila. Just I've been harvesting on their patch, and they don't like it. I can simply give it all to them, not a problem.

They didn't even want all of it – just a half share. But they had noticed Aila.

"You're something to do with that girl, aren't you?"

No sense denying it, but no sense confirming it, either.

"That girl?"

"She was here three weeks ago, just for a few days. Collected ekraahi one day. She's a pretty girl, we let her have them. Then the next day she was up on the cliffs, auking. She's not just a pretty girl, she's the best auker we've seen in years. Never seen a girl doing it before, just heard stories about one who used to do it years ago, then she disappeared. She was supposed to have been the best auker ever, too. But that was before our time. Anyways, we saw this girl going up the hill to the coaching inn. Now that's something we don't like so much – it's one thing a pretty girl taking a few ekraahi or a few birds and eggs, but taking them for the toffs? No, mister. We don't like that. But we like her pluck, and she's no toff herself. We wanted to talk to her, not to hurt her you understand, we wouldn't do that, just to talk. But the next day she wasn't about. We guessed she might have been plucking and gutting – she'd taken a lot of birds. So the next morning we waited not far from the inn to see what she was going to do, and caught her as she set off towards the village. Well, we didn't catch her – she spotted us and she ran like the wind! We wouldn't have touched a hair on her head, mister, but she was scared. I've never seen anyone so scared in my life. She was on the coach out, not even back the way she came, within minutes. She's worried about something, mister, she thinks someone's following her. Well if that someone's you, mister, you'd better watch out. I know a lot of very tough blokes who took a shine to that girl, and if anything happens to her, whoever happens it isn't going to live very long, I can promise you that."

Well! They're not going to help Jerem's father, that's for sure. But what can I say? Tell the truth. It can't do any harm, might help me just now, might even help more than that, who knows?

But it's pretty certainly the best policy here. Whether they'll believe me is another question. But there's no better option anyway.

"I wish I could tell her that. She'd feel a lot safer – if she was here, anyway. Yes, I'm something to do with her, I'm her betrothed. It's not me she's scared of, it's a toff that she rejected that she's scared of. Well, not him himself, his hired men. That's why she doesn't know what they look like."

"Well, if that's true, you've got a lot of good friends here, who'll help you any way they can. And if that's a lie, well, you've already heard the warning."

"I believe him, Tomaam. He's a foreigner, he doesn't know his knee from his nose around here. He's not someone's hired man, that's for sure. And like he said, if she was scared of us it's a hired man she's worried about."

"That makes sense. So what's your plan, mister? You must know the risk that someone's following you, to help them find her?"

"Yes, I know that risk, but what can I do?"

"You come with us, now. I don't think these stones have ears, but who knows? We'll talk somewhere safer."

They led me back to the harbour inn by a much shorter route, down a steep flight of stone stairs between stone walls. The innkeeper nodded at us as they led me into a back room. A few moments later he followed us in and shut the door. "Friend?" he asked.

"Yup, friend. He's her boyfriend. It's a toff she spurned that's after her. Well, his hired men."

"She didn't just spurn him, she beat him up. He tried too hard."

"That figures. But she thinks hired men are more dangerous, and she's right. Well, she can't afford bodyguards, that's obvious, but she doesn't need to, they come free. We like her."

"That's all very well if she's here, but she's not, is she?"

"No, she's not. But we've got mates everywhere – well, all along the coast, anyway. Fishing boats, you see. And we've seen that she's a coast girl, she won't be far inland if she can help it."

"And your mates have been watching out for her?"

"No, because we didn't know the story. Well, they might be, we've told a few people about her, but we've not told anyone to look out for her. Just not to hassle her. But we'll make sure they keep an eye on her now."

"So you know where she is?"

"No, we don't. Someone somewhere might, though."

"If you tell people a toff's hired men are looking for her, isn't there a risk that someone will think they can earn a pile of coins by telling the hired men where she is?"

"A pile of coins? That's a poor return on an early grave."

"There's more than a few folks have ended in early graves because they didn't think about that, Tomaam."

"That's true enough. You can even remind them, and still they don't think about it. And the idiots aren't all dead yet. So what can we do? Everything has risks."

"What were you planning to do before Tomaam and Sheyr got hold of you?"

"Well, the innkeeper's family at the other inn, where I stayed last night, had already realized I was following Griima..."

The innkeeper interrupted me. "Griima? Is that her name? She's not told Biilam her name, has she?"

"It's what she's calling herself."

"Ah, that's better. Don't tell us her real name, we don't want to know."

"They know my real name, but that can't be helped."

"What happened, happened. You can't change the past."

"They knew she was frightened, but they didn't expect her to leave so suddenly. She'd not told them much, but she'd told them my name. They didn't want to let me know she'd been there until they were sure I was me."

"Ah, so they realize she's in danger. I don't like them much, but they're not fools, and it's good to know they're on her side. And it's good to know they don't know her real name."

"We don't actually know that she is in danger, but we know it's a real possibility."

Should I tell them that Jerem's disabled now, and that it's his father who's the danger? Maybe not. It's even possible that it's not true – we've only Mashaari's word for it. Everyone thinks she's honest, but is she? Or has she perhaps been fed a lie that she's passed on innocently? Surely not – she'd find out, and they wouldn't want that. It must be true. But Aila thinks it's Jerem who's the danger – or of course Jerem's father because she beat up Jerem, even without the broken knees that she doesn't know about. Don't say anything, it's all so muddy anyway.

But actually, if it's Jerem's father trying to protect himself from her revealing that she didn't break Jerem's knees, then she's in more danger than she realizes. I should say something, if only something vague.

"She might actually be in more danger than she realizes."

"You took a while thinking about that. You know more than you're telling us, but don't worry, we don't want to know the details. We've already decided whose side we're on. But Biilam knows what you're in Griishi for. What's he expecting you to do?"

"He's expecting me to catch the Karrem coach in the morning. They were going to introduce me to the coach driver tonight, and prime him not to tell anyone anything about Griima or me."

"If you don't do that, he'll wonder why you've changed your mind. It's probably best if they don't know anything about you meeting us, so you do that. Falbaash is a good man, it's good if he knows to keep quiet – he will."

"Tomaam – you could go to Karrem tomorrow, couldn't you? Then you'd know if anyone doubtful had been on the coach, or watching in Karrem when it arrived. And you could probably catch Falbaash and have a word with him, too."

"I could, but people might notice. I almost never go anywhere by coach, you know me. It'd be better if you went, Aibram. I'll look after the inn for you as usual. Nobody would think twice about you going."

"True enough. And I can stay in the same inn as our man here, and still not attract attention. You'd stay down by the waterside, wouldn't you?"

"Surely I would. It'd be the talk of Karrem if I stayed anywhere else. As soon as you get back, though, I'll get a boat up to Karrem and talk to the chaps there. Selected chaps, mister, don't you worry. If you're still there, we'll put a tail on you, then we can spot if anyone else is tailing you. We'll catch your tail soon enough anyway, Falbaash will have the sense to know who he should and who he shouldn't tell where you've gone. Then if this chap's got any hired men after you, they'll regret the day they took his coins. Not for long, though."

Blimey. What have I got myself into here? At least I think the stronger gang is on my side, by the sound of it. Talk about confidence! I wish I could discuss this with Graamon, or even Peyr. But I can't, I've just got to trust my own judgement. If I've got any choice in the matter at all any more anyway. I'm not sure I have. I'm being swept along by the tide again. Such is life.

"It's probably best if you don't spend too long here. You never know whether any of Biilam's family might have seen you come in here, and they'd wonder why you were so long. I bet they suggested you come here for lunch, but they wouldn't expect you to be here all day. I think the plans are decided, and I'll have plenty of time to talk to you tomorrow evening. Best if we don't even know each other on the coach, whoever's on it."

"I was going to take these ekraahi up to Biilam, and this seaweed. He wasn't expecting it or anything, I just decided to collect it on a whim. But if you can use it here, I'd prefer that."

Tomaam laughed. "No, we've got our half. Biilam's welcome to the rest. Someone might tell him you were collecting. We wouldn't want him to think we'd taken it all, and he knows we wouldn't have bought it. He'll probably pay you for them. Don't complain!"

"You'd better go and act the casual visitor for the rest of the day, if that's what Biilam's expecting. And I'm sure he's right if he thinks that's the best way to make sure the toffs take no notice of you."

I'd seen just about all of Griishi already. I climbed up onto the top of the hill at the point, and looked back towards the land. The mountains were visible in the distance. There was only one road into Griishi, which was at the end of a long peninsula between two huge bays. Other than Griishi, I could see no sign of human habitation. It was obvious that the hill I was on had been an island when sea level was higher, and the great expanse of more or less flat farmland that stretched to the north all the way to the foot of the mountains had been the sea bed.

I knew I'd normally find it all very interesting, and if I hadn't been so preoccupied with weightier matters, there'd have been a lot to see. I wanted to go back to the inn, but I knew I'd got to act the casual visitor. But it wasn't easy. Eventually I gave in, and trudged slowly back down.

Kiimi met me at the door. "Did you see my uncle? He went down into town, looking for you."

"No, I was up on the hill, it's a while since I was in town. Do you know if it was urgent? I could go down into town myself and see if I can see him."

"No, I think it's better if you wait here for him. I'll send Sheymaal down to tell him you're here. Get inside and get warm by the fire, I'll get you some skiir."

I sat and stared into the fire. *I wonder what this is all about?* I'd no idea what it could possibly be. *There's no point speculating, just have to wait and see.*

Biilam didn't take long to arrive. I asked him what he wanted me for. "Oh, it's nothing. I was a bit worried about you, that's all. Sheymaal saw you out on the point earlier on. He thought you might have been collecting ekraahi."

"I was. And seaweed. It's in my bag – half of it. I gather the local fishermen expect half of it as their share."

Biilam laughed a relieved sounding laugh. "Good. I'm glad you had the sense not to argue."

"Oh, I wouldn't argue. If they'd wanted it all, I wouldn't have argued. I'd have felt a bit aggrieved, but I'd still just accept the situation. I'm not about to get into a fight over a bagful of shellfish. I don't even really feel aggrieved about half of it. The sea shore isn't my property."

"It's not their property either."

"Isn't it? I didn't know whether it was or not."

"If it's anyone's, it's the Borjiis'. Most of the land around here is."

"I'd object to that more than I'd begrudge the fishermen the ekraahi, to be honest. Why does the land belong to the Borjiis, any more than the ekraahi belong to the fishermen?"

"That's a good question, and I don't really have an answer. But it does."

"Says who? The Borjiis?"

"Ah, well, we can't change the ways of the world. We can't take the Borjiis' land away from them, and we can't take the fishermen's ekraahi – or not more than half of them, anyway. Not without a fight, in either case, and the only thing sure about a fight is that everybody loses."

Well, at least Biilam didn't want me for anything important.

"Did Griima have to hand over half her harvest, too?"

I knew she hadn't, or I thought I knew, but I didn't want to admit that I knew. And I did want to open the subject.

"No, they never went near her. They probably thought she was a ghost, actually. There's an old story about a girl who used to collect ekraahi and seaweed and birds and eggs around here. Best auker ever, they said. That was, oh, maybe fifty years ago. Before I was born, anyway. No-one knew who she was, she just appeared from nowhere. Didn't talk much, never told anyone anything about herself. No-one knew where she was staying. People thought maybe she was living in a cave high up on the cliffs where no-one else dared go. One of the local men fancied her, but he was too shy to say anything. Then one day he plucked up courage and tried to talk to her, but she ran away from him. Next day, she was gone. No-one ever saw her again. The chap who fancied her never got over it. He was a bit of a painter, used to sell paintings to the Borjiis' rich friends. The Borjiis have a few of his paintings still. But after she disappeared all he ever painted was portraits of her – some full face, some of her up on the cliffs, or out on the rocks collecting ekraahi. The Borjiis have a couple of them, big ones, and a few people in the village have smaller ones, too – he practically gave them away, because he painted more than the rich people wanted. The Borjiis have them up on the wall, but most people don't keep them where anyone can see them, because they think it's bad luck. Some people thought he'd killed her, but most people didn't think he could have done that, they thought she'd disappeared the way she came, running away from someone. But the rum thing is, Griima looks exactly like the girl in those pictures."

"No wonder they thought she was a ghost."

If they did. It's only Biilam's idea that they'd think that. They way they talked, I doubt it. But they didn't mention the pictures, or the likeness. And if they half think she might be a ghost, that could explain why they're so keen to help. And they might have thought at first that that was why she ran away from them like that.

"I'd like to see one of those pictures. I might like to buy one of them if anyone will sell me one – but not just now. Sometime when all this is settled, I'll be back. With her. All being well, of course."

"I don't know whether anyone would sell you one, especially if they see her with you. You don't want to go around asking about them just now, obviously!"

By sunset, Falbaash still hadn't arrived with his coach from Karrem. I asked Biilam if he was running late.

"No, it's a long road from Karrem, three full stages, not just two like the road from Laanoha. He'll be here before long I expect."

I'd not even noticed the change of horses. He must have done it when we were having lunch. Never thought about it. Always used trains for long distances in England.

It was thoroughly dark by the time Falbaash arrived. He came in and plonked himself in the same chair by the fire that Gobiir had used the previous night. "Only three passengers today. And no parcels at all. At the present rate, I'll have to cut the service back to a three day round trip, like I did last winter. Can't feed a family like this. What's a man to do?"

"Thank your luck that you don't ply the Laanoha to Gorb route, or up to Veglid?"

"Thanks for that kind thought, Biilam. At least they can charge a good price there, they know no-one's going to try to compete. My old coach wouldn't handle those roads, though.

Put four horses on the front of it and try to pull it up a hill? It'd fall to bits."

"That's reassuring words for your passenger, Falbaash."

"Oh? Have I got a passenger for tomorrow already?"

"This young man here, Owen. Actually, he wants to talk to you tonight, while there's only us around."

I can talk myself, Biilam, but actually, I'm very happy if you do the talking for me if you want to. You know this man, I don't.

Falbaash turned and looked at me. "You're a quiet one. I know, it's hard to get a word in with Biilam around."

Biilam didn't say anything. *Ah well, it's up to me then.*

"I'm trying to find my young lady. I don't know if you remember her. A young woman, not one of the regulars, about three weeks ago. Small, slender, wearing a black cloak with a hood."

I'd only found out what she'd been wearing from Gobiir and Kiimi. I'd never seen her in a black cloak.

"You've already said plenty, there's not often strangers on my coach. Yes, I remember her. Jumped on me at the last minute, as if she'd only just decided to travel. Didn't even know where I was going, had to ask. Paid for the whole way to Karrem, but then at Griimi she asked what it was called, and said not to wait for her, she'd stay there. I gave her half her money back, and she was grateful. Most folks would have wanted two thirds back. I told her she'd only gone a third of the way, too, but she was happy. Pretty girl."

"Has anyone else been asking after her?"

"Not that I've heard. Why? Is she in trouble?"

"Quite likely, but I'm not certain. If anyone else does ask, can you tell them you've never seen her?"

"Well, yes, but how do I know whether it's you or the other fellow she's trying to get away from?"

Biilam answered that one. "She stayed here four nights, Falbaash. She talked about Owen, and we're sure it's him all right."

"She's stayed in Griimi? Not been on the coach again?"

"Maybe, I don't know. No, she's not been on my coach, neither back here nor to Karrem, but I'm not the only coach that stops at Griimi. There's two coaches that run between Laanoha and Karrem, too. You'll have to ask Preysh and Kaasham if she caught either of them."

Of course. I'd forgotten about the map Kemmina helped me make. I'll have another look at that later. Kaasham? I've heard that name before.

Ah. Workshop man in Briggi of course. Seems so long ago already.

Falbaash and I were alone together later in the evening, and I quietly told him about my meeting with Tomaam and the others at the other inn. He nodded, and said he knew who he could trust and who he couldn't, and that there really wasn't any need to say any more. "Better not to. Not here."

I spent some time studying the map. I wondered how much of it I'd actually need.

My dreams were full of Aila. One moment she was high on the cliffs, with an impossibly large bag full of eggs, standing on a narrow ledge and leaning out, nonchalantly hanging on to her rope with one hand; the next she was out on the rocks, skirt tucked into her knickers, collecting ekraahi; then she was running along in the water, trying to reach the shore before the tide overwhelmed her. Then she was running alongside Peyr's engine, but we were going too fast, and she slipped as she jumped to get in. I tried to grab her, but she slipped out of my grasp. I woke up sweating. Falbaash was snoring, so at least I hadn't been shouting – or if I had, I hadn't woken him. I couldn't shake off the feeling that the tide was overwhelming her, although I knew in my head that I'd been dreaming, and that anyway she knew what she was doing when it came to tides.

Chapter 13

Breakfast. Fresh bread, smoked fish and fried eggs, washed down with skiir. Falbaash and I ate with the family. There were no other guests. I tried to pay Biilam, but he said I'd already paid in ekraahi and seaweed, and that the Borjiis were bringing friends again that night and the ekraahi would go down well.

Falbaash went to tend to his horses, then came back in to fetch me. The innkeeper from the harbour inn was already in the coach, together with the same two teenage boys who'd been in the coach from Kromaan.

They must be the Borjii boys, the ones Kemmina was talking about. They're not tailing me, surely? No, it must be coincidence, they were on the coach already this morning, and they were on the coach already in Kromaan – I think they must have come from Laanoha, in fact. But still a nuisance – they'll very likely tell their parents that I was on the coach, and where I got off.

Oh, and damn. The harbour inn innkeeper doesn't know I'm getting off at Griimi. He'll have booked through to Karrem, I'm sure.

But he hadn't booked anything. Falbaash hadn't collected the fares yet, and he collected mine first. The boys were going to Karrem.

Well, that's something of a relief, anyway. But not much.

As soon as we'd got moving, one of the boys looked me straight in the eye. "You're Owen, aren't you?"

No use denying it.

But before I could say anything, the other boy shushed him, and spoke to the innkeeper. "You can keep a secret, can't you, Aibram? From Dad, that is, or anyone who might tell him?"

Aibram laughed. "Like you two, for instance? Of course I can."

"Okay. You are Owen, aren't you?"

"Yes, although how you knew I'd love to know."

"Oh, we've got ears and eyes, Naajal and I. You can read, can you? Laana, that is."

So he knows I'm foreign, as well.

"Sort of. I'm not very good yet. I'm a bit slow, and there are lots of words I don't know."

"Okay, I'm sure that's good enough. And this is what you mustn't let Dad know, Aibram. We've got a letter from Mum for you, Owen. That's why we're here. She was sure you'd be on the coach this morning. Oh, and she says we're to give you any help we can, as long as it's something Dad won't get to hear about."

I took the letter. It was sealed along two edges with wax, just the way Aila's had been. "Thank you. You heard that I was only going to Griimi, but you've booked through to Karrem?"

"Well, we've nowhere to stay in Griimi, and we'd only have to wait there until Falbaash comes back anyway. And this way Falbaash won't guess our trip has anything to do with you. Can't help it that you heard, Aibram."

"What happens, happens. I'm sure it's of no consequence that I heard, anyway."

I don't suppose it would matter if Falbaash knew, either. But they don't know that, and I'm not about to tell them. And they've got the right instinct.

"You can open the letter, Mister Owen. Aibram can't read, and we're not looking. We've got a pretty good idea what it says anyway."

Their mother's signature, at the bottom, was written in neat cursive script, but the bulk of the letter was written in print script, like Aila's. I guessed this was for my benefit, not because writing cursive script was harder for her. This is what she wrote:

MY DEAR OWEN,

DON'T WORRY THAT I KNOW WHO YOU ARE AND WHY YOU'RE HERE, AND THAT MY BOYS DO TOO. I'M WRITING TO WARN YOU TO BE CAREFUL, ESPECIALLY FOR AILA'S SAKE.

SHE'S RUNNING AWAY BECAUSE SHE THINKS JEREM IS ANGRY WITH HER. AS FAR AS SHE KNOWS, HE COULD HAVE RECOVERED COMPLETELY.

EVERYBODY ON THE CIRCUIT KNOWS THE STORY, BUT I DON'T BELIEVE IT. IF I'M RIGHT, AILA DOESN'T KNOW HOW MUCH DANGER SHE IS IN. I DON'T BELIEVE SHE BROKE JEREM'S KNEES. I DON'T DOUBT THAT SHE BROKE HIS

HEAD, SHE'S A CAPABLE YOUNG WOMAN AND THAT WAS SURELY THE RIGHT THING TO DO. BUT WHY BREAK HIS KNEES WHEN HIS HEAD'S ALREADY BROKEN? THAT DOESN'T MAKE SENSE, AND I KNOW SHE'S A SENSIBLE GIRL. GAMAARA HAS TALKED ABOUT HER MANY TIMES.

I'M SURE IT MUST HAVE BEEN TIIRAM (THAT'S JEREM'S FATHER) WHO DID THAT. IT IS IN CHARACTER. NOW OF COURSE HE WANTS EVERYONE TO BELIEVE IT WAS AILA. HE KNOWS AILA KNOWS SHE DIDN'T BREAK JEREM'S KNEES, AND I EXPECT HE'S VERY AFRAID THAT WHEN SHE HEARS THAT PEOPLE ARE SAYING THAT, SHE'LL DENY IT, AND THEY'LL FIND OUT IT WAS HIM. SO THERE IS A VERY REAL RISK THAT HE'LL HAVE HIRED SOMEONE TO ARRANGE A NASTY ACCIDENT FOR HER. EXCEPT MAYBE IN THE HEAT OF THE MOMENT, JEREM WOULDN'T HAVE WANTED HER KILLED, I'M SURE, AND I THINK SHE'D KNOW THAT. BUT TIIRAM PROBABLY DOES WANT HER DEAD, AND SHE DOESN'T KNOW THAT.

I'M SURE THAT GAMAARA AND OTHERS ALSO SUSPECT THAT IT WAS TIIRAM, NOT AILA, WHO BROKE HIS KNEES. BUT THEY DAREN'T BELIEVE IT, CAN'T PROVE IT, AND AREN'T SAYING ANYTHING TO ANYONE — WELL, NOT THAT I'VE HEARD, ANYWAY.

MY BOYS WILL DO ANYTHING THEY CAN TO HELP — WITHIN REASON, DON'T FORGET THEY'RE ONLY BOYS. AND IF YOU CAN POSSIBLY GET HER BACK HERE TO OUR HOUSE, WE CAN KEEP HER SAFE UNTIL THE TRUTH IS PUBLIC AND SHE'S OUT OF DANGER. MY HUSBAND DOESN'T KNOW WHAT I THINK, BUT IF SHE'S HERE TO TELL HIM ABOUT THE KNEES, HE'LL BELIEVE IT. HE DOESN'T KNOW SHE WAS IN GRIISHI.

I'M ONLY SORRY WE DIDN'T KNOW THE STORY UNTIL AFTER SHE'D ALREADY LEFT GRIISHI. WE'VE NOT TOLD ANYONE SHE WAS HERE, AND WE WON'T. I CAN'T SPEAK FOR THE COACH DRIVERS, OF COURSE.

GOOD WINDS AND FAVOURABLE TIDES,

Borjii Maamatta

Well! Well, well, well. I suppose that's not surprising, and it doesn't tell me anything I didn't already suspect – except that there are rich people who are already suspicious of the official story, and prepared to take sides with us. Well, one at least. I guess "the circuit" must mean the circle of rich friends and acquaintances. I wonder how wide it spreads?

It can't be a devious method to trap me and Aila. Neither Jerem for his reasons, nor his father for his, would actually enlist the help of anyone but a hired hand. Aila's not scared that these people would do that, just that they'll gossip and disclose her whereabouts thoughtlessly.

But by what method does she expect me to be careful? She doesn't know I've got the fishermen on my tail – and until Aibram gets back to Griishi, tomorrow night, they don't know I've not gone to Karrem. But Tomaam at least won't set off for Karrem until Aibram gets back. I got the impression it would be Tomaam not his friend – Sheyr, was it? – who was going to go. But who knows how many other fishermen there are, and who they've talked to? Tomaam talked about 'a lot of tough blokes who took a shine to that girl', and I don't think that was any bluff. There were a lot of boats out fishing, to judge by the empty spaces on the quayside.

Well, I'm pretty sure I don't want these two lads to know that Aibram already knows. And Aibram doesn't know Aila's real name. It's hard to know what I can say, and to whom. But I think everybody here understands that. I'll get a chance to talk privately with Aibram in Griimi, all being well.

"Thank you. Watch out for me at Griimi on your way back tomorrow. I might have a letter for your mother, I'm not sure yet."

"We can always get off in Griimi now if you think you need our help, or if you decide you want our help after you've seen Griimi, we can get off there tomorrow. Mum said we could stay away longer if we were needed."

"That's very kind of her – and of you, and I'll remember the offer. Thank you. There's just one other thing – if anyone else asks about me or that girl, you've never seen either of us, okay? Do your best not to let them see that you're hiding anything from them, too."

"We can do that, we're very good at it. Mum already told us not to say anything to anyone. Even Dad doesn't know the half of what we do!"

We travelled in silence for a long time. Maybe I'd become more accustomed to the movement of the coach, or maybe the road or the coach was in better condition, or maybe it was just that the coach wasn't full, but I felt more comfortable, and found I was able to stare out at the countryside. It was very flat, and where there were gaps in the woodland I could see the mountains in the distance.

After a while, a nearer rocky hill began to be distinguishable against the backdrop of the more distant mountains. It gradually came to dominate the skyline on our right.

Aibram saw me looking at it. "That's Griimi point. Griimi village is just at the foot of it, at this end. The other end sticks out into the sea, just like the point at Griishi."

I remembered from the map that we joined the direct road from Kromaan a few miles before Griimi, but I was on the right side of the coach and never noticed the junction. We pulled up outside an inn at the foot of Griimi point, and we all climbed out. Falbaash unharnessed his horses and led them somewhere behind the inn. It was only about ten o'clock in the morning, but in the sunshine it was reasonably warm, and we sat on benches outside the inn and drank mugs of skiir with the innkeeper, but apart from friendly greetings all round, not a word was spoken.

After a while, the innkeeper disappeared round the back of the inn, and came out with fresh horses. Falbaash harnessed them to his coach, the boys wished me luck and said they'd see me the next day, and they were off.

The innkeeper broke the silence. "Well this is a rare pleasure, Aibram. It's not often you stay here – in fact, I don't think I remember you staying here since your sister's wedding, and when was that?"

Aibram laughed. "That's a few years ago. Her girls must be nearly ready for theirs, I reckon. There's a few likely lads sniffing around, I dare say."

"I'm sure you're right, although I've not seen them. But you don't, do you? What brings you here, anyway? And who's the stranger?"

"He's Owen, and he's what brings me here. And Owen, this is the other Tomaam. You can trust him like a brother, he's one of us."

"That doesn't sound too healthy, Aibram. Trouble?"

"Probably. We don't know for sure. You must have seen a girl arrive here from Griishi about three weeks ago – a stranger. Small..."

Tomaam reacted before Aibram had even finished. "Slender girl. Pretty. Yes, she was here for a week, stayed here with us. Griima, she was calling herself, but I don't think it was her real name. Best auker there's been here in fifty years, and that's something else. You know her, presumably, Owen?"

"Yes, surely. I'm her betrothed."

"Come with me. You too, Aibram."

The innkeeper led us into the inn, then up a flight of stairs that angled around what must have been the back of the chimney. It ended in a huge dingy room full of all kinds of things, mostly thickly covered in dust, but some apparently used more recently.

An old woman was sitting sewing at a table under a window in one gable end. She looked up briefly as we entered, then returned to her sewing. Tomaam led us to another table under the window at the other end.

Lying face up on the table was a framed picture. I could see where most of the dust had recently been wiped off the glass.

I see what Biilam meant. That's not just a bit like Aila, that's a very good painting of Aila.

She was standing on a ledge on a cliff, high above the sea, hanging onto a rope with her right hand. She had a large bag over her shoulder, and she was just putting a large speckled egg into the bag with her left hand. She was looking round straight into the face of the painter.

She was wearing a black cloak, with a hood hanging down her back.

"I can see you're quite shocked. She was, too."

"That's astonishing. Where did you get it?"

"When she found it, she thought for a moment that I must have painted it. Then she realized it was old, covered in dust. I don't know where it came from, my mother..." he nodded in the direction of the old lady "...thinks my father must have bought it somewhere, but she'd never seen it until after he died. And she'd never thought anything of it until Griima found it."

Aibram was less moved. "I didn't know you'd got one of those, Tomaam. It's one of the best I've seen, too. I wondered about mentioning them to you, Owen, but I thought better not."

Tomaam was looking at him, surprised. "There are more like this?"

Aibram was looking at Tomaam, and then me, and then back again. "You look less surprised than Tomaam, Owen. I guess Biilam must have told you about them. I don't think he's got one, though, has he?"

"Not as far as I know, no. Tomaam – you wouldn't be prepared to part with that, would you? Not now, I don't want to carry it now, and I haven't got enough coins on me to give you a fair price. Besides, I want to find the real Griima before I buy a painting of her – or whoever it was who looked so incredibly like her fifty years ago. But if you'd keep that for me, when I've found her, I'd like to come back for it."

I hadn't realized that the old lady had left her sewing, and was standing behind us, looking between us at the picture. Then she spoke.

"Young man, you know Griima, don't you? Very well, I think."

"Yes. We're betrothed."

"You know that cloak she wears? Do you know where she got it? I was thinking to ask her, then she disappeared before I got round to it."

"I've never seen it. She never wore it when we were together. But her grandmother sometimes wears one just like the one in the picture."

"Not any more. She's given it to Griima, I reckon. I reckon she'd had that cloak fifty odd years, too. Do you know where Griima's grandmother came from?"

I racked my brains. I was sure I'd heard something, but I couldn't remember what. Then a memory replayed itself in my mind.

'You don't mind me asking, I hope. How long have you lived here?' 'In Laanoha? Apart from Gran, all our lives, all of us. Gran, you tell Owen how you came here!'

"No, I don't. But I do know there's a story attached, that I haven't heard yet."

"Griima's grandmother is called Griimab Yaana, isn't she? Well, something else Yaana for a long time now, I'm sure, but she was born Griimab Yaana, I'll bet. She's my cousin. She ran away over fifty years ago, after my uncle – her Dad – died, and another man moved in with her mother. I always suspected he tried it on with Yaana, that's why she ran off."

That set Aibram off. "If I've understood this correctly, she spent the next few years in Griishi. A Griishi man, Loumim, painted this, and dozens of other pictures of her, after she ran away again when he tried to woo her. But I'm surprised no-one knew who she was, if she'd only come from Griimi."

"Oh, she hadn't. I only came here when I married Tomaam. Yaana and I were both born in Oushi. It was our great grandad who came from Griimi."

Oushi? I don't remember that from my map. I wonder where it is? But where is Aila now, if she's not here? Run away again, scared off? I hope whatever scared her isn't really a hired man of Tiiram's.

Or worse. I hope no-one's happened anything to her.

"But where's Griima now, if she's not here? Do you know which coach she went on?"

I know she didn't go back to Griishi or on to Karrem with Falbaash; but she could have gone on to Karrem with either of the other two coaches. Surely she wouldn't go to Baragi?

"I don't think she caught a coach at all. I think I'd have seen her catching a coach, but you should ask the coach drivers. I expect you've asked Falbaash already, and Preysh and Kaasham will be here at lunchtime. My wife saw her talking to a couple of fishermen the evening before she went missing, though, friendly like. I think she might have got them to take her somewhere, they were away a few days."

"Did she seem scared, to you?"

"Not exactly scared, but a bit watchful. I did notice that she always seemed to be up on this end of the hill watching the coaches when they arrived. Most of the rest of the time she was auking or collecting ekraahi and seaweed. Our smokery is better stocked than it's ever been in my time, and I wish I could do fresh ekraahi at lunch all the time, nearly everybody takes them, even at an extra half coin. She was worth every coin I paid her. I wish she'd stayed. I do wish she'd stayed, anyway, she was good to have around. Never at the inn at lunchtime, though, always up on the hill."

Aibram asked the obvious question before I got round to it. "Was there anyone other than the regulars on any of the coaches, the day before she went missing?"

"No, not that I noticed. There aren't often strangers on any of the coaches, in fact Griima and Owen are the first ones in a long time."

"Anybody rich?"

"I think it was the day before she went missing that the two Borjii boys – the same two who were on the coach with you just now – went through to Karrem. But it was raining, and they didn't get out of the coach, so she'd've had to have eyes like a hawk to have seen them from up on the hill."

The old lady coughed. "She did have eyes like a hawk. Sort of. She borrowed your father's telescope, every day after she'd found it up here. She said it was lovely, and I said she could borrow it. But she's a good girl, look, it's back in its place." She pointed out an old brass telescope, nicely polished up, lying amongst dusty items on a dusty table under the slope of the roof.

Aibram looked at me questioningly. *He's wondering what was in that letter. Well, Aibram knows about it, and he says Tomaam is one of us. I've got to assume that's true, I can't do anything without making assumptions like that.*

"Those two boys know who Griima is, but they're on our side. They came on the coach simply to give me a letter from their mother, and to offer any help they could give. They'll be on the coach back again tomorrow. Their mother knows the whole story, but I don't know how much the boys know."

"Well, if Maamatta says she's on your side, you can be sure that she really is. But I'd trust those two boys about as much as I'd trust a cobra. Maamatta thinks they're as straight as sunbeams, of course, but they're not. That's really bad news. If they can earn a few coins telling tales to someone, they won't worry about any possible consequences. What's worse, they don't need to – who'd dare to hurt them?"

"At least none of the coach drivers will trust them, either. We'll see what Preysh and Kaasham have to say in a little while. But my guess is that she's gone further east with the fishermen. People call it dangerous country beyond Oushi, but it's really probably the safest place for her. It'd be dangerous country for rich people, or anyone suspected of being their hirelings."

"I talked to Preysh in Kromaan a couple of days ago. He said he'd not picked up any strangers there. I suppose he might not have thought to mention picking up a stranger here."

"I don't know. That would be even more unusual than picking up a stranger in Kromaan. But of course if you asked about a stranger from Kromaan..."

"I asked about a stranger just a few days ago, as well, not weeks ago, so he might not have made the connection."

Aibram gave me a puzzled look, but he didn't say anything.

At Tomaam's suggestion, I stayed upstairs in the inn while he talked to the coach drivers. "That way, no-one need know you're actually here at the moment. It probably doesn't matter, but there could even be a stranger on one of the coaches today, and you never know who gossips to whom anyway. I'll talk to the drivers away from the passengers, while they're changing the horses."

Aibram stayed upstairs with me. "No sense giving anything away to anyone unnecessarily."

We waited until the passengers and drivers had been fed and had gone, before we went downstairs.

Neither Preysh nor Kaasham had taken any strangers anywhere recently, or talked to any apart from Preysh having talked to me. Both were happy to keep quiet about Tomaam asking, and happy to report to him if they did, especially anyone who was asking about other strangers.

Kaasham had seen strangers in Karrem a couple of times, but they'd not spoken to him. "He said they didn't look rich enough to have their own transport, and hadn't ridden with him or Preysh, so they must have come from Baragi, or just possibly from Mezham."

"Doesn't seem likely they're anything to do with Griima, if they didn't speak to Kaasham. Unless they'd already got what they wanted out of someone else, of course. You could go to Karrem and ask the other coach drivers about strangers, but if Griima didn't go that way, that's just attracting attention to yourself for no purpose. We should find those fishermen. Who were they, Tomaam?"

"My wife wasn't sure, they'd got their backs to her, it was only Griima she could see clearly. But all the boats in the harbour were Griimi boats, so they were local boys. And not greyhairs, either!" Tomaam laughed, and tugged at his own grey locks.

"Well, that cuts out half the fishermen, anyway!" Aibram laughed too. "So the sooner we get down to the harbour, the better. Who knows who might go out on this tide?"

"I can tell you don't come here often, Aibram. You're thinking Griishi tides – it's a couple of hours before our lads go out."

"Gah, so it is. I wasn't thinking Griishi tides, but I was thinking Griimi's were nearly an hour earlier, and they're not, they're nearly an hour later. So we've plenty of time."

"No harm getting down there and having a chat, anyway. You take him down there, Aibram. I've got lots to do here. You know the fishermen at least as well as I do, and they know you, too. I'll expect you back here if I see you, Owen, and good luck if I don't."

Aibram and I headed down towards the harbour. "Tomaam was saying it's dangerous country for rich people, where he thinks Griima's gone with the fishermen. People there won't think I'm rich, will they?"

"That's a point, actually. You don't exactly look rich, but you don't exactly look poor, either. Your clothes are a modest style, but they're new – all of them. Oh – and those boots. They do look like money. Hmm."

He stopped, looking thoughtful, then turned round. "Let's go back to the inn, and think about this. I know you want to get to Griima as soon as possible, but you don't want to look like money over there."

Tomaam was surprised to see us back so quickly, but Aibram explained what we'd been thinking about. "We could go back with Falbaash tomorrow, and take him to the cobblers and get some cheaper boots, then get a boat from Griishi. That'll help throw anyone off the trail, too."

"The boots would still be new. And all his clothes new, too? But he can't wear any of my things or your things, they'd be far too big on him. Are any of the fishermen his size? It'd save a couple of days, as well as doing a better job of making him look ordinary. And who's going to follow him if he goes by boat? The fishermen won't take anyone else once they know. They won't even tell anyone they took Owen."

"Well, some of the fishermen probably are his size, if they're not out fishing. But I don't suppose any of them have anything to spare – particularly boots"

I wasn't sure I really wanted to wear someone else's clothes. *Judd's working clothes, good quality and freshly washed, is one thing. But a fisherman's clothes, carelessly washed if at all? Swallow your pride and your prejudices, Owen. Think of Aila!*

"If I'm their size, they're my size. They can have mine. I'd like the boots back eventually, though!" *I could always buy a new pair, I suppose. I'm not sure how many weeks' worth of coins they'd cost, but what happens, happens.*

"They'll be pleased at that. It won't matter to them looking like money for a few weeks, and it's a good price for the trip, too. I suspect you've got a deal there, but we'd better get back down to the harbour and see who's about."

"Before we go, there's one big favour I'd like to ask you, Tomaam. Do you think I could borrow your father's telescope? I'll do my best to look after it, but you know I'm on a bit of risky mission."

"I'll ask my mother, but I'm sure it's okay. You're right – it could be very useful to you."

Tomaam was back with the telescope very quickly. "She says you must look after it as best you can, and it's a gift for your young lady when you find her. And here's a scruffy old rucksack, too."

Scruffy it certainly was, but it was still strong. I transferred all my things into it, and gave Tomaam mine.

"I'll keep it for you, you can collect in when you come for that painting!"

There were four boats in the harbour. There was an old man sitting on a stone bench overlooking the harbour, mending nets. Aibram and I sat down next to him.

"Well, Aibram. It's been a long time. I reckon I was a young man last time I saw you. What brings you here? One of your nieces getting married or something?"

"Not as far as I know. We don't have time for fussy fishing, we've got to get straight to business. This young man, Owen, needs our help. You remember the young lady who stayed up at the inn for a week a couple of weeks ago – spent all her time auking and collecting ekraahi? Do you have any idea where she went?"

"If you're asking that with him sitting right there, you've already decided he's a friend. Your judgement's good enough for me. Yes, I know. Mashaar and Piiram took her to Oushi. They told her they were going that way anyway, but they weren't of course, they were going out to sea. It probably cost them half a day's fishing or a bit more. But what young man can turn down a desperate plea from a pretty girl like that? Especially when they've seen what a great auker she is."

"Ah. Oushi's not so bad. We were afraid she'd gone further than that – well, half afraid, half hoping. Harder for Owen to follow if she did, but probably safer for her."

"What's she so scared of? She's no coward, I've seen her on the cliffs, so it's something real. She's not afraid to take a trip with a couple of young fishermen, either, and it's not every young woman who'd take that chance."

"It's a toff she beat up. Well, his hired men."

The old man laughed. "I can imagine why, and good for her. Well, it's just as well she didn't beat up either of those two. That'd be a hard boat to handle single-handed."

"But they wouldn't have been single handed. I'll bet she's as good with a boat as she is on the cliffs, isn't she, Owen?"

"I don't know. I've never seen her in a boat." *I've never seen her on the cliffs, either – apart from that picture. And that's not Aila, even if it probably is her grandmother.*

"I wonder if she's still in Oushi, or whether she's headed further into the wilds. She'd soon discover that Oushi's not that hard to reach overland. Troum or even Zhaam would be safer – especially if she made sure the fishermen knew to refuse to take anyone remotely suspicious by boat. I've not heard any such talk, but they wouldn't need to tell me."

"Oushi isn't on my map – nor those other places you mentioned. Can you tell me where they are? And what makes the other two harder to get to overland?"

"You've got a map? Wherever did you get that?"

"Oh, it's just a sketch. Biilam's sister-in-law helped me make it, so I'd know where the coaches went."

I got my notebook out of my pocket and showed them. The old man looked at the map, then he shut the book and looked at the cover. Finally, he reopened the book, and turned a few pages. He found the page of my notes about how to find Baam's place in Barioha.

"I can't read, but I recognize enough to know that some of this is Laana, and some is something else. What do yo make of it, Aibram?"

Aibram took the book. He evidently could read, whatever the Borjii boys thought. "Well, this page looks like a list of street names, but they're not Laanoha streets, so I don't know where they are. Maybe Barioha or Meyroha – or maybe Briggi, I guess that's probably where you come from, Owen, to judge by your boots. So this other writing – maybe it's Maara?"

How much to give away? Enough not to seem to be hiding anything, I suppose. Which means almost everything of any significance. Ah well, I'm obviously among friends really.

"You're exactly right about the boots – they're from Briggi, which is where my home is now. But the language isn't Maara. I've heard Maara spoken, but I don't understand it and I've never seen it written. That's English. I'm from England originally."

"But your young lady is a coast girl, that's very obvious."

"Yes, she's from Laanoha. And more of a coast girl than most Laanohans."

The old man laughed again. "Your young lady is the Ghost of Griishi reincarnate. If I wasn't a straight-thinking seaman, I'd have thought she was the Ghost herself until I saw her talking to the boys. You know about the Ghost?"

"I'd not heard her called that before, but I understand, yes. I've seen one of the pictures."

They helped me put Oushi and Troum and Zhaam on my map. They explained that although Oushi didn't have a regular coach service, it did have a road that wasn't too bad. You could hire a gig to take you there from Karrem, but Troum and Zhaam were only accessible by sea, or several days' hard going over jagged rocks and cliffs along the coast, or through trackless forests and swamps inland.

Aibram explained to the old man that I was trying to find Griima, and they agreed that if Griima had in fact gone further than Oushi, I would need to look more ordinary. We found that the old man's feet were the same size as mine, and we swapped boots. "I won't want to keep these, they're fitted to your feet and legs, but they're wearable. How are mine on you?"

I grinned. "Wearable!"

He put down his nets, and we all got up and walked over to the harbour wall. There were men working on two of the boats. Aibram called out, "Mashaar! Come over here a minute."

Aibram knows everybody, even though he's not here often. It's what, thirty miles from here to Griishi? Do the boats come into each other's ports quite often? I wonder why.

"Aibram! What are you doing here?"

"Coming with Owen here, to introduce him to you. First things first. You remember Griima? Of course you do – Zhor says you took her to Oushi. I expect she told you not to tell anyone. Well, Owen isn't just anyone – he's her boyfriend. Did you actually take her to Oushi, or further than that?"

"Owen, did you say? You're certain he is Owen?"

"Yes, I'm certain. Griishab Tomaam checked him out yesterday, and he's genuine, don't worry."

"Pleased to meet you Owen. Griima talked about you. Yes, we took her to Oushi, but Oushab Jalaan took her further along. Could have been Troum, or maybe even Zhaam."

"Well, Owen would like to be taken to Oushi, and introduced to Jalaan, or anyone from Oushi who would take him to where Griima is."

"It'd be cheaper to go by coach and gig, at least as far as Oushi. Ah – but I can see why you wouldn't want to."

"The other thing is, Owen needs some more ordinary clothes if he's going to Troum or Zhaam. He's willing to swap the ones he's wearing with someone. Is there anyone about his size? You're obviously much too tall."

"That's true, more's the pity. Piiram's nearly as tall as me, too – and you're too short, Zhor. Imbaal's about your size, I reckon, but he's out at the moment. I think he's expected in on this tide. As long as he comes in early, there'd be time for you to get changed before we have to go out. I don't think anyone who's here at the moment is your size. I'll go out on the other side and see if I can see him yet."

An hour later, Imbaal and I were swapping clothes. He was very pleased with his new clothes, and very happy to give Mashaar and Piiram his share of his catch to take me to Oushi. Fortunately we really were pretty much the same size and shape.

Aibram and Zhor helped Mashaar pull the boat to the harbour entrance, while I helped Piiram get the sails up. It wasn't a rig I was used to, but under Piiram's guidance I think I was able to be useful. At the harbour entrance, Mashaar leapt aboard with the tow rope. Piiram pulled on the mainsheet, and the mainsail filled. We were off. With the wind from the south, we had to beat upwind to clear the point, but then it was a beam reach to Oushi. The wind was moderate, and Mashaar reckoned it would take us five or six hours to get there, so it would be dark and half tide when we arrived. That would mean anchoring offshore, and rowing the dinghy into the harbour. "At least with it being dark, no-one will see you well enough to know you aren't just one of us. But I'll go into the inn first, and make sure there's no-one suspicious around before you come in."

As the sun went down, the wind began to diminish. Mashaar was disappointed, but not surprised. "I hope the wind doesn't drop too much. We could be later in Oushi than I'd hoped."

Lights started to appear on the shore. Mashaar lit our own light and pulled it up to the masthead. I'd not really been aware of any other boats out on the water before, but now I could see their lights, too. They were all far to the south of us, further out to sea, presumably fishing. The masthead lights were the only lights they had.

The wind was dropping minute by minute, and we were scarcely moving.

Mashaar was philosophical about it. "Oh well, what happens, happens. The wind will pick up again in the morning. There could even be an offshore breeze in an hour or so's time. We might as well get some sleep while we can."

He wound the mainsheet a couple of times round his wrist, so it would tug at his arm if the wind picked up. Then he simply curled up on the floor of the cockpit. As far as I could tell, he was asleep within moments. Piiram set a line for fish and followed suit, below deck.

I couldn't sleep. I slouched in the cockpit with the tiller under my armpit, lost in thought.

I noticed that Piiram had tied the fishing line twice – firmly to a cleat under the gunwale, and with some kind of slipknot to the mainsheet, half a metre from Mashaar's wrist. *Cunning*, I thought. *Wake Mashaar up if there's a big fish, but let the knot slip before he realizes he's been tricked.* I couldn't help smiling to myself.

I won't say anything. I haven't noticed. They've obviously got a good relationship, anyway. Are they brothers? Or just friends? I simply don't know. They don't look particularly alike, but that doesn't tell you anything.

The view of the heavens was fantastic.

If I knew the stars better, I could work out our latitude. Pah. It'd have been easier by the elevation of the sun at midday on midwinter's day – if I'd known when that was. Not that the few days my calendar might be out by would make a lot of difference. I'd have to think pretty hard to work out how long it is since I landed at Sirimi though, never mind how long I was in the air. And it wouldn't in the slightest help me to find Aila if I knew, anyway.

I woke in the middle of the night. The stars had disappeared, so had the lights on the shore, and the lights of the other boats away to the south. *Fog – but not thick enough to see the fog itself by our own masthead light.* The air was only very slightly damp, but I could see my breath.

By the light of our masthead light, I could just make out Mashaar on the cockpit floor. He'd moved right across from one side to the other, but the mainsheet was still round his wrist. I couldn't see well enough to tell whether the fishing line was still tied to it.

I woke again to the sound and smell of frying fish. It was just beginning to get light, and it was foggy. Thick fog, and not a breath of wind.

Mashaar and Piiram were sitting one each side of the cockpit, warming their hands at a little charcoal brazier in the middle of the cockpit. There were potatoes in the pan, several large pieces of fish, and some egg roe.

"Caught that last night?"

"Ah, you're awake. Yup, and there's two more bigger ones and the rest of this one down below in the ice. Lucky I woke up not long after the first one bit, or she'd probably have been the only one."

I know how that happened, but I'm saying nothing.

I noticed there was still a line over the side. *Well, while we're going nowhere, what's the point missing out on the fishing?*

"If the weather keeps on like this, you'd have been quicker getting the coach to Karrem, and hiring a gig from there this morning."

"I know why he didn't want to do that, Piiram. This way, no-one who might tell tales knows where he's headed. Anyway, who was to know we were going to get becalmed?"

"Another reason is that I need someone like you to vouch for me with whoever's going to take me on to Troum or Zhaam."

"You could always have proved who you are like you did in Griishi."

"I don't know whether I could. I think I was lucky with Tomaam and Aibram. If they hadn't spotted me and questioned me, I'd have arrived by coach in Griimi all on my own, and had no-one to vouch for me. Would you have trusted me, or just told me you didn't know anything about Griima?"

"That's a good point. It was them who approached you, not you approaching them? I wonder why they did that."

"Oh, that's easy. I was collecting ekraahi. I think they probably didn't expect a hired man to be doing that."

"Ah, I see. No, they wouldn't expect that. They wouldn't expect them to know how, nor to think of it as a way to pretend they were you. Are you an auker, too? You didn't look the part in the clothes you were wearing when I first saw you, but you'd not had them long, and you've got the build."

"No, I'd be scared silly on the cliffs. I only learnt how to collect ekraahi a few weeks ago. Griima showed me." *I would be scared silly on the cliffs, too. Yet ballooning wasn't too bad once I got used to it. Landing was the only bad bit, really. I wonder if I could learn auking?*

"You could have collected ekraahi in Griimi, and waited for one of us to pounce on you."

"That's a bit hit and miss, though. I hadn't planned it. I didn't even know I ought to be handing over a share. Biilam told me Griima had brought him ekraahi – and auks and eggs – and never mentioned anyone taking a share."

"She's an amazing auker. No-one would ask her, especially since she looks just like the Ghost. She gave us a whole bagful, too. Mum and Dad have them in the smoker at home now. And we've got some eggs she gave us on board, too. If we hadn't caught these last night, it would be eggs for breakfast now, but eggs keep better than fresh fish. Here, this roe is ready."

We ate in silence. The fish and potatoes were ready by the time we'd finished the roe, and Piiram put a pan of water on the brazier in place of the frying pan.

There wasn't much we could do. We lounged about in the cockpit as the fog got gradually brighter around us, hoping for a bite on the line or a breath of wind. The water boiled, and Piiram made an infusion with some dried leaves.

I wonder if that's the same stuff they made at Belgaam?

It wasn't the same, but it wasn't bad. I suspected it was a mild stimulant, and it was certainly a diuretic.

"I wonder how long we're going to be stuck here. Is it often like this?"

"Who knows? I've been becalmed for five days before now, but it's usually not more than a few hours. The wind's often light for a while after a calm, but there's a fair chance of an onshore breeze once the sun burns this fog off. And you can just about see the disk of the sun now."

Mashaar nodded over my shoulder, and I looked round. The sun, a slightly brighter disk showing through the fog, was behind me. We'd turned a half turn in the night.

"You're not worried about drifting onto rocks in the fog like this?"

"No. There's no wind, we're going nowhere. We were ten miles or so off the coast last night, and we won't have moved more than a mile in the night. It's all deep water around here. Too deep for an anchor – well, too deep for any rope we've got, anyway. The fog'll be gone soon, and then we'll see where we are."

Mashaar knew what he was talking about. Within minutes, we could see patches of blue above us, and the top of the fog was visibly moving. Not fast, but definitely blowing gently shorewards. Before long the whole fog right down to water level was on the move, and there were the faintest signs of ripples on the water. Mashaar motioned me away from the tiller, took hold of it, and pulled on the mainsheet. We were moving – slowly, but fast enough for the rudder to act, and slowly we turned round to face the sun.

"Well, I can't see anything yet, but this is the right general direction, and it won't be long before we can see where we are."

"Any idea how long it'll take to get to Oushi?"

"Depends how much the wind picks up. This is just an onshore breeze, nothing more than that. If that's all we get, it could take most of the day. But don't worry, Griima's pretty safe the other side of the estuary. What worries me is what you're going to do when you find her. You can't both stay out in the wilds forever. Well, I suppose you could, but would you want to? Do you know how to scrape a living there? Do you want your children to grow up as little savages?"

A few weeks ago, I'd have been happy just to be alive and free. Being a savage myself would have been absolutely fine. Little savage offspring would have been an incredible bonus. How expectations and hopes change! And what does Aila want? Can Maamatta's promise be relied upon? Should I tell these men about it?

No point telling them. It can't be relied upon in any useful way – she's got those two boys, who can't be trusted. Things could go badly wrong there. We need Graamon's help. Can we get to Baam in Barioha, without anyone catching hold of our tail? Should I ask these lads about that? No harm in it, I'm sure. They're not going to tell anyone anything.

"We've got friends in Barioha who will be able to sort things out for us if we can get there safely. How far beyond Zhaam is Barioha? Could any of the fishermen take us there?"

"Barioha is up the river, and we can't take these boats up there without knowing the river. The locals do, but nobody I know would go up there. But we can get to Mormi, at the mouth of the river. With a decent wind, it's a day's sailing from Zhaam to Mormi. You can hire a gig in Mormi, and I guess it's about three hours into Barioha from there. That's a guess, mind, I've never been. I've only been to Mormi a few times, after running before a storm."

Of course. That's why he knows Griishi so well. Any port in a storm – and Griishi's relatively close to home.

The fog went quite suddenly. Everything to the north was still hidden in a bank of fog, but it was receding northwards quite fast. The wind was picking up a little. Ahead, I could see a rocky headland in the distance.

"That's better! If this keeps up, we'll be there by late morning. It'll be low tide, so we'll have to anchor offshore and go in in the dinghy. We'll just have to hope no-one who matters sees you."

Piiram had a better suggestion. "No, Owen can stay on the boat. You and I can go ashore and see if Jalaan's there. No need for Owen to come ashore at all if he is, we can talk to Jalaan."

I'd have liked to see Oushi, but Piiram's right. Better let them do the talking anyway. Come and see Oushi with Aila sometime – but there's a whole world to see, why Oushi especially anyway? Something about it has captured my imagination, but is it really anywhere special? Yaana was born there. So? See what Aila wants to do.

Mashaar altered course slightly, heading for a spot just north of the rocky point.

We did indeed arrive at Oushi late in the morning. Piiram dropped anchor a couple of hundred metres outside the breakwater. The anchor wasn't an iron one with flukes, like the anchors I was used to in England. It was just a large lump of waterworn limestone with a hole in it.

"Dad remembers when you could come in here whatever the tide, in a bigger boat than this. Another fifteen years and they'll have to build a new breakwater further out. We've got the same problem at Griimi, of course."

And at just about every harbour in the world. You can see from the remains of their harbours, forty-five metres above sea level now, how the ancients had it easy, with sea level near enough constant for generations. They could build huge, deep harbours for huge ships, and expect them to last long enough to make the effort worthwhile.

Mashaar and Piiram climbed down into the dinghy. For a short while I could hear the neat plops of their oars as they rowed for the harbour. *Not much splash. They're good. Not surprising, I suppose.*

I kept my head below the gunwale, and wondered how long they'd be ashore.

How will Aila react when I eventually catch up with her? Will she be pleased, or angry? She's never been angry with me, but she did say I should find someone else. But she said she'd love me forever, too.

They didn't actually take very long, although of course it seemed like forever.

"Jalaan's there all right. He took her to Troum, but he can't take you, he's repairing his boat. It'll be several days before he's ready, he reckons. Griima told him you work for the Railway, though. We can't afford the time to take you for nothing, but we'll take you happily if you can pay us."

Either Imbaal's done rather well getting my clothes, or they're doing rather well if he's paying a fair price, or a bit of both. But fair play, they're doing me a huge service, and I'm better off than they are.

"Fair enough. How much do you want?"

"How does sixty coins sound?"

Ouch. It sounds a lot. But I don't really know what things cost, so I'm no judge. It might leave me a bit short, too. I can't get any more until I can get to the station in Barioha. Surely they're trying for a high price, and ready to haggle?

"It sounds a lot. I don't have that much on me."

Not quite true, but...

"Okay, make it fifty. And don't worry, we'll trust you to pay us later. We know you'll come back. Just give us ten each for pocket money for the moment, if you can."

I could, and I did.

"We can set off right now if you like, but there's no strangers around, you can come ashore for a little while if you want to."

"I expect he'd rather get moving. The wind's fairly good at the moment, it'd be a pity to waste it."

I'd have loved to have gone ashore for a while, but I wanted even more to get to Aila as soon as possible, and said so.

We had to beat upwind to get around this headland, too, but then it was a broad reach towards Troum.

"With this wind, we'll make it around sunset – probably just a little after."

What will the reception be like? Will Aila still be there, or will she have moved on again? Will she see us arriving? If she does, will she be afraid it's Jerem's man arriving? Hide somewhere to see who it is, or just get out of the way quickly? If she does see it's me, how will she react?

You can't think like that all the time. Once the fog had gone, there were wonderful views of the mountains behind us, snowy caps bright in the sunshine. In all other directions, all I could see was sea. Mashaar had no navigational aids whatsoever, but was clearly confident he knew where he was headed.

The wind kept pretty much the same all day, and Mashaar's prediction wasn't far off. A rocky coast appeared ahead late in the afternoon.

Mashaar altered course a little closer to the wind. "Not bad. We're a bit too far up the estuary, but better that than risk going south of the point and missing it altogether!"

We still had a few miles to go to reach the coast. By the time the sun went down, I still couldn't see any sign of a settlement, or indeed any sign of human life on the coast at all. The wind had dropped to a gentle breeze. But Mashaar said we were almost there.

There were quite a few stars in the sky when Mashaar announced that we were just off Troum. The moon was low in the west, little more than a fingernail. I couldn't see a thing on the coast.

"Don't they have lights in Troum?"

"Not many, and never any facing the coast. Especially no leading lights. Troum's a strange place, not good to turn up after dark. It's best if we anchor a little way off, and row in in the morning."

It was only then that I realized he'd not lit a masthead light, either.

Mashaar brought us round into the wind, what little was left of it, and Piiram lowered the anchor stone over the bows.

I could see that he was feeling for the bottom. When he found it, he checked how much rope he had left, and seemed satisfied. He chucked the spare rope over the side. "Deep enough here, and the bottom's soft."

"The bottom's soft everywhere here, as long as you're not too close in."

"Doesn't that stone drag a bit?"

"Oh, yes, it drags a bit. We might have moved fifty metres by morning, more if there's a real blow. But if there's a real blow,

you want it to drag. Better to drag it than go to the bottom where
you are. But the water's deep enough to know we're not near
any mud banks, and there are no rocks this far from the coast
around here."

Piiram started frying fish and potatoes again. Mashaar baited
a series of hooks on a line that had several small floats, and cast
it over the side. "More hope than expectation. This isn't a very
good spot."

There was something calming about sitting in the cockpit
under the stars, with the glow of the brazier almost the only
light. We ate in silence.

Piiram made the leaf infusion again, and we sat sipping. The
wind had dropped to nothing again.

After a while Mashaar broke the silence. "You're not from
anywhere around here, are you? I thought at first you were from
Briggi, once I realized you'd swapped boots with Zhor. But
you're not. Briggi men talk a little oddly, but Laana isn't your
mother tongue at all, is it? Nor Maara, for that matter, I'm used
to the way Maaramen talk. I can't place your way of talking at
all."

"That's not really surprising. I'm from England, and as far as
I know I'm the only Englishman anywhere around here."

"Never even heard of it. Whereabouts is it? It must be a long
way off."

"I don't really know whereabouts it is, from here. And it is a
long way off, but I don't know how far."

"How the devil did you get here, then?"

"That's a long story."

"We've got all night."

I owed them that much. When I'd finished, Piiram wanted to
know how I'd met Griima, but Mashaar shushed him. "I think
it's best if we don't know too much."

I was quite relieved. I didn't want to tell too much, but nor I
didn't want to refuse.

Chapter 14

It was foggy again in the morning. Piiram fried fish and potatoes again. "We can't go anywhere until we can see the sun, at least. I haven't got a clue which is the way towards the shore. It's so still I can't even hear the waves hitting the rocks. But anyway, it's best to wait until the fog clears, or at least gets a bit thinner. We don't want them to think we're sneaking up on them."

Blimey. What a place. No lights in the evening, don't arrive in the evening, and don't arrive in fog. Talk about distrust! Maybe they've got good reason.

'Dangerous place if you look like money...'

"What would they do to us if they thought we were sneaking up on them?"

"Who knows? I wouldn't want to be the one to find out. But if we're straightforward with them, and they can see we're being straightforward with them, they'll be straightforward with us."

By the time we'd finished breakfast, the sun was a dim circle in the sky, and the coast was vaguely visible as a fuzzy, darker bit of fog.

"If we wait another few minutes before setting off, they'll be able to see it's just three chaps in a dinghy before we get too close in. We'll just have hot water, Piiram, don't put anything in it."

The fog lifted as we approached the shore, but I couldn't see any sign of human habitation. As we got closer, I realized that there were people sitting on some of the rocks, watching us, but I still couldn't see any buildings. We were heading for a gap in the rocks, maybe seven or eight metres wide.

"They'd have recognized Jalaan by now, but they don't know us so well. We've only been here a few times before. It's not the easiest place to run to in bad weather. At least they don't mind if you bring a boat right in if you have to, they even put up leading lights during storms. They'd have been very suspicious if we'd brought it in last night. There's not enough wind this morning, even if we wanted to."

Then suddenly I spotted Aila, high up on the rocks, much further away than all the other people. She'd already seen me, and was running, leaping from rock to rock. Then she disappeared behind some rocks, and didn't reappear.

Piiram had seen her, too. "That was Griima running, wasn't it? She must have seen you. She's heading for the quayside, we'll be there in a minute."

My heart was pounding in my chest. I felt as if I would burst.

The rocks either side of the inlet towered over us, and the inlet seemed to go on forever. Then suddenly it opened out into the most beautiful natural harbour. Piiram threw the painter to a young man on the quayside, who tied it round a stone bollard. As we clambered out onto the quay, Aila appeared at a run.

She ran straight up to me, flung her arms around me, and buried her face in my chest. I put my arms around her and held her tight. She was breathing hard from running. I could feel the tears running down my face.

Then she was leaning back in my arms, looking up at me with tears in her eyes, too. "What are you doing here? I told you to go and find somebody else! Didn't you get my letter?"

"Yes, I got it. You didn't think I'd really do that, did you?"

"Yes! No! I don't know. You're a naughty boy, anyway!" She buried her face in my chest again and held me tight. I could feel her breath catching in great sobs.

She looked up at me again. "But what can we do? Where can we go? You shouldn't have come, it just puts you in danger too. There's no point getting both of us killed."

"But we can do something. We've got friends. Lots of them."

"So we get our friends killed, too? Do you know what happened to Jalaan?"

"Nothing's happened to Jalaan. Mashaar and Piiram talked to him yesterday."

She was beginning to calm down a little. "Come into the inn. They'll get you a skiir. I could do with one, too."

She seemed to see Mashaar and Piiram for the first time, and reached out towards them. "I don't know how to thank you two. I told you not to tell anyone you'd seen me, but I'm so glad you told Owen. You come and have some skiir, too."

Somehow I hadn't expected Troum to have an inn.

The whole village seemed to face in towards the harbour. It reminded me of the village on the Sirimi road, and I wondered for a moment why, then realized. There was no glass in the windows, the buildings were the same rough cut grey limestone, and none of the roofs protruded above the line of the rocks behind. I realized that we had an audience.

Aila led the way up a flight of stone stairs between two houses, onto a narrow alleyway behind them. The inn, which didn't look any different from the houses, was just the other side of the alleyway.

"Have you three had anything to eat this morning? I'm well in credit here, and Bashaamu's always got stew on the go."

We had, but Piiram was willing to fill up again, and Mashaar said he wouldn't mind a half portion. I really didn't feel hungry at all. I just wanted to be with Aila. And we needed to talk, too.

"He tried to kill me. Twice, now. And he didn't care if he killed Jalaan in the process."

"Who did?" I was fairly sure I already knew.

"Jerem's man, of course. Or more likely, his father's, if Jerem's dead."

What to say, and what not to say? I really want to tell her in private, but I can't say that in front of all these people. If I tell her here about Jerem's legs, then everyone here will know. But so what? They've tried to kill her already. It can't get any worse than it is. And these people are unlikely to talk to anyone else anyway.

"Jerem's not dead. He's a gibbering idiot now, and he'll never walk again. But it wasn't you who smashed his knees, was it?"

Aila looked thunderstruck. "Smashed his knees? No! Why would I do that? I hit him on the head, and he fell down. I didn't know if he was alive or dead, but he wasn't moving. I just ran out of the house and hid until I heard Berraami's train coming. Surely Berraami told you the story?"

"Yes, that's exactly the story she told me. But Mashaari went round to your place a few hours after you left..."

"I know. I saw her. That's when I knew I had to leave."

"Ah. I did wonder about the coincidence of the timing. Anyway, Mashaari told your Mum and Gran that you'd smashed Jerem's knees as well. They seem to have just accepted Mashaari's word for that, but it seemed strange to me. Then when I talked with Birgom, he didn't believe you'd have done that. Nor did Maamatta..."

"Who's Maamatta?"

"Borjii Maamatta. The lady of the wealthy family in Griishi..."

"You've been to Griishi? And talked with the rich people?"

"I've been to Griishi, but I've never talked to the rich people there, no – well, apart from the two boys. They gave me a letter from their mother. Here, you read it." I fished Maamatta's letter out of my bag.

"Aibram warned me not to trust the boys, though."

"I don't know who Aibram is, either, Owen. We've got lots to tell each other, I know. But let me read this first."

People were crowding round us, fascinated. I was pretty sure none of them could read.

Suddenly Aila thrust the letter into my hand. "Here, you read it to me. I can't see, I'm crying too much."

She grabbed me round the chest and put her head on my shoulder. I read it to her quietly. I was sure everyone could hear me, anyway. They weren't making a sound themselves. I carefully changed 'Aila' to 'Griima' throughout as I read.

MY DEAR OWEN,

DON'T WORRY THAT I KNOW WHO YOU ARE AND WHY YOU'RE HERE, AND THAT MY BOYS DO TOO. I'M WRITING TO WARN YOU TO BE CAREFUL, ESPECIALLY FOR GRIIMA'S SAKE.

SHE'S RUNNING AWAY BECAUSE SHE THINKS JEREM IS ANGRY WITH HER. AS FAR AS SHE KNOWS, HE COULD HAVE RECOVERED COMPLETELY.

EVERYBODY ON THE CIRCUIT KNOWS THE STORY, BUT I DON'T BELIEVE IT. IF I'M RIGHT, GRIIMA DOESN'T KNOW HOW MUCH DANGER SHE IS IN. I DON'T BELIEVE SHE BROKE JEREM'S KNEES. I DON'T DOUBT THAT SHE BROKE HIS HEAD, SHE'S A CAPABLE YOUNG WOMAN AND THAT WAS SURELY THE RIGHT THING TO DO. BUT WHY BREAK HIS KNEES WHEN HIS HEAD'S ALREADY

BROKEN? THAT DOESN'T MAKE SENSE, AND I KNOW SHE'S A SENSIBLE GIRL.
GAMAARA HAS TALKED ABOUT HER MANY TIMES.

I'M SURE IT MUST HAVE BEEN TIIRAM (THAT'S JEREM'S FATHER) WHO DID
THAT. IT IS IN CHARACTER. NOW OF COURSE HE WANTS EVERYONE TO
BELIEVE IT WAS GRIIMA. HE KNOWS GRIIMA KNOWS SHE DIDN'T BREAK
JEREM'S KNEES, AND I EXPECT HE'S VERY AFRAID THAT WHEN SHE HEARS
THAT PEOPLE ARE SAYING THAT, SHE'LL DENY IT, AND THEY'LL FIND OUT IT
WAS HIM. SO THERE IS A VERY REAL RISK THAT HE'LL HAVE HIRED SOMEONE
TO ARRANGE A NASTY ACCIDENT FOR HER. EXCEPT MAYBE IN THE HEAT OF
THE MOMENT, JEREM WOULDN'T HAVE WANTED HER KILLED, I'M SURE, AND I
THINK SHE'D KNOW THAT. BUT TIIRAM PROBABLY DOES WANT HER DEAD,
AND SHE DOESN'T KNOW THAT.

I'M SURE THAT GAMAARA AND OTHERS ALSO SUSPECT THAT IT WAS
TIIRAM, NOT GRIIMA, WHO BROKE HIS KNEES. BUT THEY DAREN'T BELIEVE IT,
CAN'T PROVE IT, AND AREN'T SAYING ANYTHING TO ANYONE — WELL, NOT
THAT I'VE HEARD, ANYWAY.

MY BOYS WILL DO ANYTHING THEY CAN TO HELP — WITHIN REASON,
DON'T FORGET THEY'RE ONLY BOYS. AND IF YOU CAN POSSIBLY GET HER
BACK HERE TO OUR HOUSE, WE CAN KEEP HER SAFE UNTIL THE TRUTH IS
PUBLIC AND SHE'S OUT OF DANGER. MY HUSBAND DOESN'T KNOW WHAT I
THINK, BUT IF SHE'S HERE TO TELL HIM ABOUT THE KNEES, HE'LL BELIEVE
IT. HE DOESN'T KNOW SHE WAS IN GRIISHI, EITHER.

I'M ONLY SORRY WE DIDN'T KNOW THE STORY UNTIL AFTER SHE'D
ALREADY LEFT GRIISHI. WE'VE NOT TOLD ANYONE SHE WAS HERE, AND WE
WON'T. I CAN'T SPEAK FOR THE COACH DRIVERS, OF COURSE.

GOOD WINDS AND FAVOURABLE TIDES,

Borjii Maamatta

"Your reading is fantastic, Owen. You've been studying hard,
I can tell."

"We were snowed in in Briggi for four weeks. What else was
there to do? Well, really there was lots to do, but I did spend a
lot of time studying, yes. I didn't know anything had happened
to you until we got through to Tambuk, where Berraami was
stuck."

"So what should we do now? Should we get Mashaar and
Piiram to take us back to Griishi, to Maamatta?"

"No, I don't think so. Maamatta won't believe that her boys can't be trusted, but Aibram is sure they can't be. He thinks they'd tell anyone anything for a few coins, because they know no-one would dare touch them. Graamon has a friend in Barioha who'll help us, though. Mashaar and Piiram will take us to where we can get a gig into Barioha. I hope Jerem's father doesn't have any friends here listening to us."

"I'm pretty sure he doesn't. Oh, I've so much to tell you, Owen. But Maamatta has it exactly right, I'm sure. And Tiiram's man did find me, and he's tried to kill me twice now, but he won't try again. But sooner or later another one will come looking for him, and with murder in his head."

"He won't try again? He's dead?"

"I doubt if he's dead yet. He's only been there three days. But he won't last long."

"Where is he? Are you sure he can't escape from wherever he is?"

"No, he doesn't have a boat. And he doesn't have any fresh water, either – or not more than he was carrying, and he probably wasn't carrying any. He didn't expect to be stuck there."

"Stuck where? Where is he? How did he get stuck?"

Aila started crying again. *She's remembering something that happened. What happened? Patience, Owen. She'll tell you everything in her own time.*

After a little while, she took another sip of skiir, and pulled herself together. "The first thing that happened was sailing over here with Jalaan. We were about halfway across when the rudder broke off. Jalaan spotted it floating a little way astern, and spilled the wind to slow us down, but of course he couldn't bring the boat round into the wind, so we were just blowing with the wind. The broken rudder was too far away already to retrieve it, we were blowing along much faster than anyone could possibly swim, and we didn't have a long enough rope to swim for it with a rope to get back with. We thought we were finished, and would get smashed to pieces on the rocks halfway between Troum and the river mouth. But we were lucky, we got caught on a mud bank instead, and it was half tide, going down. Jalaan managed to break a plank out of the cabin roof, and lashed it onto the stump of the rudder. We waited for the tide to float us again, and managed to limp in here. He said the boat was handling like a grumpy goat, but he managed, and here I am. They made a better temporary rudder for him here, but they could see that the original break was deliberate sabotage. They looked the boat over thoroughly, but couldn't find anything else. You said you'd talked to Jalaan?"

"No, but Mashaar and Piiram have."

"Yes, he said he had some repairs to do that would take him a few days. He didn't say anything about sabotage."

"Oh, and that was ages ago! Surely it wouldn't take so long to make a new rudder, and repair where he broke the plank out?"

"No, that sounds like two or three days' work to me. Maybe there was some other bit of sabotage, that they didn't notice here. Or maybe it was nothing to do with it, just coincidence. We all have to do repairs sometimes."

"So how did Tiiram's man end up stuck wherever he is?"

Aila took another sip of skiir. "Nobody expected him to follow me here. We all assumed he'd think he'd done his job, but he obviously watched to see if Jalaan came home. Or he got word from someone. And someone must have leaked where Jalaan had taken me, too – or he made a good guess. Anyway, he came round overland, on horseback. That's quite a trip, it's a long way, through uninhabited, trackless, really rough country. At first we'd no idea how he got here, but Biishu found the horse. It's branded Mezham, so someone there will be getting pretty angry soon, if they're not already, unless he's left a big deposit. I was the first to see him. I was out auking on the point. It's an island. I saw someone coming over in a kayak, but they obviously weren't very expert with it, so I knew it wasn't anyone from Troum. So I didn't let him see that I'd seen him. I carried on auking, but kept an eye on what he was doing. He started to scramble up to the top, and then I knew. I made sure I was secure, and tied the bottom of my rope to a good rock where I was. I'd guessed right. My rope came tumbling down. He was trying to arrange another accident for me, but he'd misjudged. I was down that rope like the wind, and had my kayak and his long before he could get down from the top. He's stuck on the point without a kayak now, and I'm back here."

"So what will you do with him now?"

"Everyone here says we should just leave him there. He'll be dead in a week or two at most. It's obvious he was trying to kill me."

"Hmm. Alive, he could be very good evidence against Tiiram. Is there any way we can keep him alive without risking him getting away, or hurting anyone?"

"What use is evidence against Tiiram? He's rich, it doesn't matter how good the evidence is."

"I'm not so sure. Think about Maamatta's letter. If the rich themselves believe he's guilty, then he's on his own. And Graamon has a lot of influence with a lot of rich people."

"I hope you're right. It's our only hope. But whether there's any way to keep him alive safely, I don't know."

Aila looked round at the ring of faces surrounding us, so I did too. Most were looking rather blank, but a few looked thoughtful.

Mashaar was the first to speak. "I don't think so, not here. And there's no safe way to move him anywhere he could be kept alive. Leave him to the birds. It means the point's out of bounds for auking until he's dead, but that's not such a big thing. People leave it alone for days at a time anyway, I'm sure. But his horse, and the people he hired it from, are pretty good evidence themselves."

"The people he hired the horse from don't know who sent him, as evidence they're not good as he is."

"If he hired it anyway. What's the betting he stole it? He stole the kayak to get out to the point."

"There's no risk he could swim back from the point, is there? Or even that he's done it already?"

"He's not tried yet, anyway. He's just sitting there staring at whoever goes to look at him. I think he's expecting to be rescued eventually. Maybe he can't swim, or maybe he realizes that if he tries, someone will stick an arrow in him. It'd be a hell of a place to swim across, anyway, with tidal currents and cross seas, and nowhere to climb ashore safely on the mainland side.

He'd have to swim all the way round to Troum harbour. I've never heard of anyone doing it."

Mashaar said that if we wanted them to take us to Mormi, it would be good not to waste the wind that he thought was beginning to get up. Not only were we inside the inn, but the inn itself was in a deep hollow amongst the rocks; so how he knew the wind was getting up, I don't know. But we all went outside, and then you could tell that he was right.

Aila was clinging tight to my side. "I shall miss the people here, Owen. There's something about Troum. The people here have been incredibly good to me. But I know. We should get to Barioha as quickly as we can, before Tiiram becomes too concerned about where his man's got to."

The farewells were tearful on both sides, with lots of hugging. It seemed that the whole village had taken Aila – Griima – to its heart. Even Mashaar, Piiram and I got hugs. Mashaar and Piiram were given heartfelt thanks, and I was told to "Look after her!"

I'd like to come back here. We will, one day. In fact, I think I wouldn't mind living here, it's a lovely place full of lovely people. But what about Graamon, and the research institute, and Briggi, and Viina's lovely room, and Yaana and Yaani and Peyr and Grim in Laanoha? – and Birgom. Got to talk to Aila about all this, but this isn't the time. Oh, and there's that question of bringing up children as little savages.

Is there anything really so wrong with bringing up children as little savages anyway?

The dinghy wasn't big enough for four – it was really only designed for two, but I sat in the stern, and one of the village women brought Aila in a canoe.

The wind was from a little east of south, but the point at Troum was more east than south of the village, so we didn't need to tack to clear the point. Sailing close hauled, we ran parallel to the coast towards the point.

"You two keep your heads down," Mashaar said. "It's probably better if Tiiram's man doesn't see you."

"I don't see that it matters, he'll be dead soon," Aila said, but she snuggled down beside me in the bottom of the cockpit anyway.

"That's very likely, but just in case he somehow gets away, it's better if he doesn't know you're with us."

We heard him shouting to us to stop and pick him up as we sailed past, but Mashaar didn't even let him see that he'd heard.

"That's one risk, of course, that someone will stop and pick him up. I'm sure the two chaps sitting the other side of the channel watching him will shout to anyone to leave him where he is, but not everyone might take any notice of them. It's not a big risk, though. Very few boats come here apart from the Troum people themselves. I don't think any of the fishermen would pick him up if the Troum people said not to, and the chance of anyone else coming here in the next little while is pretty remote."

I still felt very uncomfortable just leaving the man to die for lack of water. *But he tried to kill Aila. Why should I feel sorry for him?*

Piiram had another thought. "If it rains, he'll be able to find some water collected somewhere. At this time of year, it's likely to rain any time."

Mashaar laughed. "So he'll maybe last a few days longer. Lucky man. Don't worry about him, he's as good as dead already. Maybe if it rains often enough, he'll last until he starves instead. I doubt he's capable of getting at the eggs, even with Griima's rope dangling there for him. I wonder how long you can survive on raw eggs and rainwater?"

Aila whispered in my ear, "I wish they'd stop talking about him. I don't want to think about him."

But she couldn't help it. "Even if he manages to climb the cliffs, egg time will be over in two or three weeks, unless there's a bad spell of weather and the birds have to start again. Then he's got to eat chicks. Even an expert can only catch adult birds when they're sitting eggs. He could try ekraahi, but you've got to cook them well or they're a sure recipe for the worst bad stomach you can imagine. I wouldn't like to have to eat them raw!"

Near Laanoha, that's no doubt true. Here, it might not be. But I won't say anything.

From the floor of the cockpit, we could see the upper part of the cliffs. I could see birds perched on ledges, and white streaks of droppings below every ledge. I imagined Aila up on the cliffs, clinging on to a rope with one hand, and catching birds or collecting eggs with the other. In my mind's eye, I could see the picture I'd seen in the attic in Griimi. Just as it matched Aila perfectly, it matched these cliffs perfectly, although I knew it had been painted in Griishi, and its cliffs were the Griishi cliffs.

But Aila isn't up on those cliffs now, she's right beside me, with her shoulder under my armpit, and her head resting on my neck. I held her more tightly.

We were leaving the cliffs behind. The wind freshened and veered due south, but Mashaar held his course for a while before turning a little north of east. I guessed that Mashaar knew the coast well, and that there were nasty rocks well out to sea on the line of the cliffs. *Maybe he can even see the rocks under the water by the way the waves behave above them.*

The sun was shining, the sky was blue with a few white clouds scurrying northwards, and Aila was snuggling against me. I felt almost happy. But I still had nagging doubts about how the Tiiram situation would work out. *Are we doing the best thing? Hmm. I don't see how any other course would be better.*

"If you two want to sit up, we're well out of his sight now. Have been for a while."

"Let's. I'd like to see the coast along here. This stretch is famously wild. You want to hear Gran's tales!"

"That's better. The trim of the boat's better with you two up there. We'll make an extra half knot like this."

Troum point was already shrinking behind us, and we couldn't actually see anything else but sea all around.

"It'll be another hour before you can see Zhaam point, and Troum point will have nearly disappeared by then. We'd have to sail closer in to see the coast, and it'd take longer to get to Mormi. If the wind keeps up, we might make Mormi late tonight, but if it drops overnight like it has the last few nights it could easily be two days before we get there."

"It might be safer just to stay the night at Zhaam when we get there, brother. I don't think I fancy a night halfway across the bay."

"Fair enough. I can't say the prospect appeals to me much, either."

So they are brothers – unless they use the word the same way as people do in England. I wonder what's so terrible about a night halfway across the bay?

I do believe Aila's gone to sleep. I twisted myself round to hold her more securely. *I wonder how much she's been sleeping recently? I bet she's not been sleeping well at all.*

We'd be better off on the cockpit floor, but I don't want to wake her up to move her.

Mashaar had noticed, too. "She's nodded off? Probably a good thing. I bet she's scarcely slept a wink since Jalaan lost his rudder."

"I was just thinking the exact same thing."

"Piiram's probably right that it'll be better to spend the night at Zhaam than on the open water, but I hope she won't feel insecure there again."

"Hard to know. But it's pretty unlikely that Tiiram would have sent more than one man, unless he sent them together. And if there'd been two together, the other man wouldn't have left that horse around for them to find. I'm pretty sure we're safe, at least until Tiiram starts to wonder what's happened to his man. And we should be safely in Barioha before then."

"It's one thing to know something in your head, it's quite another what you feel."

"That's very true. At least I think she must be feeling reasonably secure just now."

"Just having you to hold on to must make a huge difference."

"That's probably true, even if she can probably look after herself better than I can."

Mashaar laughed quietly. "What happens, happens. You never know how good you are in a situation you've never been in before until you're in it. I don't know how many men would have dared float halfway round the world hanging from an oversize paper lantern!"

"You do what you have to when you can't think of any other option."

"But you're right about Griima. She foxed that man perfectly beautifully. He probably thinks she planned it all, and led him out there on purpose."

"I haven't actually asked her. Maybe she did."

"No, I don't think so. I don't think she knew he was in the area until she saw him in the kayak. Lucky she saw him."

I shuddered involuntarily at the idea that she might not have seen him, and that he might have succeeded in making her fall. Aila stirred and mumbled something, but didn't wake.

We sailed on in silence, apart from the slap, slap, slap of the waves against the hull.

Troum point shrank behind us, and another headland appeared in the distance dead ahead. Mashaar altered course very slightly, heading just inland of the point.

"That's Zhaam point. We're making good time. But Piiram's right, better not to try to get to Mormi in one go. It's not as though we're pressed for time now."

Funny how he seemed so itchy to get away from Troum, but now we're not pressed for time. He seems very confident of his assessment of situations, and he seems genuinely to have a good grip on reality. I wonder why the change? No sense asking; he'll tell me if he wants to.

I could see Piiram's head and shoulders over the top of the cabin. He must have been sitting on the foredeck, leaning back on the cabin, constantly on the lookout ahead. Aila was sound asleep; Mashaar seemed lost in thought, but holding our course beautifully steady.

The wind was cold, but the sun was bright, and warm on my shoulders. I dozed.

The topography here isn't like England. In England, we have a line of big cliffs with platforms at their feet at about a forty-five metres above sea level. According to Godfrey, it's an old sea coast that had stayed pretty constant probably for thousands of years, and surely that's confirmed by all the remains of things the ancients did along that line. Here, they've got that at about the same height, but there's another one pretty much at current sea level. It's not that sea level here is constant, it's falling at about the same rate it is in England, which probably means the sea here connects with the sea there eventually – although the connection could be under the ice, which would explain why English sailors are so rare, they'd have had to come overland somewhere as well as probably two long sea crossings. But if sea level's not been roughly constant at the present level for millennia, why the cliffs and platform at sea level? The only explanation I can think of is that at some time in the distant past, long before even the period of stable sea level we'd already worked out, there must have been an earlier period of stable sea level, at roughly the level we're at now. But if that's the case, why isn't there a similar line on the English coast?

Ah. One possibility is that the connection between the sea here and the sea there isn't as deep as that, and once sea level drops much below where it is now, the two seas aren't connected any more. Or maybe at some point the sea froze right down to the sea bed in the connecting channel. Oh, and there's another possibility – the level of the land itself might change slowly, too. In fact, we can be pretty sure it does, as the weight of ice pushes it down – that's what all the earthquakes are all about, and why they're stronger the closer to the ice you get. We ought to try to devise some way of measuring the compressibility of different kinds of rock – although it must involve creep as well as elastic compressibility. Well, we know it does – look at all the bendy strata that must have been laid down horizontal originally. I wish I could talk to Godfrey about that, he knows much more than I do. I wonder how much anyone here knows?

I ought to write all these thoughts in my notebook, but I can't with Aila sleeping on me like this. I must as soon as I get a chance though, it's exactly the stuff Graamon wants – oh, and Baam will want it, too, especially information about England.

A sudden thought struck me. *Birgom's not originally an English sailor, is he?*

Hmm. If he is, where did he get the name Birgom? Where did he get the name Mezhab? Hmm – where did I get the name Mezhab? And the name Mezhab originally meant 'from Mezham', apparently. And if he's originally an English sailor, how did he get Laanoha papers? Well, how have I got railway papers? Hmm.

Hmm.

Zhaam point was growing slowly; I looked behind, and Troum point had vanished. Apart from Zhaam point, all I could see in all directions was water and sky.

Blue sky, with just a few small white clouds scurrying northwards. Oh, and a couple of gulls, apparently riding a wave of air deep in the lee of the sail. Oh to be able to see the pattern of movement of the air! Can the gulls see it somehow, or do they have an instinct for it, or just years of experience?

And was that a sail, far behind us? Right on the limits of visibility, if it was. I can't see it at all, now. And I can't reach my bag, to get Aila's telescope. When should I give that to her? Privately would be best, best not to get it out anyway.

A sudden realization shocked me awake. *I wonder how good Mashaar's eyesight is? Obvious thing to do is ask him!*

"How good's your eyesight, Mashaar? I thought I saw a sail in the far distance behind us! Too far behind for me to be sure, and I can't see it at all now."

Mashaar looked behind. "I can't see anything now, either. But Piiram's eyesight is much better than mine. Piiram! Come astern a minute!"

The shout woke Aila, and she sat up as. Piiram got up and came into the cockpit.

"Can you see a sail in the distance, behind us? Owen thought he saw one, but too far away for him to be sure."

Piiram scanned the horizon astern, then fixed on a point almost dead astern, just where I thought I'd seen it.

"Could be. Dead astern. I can't be sure, either, but it looks like it."

Mashaar was a bit worried. "Well, we haven't passed anyone fishing, so it's someone else coming this way from Troum. Who, and why? I wouldn't expect anyone coming out of Troum to head in this direction going fishing, I'd expect them to beat southwards for the best chance of a good run home later. I hope no-one picked that villain up and got persuaded to follow us. Bad luck it's so soon after we left, if so."

Piiram had another thought. "Griima, you didn't get the impression there was anyone in Troum who might think to earn themselves a few coins helping him, did you? That would explain the timing, Mashaar."

"I really don't know. They all seemed to be so good with me, and probably most of them were. But how can you tell if there's the odd one or two biding their time, waiting for an opportunity to take advantage? But everybody in Troum would know about it if anyone picked him up, so they'd have had to persuade the whole village."

"Or not have thought through the consequences properly, or decided to argue the point later when they'd got the coins, or try to make a new life somewhere else. I wouldn't bet against it."

"And I thought we were well on our way to safety."

"Well, we pretty certainly are. This is a good boat. We won't stop at Zhaam, and we'll put on the best speed we can."

Piiram was already below decks, sorting something out. I wondered what. Mashaar had already altered course to clear Zhaam point.

Then something occurred to me. "Pass me my bag, Aila." *Oops. Did anyone notice? Don't draw attention to it by correcting yourself.*

If they did notice, they never mentioned it. Aila passed me my bag. "I've got a present for you, from the Griimi innkeeper's mother. I was going to wait for a private time to give it to you, but it would be very useful just now."

I got out the telescope and gave it to Aila. She burst into tears, and I put my arm round her again. "Oh, I could hug her, Owen. What a really, really kind thought! Here, give it to Piiram, he'll see better than I could." She handed the telescope back to me, and I called Piiram up out of the cabin and passed it to him.

"Wow! That's just what we need! That's Tomaam's Dad's telescope, isn't it, Mashaar?"

"Yes, apparently his Mum gave it to Owen as a present for Griima. She must have thought a lot of you, Griima. Well, we all do."

"I used to borrow it when I was out on the cliffs at Griimi, to look out for anyone getting on or off coaches."

Piiram climbed onto the cabin roof. He stood just forward of
the mast and held onto the halyard with one hand. He tried to
hold the telescope to his eye with the other hand.

"It's no good, I can't hold it steady enough. I'll have to lie flat
and use both hands, but I wanted the extra height. If it's there, it
keeps dipping below the horizon."

He lay flat on the cabin roof. Resting his elbows on the roof
and holding the telescope in both hands, he managed to hold it
reasonably steady.

"Blimey. Everything doesn't half jump about when you're
looking through a telescope. And it's hard to get it pointing in
exactly the right direction. Even just holding it on the horizon is
hard, so I can't be sure I'm scanning the whole...ah, yup, there's
definitely a sail! That's all we need to know, unless it gets any
closer. I'm coming down, and I'll get a trapeze set up. We'll
leave them so far behind they won't know where we've gone.
Oh, and we must put a lanyard on this. We don't want to lose it
over the side!"

"Can you two hike as well, do you think? If you can, I'll jury
up some kind of a foresail, too. She wasn't built for speed, but
she's a good boat and strong enough to make the best of this
wind, and their boat won't be any better."

Aila didn't even know what hiking meant, but soon learnt,
and took to it like a natural, which didn't surprise any of us. I'd
only ever seen her on the cliffs in my mind's eye, and a picture
of her grandmother, but the other two had seen it in reality. Aila
and I were soon hanging out as far as we could, while Piiram

rummaged around below to find a piece of sail to tie on the forestay.

"Well, it's not the best foresail you've ever seen, but it's the best I can manage. We ought to make ourselves a proper one sometime, Mashaar."

"How often do we go racing, Piiram?"

Piiram laughed. "I never thought we would. If it wasn't so serious, it could be quite fun."

"Well, I've never seen hikers on a fishing boat before, and you're not having as much effect as they seem to on a toff's dinghy, but it's making a difference. Quite a difference."

It was. It was also hard work. I could see how a better harness could make it a lot easier, but Piiram had done very well at short notice, and I was impressed. We were making a very good speed for a little round-bottomed fishing boat in only a moderate wind.

Mashaar was having a hard time at the tiller, too. "She's hard to keep on course like this! We could do with a rib along the bottom of that foresail, she flaps like billy-oh! But I'm sure she's helping a lot."

"I'm not putting one on now! I don't think we've got anything that would do the job. The tender oars are too long, and I can't think of anything else."

"No, don't worry. But if we ever make a proper one, we should think about that. But we'll probably never be in a race again, so why bother? Just a waste of time."

"Oh, I don't know. Saving half an hour getting to good fishing grounds would pay the effort back quite quickly, really."

"Maybe. We'll think about that later. Could it really save that much time? We'll see how much difference it really makes – but we'd only have one hiker, not three, and we'll never know whether it's the foresail or the hikers that make most of the difference."

Blimey. I wonder how long I can keep this up? The other two don't seem to be having any problem. Yet? Or just not showing it. I don't suppose I'm showing it, either. Courage! That could be the chap who tried to kill Aila following us.

It was actually Aila who buckled first, after about half an hour. I was the rearmost of the three of us, looking back to see if

I could catch a glimpse of sails astern; Piiram was in front, doing his best to do lookout duty forward. I suddenly felt Aila slip away from beside me, and turned round quickly. She'd fainted, and was in the water.

Mashaar had seen what had happened, and hove to quickly. Piiram was in the water beside Aila and had made sure her face was out of the water before I'd had time to think beyond thanking goodness we'd put on safety ropes. Then he grabbed the side of the boat with one hand and hauled her up to where Mashaar could grab her and haul her aboard.

She'd recovered consciousness, but was dazed and confused.

Piiram scrambled down into the cabin, shouting to me to get her wet clothes off her while he found something dry. Mashaar was already getting us under way again.

Aila started stripping her clothes off herself. Piiram was back up the companionway with a blanket before she'd finished.

"I'd better tie her clothes to the shrouds and get them dry, pass them here."

"You don't have another set, do you, Griima? Clothes on the shrouds will spoil our trim, Piiram."

"I've got a spare set in my rucksack. You'll look a bit funny in them, sweetheart, they'll be a bit big on you and a bit mannish, but they'll keep you warm enough and let us keep going as fast as we can."

Piiram dived back down into the cabin to change his own wet clothes. "I'll get back out on the trapeze, anyway. You give Griima your spare clothes, Owen, and then do you think you could come and hike with me again? You stay where you are, Griima. We don't want you to catch your death."

I gave Aila my rucksack to find my spare clothes, and then clambered out onto the side of the cabin alongside Piiram. He looked at me. "You're sure you're not going to fall in the water too? The only dry clothes we've got left are Mashaar's, and they'd be even sillier on you than yours on Griima!"

"I'll be all right. I'll go back in the cockpit before I get that bad."

"Just make sure you do!"

I managed to support myself a little more comfortably this time, and felt that I'd last quite a long time. *Every minute helps.*

Aila changed into my second set of clothes. "These are nice, Owen! Where did you get them?"

"Judd took me up to a place just under the Castle. I don't think he'd ever been inside, just seen it from the outside. The railway paid for them – two sets. I swapped the other set for these so I wouldn't look too posh in Troum, but if we're not stopping in Zhaam I don't suppose it'll matter after that."

Mashaar agreed. "No, Mormi's not like Troum and Zhaam. It's quite civilized, really – more so than Oushi even, just a gig ride from Barioha."

He said something I couldn't hear to Aila, and she climbed down into the cabin. "Whereabouts is it?"

"Oh – isn't it on the table?"

"No – oh, I see it. It's fallen on the floor. Got it."

She came back up with a reel of cord. Mashaar pulled a knife out of a sheath on his belt and handed it to her, handle first. She cut a length of cord, passed the knife back to him, then disappeared into the cabin again. A few minutes later she reappeared, with the telescope dangling round her neck.

"That's better. We won't lose it now."

"How are you feeling now?"

"Absolutely fine. I don't know what happened to me."

"Oh, I can guess. Hiking's not like cliff hopping. Cliffs don't pitch and roll quite as much as small boats! And you're tired, and you were probably cold, too. Are you warmed up a bit yet?"

"Not too bad. But I might snuggle up in that blanket again, as well as Owen's lovely clothes."

She parked herself in the corner of the cockpit seat, by the top of companionway on the windward side, close to my feet.

Mashaar approved. "That's the best spot for the trim, short of being out on a trapeze."

"I'm not as high as Piiram was, on the top of the cabin. I don't know how far astern I can see."

"Have a go. See what you can see with the telescope."

Aila put it to her eye. "Piiram's right. It's not as easy as it was on the point."

Then, after a moment, "I'm managing to hold the horizon all right, so I can scan along it without missing any. Can't see a sail anywhere from this height. I'll go up on the cabin roof in a bit."

But she didn't; she was soon fast asleep again.

Piiram suddenly called out, "Sails ahead! It's the Zhaam boats, I reckon, fishing. Do you think we should avoid them, Mashaar? Or should we talk to them?"

"No sense trying to avoid them. If they see us doing that, they could intercept us pretty easily if they wanted to. We can try sailing straight past quite close, and shout to them as we pass, or we can luff a bit and talk even if they don't seem to care. Probably best to do that – we might even be able to persuade them to delay anyone who's following us. Owen, do you think you can get the telescope off Griima, and give it to Piiram? Get up on the cabin roof and see if you can see anything astern, Piiram. Once we're past Zhaam, we won't know for ages whether it's just Zhaam boats we're seeing or someone following us."

Aila stirred as I took the telescope, but didn't wake. Piiram put the lanyard round his neck and went up on the roof. It took him a couple of minutes to be sure he'd scanned enough of the horizon to be sure, but he eventually expressed his satisfaction that if they were following us at all, we'd left them well behind.

"Good, good. We'll get the Zhaam men to tell them we've gone into Zhaam. That'll waste them an hour at least."

"Hmm. Not so sure. They'll be sore as hell when they find out they've been tricked."

"Yup. And then what will they do? Take on the whole population of Zhaam? If we can make that man burst a blood vessel, so much the better."

"I suppose so. It just makes me itchy, that's all."

Aila had woken up again by the time we reached the Zhaam fishing fleet. One of the boats came to meet us, and we hove to alongside each other. I climbed down into the cockpit.

Mashaar greeted them in a language I didn't know, and they talked for a while. Then one of the two men on the other boat clambered across onto our boat, took me by the hand, shook it vigorously, and addressed me in broken Laana. "Good luck, young man."

He turned to Aila. She extracted her arm from her blanket, and offered him her hand. He looked a little surprised, but took it, and shook it much more gently than he'd shaken mine. "And good luck to you, young lady. For the Ghost's granddaughter, we'd sink anyone who was causing you trouble, but we don't want a war with Troum. But don't worry, any man on that boat who isn't a Troum fisherman won't get beyond Zhaam."

He nodded to Mashaar, said something in the other language again, and returned to his own boat.

The two vessels turned to the east together. Mashaar adjusted the sheets and the sails filled, and we left the Zhaam boat behind. They waved, and Piiram and I waved back.

Piiram had been on the cabin roof the whole while. He put the telescope to his eye again, and scanned the horizon. "Still no sign. I wonder if we've been worrying about nothing."

Mashaar wasn't sure. "I can't imagine what it was doing coming this way. It's possible the Troum men know some reef that's good for fishing somewhere out this way, but I've not heard of it."

"Well, by the sound of it, we can pretty much rely on the Zhaam lads stopping them, anyway."

"What was he saying? I couldn't understand a word when you were talking with him."

Mashaar laughed. "That was Maara, more or less. Zhaama really, but it's not a lot different. He said they'd tell anyone following us that we'd gone into Zhaam, then blockade them in and make them hand over anyone who wasn't a fisherman. I'm not sure what he said they'd do to him, but it didn't sound gentlemanly, whatever it was. If it was a Troum fishing boat, they'd let it go, with just the Troum men, after a couple of days, under strict instructions to go home and not to follow us. I didn't know whether they knew the Ghost story here, but I hoped they would, and he did. Worked like a charm."

Piiram suddenly had doubts. "It's probably okay. I hope so, but I wouldn't rely too heavily on them. He could have seen an opportunity to make a few coins, and if he hasn't seen it already, he might see it before the other boat arrives."

Mashaar nodded. "I thought of that possibility, too, but I wasn't going to mention it. I don't think it's very likely. If Tiiram's man's got any coins on him, they can just take them, he can't stop them. And if he hasn't, they're not going to believe any promises of getting paid later! But we'll make the best time we can anyway. If it is him following us, he's managed to persuade someone in Troum, somehow. You two get back on the trapeze. No, not you Aila. You should try and get some sleep."

After the point, Mashaar altered course somewhat to the north. "The trouble with doing this passage in the dark is that there are no lights along this stretch of the coast, not until you get to Mormi. You don't want to get too far offshore or you can miss Mormi altogether, but you don't want to get too close in either, there are rocks. It wouldn't be too bad in moonlight, but there's no moon tonight. At least it's not cloudy. I won't light the masthead light until we see Mormi lights though, give everybody's eyes the best chance to see the coast. I don't think we can keep the foresail after sunset, it makes my steering too wobbly, and it'll probably be best if you two stop hiking, too. The next couple of hours should get us a good long way, anyway. I just hope the wind holds up after sunset. It's stronger now than it was earlier, or yesterday, so I'm hopeful."

My arms and back were aching more than I could ever remember, and my feet were numb, by the time Piiram decided it was time to call it a day. But I'd held out, and I was quietly pleased with myself.

I hope the Zhaam men are as good as their leader's word. Was he a leader of some sort? He obviously felt he was in a position to speak for them all. If he wasn't, what then? Well, hopefully we're a long way ahead. Will we be able to get a gig in the middle of a moonless night? And if not, what will that chap do if he arrives in Mormi before we've managed to get away? We might actually be better off getting becalmed and arriving in the morning – anyone following us would be becalmed, too. No point saying anything; what will happen, will happen.

Piiram took down the foresail. The wind weakened somewhat as the light faded behind us, but it didn't give out altogether. The crash, crash, crash of the waves against the hull gradually diminished to the slap, slap, slap I was more used to.

Piiram made the usual fried fish and potato meal, then came and sat beside me and Aila while we ate.

As it got really dark, I could see what Mashaar meant. I could only just make out the coast as a blacker band along the horizon. The sky was clear enough, with a sprinkling of stars right down to the horizon, and nearby the sea was alight with dancing reflected stars, but further away the sea itself was almost as black as the coast.

Three pairs of eyes peered into the blackness. Aila was fast asleep again, her head now resting on my lap. She'd started to snore gently, a reassuring sound – but I hadn't heard her snoring in Laanoha. *I hope she's not caught a chill. Maybe it's just the position she's lying in.*

I couldn't help it. I went to sleep, too.

I was cold. I opened my eyes, but all was utter blackness. There was no sign of stars, the pitching and rolling of the boat was barely noticeable, and almost the only sound was Aila's gentle snoring.

My left arm was warm on Aila's tummy. My right arm was tangled in rough cloth. Eventually I managed to free it, and brought my hand up to my face. There was dew in my beard, and my face was wet. Feeling around with my free hand, I realized that someone – probably Piiram – had tucked an oilskin blanket in around me and Aila, carefully not covering her face, but managing to get it around my upper back where it was above the coaming, and then round in front of me and across my chest, tucked in behind Aila's head. *A very carefully done job. What a hero.*

Whether Piiram was sitting the other side of Aila where he had been, I couldn't tell; nor could I tell whether Mashaar was still sitting in the stern by the tiller. I suspected that they might have been in the cabin, probably with a line to the boom round a wrist, to wake them at the first breath of wind.

Well, I'm cold, but not dangerously so. Aila's snoring sounds healthy enough. Best not to move more than I have to. At least this means we'll probably arrive in Mormi at a better time, and anyone chasing us must be just as becalmed as we are.

I tried get my right arm into the blanket again. It was difficult without the help of my left arm, but I didn't want to disturb Aila. I managed after a fashion eventually – not as good as it had been before I moved, but better than nothing. I tried to get back to sleep again, but didn't succeed for a while.

I really must get my thoughts written down. When am I going to get a chance?

There's all that stuff about the ancients' railways that Godfrey was telling me about, too. Did the ancients have railways in this area? Are there remains of ancient railways here? Are they even more decayed and buried and difficult to recognize than they are in England? Were any of them high enough up to escape the water during the high sea level period? Or at least high enough to have been flooded only for a relatively short time, and so not be too badly affected? Does anyone here know about them, if there are any?

Are there any accursed sites anywhere here? What were they really? I don't believe in that ancient curse nonsense – but people really do get sick and die if they try to investigate the sites, so I'm not going to. But are there any here, and does anyone here know more about them than they know in England?

*Interesting – I'm thinking of the English as **they**, now. Not just interesting – good, really.*

Chapter 15

There was the faintest hint of daylight when I woke again. Mashaar was squatting in the middle of the cockpit with a lantern beside him, trying to get the brazier going. Aila was sitting in the stern by the tiller, slicing potatoes. Piiram was sitting twisted round on the seat opposite me, gutting a large fish over the side.

Someone had tucked the blanket round me again after Aila had got up, and it was quite difficult to free my arms. Aila saw me struggling and leant over and helped me.

Mashaar looked up. "Ah, you're awake. I wish I knew your language, whatever it was you called it. You were telling a fine story last night, but I couldn't pick out a single word."

Aila laughed. "You woke us all up, but it doesn't matter. It was lovely to hear your voice rambling on like that. Do you often talk in your sleep?"

"I don't know. I've never listened. At home in Laanoha the first night I knew you'd gone missing, I was shouting and woke everybody up, but apart from that no-one's ever mentioned it. So I think probably not, although in England I always slept in a room on my own for the last few years, so there'd have been no-one to say anything."

"Shouting? You sounded quite contented last night."

"That was probably after I woke in the middle of the night then. I felt much more relaxed when I realized we were becalmed."

"Yup. If there's anyone following, they're becalmed too. It's better that we arrive an hour or two ahead of them in daylight when you can get a gig, than at night when you'd just be stuck in Mormi waiting for them to catch up. Ideal – as long as it clears reasonably soon. Ah, that's better."

He'd managed to get enough charcoal going to start warming the pan. "You couldn't fry over that yet, but it'll get to frying heat quicker from warm than from cold. It won't be long now."

They could do with a pair of bellows or something. Even just a blowpipe would be an improvement on pursed lips.

"How much further did we get after I went to sleep? We seemed to be going so well, then I woke up in the middle of the night and we'd stopped, and I couldn't see a thing."

"Until the last minute, I though we were going to make it. We could see the lights in Mormi, but still much too far to pick out the leading lights when the wind dropped to nothing. I didn't see the fog until I woke up this morning at first light. There's a surface current of fresh water from the river here, so we'll have drifted south a bit during the night. But I dropped a sea anchor below the current, so we shouldn't have gone far. It's very variable anyway, sometimes wide and slow, sometimes only a narrow stream but going a fair bit faster. We won't know until this fog lifts."

The fog began to thin as we were eating breakfast, and soon we could discern the direction towards the coast, although we couldn't see any detail on it at all for a while.

Before we'd finished, Mashaar announced that he could see Mormi point, and that he thought we were about two and a half miles out of Mormi. "Not a breath of wind yet. Who knows when the wind will come? I think we should start rowing her in, Piiram. We'll be there in under two hours, I reckon, even if the wind doesn't pick up."

They started to get up, but Aila told them they should finish their breakfasts first, and they sat down again.

"You're right, Griima. I don't know how far away anyone following us is, if there is anyone, but they can't row in from there, wherever it is. If the wind doesn't pick up, they're going nowhere. And if it does, we'll be in Mormi in no time."

"Can you row, Owen? You and I could take a turn and give them a rest if you can."

"No, don't do that, Griima. Piiram and I are bigger and heavier than either of you, it'll be quicker with us at the oars. You could get up on the cabin roof with the telescope as soon as the fog's lifted enough for it to be worth it. I'd like to know if there is anyone out there, and you can both take a look at Mormi as we approach, too. Mormi's not like Troum or Zhaam though, coming in here is pretty routine."

Mashaar hauled his sea anchor aboard. It was the same piece of canvas Piiram had used for a foresail the day before, stretched between a rope from the stern and another from the bow, and weighed down with the anchor stone on one rope and another, smaller stone on the other. "Too deep here to put the anchor on the bottom."

While Mashaar was doing that, Piiram lashed the tiller straight ahead, then undid the dinghy's painter and took it round to the bow.

"Owen – you come and sit on the foredeck, and you can keep us on course." He pointed out the landmarks I was to try to keep in line, and explained the calls to use to direct them. "When we get close to the village, there are streets at right angles to the sea. One of them is wider than the others, with the only big building in the village at the top end of it. As soon as we're in line with that street, we turn and head straight for the coast along that line. Okay?"

"I think so!"

"Griima, you get on the cabin roof with the telescope, and see what you can see."

Mashaar and Piiram clambered down into the dinghy, and were soon pulling hard. Once we'd got on course, they pulled beautifully evenly, and I didn't have to call out corrections very often at all. I wondered why we didn't use hand signals, though – it was definitely hard on the voice.

From the cabin roof, Aila couldn't see much in the direction of Zhaam. "Can't tell where the sea finishes and the sky begins, just fog at that distance."

She turned and took a look at the coast we were approaching. "Aha. I can see the village now. I think I see six masts sticking up behind a breakwater. It's not a natural harbour like Troum, then."

Piiram shouted back, "Sorry, Grima, couldn't hear what you said."

Aila repeated herself, a bit louder.

"No, Troum's the only place I know with a harbour like that. Well, Zhaam used to have, but it's dry now except at high tide. They've built a breakwater, but what they'll do when that's dry I don't know, the bottom shelves away really steeply only a few metres beyond the breakwater. Here at Mormi, they'll have a brilliant natural harbour in fifteen or twenty years' time, but just now you've got to be really careful to keep in the deep channel, it's rocks and reefs everywhere else."

Aila turned back to look back towards Zhaam again. "I think I can make out the horizon now. No sails, unless they're edge on to us. With no wind, they could be lying any which way."

"Well, keep looking every now and then. If they're edge-on just now, they'll swing into sight eventually, unless they're holding them that way on purpose. I can't see why they'd bother. They can't have guessed that we've got a telescope."

There was still no sign of a sail to the west by the time we reached the point where we had to turn to go into Mormi.

"Well, as long as there's at least one gig in Mormi at the moment, you're home and dry, Griima. Oh, good, it's high tide, near enough. I never know what the tide times are here, only been here a few times before. At least nobody else will be coming in or out with no wind like this."

"You two will head home as soon as there's a breath of wind?"

"Yes, for sure. We'll come into the village with you now, though, nothing to do down here until there's some wind. Griima, can you tie Piiram's wet clothes on the forestay? They might dry while we're ashore. There wasn't much point earlier on with all that fog."

There was only room along the inside of the breakwater for the six boats that were already tied there. Mashaar and Piiram towed their boat into the middle of the harbour, then Mashaar climbed aboard and lowered the anchor stone over the bows. He felt for the bottom, and gave it an extra metre and a half before making fast. "The first time I was here, you could tie up at the village side of the harbour, but the water's too shallow that side now. We could get in there now, but in a couple of hours we'd be sitting on the bottom, waiting for the tide to float us again."

He rowed Aila and me ashore in the dinghy, and then went back for Piiram, who'd been tidying things up a bit on the boat.

"Well, I've no idea who has a gig, or where they live, but I know where the inn is, and they'll know."

The innkeeper was very friendly, and laughed good naturedly at Aila in my clothes. "I can see why, though. It's lucky one of your men had a spare set!"

Aila had tied her wet clothes together in a gently dripping bundle. She pretended to be indignant. "Only one of these chaps is my man! The other two are friends of ours."

The innkeeper produced four mugs of skiir without even being asked, and Mashaar asked him where we could hire a gig. "Just for these two, they need to get into Barioha as quickly as possible."

"I'm not sure whose gigs are here at the moment. I'll send my lad round to find one for you. You wait here, he won't be long."

He turned and shouted up the stairs, "Baasham! Run up the hill and see if Naajal's at home. If he is, get him down here with his gig as quick as you can. If not, go round to the others and see who's got one at home."

Then he turned back to us. "Naajal's got the best gig – and the best horse. You don't mind an extra two coins for the trip into Barioha, I hope – you said you were in a hurry."

"No, that's fine. We are in a hurry."

I paid the innkeeper for the skiir, and gave him a half coin for his lad.

The lad was back in a matter of minutes. "Naajal will be down here in about ten minutes. He said everything's ready to go, he was going to go to Barioha himself today, and he's happy to take them."

The innkeeper and the lad went back inside the inn, and the four of us sat on a bench outside the front, sipping our skiir.

"I don't know how to thank you two. I couldn't ask for better friends." Aila was nodding vigorously.

"It just seemed like the right thing to do. Quite an adventure, really. You'll come and see us as soon as everything's sorted out, anyway, I know." He laughed. "Oh, and you owe us thirty coins!"

"I reckon I owe you a fair bit more than that. I was going to pay you just to take me from Oushi to Troum."

"Yes, but you were a fare paying passenger then, you're an old friend now. We were overcharging you. We realized you didn't know how much it ought to be. Imbaal owes us a good amount for your clothes, too – not that he can pay us anything but a share of his next few catches."

"If that chap is following us, you're not going to get into trouble at Zhaam or Troum, if he's managed to persuade them we're the baddies?"

"Probably not, but we won't take a chance on that. We'll head south, out to sea, from here, and give them a wide berth. We'll get some good fishing done on the way home."

We saw the gig coming down the hill. Aila jumped up, and gave first Mashaar and then Piiram a big hug and a kiss on the cheek. "I shall miss you both. And thank you so very, very much."

"We'll miss you two, too. It'll feel lonely on the boat with just the two of us now. But you'll come and see us in a few weeks' time, I know."

I pressed another four fives into Mashaar's hand. "I can spare that much now. We'll be in Barioha soon, and I can get some more."

I think all of us had tears in our eyes as Aila and I climbed onto the gig.

"Good winds and favourable tides!" they shouted as we set off, and Aila shouted the same back to them. We waved until they were out of sight round a bend in the road.

The fog had burned off completely, and the sky was blue from horizon to horizon. There wasn't a lot of wind, but there was beginning to be a little, and we imagined that Mashaar and Piiram would probably have set sail already. Aila kept looking back, to see whether she could see them, but the village itself, and the harbour, had disappeared behind a shoulder of land almost immediately after we left the village. She never saw a sail out on the water.

For the first mile or so, the road climbed gently away from the sea, winding in and out of ravines and round spurs. Eventually we reached the top, and came out onto flat country. It was a patchwork of copses and small fields. The fields were mostly bare wet soil, but a few showed the first green shoots of some crop.

The horse knew exactly where she was going. Naajal, sitting at the right hand end of the seat, had the reins in his hands, but they were permanently slack. He was quite a young man, and rather taciturn. Eventually he turned to me, and asked, "Whereabouts in Barioha are you going? There's a junction in about a mile, and the two ends of the town are best approached on different roads."

"We want to go the railway station."

I didn't want him to take us to Baam's house. I had instructions in my notebook for how to get there from the railway station. On the off-chance that we were still being followed, the fewer people knew exactly where we'd gone, the better.

"You don't look as though you could afford a ticket!"

Hmm. What to say to that? I don't want to give away the fact that I work for the railway.

But Aila was quicker than me. "My Dad's an engine driver."

Very good. True, and totally misleading.

*Hmm – on second thoughts, I **hope** it's very good. He's rather posh. I hope he's not connected to the...Circuit? Is that what Maamatta called it in her letter?*

Well, he's not reacting, so if he's heard the story, either he's not made the connection, or he doesn't care...eek...or he's going to take us somewhere we really, really don't want to go. Oh help!

I hope I'm just being paranoid. But is there anything we can do about it anyway?

I realized that Naajal was being as thoughtful as I was, which worried me. Maybe he *was* reacting.

After a full minute, he turned to us again. "I think I know who you are. You're Riish Aila, aren't you, who used to work for Baragab Gamaara? Don't worry, I shan't tell anyone that I've seen you. I think I understand the situation, I can read between the lines. If there's any way I can help you, don't hesitate to ask. In particular, my friend's daughter probably has some spare clothes that would fit you. Would you like to stop by there before I take you to the station?"

Aila looked at Naajal, then looked at me. She weighed the situation up more quickly than I did.

She turned to him, "You're right, of course, and that would be very kind, thank you."

Then she burst into tears, put her arms round me, and buried her face in my chest.

Well, if we're trusting him, we might as well trust him.

"Actually, if you could take us to our friend Baam's house rather than the station, that would be better for us. I've got the directions in my notebook."

Aila looked up at me, as if to question whether that was wise – and then I could see in her face her sudden realization that she'd already committed us to trusting Naajal completely.

I've scarcely had time to tell Aila anything yet. She's heard we've got friends in Barioha who will help, but I don't think I mentioned their names. She doesn't know about Biiniha's room in Briggi, and in no time at all we're going to meet Biiniha herself.

"Sweetheart, I've so much to tell you..."

"I know, and I've still got lots to tell you."

"Graamon told me his friend Baam would help me if I ever I needed help in Barioha. And he's married to Graamon's landlady's daughter, Biiniha. And Graamon's landlady is my landlady too now, and yours as soon as we're married, at least until we get a place of our own. And the room we've got used to be Biiniha's room until she and Baam got married, and it's the most lovely room you've ever seen. I do hope you'll like it. Oh, and Viina – that's our landlady – says that if you want to start a kindergarten in Briggi, she'd be delighted to help, and she knows there's plenty of demand."

I was out of breath. Aila was looking at me with big eyes. Naajal was looking at his shoes. The horse had just made up her mind that since Naajal hadn't indicated anything different to her, she was to take the left-hand fork, where she usually went. She was right.

Epilogue

That's really the end of the story. The big adventure was over. Of course, as the cliché goes, another adventure was just beginning. But you might like to know a bit about what happened next.

Word of our arrival was sent to Graamon in Meyroha, and he came to Barioha. He and Baam petitioned Barioha Castle, and Aila's story was heard and debated there. A guard was sent to Mezham, where he found the people who had hired a horse to a man answering Aila's description of her attacker, and whose horse had not been returned. A delegation went to Baragi, and confronted Tiiram. They did in fact get enough sense out of Jerem to confirm that it was his father, not Aila, who had smashed his knees.

Gamaara threw Tiiram out. He was stripped of his Castle papers, and all his property was given to Gamaara. He was dressed in beggar's clothes and sent to Gorb, which is about as far out in the wilds as you can get by coach. The coach drivers were given strict instructions not to allow him to travel. I've no idea what happened to him after that, but we've never heard of him since.

Gamaara sent the price of a horse to the people in Mezham, and identified the hired man as a chap who'd lived in Baragi for a long time, but who had no known relatives living in the area.

Graamon, Baam, Biiniha, Aila and I went in style, by passenger train, to Laanoha. The news had reached family and friends ahead of us, and there was a huge party in Peyr's room.

At Yaana's suggestion and by common consent, the party turned into our wedding halfway through the evening. Aila was probably already carrying Aariini, our firstborn, but nobody knew or would have cared if they had known – it's not like England here.

The only thing that marred the occasion, and very sad we were about it, was that Birgom had died just a few days after I left Laanoha. At least he'd died peacefully in his sleep. Viilam thought he was ninety-six years old, a fact that I subsequently confirmed from his diary, which Viilam gave to me. Birgom's diary was almost entirely written in English, so I was the only person who could read it. But that's another story in itself.

Aila and I revisited Griimi, Oushi, and finally Griishi – and no doubt will again. We invited Yaana to come with us, but after wavering for a while she decided not to come. We've not been to Troum again yet, but we intend to some day.

Griimab Tomaam's mother gave us her painting, and sent her greetings to Yaana. We talked at length with Mashaar and Piiram, but went by coach with Falbaash to Oushi where I met Jalaan for the first time. He told us he'd heard from the Troum fishermen that Tiiram's man had died only a week or so after we left Troum. We've never discovered who we'd seen behind us as we went from Troum towards Zhaam. We've almost begun to think we imagined it.

We learnt another thing about Troum as an indirect consequence: their method of disposing of the dead. They feed them to their pigs, well cooked if they died of disease, otherwise raw. Is this a health hazard to the humans who subsequently eat well-cooked pork? No-one seems to be aware of any evidence that it is.

We visited the Borjiis in Griishi, and Maamatta gave us another painting.

Yaana was tickled pink to learn that she was a legend amongst the fishermen all the way from Griishi to Zhaam, all the more so when she saw the paintings. One of them now hangs on Yaana's wall in Laanoha, and one on ours in Briggi.

We'll be leaving Briggi eventually. With Graamon, Baam and a few others, I'm on a committee setting up that research institute. It's going to be in Maaram.

The railway is going to connect Maaram. Work has begun on a tunnel between Belgaam and Maaram, and on surveying for a route from Maaram direct to Barioha.

The rock cuttings between Tambuk and Briggi have been roofed over.

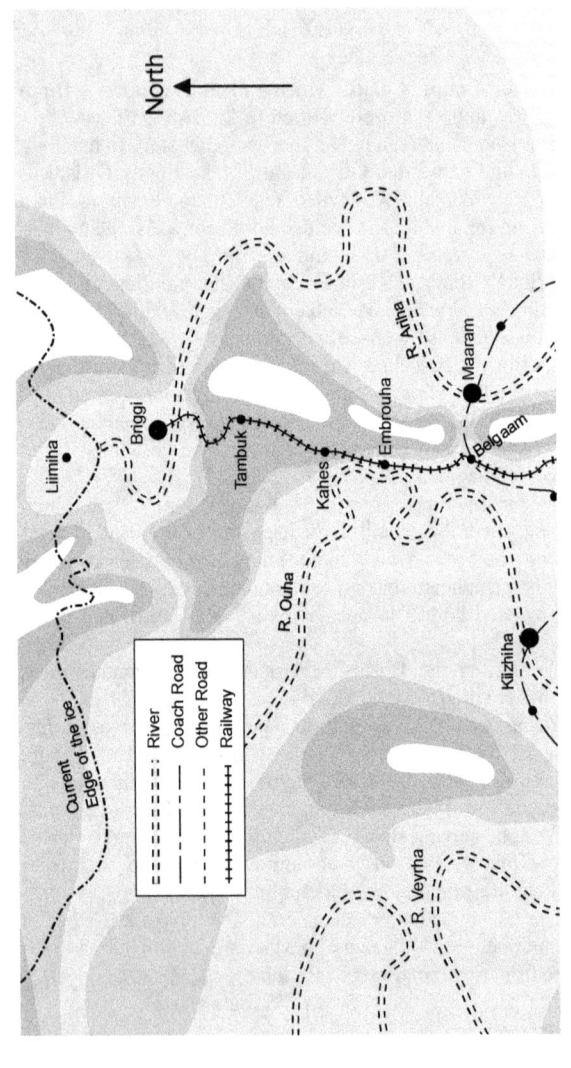

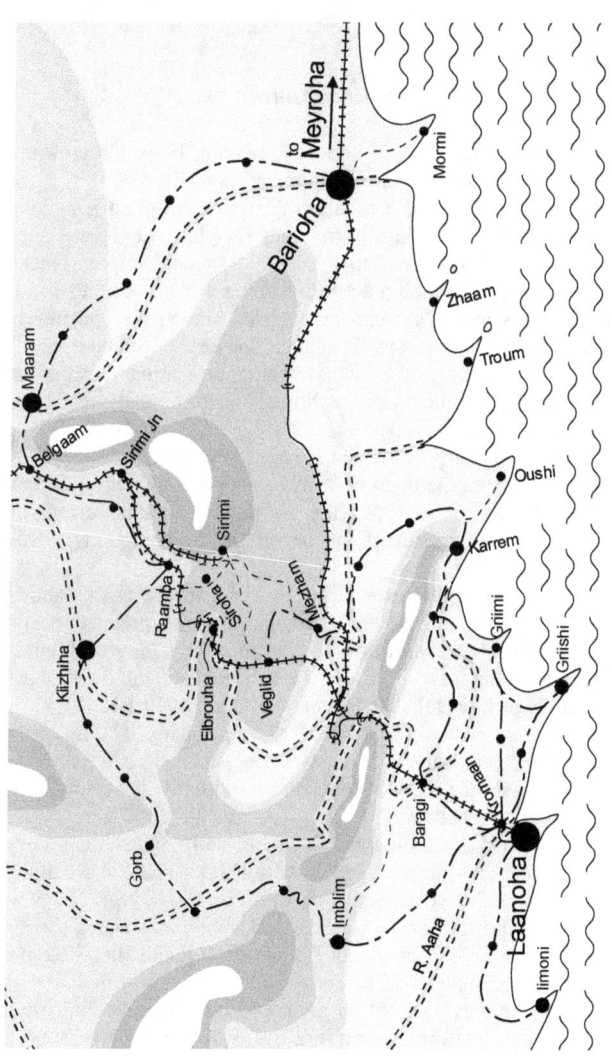

There is a colour version of this map at
http://clive.semmens.org.uk/Exile/Map.html

About the author:

Clive K. Semmens was born in London in 1949, and grew up in Yorkshire and then Hertfordshire, in England.

In 1967, he gained a scholarship from the United Kingdom Atomic Energy Authority to study Nuclear Engineering, a course intended to lead to a career designing nuclear power stations and associated infrastructure. His studies and experiences in the nuclear industry led him to the conclusion that nuclear power is a *very* bad idea, and he changed course.

After that, he had a wide-ranging professional career in engineering, education, technical writing and academic publishing.

He's particularly interested in people and their lives, trying to see things from the point of view of people from very different backgrounds, to avoid as far as possible making errors of judgement arising out of the unconscious assumptions of his own background.

He is also very interested in the world around people and is well versed in the issues surrounding energy production and consumption, resource consumption, and environmental pollution. He was the Green Party candidate for South East Cambridgeshire at the 2015 general election in the UK.

He first visited India in 1983. He rapidly got involved providing technical advice for a charity, and met his future wife, who hails from a remote village in central India. They now have two grown-up children.

Today they are retired and live in a small English town. They still travel, and he takes part in political, technical and cultural discussions and writes essays, short stories and novels.

Clive knows French, German and Hindi well enough to be useful, but in his own words "would certainly not describe himself as completely fluent or accurate in any of them."

He describes his hobbies as innovative DIY (anything from micro-electronics to major building projects), travel, photography, reading and writing.

Also by Clive K. Semmens

Novels

The Reminiscences of Penny Lane, ISBN 978-0-9564897-4-6

Pawns, ISBN 978-0-9564897-9-1

Going Forth (a sequel to *Pawns*), ISBN 978-1-326-23956-5

Short Stories

These anthologies each contain several of Clive's short stories, together with stories by others:

Different Minds Different Lives, ISBN 978-3-942357-26-5

Kaleidoscope, ISBN 978-3-942357-30-2

www.ingramcontent.com/pod-product-compliance
Lightning Source LLC
Chambersburg PA
CBHW051241260626
47162CB00002B/543